Praise for *Discovery* by Karina

"Karina Fabian's Discovery is a suspenseful space adventure with deep roots that extend to questions about life, death, faith, and purpose. With the dexterity of an Isaac Asimov or Larry Niven, Fabian makes the science and speculative science of the story accessible, deftly weaving it into the fabric of the story."

Tom Doran, author of *Toward the Gleam*

"Engaging with a powerful undertone of fun, this is a book whose pages will fly through your hands and whose words will paint vivid scenes in your imagination."

Sarah Reinhard, author and writer, SnoringScholar.com

"WOW lots of surprises...this is an exciting, thought-provoking read!"

Forrest W. Schultz, Science Fiction and Fantasy Reviews

"I believe this book will be a classic in Catholic science-fiction, to rank with "A Canticle for Leibowitz". I started to read this as a favor to the author, and was put off initially—'oh no! not another one about nuns who regret their vocation', but then it was hard to put down. That plot is extremely well-crafted, the characters are believable and three-dimensional and the implications for Catholic faith are stirring. We wonder about whether extra-terrestrial sentient beings could have souls; this book will put that doubt to rest."

Robert Kurland, author of *Science Versus the Church*

"Here's something different: a first contact story where the most terrifying things are our own motives and actions. Well-drawn characters and surprising events give the plot real impetus."

Dr. Simon Morden, Philip K Dick-winning author of the Metrozone Series and *Down Station*

Discovery

A Novel

By

Karina Fabian

FQ Publishing
Pakenham, Ontario

Discovery

copyright 2016 Karina Fabian

Published by Full Quiver Publishing

Award-winning publisher

PO Box 244

Pakenham, Ontario K0A 2X0

www.fullquiverpublishing.com

ISBN Number: 978-1-987970-01-2

Printed and bound in the USA

Cover design: James Hrkach, Karina Fabian

Front and Back Cover Art: James Hrkach

NATIONAL LIBRARY OF CANADA

CATALOGUING IN PUBLICATION

Published by FQ Publishing

A Division of Innate Productions

Dedicated to all the men and women who work to make the dream of manned space a reality, especially those who understand that faith has a place among the stars.

St. Joseph de Cupertino, pray for us.

Chapter One

Despite years of working in space, putting on the helmet inevitably gave Sister Rita a moment of claustrophobic unease. It didn't help that Sister Ann always performed the task with the same solemnity as a priest performing Extreme Unction.

She heard the *snick!* of the locking collar engaging and felt a slight hiss of air. She opened her eyes. Ann had moved behind her and was checking the equipment on her back.

"Heads-up," Rita muttered, and a display appeared to the right of her helmet. As usual, the monitors showed everything within normal. She released the rest of the breath she'd been holding. Sister Thomas, the pilot and leader of Team Basilica, called for a comms check and said a prayer for a successful rescue.

"Amen." Ann's light voice sounded grave, yet so young.

"Amen," Rita replied, making the sign of the cross. Did her arms move so smoothly because of the new suit, or was it a sign, finally, that she was, indeed, where God meant for her to be?

Ann jarred her from her musings by enveloping her in a hug. She bumped her helmet against Rita's so that Rita could hear her voice through the faceplate as well as the radio. "Happy anniversary!"

"Is it?" Outside the airlock of their rescue shuttle lay the ruins of a mining colony with people injured, maybe dying. Her anniversary Mass had been interrupted by wailing alarms that sent the entire convent scrambling to the rescue. Perhaps it was an appropriate way to celebrate her third anniversary as a sister in the Order of Our Lady of the Rescue, but *happy*?

"You're with us," Ann said, "and you're doing the most important work in the 'verse: saving lives in the name of God!"

"She's got you there," Tommie added wryly.

This is not the time for doubt or self-pity. I need to concentrate on the job. She gave Ann a smile she hoped looked more confident and sincere than it felt. Ann returned it with one of her own, her large blue eyes shining with excitement. Ann lived for the rescue.

In the suit, Rita couldn't hear her boots hitting the floor as she entered the bay to check the rover, but she did find their impact reassuring. Ann ran checks on the systems, while Rita inspected the exterior.

A far cry from the stripped-down car the original astronauts used to drive around the moon, the MicroGrav Rover was not much more than an aluminum framework with a central pressurized air container for the reaction mass and directional jets. Three years ago, she hadn't even known what reaction mass was; now she thought about it in the same casual way she thought of the fuel cell in her old Honda back on Earth. Wheels and treads were useless in microgravity when the MiGR could just skim the surface. The frame rested on a pedestal, and she crouched under it to check the underbelly. She called up pictures and specs on her suit visor to make sure she didn't miss anything. Despite the fact that it looked like something an ambitious child might construct out of old pipes, this MiGR, a donation from ColeCorp, was state-of-the-art. Despite its nickname, there was nothing meager about the MiGR. Ann always got the new equipment first to put it through its paces to find and fix all the bugs before passing it on to the other sisters.

Twenty-one going on twelve, with the brain thrust of R. Charles Hawkins and the spiritual peace of Our Lady, Rita thought, then squashed the surge of envy. Checklist completed, Rita slid into the passenger seat, buckled herself in snugly, and attached her safety line to the ring on the frame. Ann tugged the line, and Rita did the same for hers. "Tommie? We're ready."

"Copy. Opening the hangar doors."

The gray landscape of Rocky Flats spread out before them, stark and forbidding against the starry black sky. The horizon cut a sharp, definite line. Its desolation struck Rita, making her feel awed, yet suddenly and sickeningly alone.

"It took me a long time to discover that barrenness is the pause of the tree before putting out its fruit," Ann said solemnly.

Rita blinked, surprised at the sophistication of her statement. Then Tommie exclaimed, "Brother Jubal, right?" and Rita realized Ann had quoted again. The young sister consumed Catholic writings the way she did technical manuals...and, thanks to an eidetic memory, could summon the most minute of technical details or the most esoteric of quotations at will. Tommie had made a guessing game of it.

"Yes! From his *Diary at Aristarchus Plateau*," Ann answered. Under her skilled piloting, the MiGR rose and flowed out the door. "We've cleared the ramp, Tommie. ETA to the accident site, seven minutes."

"Copy that, Ann. I'll have *Basilica* prepped for your return. God be with you."

Rita squirmed slightly in her seat, all too aware of the narrow box on her back that held the equipment that kept her alive. She closed her eyes, intending to pray, but thinking instead about the first time she'd ever heard of Rocky Flats Station. The stark gray and black of the asteroid around her faded to the beige and blues of the food court at Terra Technical University, the silence to the din of busy students and faculty, the tension to the happy excitement and the thrill of discovery. The news of a new mineral, dubbed colite as an obvious nod to space baron Augustus Cole, had been confirmed, and the buzz spread across several departments. Astrophysics speculated on what it would mean for the stalled space economy, while Geology wondered how they could get a sample for study. Rita, then a sister with an Earth-confined order, taught in the Geology Department. She was content to read about it in academic journals and teach her students in the hopes that, one day, they would unlock its mysteries. Her best friend James, however, had teased her that they should take a trip to the asteroid station and see it for themselves. She'd thrown a fry at him and declared that she was very happy to keep her feet on Terra Firma.

And yet, less than a year later, she fled the Earth and James and took new vows with Our Lady of the Rescue. Her geology degree won her a position at St. Joseph de Cupertino convent station, servicing Rocky Flats. If some of her friends could see her, they'd say she was living a dream.

But not now. That morning, a malfunctioning robotic freighter had driven itself into the station. Although it missed the main bubble, it collapsed the surface of the asteroid around it, so that the dome was tilted precariously over a mine beneath. On Earth, or anywhere with significant gravity, the dome would have slipped, tumbled, and smashed; here it hovered, propped against the rocket. If anyone in the main dome survived, had they found a safe place to await rescue?

The impact had severed the lines holding some of the domes to the asteroid, and they had floated off like a child's balloons. The collection canopy had been knocked askew, and the dirt and debris it had contained covered the area in a dangerous fog. Because of the mess, the low visibility, and the fact that the impact had set the asteroid itself to gyrating, they'd had to make a bumpy landing kilometers from the damaged station. Even now, Ann jinked the MiGR now and again to avoid hitting a large piece of floating rock.

Billions of dollars and years of work, destroyed in minutes. But maybe no lives, especially if the sisters could get to them in time.

Happy Anniversary.

Rita glanced at Ann and saw that her lips were moving. Although she wasn't completely proficient at reading lips, Rita could tell she wasn't just repeating some rote prayer or meditation. Still, if she were speaking with any of the Rescue Sisters or with the mining team, Rita would have been included in the conversation. "Ann? Are you worried?" If Ann were worried, the situation was even worse than she'd expected.

However, the young sister had other things on her mind. "Did you know Brother Jubal didn't like people very much? He had hoped to spend his life in solitude at the Oceanus hermitage. Know what else he wrote?

I came as a wanderer,
found You, Beloved, here
in a dead world poised
on the edge of eternity.

"Yet God called him to go minister to the Drake Lunar station. He left the life he loved and, as a result, came to love life more."

Before Rita could digest her words, they crested the hill, and the station — or what was left it — came into view. While Rita stared slack-jawed at the damage, Ann flipped on the sensor equipment and began speaking over the general comms. "Survivors of Dome One, this is Sister Ann of the Order of Our Lady of the Rescue. Please respond."

"Sister Ann!" came the crackly reply. "GenSup Hayden. Are we ever glad to hear you! The station comms are down. All we've got are suit comms. I can't reach my people in the other domes. Do you know their status?"

"The antenna was dislodged from the asteroid. It's on its way to Silverstone, but we should be able to intercept," Ann replied. "*The Cardinal Newman* and the *St. Gillian* are catching Dome Six. It's been knocked off-rock, but the seven crewmen within are fine."

"Joyriders. And the others?"

"Dome Three and Four reported none injured and stable environment. The crew of Three has suited and is making their way out. Dome Two reported stable environment, but one person with a concussion and one with possible internal injuries. You took the worst hit, even considering Six."

"Tell us about it. We're sitting on the junction of the wall and floor. We've got two injured but ambulatory, but only four suits for eleven — repeat, that's seven crewmen unsuited — and the ventilation's shut down. That's no new oxygen, no scrubbers. Did you bring bags?"

Finally, Rita found her voice. "This is Sister Rita. We brought enough for everyone. They'll be cozy, but it's a short trip."

"Good, 'cause I'm not sure how long we have. The vent cut off about three minutes ago."

Ann ran calculations in her head while Rita tried to call up the information on her suit. As usual, Ann beat her. "About twelve more minutes, then. Save your air. We'll contact you when we get to the dome. Don't worry. We have plenty of time."

Despite Ann's promise, Rita had to swallow back her misgivings when they reached the edge of the chasm that exposed the hollowed-out mine below the station. Checking twice to make sure she was tied to the anchored MiGR, she shuffled carefully to the edge and looked down. The mine had to be at least half a mile deep — a huge, dug out cylinder, with a freighter jammed diagonally into it, and the dome resting diagonally on that. The whole thing looked precariously balanced, like the start of a house of cards. The collection canopy covered most of the dome. To drive to it and then cut through and establish an airlock would take more time than the captive crew had.

"There's our door," Ann said. She spoke a command to her helmet, and it relayed an image of the part of the dome hanging over the abyss. It magnified to show an airlock, its panel light green and indicating it still functioned. "I'll jump over and attach a tow line, so that we can relay the survivors in the bags to you."

Jump over a quarter mile? Rita was finally learning to quell her Earthborn reactions to such a suggestion and replace it with the concerns of a spacer. "Are we sure the dome is stable enough for the impact when you land?"

"I think the ship will hold it in place. Besides, if we attach a motor cable and the equipment to my belt, I can use the HMU."

The HMU, or Hand Maneuvering Unit, was a simple compressed-air canister that provided a brief spurt of force to push the person in the opposite direction. Simple in theory, yet difficult in practice. In zero-G, every action did have an equal and opposite reaction, but that didn't mean that if you pointed the HMU in one direction, you'd automatically go the other. If the unit was not held near the center of gravity — or if the angle was off, your body wasn't balanced, or any other number of *ifs* — you could send yourself spinning instead of flying. Rita practiced with the units thrice a week, yet still had problems. Ann, of course, operated the device as easily as the MiGR.

Rita unwound the cable from the rover and attached it to a ring on Ann's suit. Another ring took seven rescue bags, and a third held a medical kit. Carefully, they added some O2 canisters and tools, checking balance after each addition. Rita gave Ann two cans of stickie, a plasticine glue used for everything from emergency suit repair to sticking things in place. Meanwhile, four of the crewmen in the dome suited up. Hayden warned them that one of the newer members was starting to get panicky.

At six minutes of air left for the trapped crew, Ann backed up to the edge of the precipice. With a grin like a child going on a merry-go-round, she cradled the HMU against her sternum and pressed the button. The burst of air pushed her off the edge.

Rita resisted the urge to warn her that she was going too fast. Ann handled zero-G maneuvers like a prima ballerina, like she was born to move in space. Her faceplate darkened, and Rita knew she had called up the view behind her. Another shot, and she was angling toward the door. At the last minute, she ducked, rolled, and caught the handle as a final short burst slowed her, so she settled against the dome like a feather landing on a cushion.

"You see? God is with us, Sister. I've attached the pulley."

Rita released the breath she was holding.

While she tested the cable operation, Rita listened to Ann report her progress through the hallways now tilted at a thirty-five degree angle. Ann explained the procedure to the suited crew, then the unsuited survivors, using her spacesuit's intercom. Another "Twice and Thrice" precaution, since all the miners had quarterly evacuation training. Even though Rita could only hear one side of the conversation, it was obvious that the panicky crewman, Cay Littlefield, was giving them trouble and insisting on a suit, despite the fact that none would fit him.

"The bags are very safe," Ann cajoled. "I've ridden in them lots of times. They're fun."

Rita groaned inwardly. Fun? Not the word to pacify a panicky spacer. Ann kept speaking in her bright, reasonable voice, and Cay kept arguing.

"We're wasting air," Hayden finally exploded. "Littlefield, get in the bag or I'll have you sedated, and you can explain your cowardice to your girl back home."

A few minutes later, Hayden reported to the door with one bag. He exited first, the bag's tow line clipped to his suit. He clipped himself to the door handle, then attached the bag's line to the cable before giving it a tug to pull the balloon out of the lock. For a moment, Rita saw the woman inside, curled up with her arms around her knees, but her head back and staring around her. Then the material opaqued until it looked like a man-sized silver balloon with a box of flashing lights attached to the bottom. Rita started the cable, and the balloon made its way toward her.

Hayden looked at the damage around him and swore one tight, angry word before disappearing back into the airlock. She heard him asking Ann if she needed help. Littlefield was complaining the bag was too small and that he wouldn't have enough air. Between reassurances, Ann kept chiding him to remain still. Through it all, she kept talking in her usual serene voice.

"Rita, we're at the airlock. Cay, I'm going to open the airlock. I'll attach myself to the door, detach you from my belt, and hook you onto the cable. Then you have a short ride to Sister Rita. I need you to be very still while I transfer the line, copy?"

Some incoherent uttering, then "Copy."

"I'm opening the door... I'm attached, Rita. Cay, I'm transferring the hoo—"

"No! Stop. Take me back. I can't breathe!"

"Cay! Please stop moving!"

"Help me!"

The bag bounced out of the airlock. It bulged and twisted weirdly as the man inside struggled in a full panic. Ann held the tether with one hand and grasped the cable with the other, fighting the momentum that threatened to pull it out of her grasp. The bag reached the end of its tether and rebounded, bouncing into Ann. She lost her grip on the cable as she slammed into the door. The HMU attached to her belt hit the handle. The button compressed and stuck, sending her into a dizzying set of zips and rolls, bashing her against the dome and shooting her in the opposite direction until her tether yanked her in a new way. Cay began to scream in earnest, but Ann went silent, and Rita didn't dare speak, for fear of breaking her concentration. The young sister tried to reach the HMU with her right hand, while controlling her gyrations with movements of her left arm and legs. Each move made Cay panic more, and his own struggles added to the confusion. When a lucky combination HMU burst and ricochet off the dome pushed Ann in Rita's direction, she flung the tether hook toward her.

"Catch!"

Rita stared open-mouthed as the balloon sailed toward her, pulled by the hook. The trajectory was off. It was going to miss her. *Cay* was going to miss her.

"Oh, St. Jude, pray for us!" She tugged her line to make sure she was hooked to the rover, fought the urge to leap, and gently pushed herself toward the balloon with her ankles rather than her knees.

St. Jude must have, indeed, been guiding her, for she caught the balloon by the control box. She checked the systems — all normal, though Cay was eating up oxygen at a phenomenal rate. "Cay? Cay!"

"I can't breathe! I've gone blind! I'm gonna die! I'mgonnadieI'mgonna!"

His voice squeaked. He didn't sound older than eighteen. If he kept this up, he wouldn't see nineteen. "Calm down, or you'll jerk out of my grasp. You're breathing fine. No more panicking."

"Code One: A Spacer never panics. Code One: A Spacer never panics!"

Like yelling the code is going to stop you. She racked her brain for a way to distract him. "Cay! What's your girlfriend's name?"

"What?"

Surprise made him still, and she dared to let go of the box with one hand to grab the balloon tether and attach it to her belt. The cable to the rover started pulling her in. "Your girl. Hayden mentioned her. What's her name? What's she like?"

"I...I don't..."

She forced her voice to a light, teasing tone, the one her grandmother used to use on her. "You don't know? Maybe it's not so serious then."

"No! She's everything to me. She's the whole reason I came to Rocky Flats." As Cay protested his undying love, his breathing slowed, and even better, his frantic struggling stopped. The cable brought them back to the MiGR. Rita couldn't get her feet to touch the ground again, but it hardly mattered. Grabbing the handholds and making encouraging comments whenever Cay slowed in his dialogue, she made her way to the back of the MiGR.

Ann screamed.

"Ann! What happened?" Rita yelled.

Only strangled gasps answered her.

Tommie repeated her question with demands for status when Ann didn't immediately reply. Over that, Cay had broken his monologue to ask as well. Rita overrode his suit to cut off his panicked cries. She doubled her pace to the MiGR, where she attached Cay's balloon, giving it a quick yank to double check the hold. Through it all, she only heard strangled gasps and Tommie's demand to know what's happening.

"Ann, talk to me!" She turned toward the dome so fast, she had to catch herself on the rover to keep from spinning, and even then, it took a moment to stop herself. The whole time, Ann's strange, pained breathing filled her helmet. "Ann, what's wrong?"

She focused on a still form clinging to some wreckage. She magnified. Ann was braced against a broken strut, holding herself steady with one hand while her other hand fumbled with the can of stickie. Globs of red floated from the strut, spattering when they impacted the debris.

Ann wasn't bracing herself against the strut. She was impaled by it.

Chapter Two

James broke the surface of the water and scanned the sea for his boat. The zodiac, *ColeMiner's Daughter*, bobbed up and down in the gentle waves. He ducked under and covered the short distance, coming up just below the ladder. A couple of boat-hands leaned over the side.

He checked the heads-up display to make sure his suit had adjusted its internal pressure to match the air pressure outside, then cracked the seal of his helmet and flipped back the visor.

"What's going on?" he asked the senior of the two.

"No se'," the man replied, and in the pidgin of English, Spanish and Tagalog that had become the native dialect in the area, explained that they had orders to retrieve him and bring him back to *ColeMiner*. No, they weren't supposed to accept his protests; no, he couldn't use the radio to call the bigger ship. James had to go to the ship and find out himself.

"It's not an emergency, is it?" James asked. "It's not my mother?"

The old man's eyes widened, and he sputtered hasty denials, his hands accenting each one. Still, he insisted, James had to go to the ship, and he had to go right now.

"Fine! Fine. *Andale!*" The sooner they got to the ship and he found out what this was about, the sooner he could get back under. They'd just finished recording the ballroom of the sunken ship and were starting on the inventory. Even though the whole assignment had left him feeling more like a treasure hunter than an archaeologist, it did have its own fascination.

He could have used the dive suit's engines to "fly" him back to the *ColeMiner*, but that would have wasted fuel and air, so he awkwardly clambered over the side in the bulky, semi-hard suit, and, helped by the men, settled into a sitting position without toppling or capsizing the boat. So graceful in the water, so lumbering on land... no wonder they called the suits "penguins."

As the old man helped him remove the helmet, his assistant took the engine, and soon they were speeding toward the main ship. James pulled the cap off his head, letting the breeze blow his sandy blond hair dry. He draped his arm over the side and gazed out at the blue-on-blue of sea and sky. So beautiful. So calm. He tried to let that calm enter his soul. Below him on the ocean's floor lay the remains of three hundred and sixty-four people. Had they enjoyed a view like this, not knowing that only hours later, an explosion would rip the hull of their yacht in the midst of its maiden voyage and send them to their deaths? All those people, so many dreams...

Give it a rest, James. It was two hundred years ago. And it's not their lost dreams that have you in this mood. Three years since she just disappeared. You think you'd be over it by now. Still, he brooded over the view until a familiar "Ahoy!" made him look up.

The thick rubber sole of an expensive boat shoe with AC molded into the bottom had planted itself on the top rung of the *ColeMiner's* ladder. James shook his head, grinning now, as the men attached the lifting harness the crewman of the *ColeMiner* had lowered for him. As he came level with the deck, Augustus Cole grasped his arm at the wrist.

"Find Atlantis yet?" Augustus asked.

"You didn't ask me to find Atlantis," James countered as men swarmed around him, undoing catches and cracking the suit at the waist. He bent forward, then slid out, first the arms and torso, then grabbing hold of the suit's waist and stepping out of the legs. "You asked me to find a ship, and I did."

"I asked you to find my great-great-grandmother." Augustus snapped his fingers, and a crewman dashed up with a towel in one hand and T-shirt and sweat pants in the other.

James didn't even ask what the rush was; he just slipped out of the wetsuit and started toweling off, pulling the sweat pants on over his swim trunks. Augustus would explain in time.

"That is going to take a little longer," he told his boss, as he stuck his feet into flip-flops. "It looks like the explosion happened during a dinner-dance. Hardly anyone was in their rooms. Unless her wedding ring's managed to stay on all this time, we may have to exhume the bodies and conduct DNA tests. We expected that, though, and brought the equipment with us."

"Can your team handle it from here?"

James pulled on his T-shirt. "You firing me?" he asked through the fabric.

"Of course not." But Augustus' eyes twinkled. Despite the fact that he was one of the richest and most powerful men in the world — in the solar system for that matter, ColeCorp had more assets in space than on Earth — Augustus Cole was a child at heart. He had a secret and was just waiting for James to give him the right cue.

James didn't mind playing his straight man; maybe that's why Augustus had made him his pet archaeologist. "You want me to find Atlantis?"

Augustus laughed and put a friendly arm around James' shoulder, leading him down to the ship's offices. He said nothing more until they got to the conference room. He held the door open for James, and when they had stepped through, announced, "Gentlemen, I'd like you to meet Dr. James Smith. He thinks I want him to find Atlantis."

Two men sat at the table. The younger dressed in jeans and a gray collared shirt with the Luna Technological University logo over the pocket; his mousy brown hair and pale brown eyes combined with a tense, nervous posture reminded James of many worried grad students he had known. The older, a fifty-something man dressed in a similar shirt but with tweed pants, nodded James' way. His relaxed, full-throated chuckle was for Cole's benefit.

Augustus continued, "James, this is Dr. William Thoren, Dean of Astrophysics at LunaTech, and this is Chris Davidson."

"My protégé," Thoren added when Augustus paused.

The entrepreneur's eyes flicked in annoyance. He hated having his dramatic moments spoiled. Nonetheless, he continued on as if the dean had not spoken. "Chris has been working on a rather uninspiring project for his doctorate that has had a surprising result. But wait!"

With that impish grin, he reached into his pockets and pulled out four small devices, which he set at four points of the room. When he pressed the remote in his hand, they heard a brief hum, then a shimmery fog formed a dome over them. No one outside the dome would be able to hear them and would only see vague shapes.

Scientists from the moon? Security fields? Well, if Augustus wants my attention, he's got it. James took a seat at the table and cocked a brow at Augustus. "So you've found the Lost City of Atlantis in space?"

"Close, my friend. Close. Chris?"

Chris gave a brief glance at his supervisor, and Thoren nodded in a benign "carry on." He pulled out a handheld computer, set it on the small table, and pressed some buttons. A holographic map of the solar system from the Sun to the asteroid belt appeared, beautifully detailed and large enough that James had to sit back a bit.

"Sir, are you familiar with the Kuiper Belt?" Chris asked.

James shrugged. *What's going on?* "Ky-per Belt? That's not like the asteroid belt?"

"This is the asteroid belt." Chris set his finger on the thin line of rocks just past Mars' orbit. He slowly pulled his finger toward himself. As he did, planets rushed past James' field of vision: Jupiter, Saturn, Uranus, Neptune, Pluto. A moment of black space, then the image stopped at a smattering of dots of various sizes.

"This is the Kuiper Belt. K-U-I-P-E-R, even though it's pronounced 'Ky-per.' It's really just the rubble left over from the formation of the solar system. Most of it isn't even rock, but ice. Comets come from here. We don't hear much about it because the distances even from the Outer Planets mean it's not really cost-effective to live or work there. And since the commercialization of space, most people don't even care..."

"Excuse me, Chris, but why am I getting an astronomy lesson?"

The entrepreneur grinned. "Give him a minute." He jerked his head encouragingly at the grad student, who gave him a shy smile in return.

From the corner of his eye, James saw Thoren glower; then, the expression was smoothed away.

Chris didn't notice. "Okay, the last time anyone has bothered to explore the Kuiper Belt was with the Seeker Probe of 2215. The American President, Linda Montero-Fadil, pretty much pushed it through on personality and stubbornness, but they called it Fadil's Folly..."

Thoren cleared his throat.

"Anyway!" Chris started, then floundered a moment, his train of thought derailed. He took a breath, touched an area of the map with two fingers and pulled it apart, expanding that area. He did it again and again, then rotated it and circled an object with a dark center. The rest of the map fell away.

"This is 2217RB86. Seeker did a flyby of it and its Ky-boes. That's what you call, um, neighboring objects in the Kuiper Belt. That's what we call them at the university. So, this Ky-bo caught my attention because it's got some very unusual readings, especially around this dark dot... I won't bore you with the details. The point is, Dr. Thoren was able to get us some time on Old COOT — that's a telescope on L5 Station — and um..." He stopped to glance around, as if making sure the security field was still in place. Then he pressed another button and pulled up a different, sharper image of the Ky-bo.

"We found this."

"Oh, my." James leaned forward, his nose only inches from the image. The dark circle had resolved into six crescent arms jutting from a sphere. One arm was partially dug into the rock.

"He didn't find Atlantis." Augustus smirked.

No, he didn't.

Chris Davidson had discovered an alien starship.

"I, I, uh..." James found himself stammering worse than Chris. He wiped his face with one hand. "That's...amazing. But I don't understand. I mean, I don't understand why you're telling me."

Augustus rubbed his hands together in the way he always did when he was excited. "It's my university. Well, sort of, but even better, I sponsored this particular project. And I'm the one with the bankroll. I say you go explore it for me."

James' jaw dropped. He met Augustus' eyes over the hologram of the alien craft millions of miles from the ship on which they sat. Augustus still had that grin, but his eyes were dead serious.

"You like a challenge, Dr. James Smith. What could be more challenging than exploring an alien starship?"

* * *

James stood on the forecastle deck and leaned against the railing, staring out at the dark sea. After three hours of briefings, they had taken a recess, and Augustus and his lunar guests had retired to a private dinner with the captain. James had bowed out, preferring to meet with his team and get an update on the excavation. He'd been sworn to secrecy, so when they'd asked about his sudden recall, he'd brushed it off as "another wild idea from the boss." They'd left it at that. They all knew Augustus' reputation for going off on tangents. Even so, he'd been glad when everyone had retired to their rooms or to play quiet games in the commons, and he'd had a chance to be alone.

The breeze had picked up, ruffling his windbreaker in a stuttering complement to the smooth lapping of the waves. From this side of the ship, he couldn't see the moon or its reflection on the water, which suited him just fine. He'd had enough of space for a while.

Dr. Thoren and Chris had explained the mission to him, thoroughly, with Thoren casting dark glances Augustus' way whenever he thought the entrepreneur wasn't looking. Obviously, as mission commander, he preferred more secrecy. Chris, on the other hand, lapped up Augustus' encouragement and went into great detail. The technical parts went over James' head; he'd have a lot of studying when he agreed to this mission. *If* he agreed to the mission. The basics, however, were clear: he'd be joining a team of scientists, some from major universities in the solar system or the orbiting colonies, a few from Earth, plus a mining crew and some sisters from the Order of Our Lady of the Rescue. The scientists, including engineers, xenobiologists and even language experts, would study the ship; the miners were supposed to extract it if possible. The "Rescue Sisters" would provide training and safety. His job, as Augustus put it, was to "coordinate the dig."

The dig. James snorted to himself. Some dig. Cutting into the hull of an alien craft, no idea or even a guess at what they might find. Only some fabric and equipment between him and sudden death...

"Enticing, isn't it?"

James glanced back, saw Augustus approach. He took a similar posture beside James, resting elbows on the railing, slightly hunched. Had it not been for the difference in style and expense of their outfits and hairstyles, they could have been twins.

Half a dozen replies flitted through James' mind, most sarcastic, but he didn't bother. Augustus had his mind made up. This was a dream come true; only an idiot would disagree. The question was, was James an idiot? He turned back to the ocean view.

"Six months," he said. "It's too long. My mother…"

"She doesn't remember you," Augustus cut in. "I checked with her doctors before I came here."

James spun. "You had no right!"

His boss and friend held up his hands. "Did you think I would propose this to you if there was any hope of your reaching her? I'm not totally insensitive."

James couldn't look at him. He turned back to the sea. "What did the doctor say?"

"She's comfortable, happy most of the time, when she's not confused. She enjoys the facility's dog; he seems to be the only constant for her now. Each day is a new day to her, and she meets everyone for the first time. Pretty much like she was before you left on this job."

"Drive the knife in a little more," James grumbled.

Augustus set a hand on his shoulder and, as much as he wanted to shrug it off, he found he didn't have the heart to do it. "James, I know this isn't easy, and I know how callous this will sound, but you need to look at a bigger picture here. You can't help her."

"Can you?"

Augustus sighed and dropped his arm. "If I thought my money could make a difference, I'd give it to you. Not just because this project is that important, but because you're my friend. You found her a good facility, one of the best. The people are top-notch, and they care about her. And your sister's there now, right?"

"She has to get back to her job."

"No, she doesn't. *That* I can make happen. Get her a nice apartment if she's tired of your place, work if she wants it. She's an artist, right?"

"Murals." James closed his eyes. He hated Augustus' ability to pinpoint weaknesses. His sister hadn't had a commission in months.

"I've seen her work. 'An innovative foray into the primitive,' I think the *New York Art Scene* put it. Personally, I think her canvases are too small, and I can take care of that. I have some buildings in that area that could use some primitive innovation. Could be fun."

"But only if I do this," James concluded. When Augustus didn't contradict him, he sighed. "Six months."

"Closer to eight," Augustus replied. "Three there and three back, plus two or three weeks on site. And you'll go up early to the moon and get a crash course in spacesuit wear and zero-G maneuvers. Should be a piece of cake, since you scuba so well."

"Did you have to say crash? You really brought a spaceship out of *salvage* for this?"

"Hey, do you know how hard it is to find a ship on short notice that can make that kind of run? The *Edwina Taggert* is a great ship. She's been doing cruises to Saturn and back for two decades. First class engines, even if outdated. They'd started scrapping her insides, which made refit into a research vessel easier. It's not her fault her company went under."

"Was it yours?"

"No, O Father Confessor, it was not."

"I'm not a priest," James grumbled. "I didn't even finish seminary."

Augustus leaned forward, trying to catch his eye, and James turned his face away. Low to the horizon, a small, bright light tracked across the sky. LEO-York. Cole's family had built that city, then Augustus had sold all his real estate and rights in order to invest in asteroid mining — or asteroid miners. He had cooperative agreements with various small ops that the press heralded as "unconventional." James remembered laughing about it to Rita. Now he worked for the man, even considered him a friend. And Rita?

He pulled his mind away from the thoughts that had haunted him all day. Three years ago today, she'd walked out of his life. Off the face of the Earth, it seemed. Why should it still hurt to think about her?

Augustus can't do anything in a conventional way. A cruise ship for a research vessel.

An archaeologist to explore an alien ship.

He turned to face Augustus, one elbow on the railing. "Why me? Why an archaeologist?"

"You mean other than because it makes Thoren vent air?" When James didn't laugh, he cleared his throat and spoke seriously, again positioning himself to match James' posture. "An engineer gets given a piece of equipment and told to figure out what it is. What is he going to do?"

James shrugged. "Push buttons? Take it apart?"

"Exactly! Give a biologist a new specimen, what will she do?"

"Autopsy?"

Augustus stopped leaning on the railing, his hands in front of him, palms together, fingers pointed toward James. "Right! That's what we have going up so far. But James, this is more than equipment or a new species — this is a peek at a new civilization! Who do you send in to study that?"

James pushed himself off the railing. "An archaeologist."

"Now you're getting it! This is something no one — no one in all of history — has ever done! There are no procedure manuals, no rule books. I gave Thoren the authority to pick his research team, and he's got a pretty good bunch. But if they go into that ship without someone who knows what it's like to enter a, a temple, they are going to traipse in like treasure hunters. Remember that lecture you gave? You held up a thin narrow tube and asked us what it was."

James nodded. It was one of his standard openings about the importance of not making assumptions. Some folks would see a straw; others tubing for some piece of equipment; someone even mentioned the breathing tube for a tracheotomy. "They would be so intent on their own specialties, they won't take time to put things in context."

"They wouldn't know how. But you do."

"I prefer Hierakonpolis."

Augustus waved his hand dismissively. "Egypt's been done. You wouldn't just be studying history. You'd be *making* history. You like challenges."

Augustus grinned at him, and James found himself grinning back. A completely new civilization, his to discover. Still. "I need to think."

"We've got a short launch window before we have to add months to the flight plan. You have three days to decide." With that, Augustus turned back toward the ocean, leaning against the railing as before. After a moment, James joined him. They lingered, enjoying the breeze, the sound of the waves, the starlight on the dark water.

Augustus asked, "Remember that night in Luxor?"

James chuckled. "I remember the hangover. What was that stuff we were drinking?"

"Local specialty, just for us tourist-types. You talked about a woman."

"Rita. That, that was a long time ago."

"Yet you still have a photo of her on your computer." He blithely ignored James' glare, gazing at the ocean with feigned innocence. "What if I told you I know where she is, and I can get her on the mission for you?"

Chapter Three

The *OLR Basilica* approached St. Joseph de Cupertino convent station at past the highest recommended speed. As the airlock arm extended outward, the shuttle turned hard, the braking and maneuvering jets firing in a controlled frenzy. It settled onto the asteroid beside the station in perfect position and with a feather-light touch of its skids.

Inside the shuttle, Sister Rita let out a sigh of relief. At least one thing went right today. Tommie was the best pilot in the convent.

I'm surrounded by the best, she thought, *but it doesn't keep terrible things from happening.*

A hiss of pain from Sister Ann forced her mind away from such thoughts, and she gripped her injured partner's hand a little harder, careful of the IV.

"Ann, are you okay?" It was a stupid question. The broken piece of strut protruded from her side like a lance. A messy glob of plasticine glue pasted it to her spacesuit, holding it in place and sealing the tear that would have bled out all her air, as well as her blood. Ann was still in her suit, gloves and helmet off, snoopy cap still on at her insistence, so she could hear the progress of the other sisters on the rescue.

"The *St. Gillian* caught Dome Six," Ann reported and smiled. "Sister Quartermaster is scolding it for wandering!" She giggled, then winced.

Rita gave a distracted chuckle as she checked Ann's vitals on the medical scanner. It was easier than looking at that horrible mess of emergency first aid she'd done to her friend. The monitors spoke to her of pain and delirium and a body fighting off shock. The medpod of Ann's suit was dosing her, Rita could see that, but it refused to tell her with what or how much. Even though she longed to relieve her friend's pain, she was even more afraid of adding medications when the malfunctioning medpod might be administering regular injections according to some schedule of its own design. Stupid computers!

A spike in Ann's vitals said the medpod had injected her with something...but what? *Why couldn't we have gone after Six? Hurry up, Tommie!*

Tommie reported the airlock mated and pressurizing. Rita felt the slight shift in her weight as the ship's artificial gravity matched the convent station's.

"*I came as a wanderer/found You, Beloved, here/in a dead world poised/on the edge of eternity*," Ann murmured. "Sister Quartermaster could scold you."

Rita glanced from the readouts to see Ann staring at her. "What?"

"*Let the soul remember that she was first sought, and first loved, and that is because of this that she seeks and loves...* You wandered so far, but He was always right there," Ann muttered. Her eyes clouded, then cleared, and she tilted her head to where eleven miners sat in jump seats along the wall of the shuttle's bay or in the microgravity rover now secured to the deck.

"Andi?" she called.

A young woman in a spacesuit decorated with the Andromeda galaxy unhooked herself and hastened to take Ann's hand. "Here, Ann."

"They caught Six. Everyone's okay."

"I know." Andi tapped her own headset. "I'm listening, too. Now you just be still."

Ann smiled. "*Be still and know I am God.* We're not still enough. We pierced God with a lance, and blood and water poured from His side. I'm human; fifty-seven percent water, and I only bleed. Nanoweave of the skinsuit's applying point-nine-five pounds of pressure to slow the bleeding. No pouring. Side, not stomach. Missed the vital organs. He pushed me."

Rita and Andi both glanced at the young miner folded over in his seat, sobbing quietly.

Rita shushed Ann. "It was an accident. He didn't mean for you to get hurt. He panicked."

"Silly! Angels don't panic." A loud laugh escaped Ann's mouth, making her gasp in pain.

The miners looked up, including the distraught Cay Littlefield.

"*Angel of God, my guardian dear...* He shoved me starboard. Starboard, starboard. Starboard three thruster didn't fire as strong as the rest; did you feel it? Tommie had to fire twice, to push us into place. Dust from the accident site. Dust to dust... We should be careful in case there's colite dust."

The airlock opened, and Sister Lucinda, the station doctor, rushed in with three sisters following at her heels.

Rita stepped back and let Lucinda take her spot at Ann's side, doing her best to be still as the older sister read Ann's vitals off the screen. Meanwhile, the other sisters, EMTs, fanned out among the miners to check their injuries. Rita had done only the quickest of triage to make sure none were badly hurt before returning to Ann.

Ann was murmuring about the price of colite and how they had to modify the overhaul procedures to make sure they collected the dirt on the shuttle for examination. In between listing procedures, she murmured reassurances to her guardian angel.

Sister Lucinda asked, "Skinsuit still not talking?"

"Vitals, yes. Medpod, no. It just gave her something, but I don't know what." Her calm tone surprised her. She really wanted to howl like a child and demand Sister Lucinda make it better, or at least reassure her that she hadn't screwed up.

Lucinda, however, only grunted as she reached into her pouch and pulled out a syringe and a bottle. She filled the syringe, then administered the anesthetic through the IV. "Time to sleep now, Annie, while I get this thing out of you."

"Will I bleed?"

"Some."

"Okay, but no water. That would be blasphemous. Blood and water and fire... His heart's so full..." Her eyelids drooped.

"Can I come with her as far as OR?" Andi asked.

Lucinda smiled warmly. "I think Ann would like that, wouldn't you, dear?"

Ann murmured something that was probably an assent, and Andi and Lucinda wheeled her out of the shuttle.

Rita watched them go, feeling like some kind of support had been pulled out from under her. A terrible urge to sit on the cold deck and rock and cry gripped her. Should she have given Ann something? She'd wanted her to stay conscious, stay babbling, even when she didn't like what she heard. She'd been studying emergency medicine for two years now, but it hadn't prepared her for this.

Her sisters were guiding the others out. Rita saw one of the miners try to take Cay by the elbow. The young man shrugged out of his grasp. His would-be companion didn't argue, but spun on his heel and left him. The rest of their teammates ignored him.

Rita stifled her tears. Cay couldn't be more than eighteen, and he was going to hate himself forever unless someone did something about it.

She intercepted the general supervisor before he got to the airlock. Hayden followed her gaze toward his subordinate and let a sigh out through his teeth. Together, they sat down on the jump seats on either side of Cay.

"I'm sorry," he whispered. "I thought we were going to die. They put me in that bag, and I couldn't see, and I thought I was going to float away..."

"You almost did," Hayden growled. "Kicking Sister Ann like that. If it hadn't been for Sister Rita, they'd have had to retrieve you with Dome Six."

Rita glared at Hayden over Cay's crumpled form. She rubbed the boy's back, feeling how his shoulder blades poked out. At six-ten, he hadn't fit well in the rescue bag. She wondered if he was claustrophobic. "Cay. You were scared. It happens."

"I went *couritza!*"

Scared enough to endanger himself or others. Rita couldn't argue with that. "It happens. But what happened to Ann isn't totally your fault."

He sobbed. "I never should have left Mars. You don't understand."

"That's not true. I'm a greenfoot, Cay. Do you know how many times I've freaked out since leaving Earth?"

"You're Catholic. It's different for me. Code One: A Spacer Never Panics. It's so true. The Code is life. I failed the Code!"

A Codist? Hot anger, fueled by stress and fear, flared in Rita. She grabbed Cay by the shoulders and forced him to look at her. "Is that what this is about? Not that Ann was hurt, but that you failed your silly code?"

"Rita," Hayden warned.

She didn't hear him. The temper her father used to say went with her red hair had taken hold. "Cay, listen to me. The Code is a series of rules for living in space. That's it. They can protect lives. They can save lives, but they are *not* life. And if you start measuring your life by how well you can adhere to a bunch of, of *safety regulations*, then you will fall short! Now get up!"

Cay blinked at her, confused. "Where are we going?"

"You are going to Sickbay to get checked out. I need to stay and secure the shuttle. And Cay, you'd better think about what you have to fall back on when you 'fail the Code,' or you will not last long here."

Hayden rose, pulling Cay up with him. "Can't argue with that. Let's go, Cay."

Rita watched them with narrowed eyes until the airlock cycled shut behind them.

"That went well." Tommie's voice came from behind her.

The third member of Team Basilica leaned her stocky frame against the wall near the entrance to the shuttle proper, one knee bent, foot hooked on the bar that ran the length of the bay walls, arms crossed loosely. Typical spacer stance, and one Rita still found uncomfortable.

Rita sank back into the seat and put her head in her hands. "You're right. But did you hear him? Whining about failing when Ann was lying there with that..." Rita bit back a sob.

Tommie sat down beside her. "Annie's tough. She'll be okay. Cay feels horrible about what happened to Ann — and his part in it."

"I know."

"That's some pretty heavy guilt, so he's deflecting his attention. People do that."

Rita sighed and leaned back, resting her head against the wall. "You're right. I shouldn't have lost my temper. I just have so little patience for Codists. It's like making a religion around jaywalking ordinances."

"I have no idea what jaywalking is." Tommie grinned, and her dark eyes glinted with amusement. The closest Tommie had gotten to Earth in her 57 years of life was Phobos, and even then, she hadn't had any interest in leaving Mars' moon to visit the Red Planet, much less travel on to Earth.

Rita shook her head dismissively. "Earth thing. I shouldn't have lost my temper. I'll talk to him later. I dunno. Maybe I was doing some deflecting myself."

"You were right not to give Ann anything. The suit was medicating her. That's its job. Don't let Lucinda's brusqueness get to you. You know how she is with EMTs."

I shouldn't need Lucinda's reassurances. Rita looked at her hands, clenched on her knees. When she breathed out, it was hard and shaky.

Tommie squeezed Rita's shoulder. "Ann's going to be all right. She's a lot tougher than she looks," she repeated.

Rita barked out a harsh laugh. "You don't need to tell me. You didn't see her, delaying her suit's painkillers so she could have a clear head while she sprayed stickie over the bar and her suit. Then she just stayed there, still as a statue, reciting the Divine Mercy chaplet until Hayden could cut her free, while I was stuck watching from the other side of the chasm. I couldn't do anything!"

"You made sure the others were safe. You got her to *Basilica*. You took care of her here, and you kept her conscious and lucid."

Now Rita's laugh was brighter. "Lucid? Did you understand what she was talking about?"

Tommie raised her brows in a Spacer's shrug. "I'm sure it all makes sense in Ann's world. Want some help securing the bay?"

Rita shook her head in a gravfoot negative. "No. Frankly, I...could use a few minutes alone."

"Not too long. As soon as the *St. Gillian* returns with Six, Mother Superior's no doubt going to want a debrief." Tommie gave Rita's shoulder a second squeeze and left, her smooth gait telling of her years of military training. Was that why she could be so calm about all this?

Rita watched the airlock close, then let her eyes wander around the bay. It wouldn't take long to secure the area; just putting things away and doing the initial inventory of items used and items remaining. She'd do a second inventory after she knew Ann was all right and ask Tommie to double check. *Twice and thrice and yet again, so sayeth the Spacer's Code.*

It's so gray here, she thought. *Grays upon blacks upon whites. Black habits with black skinsuits beneath. Why couldn't St. Gillian have chosen something with more color?* She'd already broken convention for practicality by selecting a T-shirt and pants rather than the traditional habit. *Would it have hurt to have chosen a sunny sky blue? Or yellow. Yellow and orange...warm, vibrant colors. Something to counter all the gray.*

Even the rescue balloons, now in a neat stack waiting to be serviced, were silver. Rita rose and picked up one, touching the thin, but tough, fabric. Lighter than a bed sheet, yet it could hold an atmosphere and heat well enough to keep a person alive for half an hour, longer if you switched the O2 tanks. Ann had called them "pretty silver wombs."

Rita dropped the balloon and pressed the heels of her hands against her eyes. *What am I doing here? Am I just deflecting? Wandering, like Ann said?*

You're running, a small, scolding voice in her mind answered. *The question is, why?*

Awkwardly, Rita reached into her suit and pulled out a photo from the inner pocket. Autumn at the lake, with the golds and reds of the foliage of the trees reflecting off the still waters, the blue sky with fluffy clouds. Under one stately oak, the TerraTech University-Indiana youth group crowded together, all smiles and linked arms. In the photo, she smiled with them, a happy sister in the modern, conservative dress of her order, one arm around the waist of the group leader, the other around the university's "priest," a seminarian studying for his ordination while teaching.

"Oh, James." Her whisper sounded too loud in the empty shuttle bay, and she bit her lip. *I did this for you, you know. I had to leave, get as far away as possible.*

The stern voice spoke, each phrase piercing her like thorns. *You left everything — your home, your career, the Order of the Blessed Virgin Mary, the Earth. All to become a greenfoot novice of the Rescue Sisters on an asteroid convent on the edge of nowhere. Was it worth it?*

She traced the line of his jaw with her finger. *He'd have come after me, otherwise. I know him. He's tenacious.*

Her mind flashed back to how he'd looked at her the day he'd told her he was having doubts about his vocation. "I'm going back to my Order over Spring Break. When I return...we need to talk."

She'd felt such a lurch in her stomach.

Fear or desire? the voice persisted. *You wanted him to forget you, but why can't you forget him?*

"I came as a wanderer/found You, Beloved, here/in a dead world poised/on the edge of eternity." Does Ann know? She maintains the suits. Had she seen the photo and jumped to conclusions? And what did she mean, he was always right there?

Chapter Four

"Hey! Mr. Smith, wake up. We're almost there!"

The prodding of the boy next to him pulled James from his sleep, causing his dream to fade. He grumbled and twisted, the shoulder restraints preventing him from fully turning his back on his fellow traveler. He fought to recapture his dream. It felt so important. Something about Rita and green cheese...

"Come on! You're going to miss it!" The nine-year-old tapped on his shoulder like knocking on a door. On the other side, his mom admonished, "Cory!"

Rita, wearing a spacesuit, a pickax in one hand and a chunk of colite in the other. She held it out to him...

Cory jabbed him harder. "You gotta see this. It's the Aristarchus Plateau. Wake up!"

"Five minutes," he muttered, still half-asleep. He had to see how this ended.

He was standing on an asteroid in his underwear, holding a hunk of Swiss cheese. There was a crowd around him, laughing. Rita, old teachers, past students, Jesuits. Saints? Brother Jubal pointed at him and folded over with mirth.

Cory didn't need to poke him again. His eyes flew open, and he moaned.

"I'm sorry, Dr. Smith," Cory's mom apologized. She waited a moment, then jabbed her son with her elbow. He repeated his mother's apology.

James shook his head. The motion set his hair floating. "No, it's fine. Just a weird dream is all."

Cory grabbed his arm and pointed to the screen in front of them. "Look! It's the crater!"

The Aristarchus Crater, one of the best-known features of the moon, loomed huge and forbidding on the screen as the shuttle passed over.

How big was the meteor that created it? Rita would know, wouldn't she? James stared, mesmerized. The angle of the sun cast harsh shadows inside it. The shadow of the shuttle looked like a small raven diving, then skimming the bottom, heading to a sea of black.

Big ones are rare, but small ones? There's no atmosphere to protect the moon. There's no air.

The black edge swallowed the raven, who gave itself willingly to the dark. James shivered.

God, what am I doing here? I'm an archaeologist, not a spacefaring adventurer. How could I let Augustus talk me into this? He didn't even tell me anything about Rita, just that he'd found her and would get her on this mission. She could be married with kids, for all I know! No, he wouldn't do that to me — would he? Lord, it's not fair to ask, but if you could send me a sign...

"Dr. Smith, are you all right?" Cory's mother asked.

Cory, however, picked up on James' mood. "Spooky, huh?" he said, then giggled, relishing the thought.

James tore his gaze from the screen, admonishing himself. No one had twisted his arm. He chose to accept this mission — and not just because of Rita. The best part of his career was when he got to learn about lost civilizations. How could he have turned down the chance to be the first to explore an alien one?

He turned to the boy and said in his spookiest voice, "Maybe they throw the naughty boys down there. Ooooooh!" He arched his fingers like claws and leaned toward Cory.

Cory burst out laughing. "Who cares? One-sixth gravity! I can jump out!" He tried to demonstrate, but the straps held him down. His mother set her hand firmly on his shoulder and pointed to the screen.

"Look! There's Drake." She sounded more relieved than excited. An eighteen-hour shuttle flight with an overexcited nine-year-old had worn her out, despite James' help keeping the boy occupied. There were shadows under her eyes almost as dark as the one in Aristarchus Crater.

Drake, James thought. *That's why I was dreaming of Brother Jubal.*

No longer the frontier mining station of the saint's time, Drake had grown to a thriving metropolis and spaceport, spreading out across the lunar surface, and (so the flight attendant said) handling two interplanetary shuttles a day and dozens of local flights weekly. Despite appearances, the majority of the habitation areas were below the surface, including the ColeCorp Mining Consortium, the business offices of DiHydrogenMonoxide, Inc., and Luna Technological University. She'd also told them Drake still hosted several hermitages and, to this day, men and women from around the system come here to find solitude among the stars. She seemed to find it ironic.

And I'm traveling to the stars to end my solitude, James thought. Now there's irony.

Except for a slight jerk when the braking jets fired, the landing was smoother than any James had experienced on Earth. The passengers, forty in all, clapped to show their appreciation. A brief reminder to stay in their seats while the artificial gravity was activated on the landing pad, then a gradual heaviness as they again felt their full weight, and finally they were thanked and bid adieu. People rose, their minds already turned to getting luggage and finding a hotel or boarding the next flight. He helped Cory and his mom get their things. They headed down a hallway and queued up with people from other arriving shuttles, anxious to get through customs. Two hundred and forty thousand miles from Earth, a mile, maybe two, underground, artificial gravity, canned air...and he may as well have been going through customs at JFK. Once through, they shared brief hugs, and he knelt in front of Cory and adjusted his light jacket.

"Take care of your mom," he admonished.

"I will." Now that they were parting ways, the boy was subdued.

"And say your prayers. Remember what I said."

"With God's help, you can get through anything. I will." Cory again threw his arms around him and squeezed.

"You'll love it in space," James said with a conviction he didn't feel. "Just don't go jumping out of any craters."

"No promises!" Cory replied, his mischief back, and his mother sighed and took his hand. The two joined the swarm of tired travelers heading to the elevators leading deeper into the station. James hesitated, unsure where he should go.

Someone called his name. He searched the crowd and saw Chris Davidson, waving his hand over his head.

Was I ever that young? James thought as he went to him. The return to normal gravity after nearly a day at free-fall had left him feeling old and slow. He half-wished Drake didn't have artificial gravity, and he could skip about at one-sixth his weight. He repositioned his bag on his shoulder, his arms protesting at the work, and headed over to Chris, thinking that he might give into the feeling and ask to take a nap before whatever they had planned.

"Enjoy your trip, sir?" Chris asked as they shook hands.

"It was interesting at first. Then, just long."

Chris nodded and gave a sympathetic smile that disappeared quickly. "Um, so Dr. Thoren has arranged for you to meet the rest of the team members..." His voice trailed off, and he waved a hand toward the elevators.

"You mean right now?"

"Um, yes, sir, Dr. Smith."

James sighed. "First of all, it's James. Second, I'd like to at least go to my room, dump my stuff, and change. Get a quick shower, if that's allowable."

"Well, we have sonic showers, but..."

"A quick one, then. I think he'd rather I be a bit late than show up smelling like twenty-four hours of travel."

Chris' expression said he wasn't sure about that, but he led James to his room. It was more like a walk-in closet. A long narrow table protruded from the wall, flanked by a three-drawer dresser that bore a dock for powering tablets and a wristcomp. Chris pulled the table, and a bed folded out of the wall, with the table making its legs. The simple chair folded into a square that made an end table or ottoman. Then he pulled down panels on one wall to show the sink and commode. The shower was a sonic nozzle protruding from the ceiling above the commode.

"It's not much, but by Luna standards..." Chris started.

"Hey, there's no sand, no bugs, and no snakes wanting to share my sleeping bag. It's great."

Chris demonstrated the controls and offered to wait outside. As the tickly waves removed the dirt and sweat, which were sucked up by a fan at his feet, James mused over what he'd just said. *No snakes in space. Rita must enjoy that.*

The thought that Rita might be there made his stomach lurch. What would he say? He clenched his fists. He'd dreamed a hundred scenarios — even standing in his skivvies holding cheese, for pity's sake! He couldn't know which would play out until he actually saw her. He took a long breath and forced himself to exhale slowly. Not the skivvies, at least.

He dressed in a long-sleeved collared shirt and beige pants and pulled his wristcomp from where Chris had set it in the docking station. As soon as he strapped it to his wrist, a message popped up informing him that an agenda and a full map had been downloaded, complete with marked locations and links to vitae of each meeting's attendees. He almost asked it to find Rita Aguilar, but a flashing notice reminded him he was late for his first meeting.

With a roll of his eyes, he left the room and let Chris escort him to Thoren's meet-and-greet.

Rather than the informal get-together he'd expected, James found himself surprised to see the ten or so people seated in an auditorium-style classroom, reading displays on pads or wristcomps as Thoren led the briefing. Conversation stopped as they entered, and he could almost feel Chris shrink back.

"So good of you to join us, Dr. Smith," Thoren said, a false smile on his lips. "The shuttle was delayed?"

"No. I wanted to get a shower first," James said as he scanned the faces. *Where was she?*

"I see. Well, no matter. We were able to cover some items that do not concern you as we waited." Thoren turned to face him, hands held loosely, level with his sternum. "I greet you under the auspices of the Code, which promises safety and demands obedience. For the Code is Life."

"The Code is Life," some of the others repeated.

He didn't see Rita. "Um, sorry?"

Thoren bowed his head indulgently. "It is a standard Spacer greeting."

From the audience, an older man with thinning blond hair and a strong square face just giving in to middle age softness snorted. "A Codist greeting, you mean, Thoren."

Thoren countered smoothly, "Just as a Jew might greet you with 'Shalom,' or the Chinese with a bow —"

In the front row, a tanned man with dark hair and oriental features chimed in, "And we surfers do this!" He made a funny gesture with his hand. Beside him, a taller man with a large smile mimicked the gesture. Their hands met and they laughed as though they were far younger than the academic doctors they had to be.

Thoren again made his slow nod. "Just so. You are not familiar with Codism?"

"Uh, no. Catholic. Not a lot of Codists in archaeology," James answered, his eyes still scanning the crowd. *Had Cole lied?* "Is this everyone?"

Thoren frowned, and James realized how impertinent his question sounded. However, the mission leader merely cleared his throat. "In fact, the recovery crew, a group of miners from a station called Rocky Flats, will join us."

"Rocky Flats?" James almost shrieked. "That's where they mine colite!"

"You're familiar with the ore?"

"I, uh, had a geologist friend who was interested in it."

Thoren's frown became a superior smirk and, despite his distractions, James felt his hackles rise. "As are most geologists. It seems there was an accident two weeks ago, destroying a significant portion of their station. Augustus — Mr. Cole, that is — has offered to help them rebuild in return for their help in recovering the ship."

"I see." *Rita, is that where you are? I used to tease you about going there, studying colite firsthand... But you loved the earth.*

"If there are no more questions?" Without waiting for an answer, Thoren turned back to the group and introduced James as the archaeologist he had brought in to supervise the exploration.

James stopped his jaw from dropping at Thoren's audacity. "Just give him rope," Augustus had said. Despite the entrepreneur's amused tone, James had realized then he didn't like Thoren much. *Guess even Augustus has to play politics.* So James smiled and nodded as Thoren introduced the rest of "his" team:

Ian Hu, drive systems specialist, again greeted him with the surfer's wave. "The hidden genius of the group," he added to Thoren's introduction. He stood to bow and said, "In the name of Code Six, I say *salaam, shalom, wazzup?,* and bless you!"

Reg Alexander, civil engineering lead, stood and took James' hand. "He's always like that. Be ready," he said with a jerk of his head toward Ian, who grinned.

Gordon Radell, who looked far too athletic for the sedentary work of a cryptographer, gave James a nod. Seated in the row behind him and wearing a flowing skirt and bell-sleeved shirt that had become popular again in the United States, zoologist Kelley Riggens toyed with a pentagram necklace as she gave him a warm smile. Beside her, Zabrina Muha, microbiologist, waved her fingers. Both, Thoren explained, had advanced degrees in xenobiology as well.

Merl Pritchard, the older gentleman who called Thoren out for his Codist greeting, gave James a thumbs-up and a smile, as Thoren introduced him as the mission's linguist. James smiled back. Finally, someone not in a hard science or engineering. He was beginning to feel outnumbered.

"And over here," Thoren waved toward the corner of the room, "we have our documentarist, Sean Ostrand."

Sean abandoned his VR equipment and hastened to pump James' hand. "An honor, Dr. Smith! An absolute honor to join you on this historic journey! I'm going to want to talk to you about V-Recking the interior of the ship. The magnitude of what we have here!"

"Thank you, Sean," Thoren said, and, dismissed, the young man returned to his camera.

James schooled his face into neutrality. He'd thought Chris seemed young!

With a magnanimous gesture, Thoren indicated James could take a seat between Ian and Reg.

Ian leaned toward him. "Don't act too excited, or Thoren will beat it out of you. 'Staid' is the word of the mission."

James smirked in reply, but watching Chris standing half behind the desk and looking at his mentor with anxious eyes, he had to wonder how true Ian's joke was.

"In your absence," Thoren began, with just a bit of a martyr tone, "we've been discussing the modifications to the *Edwina Taggert.*"

On the pad in front of Thoren popped up a holoimage of the ship that could have been pulled from a pulp fiction novel of the early twentieth century. It spun slowly to reveal a woman painted on its hull. Something clicked in James' memory.

"Edwina Taggert?" James blurted out. "The hologame actress for the Lola Quintain games?"

"Actually," Sean jumped in before Thoren could say something "staid," "the luxury liner based on the hologames. How stellar can we get?"

"We need her engines," Ian cut in, serious now that they were talking about engineering. "The Kuiper Belt is a *looong* way away. Her VASIMR engines will get us to .7c. Of course, no sooner do we get that fast, than we flip and use the engines to decelerate us to match speed with our target..."

James hardly heard him. Rita's brother loved the Lola Quintain games; Rita was always trying to find him some silly Lola thing to add to his collection. *Surely something as silly as a game would not draw Rita off-planet, but what if it was Joseph's idea, and he dragged Rita along? Maybe. They were always close. But could I have spooked her that much?*

James banished his thoughts before they led him down a dark path.

"As well," Thoren concluded, "the ship was purchased from the Landra clan, who recently acquired it as salvage."

"You never told us if any zerogs are going to be on the crew." Merl's voice suggested he wasn't too keen on having zero gravity humans on board.

"We'd not discussed ship's crew, but their biographies are in your files if you are interested. The chief medical officer is from the Landra clan. However, she was with the *Edwina Taggert* for ten years before its decommissioning. I'm sure she's quite accustomed to normal humans," Thoren told them.

"So," James asked, trying to sound casual, "what else do we know about the others who are joining us? We have the crew for the ship, the miners..."

"They're known as the recovery team for this mission. And a small team from the Order of Our Lady of the Rescue," Thoren finished. "They will be ensuring the safety of the mission."

The conversation shifted then to the preliminary training for the planetbound and moonbound people — called "dirtsiders" or "gravfeet," Gordon told James — and then to the modifications done to convert the *ET* conference rooms into working labs. Thoren directed them to look over their schedules, which included the first Extra-Vehicular Activity Basics class right after lunch.

"We have a mere ten days to prepare ourselves before we board the *Edwina Taggert*. Study, prepare, gather what you need, but remember: This is of the utmost secrecy. Discussing this mission with anyone not directly involved will get you removed from the mission — and from any chance of researching the ship when it is eventually brought in-system."

Everyone rose. Ian clapped a hand on James' shoulder. "Come on, greenfoot. Let's get you a suit."

"You're a greenfoot, too," Reg noted as he led them out the door.

"I resent that!" Ian retorted, humor in his voice. "My feet are blue or green, depending on whether I'm in the water. Or sandy brown if I'm on the beach. I love the beach! I never feel so clean as when I'm in the water." Ian kept up a steady stream of chatter, occasionally interrupted by teasing from Reg, until they got to the small office where James was sized and outfitted for his spacesuit.

Only when James was donning the fully assembled suit, thinking how different it felt from the penguin he wore on dives, did he realize that he never did find out if Rita was part of the ship's crew or the recovery team.

Chapter Five

Rita puffed a sigh as she settled another box back into place and leaned against it, looking at the ordered chaos of boxes and bags, equipment and items that crowded the cargo bay of *Basilica*. Emergency medical kits cozied up to spacesuits; rolls of wire encircled tanks, and were all very compact and neat yet lacking rhyme or reason.

"This is ridiculous!" she exploded. "Who in their right mind gives a mission profile of 'Teach and conduct EVA?' We're exploring an alien ship, so just be ready for the weird?"

"Mr. Cole." Ann's voice came from down the aisle where she was checking the upper shelves. "Besides, half the Rocky Flats team is going, too. We couldn't refuse them."

"Right. Rocky Flats, 'the *Edwina Taggert* crew, plus twenty others.' And who are these others?"

"Dr. William Thoren and Chris Davidson." Ann stopped.

"Exactly. Two names, and statistics for the rest — this many women, that many men, this many gravfeet, that many with experience working in space. It's like Cole didn't want us to know who was on the mission." She knew she wasn't being fair; more likely, he didn't consider specific personalities important.

"It'll be an adventure," Ann said.

"Adventure. Haven't we had enough adventure for a while?" Rita glanced down the narrow walkway between shelves to where Ann craned her head back to look at Rita upside-down. Her pale hair floated about her like a halo, but she looked like a kid in a playground more than an angel. Rita felt an annoying flare of maternal instinct.

"Ann, please be careful!"

Ann was already pulling out a box to look behind it. Rita could see the luminary tattoo on her wrist glowing bead by bead as it tracked the rosary prayers. Inventory, conversation, and prayer. Rita wished she could multi-task so well.

Ann said, "I'm fine. I actually feel better than the time the snake bit me."

"I thought we agreed never to mention the snakes." Rita shuddered. What if the aliens were like snakes?

"You're right, but this is better than then, and Sister Lucinda said I'm cleared for light duty."

"And gallivanting off to the Kuiper Belt to explore an alien ship is 'light duty'?"

"We'll just be doing training for three months. I'll be perfectly fine by then!"

Which was just the counter Mother Superior gave us when Tommie and I protested this assignment, Rita thought, remembering when she told them.

Rita could still see the angry fire in Tommie's eyes when she had crossed her arms and declared, "Not Ann."

Mother Superior raised one fine eyebrow at Rita's team leader. "Ann will be fine. I have already discussed this with Sister Lucinda. She will be able to travel, and there is a skilled surgeon on the ship."

"Not Ann," Tommie had repeated. "You know why better than any of us."

Finally, Mother Superior had leaned over her desk, an uncharacteristically large gesture for the small Asian. "It is not as if we are sending her to Phobos, Sister Thomas. You will be traveling with a small group of researchers and people we know and trust to the far end of the solar system. She will be fine. Your team was requested by name. You have your assignment. You have one week, so I suggest you start planning what you will bring. Talk to the Quartermaster." She'd sat back in her chair and turned to her computer, dismissing them. Rita had risen to go, but Tommie stayed behind and, when the door closed, she heard the argument start.

Rita had gone to arrange a time to meet with Sister Quartermaster. Thus fulfilling Mother Superior's command in fact, if not spirit, she waited in the dorm until Tommie stormed in.

"Are we off the assignment?" She set down her book, a time-travel novel, because she didn't want to think about aliens.

"No," Tommie growled and sat hard on her bed. She grabbed her pillow and shoved it against the wall, then slumped against it.

Why was she so angry? "Tommie, listen, if Lucinda says —"

Almost on top of Rita's reassurance, Tommie started, "Listen to me, Rita, we have got to keep Ann close. I don't like this. She shouldn't wander."

I came as a wanderer... The memory of Ann's quoting had floated to Rita's mind. Was that it? "Oh, Tommie, I know Ann is a little...odd...but she'll be fine. Frankly, I can see why they chose her — she's such a technical genius! I'm the third wheel here."

Tommie sat back up and regarded Rita with hard, narrowed eyes. "Well, someone thinks pretty highly of you. Ann and I are going because we're your teammates — and Augustus Cole requested you by name."

Ann's words brought Rita back to the present. "Render unto Caesar."

"Augustus Cole is not Caesar."

"Out here in the Black he is."

Ann sounded so matter-of-fact about it. Rita wished she could feel such aplomb. She picked up what looked like a butterfly net and turned it over in her hands. *What could we possibly do with this? Sister Quartermaster's got everything packed in here, including the kitchen sink.*

She slid the pole back in next to the portable emergency eyewash station.

What are we doing here? What am I doing here? I don't even know Cole. What's he want with me?

Thinking about it would just make her crazy. She started to grab something from the next shelf up and realized she'd already checked there twice. "Well, the third crate of lights is not here. Could Sister Quartermaster have miscounted? We were tossing things in helter-skelter — by Rescue Sisters standards, I mean. You should have seen me back home on Earth. I'm sure Saint Anthony was tired of my asking where my keys had gone."

Still hanging from the ceiling, with her feet and one hand in loops, Ann pushed aside a box. "*Solicitude for material things distracts the soul and divides it.* It's not here, either. We'll have to improvise; I'm sure the *Edwina Taggert* will provide. You had actual keys? What did you use them for?"

"What didn't I use keys for? There was my car, my house, my office..."

"And you'd lose them?"

Tommie's voice over the intercom prevented Rita from replying. "Sisters, it's almost time to pace the *Edwina Taggert* and dock. Come up to the bridge."

Ann pulled her feet out of their loops and lowered herself smoothly to the floor. *Like a gymnast*, Rita thought, with a tinge of envy mixed with admiration. Still, when Ann chose to use the hand straps to go down the hall like a kid on monkey bars, she joined her. After all, it was pretty easy when she only weighed about twenty percent of normal.

"There she is, home for the next few months," Tommie said as they glided in. She, of course, was strapped into her seat, her hand on the joystick control that guided their ship. "What do you think?"

Rita looked out the viewscreen at the bullet-shaped behemoth with a shiny metallic finish and red piping along the three fins that flared over the "bottom" third of the ship.

"It's huge," Rita whispered, then laughed. "Look at the stabilizer fins, though! It's just like the *Star of Vengeance* in the Lola Quintain hologames. My brother will be in orbit when I tell him." She pressed some buttons on the console to get pictures for him.

"When you can tell him. It gets better. Look!" Tommie focused the forward screens on the stories-high painting on the nose cone: A buxom woman with skin the color of instant coffee dressed in a hardshell spacesuit that hugged her curves, posing beside the words *Edwina Taggert*.

"Well, that's certainly..." She tried to think of an appropriate word and ended up snorting through her nose and falling into giggles. She teased her brother about having a crush on Lola. Seeing her splashed across the hull of a ship made it seem even more ludicrous.

"And this is what ColeCorp bought for their important mission?" Tommie asked. She tried — and failed — to sound stern.

"I guess the secret's safe!" Rita managed to gasp out. The magnitude of their mission, the worry about her role in it, and the lack of sleep from the preparation had left her feeling punchy. Weird dreams she only half-remembered had robbed her furtive naps of any restfulness. At least the only time she had thought of James was when she prayed, and then only to notice that she hadn't thought of him. Laughter brought welcome release.

Ann regarded the picture with cocked head. "Who would make a spacesuit so tight?" she asked. "Why is it painted like metal underwear?"

Rita's giggles became shrieks of laughter, and she covered her mouth. "I'm sorry! I'm sorry. It's not that funny, really."

Rita noticed Tommie chewing the inside of her cheek to keep from laughing. "Yes, it is. But I need you two in your seats and quiet for docking. Despite what I told the *ET*, this is a little more complex than landing on a comet."

The two complied, Rita wiping her eyes with her sleeve. Ann kept frowning at the ship.

Rita stifled a snicker. "Ann, if you really want to know about Lola, I can tell you what I remember. My brother loved those games. Still does, actually. What I don't understand is why anyone would buy a cruise ship for a scientific expedition. And one like that?"

"Don't judge it by its shell," Tommie warned. Her hands flew over the keyboard controls, and the visual display moved to a corner of the viewscreen so that a computer-generated schematic of the docking dominated the center screen. *Basilica* seemed very small alongside the cruise ship.

Ann's voice took a flat tone. "IndyPhobos Retroshell bearing three ColeCorp Hulkhauler II VASIMR engines capable of 1.5g constant acceleration, with dual Kayfarer hydrogen fusion drives for emergency deceleration and boost. Standard Quantum Networks communications package. Gross volume: two hundred ninety-four thousand, six hundred seventy cubic meters. Two docking bays capable of holding five Esprit-class private yachts, each bay equipped with a Minnownet MagArm to assist in docking."

Tommie snorted. *Edwina Taggert* had offered the use of the magnetic arm to dock *Basilica*. However, when they found out the size of the OLR ship, and she learned of the inexperience of the crewman in handling the equipment, they mutually agreed on her docking manually.

"Seventy-five TorpedoLife escape pods with twelve person capacity situated at key points throughout the passenger and common grounds," Ann continued. "Six separate hydroponics and garden areas provide fresh produce and O2 production. Recycling system was refurbished four years ago. Sickbay is equipped to handle everything short of transplant surgery; three stasis chambers for emergencies."

"See?" Tommie said. "She's a powerhouse."

Ann continued, "Hawkins/Jacobs 7 gravity generator. Three-storey grand lobby. Viewing room in the nose of the ship, with additional viewing rooms along port and starboard. Valle Marinaris 25,000 square-foot day spa with Olympic-sized pool and full fitness center. The reaction mass tank contains forty percent overage and doubles as a scuba reef with live fish, rays, and a domesticated shark. Oh, I wish they were still there!"

Rita yelped. "Sharks? No thanks! Snakes in space were bad enough."

"Very good point. Amusement deck contains an amphitheater with two hundred and fifty capacity; a zero-G fun deck. We can use that for training, perhaps. Virtual sports, the Nova Casino, and a two-level variable-gravity disco. And of course, the splat court."

"Is that why Sister Quartermaster packed your gear?" Rita asked.

Almost on top of her question, Tommie said, "Probably been salvaged already. Dodecks are hard to come by."

"*Faith, hope and love.* We can hope," Ann countered. "Two ballrooms, five formal dining facilities, four public Laundromats, a library with a complete set of the Library of Sol (as of last year), plus two thousand paper prints."

"Really?" Rita wondered if they were still there. She hadn't read an actual physical book in too long.

"Shopping mall. Ten passenger decks, each with its own dining facility and pub. Staterooms vary from fifteen-hundred-foot suites to single-bed cabins and house up to nine hundred eighty crew and passengers, with kennel facilities for twenty-four approved spacefaring animals and their supplies for two-month cruises of the inner system and extended cruises to Saturn and Jupiter. Yet only one chapel, multidenominational." Ann sighed, as if she couldn't understand their oversight. Nonetheless, her eyes flickered with excitement over the *ET's* hull.

"Yet they've released it to a group of seventy-five?" Rita asked.

"It was already in decommissioning; I wonder what's been removed?" Ann mused.

"As long as the engines and life support work, I'm fine," Tommie declared, "though the splat court would be nice."

She switched a dial on the console and spoke louder. "*CCS Edwina Taggert*, this is *OLR Basilica*. We've matched velocity and acceleration and are on-target. Please confirm shield frequencies."

Nervousness chased away the last of Rita's mirth. Every ship had a magnetic field to deflect radiation, but the field itself posed even greater danger to humans. Once inside the *Edwina Taggert's* field, they were protected but, in order to pass through, they had to generate their own cancellation field. If they got the harmonics wrong, the strong magnetic forces would wreak havoc with everything from nerve impulses to blood cells. She'd learned this in basic training, but had been so overwhelmed at the time, she hadn't thought much about it. She wished Tommie hadn't reminded her of it last night.

"That's the easy part," Tommie had confided to her over dinner. "Computers handle that. I get to make sure we keep exact pace with the *ET's* docking bay as we slide sideways into it. We'll already be moving nearly a tenth of the speed of light. I haven't done a point-c parallel dock since..." Her voice trailed off, and her eyes focused somewhere into her own past. Then she huffed, shook her head, and returned to her meal without ever telling Rita how long it had been.

Rita shivered. Maybe she was better off not knowing.

If Tommie was nervous, or excited, no one would know from her voice. "Counter-harmonics active. Confirming visual on the open bay door. Firing port thrusters."

Rita felt a lurch in her stomach as the small rockets fired, and the *Basilica* drifted into the *Edwina Taggert's* ample bay. The viewscreen, projecting forward, flared as they passed through the shields, then showed the ceiling of the docking bay. On the heads-up schematic, she watched the graphic of the *Basilica* rotate 90 degrees to match the floor of the *Edwina Taggert's* flight deck; behind it, she saw the room shifting. The effect reminded her of cresting the first large hill on a roller coaster. She hated roller coasters. She closed her eyes and jumped slightly when she felt the landing gear impact the flight deck.

Tommie flipped switches to cut engines. "*Edwina Taggert, Basilica.*

We're in."

"Confirm, *Basilica*. Excellent flying. Doors closed and green. Pressurization...complete. Atmosphere green. We are stellar. Welcome to the *Edwina Taggert*, ladies. Captain Addiman sends his compliments and will greet you with the welcoming committee. *Edwina Taggert* out."

"Acknowledged and thanks. *Basilica* out."

Ann pulled at her buckles in an ecstasy of excitement. "I can't wait to find the chapel and explore the ship and meet Captain Addiman and have them tell us about the alien ship!" She giggled. "But chapel first!"

Ann dashed to a small alcove in the control room, opened the door, and pulled out a satchel. She gave it a happy kiss before slinging it reverently over her shoulder and hurrying down the hall, again swinging hand-by-hand, despite the fact that they were under the influence of the *Edwina Taggert's* artificial gravity.

Tommie caught Rita's eye. "She wears me out, too," the older sister said, and they followed at a more reasonable pace.

When they met up with Ann at the airlock, Tommie said, "Remember, Rita: you're team leader for this mission. You first."

"Copy that — I mean roger," Rita groused. *"Copy" to hear; "roger" to obey.* After three years, she knew this, but she didn't feel qualified to lead the team normally, much less on a mission of this magnitude.

"Render unto Caesar," Ann said. "We have faith in you."

"Let's hope it's well-placed," Rita countered, though she grinned.

"You'll love it," Tommie concluded, finishing the triad with a twinkle of humor. "So, ladies, shall we, as Brother Jubal put it, 'leave the comfort of our solitude to join the Leviathan of the Noisome'?"

Ann spoke solemnly. "*Yea, my Beloved, abandon me not/For having found You in desolation and silence/I must now seek You/in the blustering crowds and the din of a drinking song.*"

"*If* the two of you are quite finished," Rita said with mock severity, and the three trooped down the cargo area and onto their "noisome Leviathan."

Chapter Six

James leaned back against the high counter of his workspace on the *Edwina Taggert* and smiled, as bemused now as he was when Thoren had first pointed out the workroom on the ship's schematic. The engineers had certainly shown their imagination in making an archaeology lab out of the kitchen that had once serviced the conference room level. Yet, it did make sense. Even though most of the refrigerator and heating enclaves were disconnected, they provided neat airtight spaces for storing objects, and the sinks were handy for washing up. With plenty of counter space for microscopes and some minor chemical testing equipment, it worked better than a lot of museum set-ups he'd worked in — and certainly better than most of the on-site labs.

Of course, he wasn't sure just how much stuff he'd get to study. Everyone agreed microbiology had first shot at any artifacts, if only to check them for potentially harmful microbes. Which, Thoren had explained, was why he was sharing his space with their documentarist.

"I hope I'm not taking too much room," Sean said as he laid out the 3-D projection map over the big table. He had to stretch onto tiptoes to smooth down a far corner. A similar screen used for two-dimensional images covered one of the walls, and he'd rearranged several of the tables to hold his computers and cameras.

"Not at all," James reassured him. "Probably most of the archeological work we'll be doing is videography, anyway, so this really is a perfect arrangement."

"Okay, then," Sean said, as he called up some footage on the flat screen and began to fiddle with the settings. "It's just you seemed kind of...down...earlier, and I thought maybe..."

"No! No, sorry, Sean. It's just... I was expecting someone to be on the recovery team. An old friend. We'd lost track of each other years ago, and I'd hoped... Never mind. Space is big." He shrugged.

"He working asteroids now?"

"She."

"Ooooh!"

James looked away from Sean's grin, idly picked up a chisel and twirled it in his fingers. Would he even need this? "It wasn't like that. We were good friends. That's all."

"Uh-huh. Well, have no fear. There are some lovely and intelligent ladies on this mission, and if you play your cards right, I'll let you see their interviews. You can have the inside track."

Sean started pulling up the files of each of the women on the mission, playing them silently in small squares on the screen.

James set the chisel down and wandered over to Sean's seat. He rested against the edge of the desk, his back to the screen, and crossed his arms. "I don't think that'll be necessary."

Sean shrugged, but his light green eyes sparkled with mirth. "Fine, Mr. Confidence. But this is an exclusive offer for my lab-mate. Although maybe I should offer to let Chris in on my interview with a certain rockjack."

Now the knowing smile tugged at James' lips. "Andromeda deChavez?"

"You noticed, too?" Sean laughed and pulled up some footage of the researchers greeting the recovery crew. A quick keyboard command, and the screen focused on Chris. A small target showed where his eyes tracked. Aside from quick, nervous glances to Thoren, his gaze remained steadfastly in Andi's direction — at least when she wasn't looking his way.

James held back a snicker. Was he ever that young?

Had I looked at Rita that way? The snicker died in his throat.

Sean typed another command, and Chris' vital signs displayed in a corner.

"How'd you do that?" James turned to stare at the screen.

In reply, Sean held up one of his cameras where James could see a switch marked VR.

"Standard virtual reality option. Records simple vitals that indicate emotion, which I can tweak, transfer or even save for other footage. I have permission from some of the team for this, and we'll remove the more personal stuff. I'm a professional. Don't let my boyish face fool you." He plugged in a linking chip, then handed a VR plug for James to put in his ear. "In the meantime, though, want to feel how bad he's got it?"

James all but smacked the lozenge-shaped device out of his hands. "Don't record like that from now on! And erase that. It's demeaning."

"Erase what?" Chris' voice came from the doorway.

Sean quickly turned off the display. "Some footage James didn't like. Wasn't his good side," Sean said blandly.

"Oh. Well, um, the *Basilica* has docked, and Dr. Thoren and Captain Addiman are going to meet the Rescue Sisters. Dr. Thoren thought you might want to record it?"

Sean shrugged and picked up the camera. James snatched it from his hands and made sure the VR switch was off, then handed it back to him with a warning glare. Sean just laughed and shook his head. He picked up a second camera and handed it to James. "Here. You can help."

James looked over the camera, which really was more of a half-mask of wire and fabric holding an eyepiece and an earphone/mic set-up.

"It's the technology used in your dive helmet, so you should be familiar with the interface," Sean told him.

"Sounds fun. There's no vital sign recording?" James slipped it on. It covered the left half of his face. He felt like some kind of cybernetic nightmare, but it was surprisingly comfortable. He played with the commands and found it did work just like the one he'd used recording the sunken ship.

"So what do you want me to record?" he asked as they started down the opulent halls of the *Edwina Taggert*. The conference level corridor was done in real wood, and the carpet absorbed the sound of their footsteps.

"Filler stuff. Crowd shots, sweep of the scene. Focus on Thoren a lot. He likes that."

Chris let out an uncharacteristic snort, and James smiled. They'd get that kid to loosen up eventually.

* * *

No "noisome Leviathan" met the three sisters, only an empty bay.

"They did say it was pressurized?" Rita asked. She hesitated at the end of the ramp.

"We're breathing," Tommie replied.

Ann grinned at them. "Maybe they're in the chapel!" She moved past them with a little extra skip in her usual gliding steps.

Rita and Tommie exchanged a glance and followed.

They were about halfway across the bay when the doors opened. A man slipped through quickly, pointing a camera at them.

Ann spun, her back to the cameraman, and looked at Tommie and Rita, her unusually large eyes even wider with worry.

Tommie muttered some words that made Rita gasp with surprise and strode forward, putting herself between Ann and the cameraman. Rita hurried after.

"We don't want to be V-Rec'd!" Tommie called out in a calm voice that nonetheless echoed in the large bay.

"Just documenting!" the cameraman called, but turned back toward the entrance nonetheless.

The doors opened with regal slowness. Rita wondered if they were programmed that way and whether the ship normally had a soundtrack to go with it. Two men stepped through and approached them side-by-side. The tall, dark-skinned man wore a naval uniform decorated in a style more befitting the nineteenth rather than twenty-third century. He moved with fluid grace for one so large. The other wore a turtleneck shirt with a mission logo on the pocket, and slacks. He moved with deliberate steps, his hands held still in front of his sternum, his head barely moving. Rita recognized him from their briefing files: Dr. Thoren.

Another cameraman followed them backward, so that he recorded them and the crowd behind. The helmet cam obscured his profile.

"There's a side exit," Ann said, her voice just over a whisper. "I could go that way and meet you at the chapel."

However, the crowd had started to surge around the two, and one miner squealed Ann's name and ran to her, her short black hair bouncing with each step. She wrapped Ann in a hug. "Oh, Ann! I didn't think they'd send you. This is going to be like on the *Diamond*, only so much better!"

Ann took Andi's arm and started pulling her away. "Do you know where the chapel is? I brought the Sacred Host."

Tommie took advantage of the confusion to approach the cameraman and repeat her request, which left Rita to face the welcoming committee alone.

Dr. Thoren cleared his throat. "Doctor Rita Aguilar, Sister Thomas Aquinas Kreuger, Sister Ann St. Joseph de Cupertino." His eyes flicked to Rita's companions with annoyance, but continued his welcome as if they stood by Rita's side. "We greet you under the auspices of the Code, which promises safety and demands obedience. For the Code is Life."

"The Code is Life," many of the researchers and a couple of the miners echoed, some automatically, some with sidelong glances to him or others, as if seeking approval.

Rita felt her hackles rise, and the words were out of her mouth before she thought about them. "And we greet all of you in the name of the Father and of the Son and of the Holy Spirit."

She made the sign of the cross. Ann paused to do the same, kissing the tattoo on her ring finger afterward. About half the miners and some of the researchers also made the sign. Rita even noted a few of Dr. Thoren's followers started to, reflexively, before aborting the attempt and returning their hands to the customary Codist position.

Thoren scowled for just a moment, but when Tommie returned to Rita's side, he put on a cordial grin and nodded to her. He held out his hand to Rita. "Doctor Aguilar. A pleasure to have another academic on this mission."

"It's *Sister* Rita, Dr. Thoren." Rita resisted the urge to call him "Mister." He shook her hand like a greenfoot: palm-to-palm instead of palm-to-wrist. She wondered if he was recognizing the fact that she was originally from

Earth, or if he himself retained the habit. She gently disengaged her hand.

"It's my understanding that you have a PhD in Geology," he protested.

"I do. However —"

"Rita? Rita, is that really you?"

Rita spun toward the familiar voice as the cameraman removed his mask.

She felt as if the gravity had changed, and the whole ship was ripped out from under her feet.

James!

For a moment she was terrified he'd embrace her, but he stopped near Thoren. It was him: those same blue eyes, his hair messy as always. The way he clenched the back of his teeth together to hold back surprise.

The oxygen supply seemed to have malfunctioned; her focus narrowed to his face, and she found it hard to catch her breath.

"What are you doing here?" she managed to gasp.

"I... ColeCorp hired me to oversee the exploration. Rita, what are *you* doing here?"

Thoren cleared his throat. "Dr. Smith will coordinate the research team's mission on the ship itself. We are prepared for our initial group mission briefing. Perhaps you can save the socializing until —"

"You know Rita?" Ann suddenly squealed and inserted herself between the two. Tommie took a step to get between her and the cameraman. Rita didn't understand Tommie's behavior. She didn't understand James in space. Her head spun. As Rita fought to recover her mental equilibrium, Ann continued. "Were you friends at TTUI?"

James blinked and stammered, "I, well, yes, I was — we worked with the youth group together."

"Wonderful! Then you *must* know where the chapel is! Won't you escort the Host with me?" Ann turned to Captain Addiman. "We brought Jesus in the Most Blessed Sacrament! I'd like to take Him to the chapel right away, and if anyone would like to join us, they're certainly welcome."

Thoren glared at Ann, a look that made Rita's hackles rise a second time. She'd been on the receiving end of looks like that as a grad student; she knew what it meant. *How did someone like you ever manage to get this far?* She welcomed the ire she felt on Ann's behalf. It distracted her from her own confusion.

Ann didn't notice. She gave Thoren an entreating smile. "Unless it's imperative we get the mission briefing now? I'm so excited to find out what we're going to do together, but..." She hugged the satchel.

"Oh, it's not a problem at all, I'm sure," Andi answered, silk in her voice.

Rita noticed now that Ann had kept her friend between her and the cameraman, as well, although he did not seem to be recording. "Like Dr. Thoren told us when we arrived, we have three months to settle in and prepare ourselves. What's half an hour? Code Six, right, Thoren?"

Thoren raised his brows, but nodded. "Of course." Like he had a choice: Code Six dictated that, where it didn't interfere with mission, people's beliefs were to be tolerated.

Chuckling, Captain Addiman finally spoke up, his voice a mellow baritone just hinting at his Caribbean accent. "Sister, it would be my honor to escort you to our little chapel. It has been too many months since I have received the Eucharist." He stuck out his elbow, and when she just looked at it, puzzled, took her hand and set it on his forearm. She gave a small "oh!" then looked at her fellow sisters.

"Go ahead," Tommie urged. "We'll finish lockdown and meet you there."

As the captain led her out, Ann reached back and grabbed James' hand. "You, too! Come on, everyone is welcome!" Several of the miners consulted with each other and followed. A few of the research team did, as well, though somewhat more skittishly, including one who had been mimicking the Codists earlier. James gave Rita one last confused look before being swallowed up again in the group.

"Please excuse our abruptness," Tommie told Thoren with forced diplomacy and a false sincerity that told Rita she was really speaking for the camera. "It wasn't intentional. We weren't expecting camera crews or a Codist greeting ritual."

Rita winced. Was she going to start her first mission as team lead dealing with a confrontation? But Thoren just watched the disbanding crowd and said nothing. He gave the sisters a distracted nod and strode out, the rest of the researchers and his cameraman following in his wake. Tommie growled in disgust.

Only a handful of miners remained, and Rita fought against the feeling that they were all looking at her. In reality, they were loitering, taking an opportunity to grumble among themselves.

"All right, secure that leak!" Galen, Rocky Flat's pilot and second in command, called out. Like Tommie, he was a short and stocky ex-military with a booming voice. "Thoren may think we have time to kill, and Andi may have rubbed his face in it, but we got half an hour or so to help our rescuers out."

The miners made various grudging noises and gathered around Tommie for directions. So much for Rita being the team leader.

Not that she minded. Rita took her chance to beat a retreat to the

Basilica. She did her best to stride, not run, and to hold her head naturally, but as soon as she was up the ramp and around a corner, she leaned heavily against the bulkhead and buried her face in her hands.

Oh, God, why did You bring him here? I don't understand. How can he be here? He's an archaeologist, for pity's sake! I can't do this. I don't know what it is You want me to do. Oh, Holy Mary, help those in need...

"Rita?" Tommie's voice made her jump.

"I'm fine." She brushed away her tears.

"Who was that?"

"Just...someone from my past. It...brought back things I'd thought I left behind. I'm okay, really..."

Tommie gave her a look that said she didn't believe any of it, but was willing to drop it for now. "We've got some of the Rocky Flats crew with exoskeletons to unload the heavy stuff. Meanwhile, if you're ready?"

She could almost hear Tommie thinking, "Suck it up, Sister, and take those feelings to God, so we can do our job."

Somehow, that made Rita feel strong enough to laugh. "Absolutely. Thoren made a point of his beliefs; I think we need to make a statement about ourselves early on. 'Dr. Aguilar,' indeed. Know why I got that degree? My order wanted me to teach at TTUI. I'm much better with high school, believe it or not." She sighed loudly, feeling some of the tension release.

"Well, you'd better be ready to handle Thoren. He's your responsibility, Team Leader."

Rita gave a "tuh!" of annoyance, but she knew Tommie was pulling her mind back to the mission. "Fine. Then you get the cameraman."

"That pup? Not a problem. Thoren is a piece of work. Why do I get the feeling Cole isn't the only one who likes to play games? That was a clever response, by the way. Pompous academic... and a Minister of the Code. How many did you count?"

Rita thought back, grateful for the change of subject. "Codists? Perhaps a dozen, at least two of which grew up Catholic."

Tommie nodded. "I saw fourteen. We've got our work cut out for us, in more ways than one."

They gave quick instructions to their volunteers on what things to unpack from the *Basilica*, checked their wrist computers for the route, then headed to the chapel.

The shuttle bay opened up to the grand lobby, a gorgeous area with a rock climbing wall and Indian artifacts.

Rita smirked, despite her mood. "One of the Lola games took place on a planet to which aliens had transplanted the populace of the ancient citadels," she told Tommie. "The rock wall had booby traps. Took Joseph weeks to get past that level. It was supposed to be a waterfall. Do you think they actually had a working waterfall here?"

Tommie shrugged. "Holographic, more than likely. Even on a cruise ship, that's a lot of water to waste."

At any rate, the waterfall was disabled, and no one manned the check-in desk that dominated a side wall. They gave the replica of the Mayan temple admiring looks as they hurried through to the corridors beyond.

They turned down a maze of long curved hallways of staterooms and suites; high-end suites, judging by the distance between the crystal doorknobs.

"What use are those?" Tommie demanded. "The doors slide automatically."

Rita shrugged. "Part of the motif?" She knocked a knuckle against a wall. It looked like oak, but gave a higher, metallic sound.

As they neared the end of the hall, they heard a low murmur of voices praying in unison and followed it down a third hallway to the chapel. Rita gasped at first to see stained glass and statues of the saints, but Tommie tapped her shoulder and pointed to a control box beside the door set to "Roman Catholic," and she realized the walls were holographic screens that changed to fit the selected religion. The pews were real enough, however, as was the altar where Sister Ann had placed the monstrance. She knelt in the aisle before it, with Captain Addiman on one side and James on the other, and was leading the dozen or so people through the Eucharistic Adoration. Tommie touched Rita's arm, and they knelt down in the back pew and joined in.

Ann's high, clear voice spoke lovingly.

In this Sacrament, sweet Jesus,
You give Your Flesh and Blood,
With Your Soul and Your Divinity,
As our own most precious food.
Yes, Jesus, I believe it,
And Your presence I adore;
And with all my heart I love You,
Help me love You more and more.

Rita glanced over her folded hands at James and saw him shifting nervously. She wondered how long it had been since he'd done this, if he even worshipped at all.

Lord, did my actions cause him to stray from You? I left to protect him, to make him forget me. I thought his superiors would talk some sense into him and then he'd find me gone and — but he left the seminary! He declined his ordination...for me?

Of course, for me. And he came back, and I was gone. No forwarding address. No way to find me. I'd begged Sister Elizabeth on that point. He must have left the university, gone into field work... God, what have I done? He would have been such a wonderful priest.

Yet, there it was in the back of her mind: the memories of him with the children of their fellow professors. He'd make a wonderful father, too. And husband. And she couldn't help but wonder...

Where is my heart, Lord? Where does it — do I — belong? Is it my spiritual needs or my temporal ones for which I should pray?

The more she wondered, the more tortured she felt, so knowing that, as usual, she was running from the problem, she turned her prayers to the needs of the Church and the conversion of sinners. *Especially those poor misguided Codists. Oh, St. Gillian, you lived according to the Spacer's Code. You were even a part of its development. Help us to show these misguided souls that man's laws are not sufficient.*

Despite her best efforts, her prayers ran in little circles and dead ends, and she was relieved when Ann began the *Prayer for Those in Agony.*

Afterward, Ann rose, blessed herself and went to move the monstrance and small tabernacle to a back shelf. Then she all but ran to Rita and Tommie and enveloped them in a joyful hug. "Doesn't Captain Addiman have the most beautiful chapel?" she exclaimed as people exited behind her.

The ship's captain stopped and laughed a deep, booming melody. "Not mine, dear sister."

"You're right. God's house is for everyone. Catholic, small c, from the Greek words *kata* and *holos,* according to the whole. Universal. Still, the Catholic, capital C, chapel is so pretty! Did you see the monstrance? What a lovely home for His Sacred Body!"

Addiman laughed again as he took her arm and led them out. "I thank you. This particular program was designed after the chapel set in *Lola Quintain VI: Quest for the Papal Crown.*"

He stopped mid-explanation and tapped at the communicator on his ear. "Addiman. Yes? I see. Yes, that is fine. We will be there shortly."

"Is it time to talk about the ship?" Ann asked eagerly.

Addiman smiled at her, bemused. With his height, he looked like a father beaming at a precocious child. "Past time, I think Dr. Thoren would say. They await us in the small auditorium."

"*I have seen the burden God has laid on the human race. He has made everything beautiful in its time. He has also set eternity in the human heart; yet no one can fathom what God has done from beginning to end.* But now we'll know a bit more!" She started down the hallway toward the auditorium, leading the captain as if she'd traipsed the halls hundreds of times already. The rest trailed behind, Tommie deliberately slow, with a hand on Andi to slow her, as well. Rita joined them.

"The ship is of the universe," Ann pondered aloud to the captain. "But it's not of the whole, so it isn't really catholic."

"In either sense of the word," Addiman suggested. "I think Dr. Thoren will find that comforting."

"Caesar, too. Control is comforting. *When we control, we find comfort; when God controls, grace...*"

Their voices became a murmur as the two rounded the corner. Tommie pulled Andi closer. "Andi, spread the word among the rockjacks who know Ann well. If that...reporter...asks about Ann's past, they are to be vague and to let me know."

"Oh, Godmom. Sean's here to document the mission. He's doing interviews, but if anybody says, 'no,' he's cool about it. Cay's already refused."

"Cay is here?" Rita asked.

Andi nodded. "GenSup Hayden thought it'd be better than having him at the rebuild. Give him a chance to rebuild his confidence, too. Don't worry about Ann, Godmom. She's safe here."

"I hope you're right."

"Faith, hope and love," Andi quipped, and Tommie raised a brow at her.

What's this all about? Rita wondered. Caught up in the little drama, she didn't notice that they had left James behind.

* * *

James watched the last of the crowd leave the chapel. He'd have to catch up to them for the meeting, but he needed a moment alone, a chance to regain his balance before he saw her again. He sat in a front pew and buried his head in his hands.

A religious! She's still a sister! When Rita hadn't shown up with the rest of the Rocky Flats crew, he'd assumed that there'd been some last minute re-assignment, or that Augustus had lied to him. James wished he had. Instead, there she was: more beautiful than ever, but just as untouchable. And for the next six months, they had no way to escape each other. What could Augustus have been thinking?

"I'm going to kill him," James muttered aloud, wincing as he remembered his surroundings.

He looked up, wiping his face with his hands, and glanced at the alcove where they'd stored the consecrated Hosts. Ann had been so excited about bringing them here, but did the sisters have any idea the trouble they'd created for themselves? True, Thoren tossed the gauntlet down first with his Codist greeting, but the little sister had led away a significant percent of the miners and researchers, and Andi, the leader of the rockjacks, had been only too happy to jump in and support her in it. A power struggle was in the making, and the sisters were either playing into it or just unaware of it.

Rita is usually savvier than that, he thought. Then her shocked, almost horrified expression flashed before his inner eye. If he'd been unbalanced, she must have been knocked out of orbit.

He balled up his fist and pounded it hard against his thigh. Maybe he wouldn't kill Augustus, but they were going to have a very unpleasant encounter when they met again.

He rose and strode out of the chapel. As the door slid shut, the lights automatically darkened, save for a single red light in one corner.

Chapter Seven

Chris stood at the holographic viewer and triple-checked the controls for the third time as people found seats for the briefing. Thoren stood just far enough from the stage that he didn't seem to be in it, but close enough that a few steps would draw all eyes to him. He checked his wristcomp again, though, whether to see the time or because he was tracking the progress of those who had followed the strange little nun to the chapel, Chris didn't know.

What was the big deal, anyway? the rebellious part of Chris wondered. *We have three months to plan and prepare this mission. Andi was right; half an hour wouldn't hurt anything.*

He hoped Dr. Thoren would relax soon. It had been an intense six weeks since they'd first turned the lenses of Old COOT toward the Ky-bo and seen the ship waiting there. Six weeks of researching while trying to keep the research secret, of briefing the right people and dealing with their reactions. Shock was easy. Curiosity welcome. Greed, he expected, and Thoren was able to leverage that in their favor nearly every time; when he couldn't, Cole would make a phone call, and the problem disappeared. Actually, that part was kind of scary; Chris tried not to think about it.

Cole had also managed to keep the military out of it. He'd laughed about that to Chris and Thoren on their way to Earth.

"After all, whose military has jurisdiction? I suppose, technically, the Ring Guard is closest, location-wise, but I don't trust them. But really, we bring any government into this, and we've got a war on our hands. A multi-state, commercial organization controlling this project is the best way to keep peace. I think God realized that, which is why you, Chris, found it with my funding." Cole had raised his glass to him then.

Cole wasn't a bad guy, Chris thought. He'd already promised Chris a portion of any profits made from the ship, from straight-out discoveries to patents to royalties from the documentary. In fact, he had the feeling his share was bigger than Thoren's. In a couple of years, he'd be set for life. He could do anything.

But what did he want to do? Astrophysics, sure, but really...

Study the unknown, and I'm doing it right now. The thought made his hands damp, and he rubbed them on his pant legs as he scanned the crowd.

Captain Addiman had arrived with the small blond sister on his arm, chatting amiably. He led her to a seat in the front and waited until she sat

Karina Fabian

before sitting beside her. He kind of reminded Chris of the pirate captain in *Lola Quintain and the Jovian Seas*, and the little sister seemed to be falling for his charms just like Lady Rosalind.

Then again, maybe not, he decided. There was something paternal about the way the Captain held her hand as she explained her bracelet tattoo.

As others came in after them, they broke off to join others in small groups. The Research team and the Recovery team (or "rockjacks" as they called themselves) seemed to stick to their own groups, with a few of the ship's crew forming an uncertain third cluster. He wondered where the sisters would fit in. *Probably with the rockjacks. Hope that doesn't cause trouble.*

James had suggested that they needed to have some mixers to get to know each other, but Thoren had nixed the idea.

"The potential for distraction and personal conflicts outweighs the potential benefits. Our missions are quite apart from each other," he'd said. "As long as the recovery team understands its place and the chain of command, all is well."

Perhaps, but Chris found himself wanting to know the miners better. He'd expected them to be hard, practical people, like the men his mom dated: common laborers who had chastised him to stop dreaming and get a real job. But interspersed among the mundane discussions of equipment, procedures, and possible profits, he heard comments like "Why do you think they were heading our way?" "What kind of world did they come from?" and "Can you imagine if we find..." Maybe there was more to them than the job?

George Powers, a loudmouth even in the best of circumstances, had worked himself into a state. He shouted, "I cannot believe we are going to be the first to encounter aliens! Actual goddamn, shittin' aliens!" Sister Ann stood and turned toward him. "Shame on you, George Powers! We don't know God's plan for those poor souls."

"Or whether they defecate," his buddy Dale added dryly, causing the room to erupt with laughter and a speculation of a different kind.

Then, again... Chris sighed.

Someone slapped a hand on his shoulder, and he jumped. He thought his heart had stopped, but when he turned and saw those big brown eyes from his dreams twinkling at him merrily, it started again with a fast pounding. Oh, he hoped there was more to at least one of the miners than just the job.

"Don't worry about George," Andi said. "He's the best iceblaster in the quadrant. He'll clean up his language now that Ann is here."

"Oh, sure!" Chris stammered. "Of course he is. You're great. I mean, you're all great. All of you. At what you do."

Andi winked at him then went to call her people to order. He realized then that the other two nuns had been with her. The red-haired one took a seat beside her colleague, but the other assessed him with a half- smile on her face.

He found himself straightening his posture. He swallowed hard.

Her grin widened just a bit, and she gave him an approving nod before going to sit beside Andi. However, Commander McVee, the first officer, intercepted the sister, grabbing her up and swinging her around. She yelped and punched rather than slapped his shoulder, but she was laughing. Then she held out her hand, palm flat, in that way aunts do when remembering someone's childhood height. He, in turn, held his hand so it just brushed the top of her short salt-and-pepper hair, and she punched him again.

Looked like there was more to the sisters than just the job.

Andi went to join them, and the nun said something that made him swing Andi around, too. Chris felt a surge of jealousy at her delight and turned his attention to the audience. Ian stared at him, chin resting on his woven fingers as he batted his eyes. Reg failed to hide his snickers as he puckered his lips in Chris' direction. How those two could be such clowns and still so respected in their fields of engineering was beyond him. If he acted like they did, Thoren would shoot him out an airlock. James walked in and made a beeline toward the pair. Caught, they ceased their teasing, and he took a seat beside them. He didn't look happy. What was wrong?

Dr. Thoren cleared his throat, and everyone found their seats, Andi by the sisters. Thoren moved to the center and looked over everyone briefly, ending with the nuns in the front seat.

"I trust your little ceremony went well?" he asked. Chris could only see his profile, but he knew the smile his advisor wore. He'd quailed under that smile, and he'd seen one grad student burst into tears.

The blond nun just smiled brightly and nodded. "It was wonderful, thank you. Perhaps next time, you'll join us?"

Thoren's grin froze, but he continued. "And everyone is comfortable?"

Again, the little sister failed to understand his intent, but answered literally. "Comfort is an interesting concept. Like time, there are occasions when it's both relative and irrelevant."

The red-haired nun (*Sister Rita*, he reminded himself) touched her arm. "Ann," she said, and Sister Ann stilled. But Chris saw Addiman smirking behind his hand.

This was going to be an...odd...briefing.

Maybe Thoren thought the same, because he gave Sister Ann a neutral nod, then backed to a corner of the stage and looked at Chris.

And apparently, I get to bear the brunt of it. Joy.

Chris pressed a button and a holographic image of the Kuiper Belt Object, and the alien ship projected onto the center stage, rotating slowly so that everyone could get a good look at the ship itself.

"Um, okay," Chris started. "So, this meeting we could make some general plans about how we'll handle the crashed ship —"

"But Mr. Davidson!" Sister Ann spoke up. "Your ship didn't crash. Did it, Tommie?"

The older nun (*Tommie? What kind of name was that for a nun?*) stood and looked at the hologram, her mouth frowning in thought.

"No. It's not a great landing, but it's not a crash. In an uncontrolled collision, that ship would have blasted that rock apart. Instead... May I?"

Chris nodded, and she walked to the display. Setting her hands on the section she wanted, she rotated it and enlarged. She pointed to one area. Chris walked around so he could see as well, scooting back when several people protested his blocking the view.

"Instead, you have one spoke that's dug into the side of the asteroid. They had to have been going pretty slow by then, or they'd have sheared off the rock, the spoke, or both. More of an angle, and they might have caught and flipped. Of course this is all looking at it like a human pilot."

"What if it's an anchor, like the screw on a Meeger?" one of the miners asked.

Tommie shrugged. "I don't see much damage at all — thinking as a human, of course. Are we sure it's a ship and not a station?"

"Uh, we're really not sure of anything," Chris answered.

Tommie grunted. "Hope for a ship. Easier to move."

"I'm all for easy!" George hollered and promptly received a number of derogatory comments.

"Focus!" Andi called. People quieted down, even the researchers. Chris had to bite back a smile that was half-wistful. *Wish people listened to me like that.*

"Are we sure it's dead?" Sister Rita asked uneasily.

Chris called up another image. This one was black against black, with only a drawn-in outline to show where the ship was. "Well, there's no way to be certain, of course, but scans don't show energy. It's as cold as space."

"On the outside, at least," Sister Ann murmured just loud enough to be heard.

"You don't think there are still things *alive* in there?" Cay's question was edged with fear. "How old is this thing, anyway?"

Chris answered the nervous rockjack. "There's no way to tell. This is the only scan of this particular Ky-bo that we know of, so at least thirty years."

"So we could be stumbling onto live aliens with advanced technology? Vac that!"

"Cay, secure that leak," Andi ordered, annoyance clear in her tone.

"But what if they are? I did not sign up to deal with extra-terrestrial monsters!"

"No one's alive," Sister Ann murmured. All the rockjacks turned to listen to her. She didn't seem to notice. "Not the people. Too far from help. No one to rescue them. They died, so far away from home. *Your providence guides our lives, and by Your command, we return to dust.*" She shivered, then kissed the cross tattoo on the back of her hand. It lit up for a second at her touch, then each circle of her bracelet started to glow purple in turn.

"Let's get Sister Thomas to fly it home!" George called.

That generated some catcalls, but Sister Thomas, who had returned to her seat, answered. "Not even I am that good."

Beside her, McVee snorted. "Dad said you could fly anything."

Apparently dissatisfied at how Chris had let the briefing get away from him, Thoren stepped in front of the display. "Extraction is, of course, desirable, but our primary mission is to explore the ship and bring back anything of value."

"That may be *your* primary mission," Andi countered, "but I think Cole will go nova if we don't bring him the whole package."

"I'm sure we can find a way for us to accomplish our mission and you to fulfill your contract," Thoren said placatingly, but Andi did not look placated.

Chris felt himself withering under Andi's angry glare, and it wasn't even directed at him! But Dr. Thoren just started discussing the exploration as if her opinion didn't matter.

Why did it matter...so much, I mean? he thought. *I hardly know her.*

She caught him staring at her from his console, and her glare turned into an eye shrug of an apology. He felt his heart lighten.

This is stupid, he thought. Why was he even thinking about her, anyway? They were worlds apart, literally and figuratively. They couldn't have a future together, and if there was one thing his last relationship had taught him, it's that he didn't want to start anything that didn't have a chance of becoming something permanent.

Maybe I'm not such a spacer, after all, he grumped.

Thoren cleared his throat, and Chris' attention jumped back to the briefing.

"Sorry," he muttered, and called up the design of the probe that Cole had sent ahead of them.

"The CL-185 launched from Massell Station, Europa, two weeks ago and should reach 2217RB86 before we do. From it, we should be able to get more detailed information about the alien craft. It will deploy six remote bots to examine each of the alien ship's arms."

From the back, Cay said, "We should have those probes check the ship's defenses."

Thoren replied with a trace of impatience. "The ship is dead. Even your nun realizes that."

"Oh, no!" Ann spoke up. "I said the people are dead. And the ship appears dead from the outside. *Only fools and managers assume appearance equals reality.*"

Her words caused a rustling among the audience, researchers and miners alike. Even Chris felt a twist in his stomach.

Thoren again cleared his throat. "Then perhaps we should not go in assuming hostile intent."

"Why not?" Cay asked, and others murmured their support. "Wouldn't it be safer than assuming everything is Green?"

"Cay, later," Andi called out, and he and the miners who agreed with him fell silent.

Thoren nodded at Andi. "Thank you. As you can see, we will have approximately two months with little data for detailed planning. Therefore, we will work on some general protocols, and I would like each research section to prepare briefings on its contribution to the mission. After all, when dealing with the unknown, knowledge is your best tool. So sayeth the Code."

"And the Code is life," Chris and several others responded.

Ian called out, pumping both fists in the air. "And otherwise —vacation!"

More people cheered and several laughed, including Sister Rita. However, she stood and turned to address the group. "Hang on, now! For all our accommodations, this is not a joy ride. Sister Thomas, Sister Ann and myself will be going through your records and making sure all of you are trained up for Outside work."

"Aw, come on!" Ian moaned. "I took the course on Drake!"

"Loops for LunaTechs isn't going to cut it on a Ky-bo." Rita crossed her arms. When the drive systems expert had slouched back into his seat, she turned to Thoren.

"Dr. Thoren, if I may, I think those briefings should also include the recovery team. After all, don't you think everyone should have a fair idea of what's going on inside and outside the ship they're working with?"

Thoren nodded. "Indeed. A sound suggestion. Andi, if you can arrange for that?"

"Dale. Briefing duty!" Andi called over her shoulder.

"Yes, ma'am!" Around him, rockjacks groaned.

After Thoren dismissed them, everyone broke up into groups. Some were talking about exploring the *Edwina Taggert* more, others about hitting the VR arcade for the next level of a Lola Quintain game. Andi left with two of the nuns, and she didn't look especially happy. Chris watched her exit.

"Excuse me, Mr. Davidson?"

"Uh, it's just Chris." He tore his eyes away from the door and met the huge and startling blue eyes of Sister Ann.

She smiled like he'd given her a great gift. "It's such a wonderful name! From *Christopholos*: bearing Christ inside. And of course, Davidson, son of David. David was a king, so it's a princely name! David was a shepherd, too. Sometimes I wonder what was harder: sheep or people?"

Before he could do more than blink, she'd turned away from him and was circling the projection of the alien ship. "May I have a copy of all of your data on the Ky-bo and the alien ship? Mr. Cole wasn't very forthcoming, though I suppose Caesar has a right to his secrets. Secrets are dangerous now that we're all together. Still, sometimes revealing secrets has its own dangers. You should talk to Andi. She's very nice, but she doesn't have a lot of patience for secrets. She knows how to keep them, though. That's the key, isn't it? Knowing when to keep secrets and when to reveal them."

"I, uh..."

Suddenly, she stopped and peered at the ship. She reached out and touched the schematic along one of the arms. She had long, delicate fingers. The program responded to her touch command, and the arm expanded. She leaned closer to it.

"Whose secrets are you hiding?" she asked.

"Uh, Sister?" Chris leaned toward her and the image, unnerved, not sure if she was talking to him or the ship. He looked where she looked. It was just a dark shape against a lighter shape. He studied her face.

She seemed to look through the image more than at it. "There are a lot of secrets on this ship. That ship. Both ships. Ships passing in the Black. But in the Black, there are stars. God gave us stars that we could look to the sky and wonder. *God gave us minds to make that wonder our own.*"

"Pardon?"

"R. Charles Hawkins. He also said, 'Only fools and managers assume appearance equals reality.' He designed the gravity generator, because he wanted us to go to the stars, and we haven't even tried."

He felt a flicker of excitement. "So the stars have come to us."

"Another star in our system? That would be disastrous," Ann said. She twisted the image so that she was looking at it from above. They hadn't been able to get that angle with Old COOT, so the computer extrapolated data to create an approximate.

"Going to the stars is safer, but not guaranteed. They went to the stars and died. *The wise man in the storm prays to God, not for safety from danger, but for deliverance from fear.* They wondered. They wandered. Did they make assumptions? Did they fear? Or pray?"

"Uh," Chris looked around the room, hoping to find someone who might help him with this odd conversation. *If* it was a conversation. Thoren lingered by the doorway, a smirk on his face, a brow raised in challenge.

Chris cleared his throat. "You don't think, perhaps, that an advanced species might outgrow the need for prayer?"

"*Prayer reveals to souls the vanity of earthly goods and pleasures. It fills them with light, strength, and consolation; and gives them a foretaste of the calm bliss of our heavenly home.* Prayer for deliverance from fear." She stood up, rubbing her side as if to ease a pain, and grinned at him. "Fear: anxiousness, fright, anxiety. But also profound respect. Reverence. A recurring theme in the Bible is 'be not afraid.' Delivered from one kind of fear, yet brought closer to the other. Oh, Chris! I do hope they prayed! To advance past fear, to forego wisdom — that's too sad!"

Then she blinked as if listening to someone else. "Ignorance, however, is dangerous. Do sheep know that? Is that why they needed a shepherd? What's this?"

"Uh..." Chris jumped mental gears to consider the small point of light she indicated with one delicate finger. It was above the horizon on the other side of the Ky-bo. "Another Ky-bo, obviously. The Fadil probe didn't study it; not on its route."

"But you're an astronomer, Christopholos! Did you get any telemetry from Old COOT?"

He caught Thoren's disapproving glare. Chris had wanted, even asked, to investigate the nearby object, but Thoren wouldn't approve the expense on side projects. "There wasn't much time."

"Well, I'm sure CL-185 can look into it. Captain Addiman!"

The captain and McVee paused in their conversation to join them.

"Captain Addiman, can we send a program change to CL-185? Scan the horizon and get some telemetry from...?" She glanced a question at Chris.

Automatically, he answered, "2217RB87." Then he realized Thoren had been clearing his throat. The mission commander moved to the group.

The commander shrugged. "Shouldn't be too hard. We can send the request to Massell Station."

Thoren again cleared his throat and stepped, so he was between everyone and the projection. "I think we should focus on the mission. Our time and resources are limited."

Sister Ann stepped sideways to peer at the projection, as if willing the answers from it. "Copy that. *It is not the time we are given that matters, but what we do with it.* All the more reason to get some telemetry, don't you agree, Chris? Besides, it could be important, and it's so close. We shouldn't make assumptions. Code Three: Assumptions kill. Do not make them. But of course, you know that! May I have the data now?"

"Oh, uh..." He pulled the chip from the projector, and the image disappeared. He handed it to Ann. He could always make himself another copy. "All the polished data is on here."

"That's a good start! We have a lot to do. *Ora et labora*: pray and work."

Thoren gave him that expectant look he knew would turn to contempt if he failed to act.

"Uh, Sister? I follow the Code."

She just beamed at him.

He tried again. "I'm not Catholic or Christian. I'm not anything." He thought about asking her how much difference that would make with Andi, then wondered for the umpteenth time why his mind kept drifting back to her.

Ann grinned at him like she thought him very silly. "You're Christopher! Christopholos!"

Instead of just taking the chip, she grabbed his hand and pulled him so that he leaned closer to her.

"Fear Andi if you like, but don't be afraid of her!" she whispered, then snatched the chip and started toward the door.

She paused at the threshold, as if remembering something, then turned back to Chris. *"Men invent new ideals because they dare not attempt old ideals. They look forward with enthusiasm, because they are afraid to look back."*

Then she smiled at Thoren, as if sharing a joke. "Comfort. The absence of discomfort. Fear is very discomforting. Be not afraid, Dr. Thoren. We'll look together. This is going to be so exciting!"

Chapter Eight

As soon as Tommie exited the theater, she said to Andi, "We need to talk. Why don't you show us our quarters?"

Despite the edge in her teammate's voice, Rita hesitated. "Should we wait for Ann? What's taking her so long?"

Andi nabbed a tall miner with swarthy Italian looks. "Lenny? Did you see Ann?"

"Yeah, she's looking at the alien ship and confusing Chris with her chatter."

Andi groaned. "Give the guy a break. Everybody needs time to get used to Annese."

Lenny chuckled. "Might help if you didn't look at him so much. Poor guy has a hard enough time concentrating."

Andi opened her mouth to protest, but nothing intelligible came out. The pinkish tinge to her cheeks didn't help her case much, either.

"Goes both ways, then? Very interesting. So, boss, you want I should wait for Ann and bring her over?"

Andi closed her mouth, then, salvaging what dignity she could, replied, "That would be fine."

Lenny snorted. "Now you just sound like Thoren."

Andi growled in her throat and spun off toward the passenger sections, each stride a testimony to pent-up fury. Tommie and Rita traded looks and followed.

They caught up, but walked in silence until they were halfway down an empty corridor.

Andi finally spoke. "If we'd turned left at that last junction, we'd have entered the hallowed halls of Research. Us 'secondary mission' rockjacks are in the coach cabins near the landing bay. You three are off in an executive suite, because it has an office attached to the bedroom." She stopped long enough to pull up a projection of the ship to show them the locations.

"Not very efficient," Tommie noted.

"Oh, it gets better. Near as we can tell, the research team's picking their own quarters anywhere on the ship. They're treating this whole thing like a school break!"

Rita looked around at the opulent wallpaper of rich gold brush patterns, the dark paneling on the lower half, the carpet thick enough to muffle Andi's angry stride. If the rooms were anything like this — and how many entertainment facilities had Ann rattled off? She wouldn't mind a little R&R herself.

"They'll be busy soon enough," Tommie reassured her but said nothing more.

Andi stopped at a corner suite with long hallways of evenly spaced doors spreading from it in three directions. "Here you are. It's already keyed to your biosigns."

Tommie approached the door, and it slid open. She stepped inside and whistled.

Rita followed. The suite opened into a large meeting area, with poufy, comfortable couches in a rich burgundy-and-gold pattern that blended well with the subdued gold tones of the walls. Oh, to see such colors again! The floor looked like hardwood but was really a microfiber. She couldn't wait to take off her shoes and wiggle her toes against it. Most of the tables and drawers were elegant but simple, except for the roll top computer station, which resembled the antique desk Rita had once seen in the TTUI university president's home.

I should stop ogling and get back to what's going on, she thought, even as her feet took her to the bedroom. Three beds lined the walls. Rita guessed they'd been traded out from another suite or suites. She wondered what the original master bed had looked like. Certainly, these had the usual sleep sacks that held you in place in case of gravity failure, but overtop were what looked like down comforters.

I'm finding the library and, if there are books, I'm grabbing a dozen, and every chance I get, I'm laying down and reading.

Tommie had followed her but slipped past and peeked into the bathroom. "Rita, I think you'll like this."

She looked in and gasped in delight. "A tub! If I should ever disappear, you'll know where to find me!"

A wave of homesickness washed over her. Tears stung her eyes.

"Yeah, *Cole's* treating us well." Andi turned on her heel and stomped back to the living room.

Tommie heaved a sigh and followed. Rita wiped her tears. So much for nostalgia, but if she should get the urge to have a quiet cry in that bathtub later, she was going to indulge herself.

"Ann to Rita." Ann's cheery voice came over Rita's wristcomp. "I've got a copy of the information, but unless they've upgraded the computers in our room, *Basilica's* are better. Do you need me right now?"

"No, we're just settling in. The room is amazing."

"Fortune 500 Executive suites done in the style exemplified in *Lola*

Quintain and the Wall Street Papers. Seven-hundred-twenty-square feet divided into living, sleeping and office spaces, furniture featuring memorygel grade seven, used for high-gravity vehicles..."

"Did you memorize the whole manual or just the brochure?" Rita accused.

"Both. I was stuck in bed for a few days. I just want to crunch some data on *Basilica*, then I can use the room computer there. I'll bring our stuff when I return."

Rita opened the bedroom closet and found their bags sitting in a row on the floor. "Looks like one of the rockjacks already took care of that."

"Copy. I'll double-check in that case. Ann out."

Rita entered the living room to catch Andi in mid-complaint.

"...and Thoren'll be perfectly happy to keep us in that corner for the rest of the trip. You know that meeting was more for your sake, right? And his agreeing to have us take part in the briefings? Trust me; he's humoring you until he figures out his game. He doesn't care about the recovery mission, except that we stay out of the way of his precious dataheads."

Tommie sat on the couch beside Andi, but held herself straight, with arms crossed. She might as well have been glaring at Andi from across a desk.

"And as the recovery team leader, what have you done about that?"

Andi tossed her dark curls. "Give me some credit, Godmom. I've tried to talk to him. But I'm a twenty-five-year-old asteroid driller, and two Master's degrees don't compare to the mighty PhDs of his team members."

"I wonder if Cole knows that?" Tommie met Rita's eyes.

Rita sat on the chair, which sank and formed around her comfortably. She tossed up her hands in surrender. "Okay, I can be *Doctor*-Sister Rita for this trip."

"Will that be enough?" Tommie asked. "Perhaps we should find someone he already trusts to help us. What about Chris Davidson? This is his discovery, after all."

Andi sighed. She stopped her pacing and dropped onto the couch beside her godmother. "Chris is nice and all. Really smart and curious, too, but he's Thoren's satellite. I don't think he's going to make a move without Thoren's approval."

Tommie frowned thoughtfully. "Perhaps we need to help him change his orbit — for his sake, as well as ours. Until then... What about Dr. Smith?"

She looked at Rita, and Rita felt a shock of guilt run through her.

"What about him?"

"You said you worked with him at TTUI. He was a professor there?"

She nodded. "Archaeology and theology." *And I just had to go to his lectures...* She could still see him, standing in front of the projection screen in his cassock, using a laser marker to draw crazy circles around one area on the schematic of an excavation. Sometimes, he'd draw a squiggle for a snake and make everyone laugh.

"Well?"

"Um..." Rita rubbed her eyes, banishing the memory. "He was always the diplomatic one, and he's a great team builder. He...worked with the Catholic social club on campus."

"James has been pretty decent to us," Andi agreed, "though he seems preoccupied. I guess that's not surprising. And, Godmom, I'm not trying to put all the dataheads in the same class. Most of them are good people, but some think we're the hired help. And most of them don't see any reason why we need to work together."

"Well, regardless of whether you're working together, we will be living together for at least half a year, and this ship isn't *that* big. We need to get out of this camp mentality. Besides, most of the researchers are dirtsiders. Even if they are working inside the ship, they'll need microgravity training, and we expect the rockjacks to help with that."

Rita added, "I don't think having the rockjacks and researchers bunked on opposite sides of the ship is so good for morale, either."

Andi's lip curled, and she slumped back in her chair, arms crossed, a darker twin to her godmother. "Oh, you'll find dataheads bunking all over the ship. Some move to a different room each night. That way, they don't have to clean up."

Tommie growled low in her throat. She never had much patience for laziness or shirking common-sense duties, like cleaning up after yourself just because no one was enforcing the rules. "That changes tomorrow morning. We need to set up room assignments and inspections, and a duties roster."

"Hold on!" Rita held up one hand. "We can't just land here and start imposing our will. I know there are good reasons, Tommie, but these are not novices or recruits. These are professionals: highly intelligent and creative people, people who are used to working on their own and living with a lot more freedom than you'll find in the asteroid belt."

"So?"

"So, we have months. We can afford to start slow and build up. Think in terms of fun, as well as work. Have you done anything recreationally with the research team yet?"

Andi snorted. "Thoren's kept them all busy and, when they are done, they break into small groups and play Lola or go on their own ways. I wouldn't be surprised if Thoren has warned them to leave us alone. Except for his Codist discussions. He's only too glad to have us come learn from his dirtside wisdom. Oh, and Merl has Sunday services and Bible study. Thoren's being tolerant. Code Six and all that."

Rita did her best to overlook Andi's sarcastic tone. She knew the rockjack leader well enough to know that, despite her frustration, she probably had Thoren pretty well pegged. After all, hadn't Rita gotten that "benign" dictator vibe off the mission commander, herself? "Well, let's find things we can do together. Starting with those mission briefings Thoren wants everyone to give. Make sure some of your people attend them and ask questions. Show them they're not just common laborers, right?"

Andi rolled her eyes. "There's nothing common about anyone on Rocky Flats."

Rita smiled, reassuringly. "True enough, but I'm willing to bet there's nothing common about any of our research team. I don't think Dr. Thoren would have a garden-variety academic on this mission."

"People he can control," Andi muttered darkly.

"Andi, do you want someone on your team that you don't trust to do what you say?" Rita reasoned, but Andi just shrugged and crossed her arms.

"I've got Cay, don't I?"

* * *

Cay Littlefield made a turn down one lavishly decorated hall into the next, less lavish one. Why the rockjacks were stuck in the cheap bunks while the dataheads were playing in the fancy suites, he didn't know. But Thoren had assigned them there, and Andi had insisted they stay together.

She's just keeping an eye on me. All I wanted was to get to the 'Belt, do a job, make a decent pay. Now I'm speeding away from civilization at .2c and accelerating...

Would he ever see Dove again? He'd promised her: one year. One year at Rocky Flats with his brother, learning the ropes, and then he'd return to Sanders Springs, Marsport, and prove to her father that he could handle their mining business. Stupid rocket had smashed all his plans along with the station. How was he going to learn mining ops now? Then Gensup Hayden put him on this assignment instead of letting him help with the rebuild. Practical experience — that's what Dove's father respected. Book learning is easy, he said. How was he going to impress Mr. Sanders now? He couldn't even tell him what they were doing.

Caught in his dark thoughts, he nearly bumped into Sister Ann.

"Hello, Cay!" She smiled at him like he was her best friend, and he found himself frozen, but whether from guilt or surprise, he didn't know. His eyes moved from her face to her abdomen.

She caught his gaze and set a hand on her side. "Don't worry. I'm fine. Sister Lucinda said light duty for a couple of weeks, so this mission is perfect, don't you think?"

"Yeah, perfect," he grunted. Yet another person happy with encountering aliens. Yet another thing to remind him of his failures. "So, no lasting damage — to your side, I mean? I'm really, really sorry."

She shook her head. "All is forgiven. It was an interesting experience. I'd read so much of the martyrs who suffered for Christ, and of course about R. Charles Hawkins. He had so many failures in his quest to develop the gravity generator. The last accident left him crippled and in constant pain. Know what he said? *Pain and fear motivate, but faith and knowledge direct. Sometimes you experience all four before you have an epiphany.*"

"Did you have an epiphany?"

Her eyes twitched to the side, and her smile faded into thoughtfulness. "I don't think I did," she said, "but I remembered Father Tran's 'Martyrdom.' *A calling so rare/suffering for His name's sake/O most holy gift!* And my guardian angel held my hands to the bar, and Saint Faustina told me the words to pray. And it hurt!" She laughed like pain was a delight.

She's spaced, Cay thought. He muttered a farewell and moved past her. He was partway down the hall when she called his name.

"Five years, three months and seven days after his accident. R. Charles had to totally rethink his plans and approach his goal with a new trajectory before he solved the problem of the gravity generator. Epiphany may be necessary, but it's not sufficient."

Spaced, he thought again as he turned away from her. *She's completely extra-solar. And we're trusting her with our lives?*

Again, he felt a clutch of fear in his stomach, along with the certainty that he would die out here in the Black.

Chapter Nine

The room's wake-up call sounded, pulling Rita from a lovely dream of being in her grandmother's home, sleeping in the genuine down bed. Like the child she was in the dream, she moaned and rolled over, pulling the covers over her head. Then wakefulness reminded her of who, what, and where she was, and she gave a different moan and opened her eyes.

From her own bed across the room, Tommie looked at her, wearing the same expression she felt on her own face.

"Maybe we should see if there are any cots around," she said.

Rita laughed. "Maybe we should see if we can take these back to the convent with us!"

She sat up, stretched, and noticed the empty and made bed on the far wall. "Where's Ann?"

They found her at the computer station, sipping tea from a large, but elegant, cup while standing in front of a projection containing at least a dozen files: one of the Ky-bo, several graphs and lists of different readings taken from the Fadil probe, and personnel files. Chris Davidson's was at the top of the virtual stack, and colored yellow. Beside that stack was another with academic papers, which had several phrases highlighted in yellow or green.

"Chris Davidson doesn't realize his genius," Ann greeted them as they entered. "*Pain and fear motivate, but faith and knowledge direct. Sometimes you experience all four before you have an epiphany.* But not Chris. He skips straight to epiphany."

Rita didn't know how to respond to that. "How long have you been up?"

"Time is relative and irrelevant. Angels move out of time. And saints. Epiphanies, too." Ann set her cup down on a side table and walked to the projection.

"The Fadil probe records have been examined at least seven times by various American government agencies and academic departments across the System. But none of them noticed anything unusual about 2217RB86, despite the evidence. Look, Rita. You'll see." With a few sweeps of her hands, she pulled down and expanded a stack of graphs. She flipped through them, but most seemed to have the average "mountain range" pattern. Rita didn't see anything and was about to remark that perhaps Ann had a little too much faith in her, when something caught her eye.

"Wait!" She went to the graph, and pointed to a particular pattern of spikes. "Isn't that colite?"

"Chris doesn't have a mineralogy degree. He's only taken a Freshman-level course. Got a C. He just knows how to recognize the extraordinary and pursue it. We should tell Andi that."

Behind them, Tommie snorted. "So what else have you found?"

She reached to the stack of academic papers in the lower left and pulled them up. She split it into two: one held term papers by Chris. The other, published articles in specialized academic journals. Rita saw that most bore Thoren's name, with Chris as contributor. Thoren's name was green, while Chris' yellow. She touched a yellow-highlighted phrase in one, and several commercial and academic journal articles showed up, as well as Chris' term papers.

Rita scanned them, but most of what she read didn't make sense to her. "I'm sorry, Ann. I don't understand."

"Neither does Thoren," Ann concluded. "He's afraid of what he doesn't understand, so he tries to control it." She pointed to one article in a popular science magazine heralding some new discovery. She traced it to the original academic article, circled the date, then pointed to a line in one of the articles by Thoren and Chris, then to a section in one of Chris' term papers, dated well before the popular article.

"Chris saw it; took it to Thoren. Thoren dismissed his intuition." She pulled up another chain of papers, then another. "And here. And here. Chris is losing faith in himself. Thoren blocks Chris' instincts; this could be a safety issue."

Ann pulled up the image of 2217RB86, circled a small dot on the horizon and flicked a nail at it. A new window sprang open with a report from Chris suggesting they request time on Old COOT to study this other Ky-bo — a request denied by Thoren.

"Pain and fear, faith and knowledge. Faith, hope, and love. The greatest of these is love. Maybe Andi can help."

"Is this going to be a problem?" Tommie pointed at the smaller object, but from the tone, Rita knew the older sister was talking about their mission commander.

"Inconclusive. More study is needed."

"So judge not, lest we be judged," Rita said.

"We have been judged." Ann shrugged. "It can be like time. We have to operate like the saints."

Rita tried to decipher that but decided it was too early in the day. "Meaning?"

"Meaning," Tommie replied, "that we have to work beyond — or maybe in spite of — any judgments made against us."

Rita sighed. She could probably handle the judgments of most of the team, but there was one...

What was I thinking, just taking off like that instead of confronting the issue? I'm such an idiot.

* * *

I'm such an idiot, James thought as he toyed with his eggs. Around him, the miners and researchers sat at the tables, eating, drinking, and mostly talking. He sat at a corner table, brooding at the familiar lunchroom scene and thinking of the lunches he'd shared with Rita at TTUI. Why did he think he was going to get those back — get her back? She'd run off while he was away, and not only didn't leave him a note, but also asked her family and friends not to tell him where she'd gone. How clear a message is that? She didn't want him. She left Earth to avoid him. Now they'd have to spend months avoiding each other.

A familiar voice said, "May I join you?"

James looked up and gaped at Rita. She wore the usual — or, to him, unusual — habit of her order: black T-shirt and pants over the standard skinsuit, her lovely red hair uncovered and cut in short waves.

"Why don't you cover your head?" he asked.

She huffed. "I'll take that as a 'yes,' then?"

Remembering his manners, he stood and gestured to the seat opposite him.

"The habit is designed to work well in stations or ships and to make it easy to get into a spacesuit fast," Rita explained as she settled into her seat and set her napkin on her lap. "There was talk in the early years about wearing the snoopy cap all the time, but it wasn't worth it. The official reason was the unneeded extra wear on the equipment, but the unofficial story was it made Saint Gillian's head itch."

"Mortification of the body?" he quipped, surprised at how easily the words came out of his mouth, and pleased when she laughed.

"There's enough potential for that out here. Trust me. Speaking of mortifications, just because we have gravity and real food does not mean I want to see you dip your fries into ketchup and then into whatever you're drinking."

He slapped his fork on the table in mock exasperation. "Milkshakes. It was always milkshakes. And you'll never let me forget that, will you?"

"Only after I succeed in erasing that memory myself."

Do you want to erase those memories? he thought. Perhaps she was wondering the same thing, because she suddenly looked away and picked at her food. It was a moment before he realized he was doing the same thing.

They spent a couple of awkward minutes pretending to eat their food, looking at the dining room, the diners...anything but each other. This was not going to be easy.

"Has it been like that all week?" Rita pointed at the others with her fork.

He followed her gaze to the center of the cafeteria, where miners had pulled several tables together to make one large square table. They were sharing jokes and laughing, while the researchers tossed them dark looks from the other tables.

"For the most part. Every now and then, someone tries to cross groups, without much success. Kind of like high school, isn't it?"

"Why are you eating alone?"

"I had breakfast with Sean this morning. Kid eats fast."

She chewed on the inside of her cheek in that way she always did when thinking.

One group of researchers got up to leave, and, as they passed the miners' table, George called out, "Hey! You leave your dishes lying around on the tables again, and we're going to dump them in your lab!"

The group gave them a dirty look, but went to pick up their plates and take them to the bus area.

Finally, Rita turned her back on the crowd and leaned in toward him.

"Listen, James. I don't understand how we both ended up here —"

He caught himself before he could confess.

"—but I'm glad you are. This mission will go a lot more smoothly if we're thinking as a team, and we have to trust each other. It doesn't look like that's happening."

It wasn't until she shifted her eyes to indicate the group that he realized she wasn't talking about them. "Oh! No, you're right. I'd been thinking that myself."

He watched the tension in her neck and shoulders ease, and she gave him a grateful smile. "Good, because we're going to need an ally among the researchers, someone who can talk to Thoren as a peer."

"You can do that. You handled plenty of deans at TTUI."

He half-expected her to blush and deny his compliment, but instead she surprised him by answering seriously. "I made a point of emphasizing my vocation over my degree, and Ann sealed our stance with the procession and prayers. Rescue Sisters have always had a minor presence on Luna. It might be a while before he takes us seriously. We need an ally."

You've changed, he thought, and it unsettled him. Still, if they were going to be stuck together for the trip, they may as well work together. In for a penny... "What do you have in mind?"

Over by the bus station, a petite woman with Oriental features picked up a tub of dirty dishes. It started to slip, but she steadied it with her knee while she got a better grip, blowing her hair out of her eyes with a loud puff at the same time. At the nearest table, several researchers were caught in conversation and didn't notice. George got up to help.

"Who's on dish duty?" Rita asked.

"That's Lt. Rose Chan. She's navigator and doubles as cook."

"Who helps her?"

James shrugged. "The crew, I guess?"

Rita pulled up a past crew roster on her wristcomp. "The *Edwina Taggert* employed forty-two crewmen, not counting wait staff and housekeepers. This mission, we have twelve."

He picked up her thinking. "Chores roster, then? I can see that. What else?"

"Some kind of team activities; make them work together now." She picked up her fork and went at her meal with renewed gusto. Between chews, she asked, "Is it true the researchers are scattered all over the ship — their living quarters, that is?"

James started again on his own food. "Mmm-hmm. Why? Want to bring them in?"

"Yes, and with the rockjacks. It's one thing to have a large ship full of people and another to have it partly manned with individuals scattered about. It'll be safer to be in a central location, maybe near the labs. Good for teambuilding, too."

"It'll be a hard sell. You're going to need a concrete reason."

Alarms interrupted him. A moment later, the strong automated voice of *Lola Quintain* spoke: "Fire on the Castaway deck. Please do not panic. Move in an orderly manner to your designated reporting area. All guests and personnel evacuate Section Five on Castaway, Babylon and Andes decks and stay clear for fire control personnel. Repeat. Fire in Room 5D on Castaway deck. Please do not panic."

Immediately, people rose from their seats, shouting with alarm.

"You were saying?" Rita said.

Over Lola's voice, Lt. Chan used the cafeteria PA system to tell everyone to stay in the room, but several people didn't listen.

Rita jumped up onto her chair. "Everyone, calm down! You!" she shouted at Ian.

He froze in his flight to the door, several others with him.

"Calm down. We're staying here."

"The ship's on fire! I don't want to be trapped."

"And where do you think you're going to go? Outside?" one of the miners sneered.

"Stow it, Lenny," Rita commanded.

From the kitchen, Lt. Chan called out. "Remember the procedures. Castaway deck is on the other side of the ship. We're safe here, if we don't panic."

The researchers passed each other nervous glances, but calmed. The rockjacks went back to sitting. James noticed a few of them talking on their wristcomps.

Rita made sure everyone was settled before stepping off her seat. "James, who do you report to?"

He stared at her blankly.

"You do have fire procedures?"

He shook his head, and she sighed. Her wristcomp beeped, and she quickly reported her situation to Sister Thomas.

"Okay then. Got a list of the research personnel on your wristcomp? Pull it up." She left him to go to use the mic. "Researchers, we need to account for everyone. I want you to call all the people on your teams and pass their locations to James. Then start contacting everyone else. Let's make sure folks are accounted for. If they want to know what to do, tell them get away from Castaway..." She paused.

"Babylon and Andes decks. Section Five," Chan said as she listened to her own comms. "We've got a fire team on the way."

"Wonderful. So get away from Andes, Babylon and Castaway. ABC-Five. They can come here if they like, as long as it doesn't mean crossing those decks. Copy?"

"Got it," people replied.

James started on the list. Sean called him, and he told him not to head to the fire with the camera. Other researchers gathered by him, some to report on friends they'd already contacted, some just to be near to hear the results.

He heard Andi tell Rita, "Our quarters are between here and Babylon. I'm telling folks to come here."

Rita called out, "Does anyone know of someone bunking on Castaway, Babylon or Andes?"

Merl said, "Babylon? What about Kelley Riggens?"

* * *

When Ann heard the alarms, she ran to the *Basilica*.

"Ann to Rita," she called into her headset as she pulled down her firefighting gear: a small tank with two masks and the belt that held a fire-resistant poncho, fire-fighting tools, and a first aid kit. Her habit was fire-resistant; she grabbed her gloves and pulled them on. "I'm at *Basilica* and gearing up. Does Captain Addiman's crew need any help?"

Without waiting for the answer, she started running toward the Castaway deck.

A moment, then a male voice came over her headset. "Sister, this is Commander McVee, First Officer. The fire suppression equipment has failed. We detect one person in the room and have prevented the secondary system from activating until we can get them out. A fire team is *en route*, but I'm sure they'd appreciate a professional."

"On my way!" She came to a corridor, turned left without bothering to consult the map on her wristcomp. The plans laid out in her mind as plainly as a head's-up display on her helmet. She broke into a smile that had to do more with excitement than joy, and when she noticed, she forced her mouth into a grimmer expression. People don't understand a grinning rescuer, Mother Superior had often chided her, but she couldn't help it. She felt so alive during a rescue!

She passed through a door and into the central core, with the rock wall spanning down the six levels and the fancy shops and casinos lining the rim, closed and dark. She tore across the walkway that stretched the chasm. She suppressed a shiver. The wailing alarms and Lola's calm intonations echoed, adding to the feeling of abandonment. So empty. So lonely. It didn't seem right.

The feeling didn't leave her, either, as she passed through the Ritz and Savoy decks. The velvet and gold wallpaper, the lush carpet that cushioned her steps like dust on an asteroid — they tickled at her mind and made the hair on the back of her neck stand up. She shook off the sudden clutch of fear. She gave a squeak when Rita's voice came over the headset.

"Ann? We think Kelley Riggens may have been in the area."

She caught her breath. "Kelley Riggens. Copy."

She felt better when she entered the bamboo-and-palm-fronded décor of the Castaway deck. Even the smoke seemed reassuring. This, she understood.

At the edge of the smoke line, a woman slumped by the wall, breathing into an oxygen mask. Ann knelt beside her. Her skin was moonlight pale, her hair dark, straight and short. Her dark eyes looked inhumanly large in her delicate face. An exoskeleton of light, but strong, metal supported her slight body.

Ann gasped. A zerog!

Ann felt her guardian angel beside her, protective, but reminding her of her job.

"Are you all right?" she asked.

The woman nodded, took a deep breath. She coughed but pulled the mask away. "Ship's doctor. My office is two halls down. I thought I could get her out, but she's locked herself in the head and refuses to move. I couldn't override the lock. Too hot. I blocked the door to keep it from closing, or the fire suppression system will pull the air out of the cabin. She can't have much time left." She broke into coughing again and raised the mask back to her face.

"You did fine. The fire team?"

The doctor shook her head and held up two graceful fingers. Two minutes before they arrive. "Stay here. I'll get the girl. Do you know her name? Is it Kelley?"

Again, she shook her head and shrugged.

Ann patted her shoulder, then stood. She donned her mask, turning on the light, then crossed herself and moved into the smoke-filled hall.

So much flammable material! The light on her headgear only cut a narrow beam through the darkness before being eaten by the smoke. Still, it was enough; God had blessed her with unusually good night vision, and she whispered a prayer to St. Clare, patron saint of eyesight. Clare: clear, bright. The path was not bright, but at least it was straight, and as she got closer, she saw the flickering column of red and orange that marked the partially open door to the fire. She peered in, squinting against the brightness of the flames arching and dancing on the bed and broken table, climbing across the walls, spreading over the ceiling. She reached into a belt pouch, took out a grenade, and pulled the pin.

"Father, Son, Holy Spirit!" She tossed the grenade into the room.

A pause, then a *thwoom!* she felt more than heard.

She peeked back in.

Droplets of fire-suppressant foam dotted the room, expanding quickly, snuffing the fire as they grew. Nonetheless, pockets of flames fought merrily for dominance. She'd bought herself some time, that's all.

She gritted her teeth and set a gloved hand on the door's edge and one on the frame and pushed them apart. Even through the gloves, she felt the heat scald her skin. She pulled away with a frustrated hiss.

St. Florian, patron of fire brigades, help me! She gripped the reluctant door again. Again the heat seared through her gloves, but this time, as she was about to pull away, she felt a pressure holding them in place. St. Florian was helping! She leaned in with her legs, and the door at last gave.

She ran across the room to the bathroom door and pounded on it.

"Hello! Kelley? Can you hear me? I'm Sister Ann! I'm here to rescue you!"

A cough and a small mewling sound.

Ann tried the door. "Unlock the door! I'll help you. It'll be all right."

The girl spoke, her voice slurred. "Hot door. Never open a hot door in a fire."

Bless her! "It's okay! Open the door, and I'll lead you out. You can do it!"

"Too hot. Fire!"

"I've got a fire-proof poncho. You'll hide under it, and I'll lead you out." She glanced around. The flames were growing in the spots the foam missed. "Hurry now! We don't have a lot of time. I'll help you, and God is with us! Please, open the door."

Small sobs answered her.

"It's okay. Just back away from the door."

She glanced at the latch, glad now that the doors had caught her eye and she'd read the specs. She'd never seen a sliding door with a knob before. It'd take too long to release the lock electronically. She pulled out a laser cutter. Her heart pounded as she directed the light against the edge of the door. Her skin tingled from the heat; sweat stung her eyes. She was smiling again. She bit down on her lips as she stuck the cutter back into the pouch and pressed both hands against the door, heaving. This time, she didn't need the saint's help.

Kelley had retreated to a large tub and had turned on the water. The tub overflowed and spread across the floor. She had to be at least ten years older than Ann, but fear made her seem much younger.

"Good for you! That was very smart! We have to leave now. Look!" She pulled out the fire poncho and unfolded it. She held it out with one hand and grabbed the second mask with the other. "This will protect you. There's fire suppression foam on the floor. The mask will help you breathe. Come on, Kelley..."

The woman stood in the bathtub, pressing herself against the corner. Ann took a step forward, coaxing.

In the other room, a ceiling tile crashed to the floor.

Kelley shrieked and ran toward the door.

Ann caught her by the waist. "Wait! Put this on!"

Kelley threw on the mask and poncho. She ran, but Ann held her hand firmly and kept up with her. The smoke seemed strange now, leering and malicious. She imagined wisps pulling at Kelley, dragging her back. Ann's back crawled with the sudden, irrational anticipation of a bulkhead exploding and dragging Kelley and her into space. The hand holding Kelley's was afire again with pain, but it was nothing to the fear gripping her heart. No one was behind them, yet she thought she heard someone screaming.

Fear and pain motivate. Help me, Guardian Angel!

When they met another suited figure heading their way, the irrational panic in Ann fled as suddenly as it had come upon her. Kelley, however, shrieked and tried to turn away from them and back to the fire. Ann imagined the smoke opening its arms to her. She whispered a plea to St. Florian and pulled on Kelley's hand.

"It's okay! Come on!" Ann led her past the firefighting team. When they left the smoke line, both she and Kelley were gasping with relief.

The doctor, still coughing and leaning heavily against the wall, but recovered, took Kelley as soon as they emerged. Ann yelped when Kelley let go of her hand. The doctor looked past Kelley's shoulder as the girl wept against it. "I want to check you, too, Sister. The captain said everyone else is accounted for," she croaked.

Ann nodded, staring in wonder at the scorched and melted streaks along her palms and the pads of her fingers, part of her mind calculating the heat and pressure it had taken to cause the damage to her gloves. The hand that held Kelley's was slick under the fire-resistant fabric. Still, she preferred pain to this fear she didn't understand. Whispering a prayer for deliverance from fear and for understanding, she followed the others into the infirmary.

The wailing of the alarm was replaced with a warm chime. "Attention. The fire has been contained and extinguished. Please do not return to Section Five of the Castaway deck until the area is cleared by the Captain. Thank you for your cooperation and enjoy your cruise."

Chapter Ten

"So! Is everyone enjoying their cruise?" Reg called down the hallway of rockjacks and dataheads who were hauling suitcases, duffle bags, and boxes into their new quarters. Groans and some personally offensive commentary answered his question.

After the fire, the "Mighty Five" (as Ian had dubbed Dr. Thoren, Sister Rita, Andi, Captain Addiman and Dr. Smith) had declared that, before they could plan the mission, they needed to make sure they could *get* to the mission alive and with ship intact. Since then, they had filled the days with safety briefings, emergency drills, and duty and chore rosters. Plus, they had everyone move into new quarters in the suite wing off the research hall. The fire had frightened everyone out of complaining — mostly — but nobody, not even the rockjacks, liked giving up their privacy.

"Me, neither," Reg muttered. He hefted his box into a more stable grasp.

In front of him, Andi carried her own bags. She turned her head back to him to give him a rueful grin, just as Ian Hu came tripping out of his quarters and bumped into her. He wrapped his arms around her, supposedly in the interest of steadying her, but she jerked back, unbalanced, to escape his embrace.

"Oops! Sorry! Let me get that for you!" Ian reached for the shoulder strap that had fallen down her arm.

She used the bag to push him away. "You wouldn't have to apologize if you'd keep your hands to yourself. And I handle heavy equipment every day. Do you really think I can't handle a bag?"

"Sorry! I'm from Hawaii! I'm not used to this lower gravity."

"It's point-nine G, and you've been on this ship for three weeks now. That excuse is obsolete."

Two doors away, Kelley, recovered from her experience, poked her head out of the room. "That's the truth, Andi. Here, I got our door. By the way, this is a 'No Ian' zone, got it?"

"There's no on your lips but yes in your eyes," Ian teased.

Despite her declaration, Kelley's eyes sparkled. She'd inadvertently started the fire by knocking over one of the many candles she'd lit for her meditation ceremony, and people still blamed her for their loss of freedom.

Ian abandoned Andi and started toward her, a flirtatious grin on his face, only to be stopped by a wall of muscle and frown.

"There's gonna be 'no' on my fist if you don't leave the girls alone, greenfoot," Lenny growled.

Dale strode between them, hands up in a pacifying gesture. "Gentlemen! Ladies! What would the sisters say if they heard you bickering so? We are a team now, forged in a common purpose..."

Andi sighed and set her luggage down and leaned against the wall to wait. Reg edged by her, hoping to sneak past to his room. He could see as well as Andi how Dale was gearing himself up for another long speech. He had had no idea spacers could be so verbose. Did they give him extra oxygen when he went out to check the mining equipment?

Dale stepped further between the two men, making Ian step back, blocking the hallway. Reg sighed with resignation.

"We should embrace this time together, a diverse people, forging a common bond for a grand goal —"

"Oh, give it a rest, Dale. We got the 'team speech' when they reassigned quarters," Ian snapped.

The stress of the last couple of weeks combined with the forced move finally wore on Reg. Even though he agreed, he snarled at his friend. "Yo, man, what are you complaining about? You only moved around the corner."

"Yeah, and I get Guido here as a bunkmate. I'd rather listen to Dale extemporize all day."

"Best news I've heard all week. Hey, Lenny, wanna trade?"

"You know the rule: one rockjack and one gravfoot per room," Lenny replied, but he gave Ian a look that said he didn't much care for the arrangements, either.

"Right. We pair Ian and Dale."

"Hey!" Ian protested.

Dale advanced on Reg with Lenny and Ian close behind. Andi took the opportunity to slip past and into her room.

Dale cleared his throat. "If I may... The leadership, the 'Mighty Five' as Ian so colorfully calls them — no doubt chose our assignments very carefully, attempting to pair complementing personalities and —" His eyes alighted on Reg's open box. "Is that a Lola Quintain manga?"

"No way, Reg! You wasted your volume on a book?" Ian laughed, but Zabrina had heard them and moved closer, too, her full lips parted, her eyes wide with wonder at the paperback. Ian did a double-take at the pretty microbiologist and stopped laughing.

"No. I found it. In the room I *used* to have!" Reg groused. He'd liked that room. Soft bed, big portal. No roomies.

"That's a real book? May I see it, please?" Zabrina asked. The others crowded in, Ian close enough that his cheek brushed against Zabrina's thick, dark hair.

"Be careful with that. One at a time. Ladies first. Here, Zabrina; hold it while I stick this in my room." Reg handed her the book, then hefted his box and backed up.

"That's my room!" Ian protested.

"Not anymore, Ian," Lenny replied.

Something was going right! Reg grinned as Lenny's words gave him one small silver lining in this whole stupid room fiasco. He grabbed Ian's bags — easily identifiable by the big flowers and surfboards pattern — and set them at Ian's feet. Ian groaned.

"Ooo! Listen to the pages," Zabrina cooed as she flipped them through her fingers.

Something caught Ian's eye, and he stuck his hand into the book, preventing her from turning the page. "Forget the pages! Look at Lola."

Andi walked out and joined the group. "I took the top bunk, Kelley. Hope that's okay. So, what's Ian ogling at now?"

"Look, Andi. Reg found a real book in his old room." Zabrina held it for her to see. She didn't protest when Ian leaned a little closer to peer over her shoulder.

Andi's eyebrows raised in approval. "Hey, vectored! I wonder what else we can find."

Zabrina passed the book on to Dale. "On those scavenging hunts the Mighty Five talked about? What are you going to have us looking for, anyway?"

"James and Rita said standard supplies, some items Ann wants for training and the mission. Lots of wiring and lamps, too."

"Perhaps we will find more books," Dale muttered as he ran his fingers over the cover reverently.

Ian cocked an eyebrow at the rockjack. "You two want to be alone?"

Dale's eyes flickered up to glare at him, but without much heat.

Andi grinned. "We should be getting lists tonight, they said. Tomorrow suit training starts. Has everyone been studying the manuals?" By "everyone," she really meant Ian and Kelley and Reg. They knew it, too. They nodded.

Nonetheless, Reg said, "The one I'm worried about is Merl. He had a rough time during 'Loops for LunaTechs.' I have the feeling he'll be spending every available minute studying if he wants to see that ship."

***

"Fine by me," Kelley muttered. Merl Pritchard was one of the ones giving her a hard time about the fire. Others had chewed her out for carelessness; some had quoted to her from the Spacer's Code that the Mighty Five were making them memorize, but Pritchard had cornered her more than once to tell her that her "heathen ways" had not just led to her downfall but were endangering them all. He should just stick to languages, or whatever it was a linguist should be doing, and stay out of her life.

Then there was the "Little Sister," Ann. She'd visited her in the infirmary: *"I wish you'd come pray with me when you're better. I'm so scared for you." She'd leaned forward and whispered, "There's something very dark around you. I saw it in the smoke — it tried to lead you back to the fire. The devil strains every nerve to secure the souls which belong to Christ. We should not grudge our toil in wresting them from Satan and giving them back to God. I'm going to pray and pray. I hope you'll come pray with me, too."*

The others seemed to like Ann well enough, but there was something creepy about her. She was too bright, like the fire. And the way she'd smiled when she busted that door down... Kelley shivered.

Andi set a hand on her shoulder, breaking her from her reverie. "Don't worry," she teased. "We'll protect you from Merl, the Big Bad Evangelist."

Reg clapped his hands together. "Well, I don't know about you guys, but I'm for getting settled in before chow. Gotta see what Chris is serving up. It's his turn passing out meals, isn't it?" He glanced at Andi, who gave him a "Why are you asking me?" look with just a tinge of guilt.

"Incidentally," he continued, "he's the other person I think is going to have trouble with Suits 101. Thoren's riding him hard about anything else he can think of, so he's not studying. Maybe you should offer to tutor him?"

"I'm sure if he needs help, he'll ask." She raised her chin slightly, then turned and went to her quarters, leaving Kelley with the others.

"She doesn't know him well enough." Reg rolled his eyes.

Ian laughed. "Well, isn't this all about getting to know each other better?" He smiled at Kelley.

Oh, please. She tossed her head in a perfect imitation of Andi and left.

Andi was in the bedroom unpacking, so Kelley gave in to her doubts and hung by the door, listening hard. What would they say about her in her absence?

She expected criticism, even if just Ian griping about her exit, but instead, they were disbanding, talking about unpacking. Ian called out loudly that he wasn't getting any say in his choice of roommate. Dale replied that Ian himself had stated he'd rather hear Dale's ponitificating. Their door closed on the rest of Dale's reply.

Kelley slumped against her own door, not sure if she felt relieved or disappointed that her exit warranted so little concern.

* * *

Dr. OvLandra set her scanner aside and took Ann's left hand, running her fingers over the palms, then turning it and tracing an old scar on the back with a long finger. "Well, Small Weight, I was concerned about what the burns were going to do, but you've healed remarkably well for a human."

"They feel fine. You and Sister Rita have taken such good care of me! You didn't need a DNA analysis after all." Mother Superior and Tommie had both warned her against allowing anyone outside the Rescue Sisters access to her DNA. Rita, as team leader, had disallowed the procedure, but Ann still felt bad for the ship's doctor.

"I suppose not." OvLandra dropped her hands. "But I shall keep an eye on you, just in case. The mission has just started, and I do believe you have a penchant for finding trouble."

"*Oh, my God, when peril stands before me, be at my side. Guide me through the dangers that I may rescue those in jeopardy and live to rescue again, in Your Most Holy Name. Amen.* I don't find trouble; trouble finds me. It's my calling."

OvLandra laughed, a warm melodious sound that bubbled up from her chest. "So it is, Small Weight. What do your parents think of this calling?"

"My parents died when I was very young. The sisters raised me."

"I'm sorry." OvLandra started to say more, but stopped and stared in curiosity as Ann's tattoo started to light up.

Ann caressed the cross lovingly. "My rosary. The sisters let me get it after my Confirmation, but I had to beg and beg for it. It's keyed to my biosigns, so it responds to my moods."

OvLandra regarded the glowing tattoo with interest. "So these are the Sorrowful Mysteries?"

"Oh, no! Joyful. See? The Presentation at the Temple."

"You don't miss your parents?"

"I don't remember them. I was very young. But they loved me, and they died trying to save me. There's only one better way to die. *So rare the calling/To suffer as the martyrs/O, most holy gift.*"

"So you wish to die?"

Ann walked her fingers over the tattoo beads on her arm. Hail Mary... "Oh, no! But if I die, I want to while helping others, and for Christ. Am I medically cleared to teach? Rita has finished the academics of EVA and will be starting the practical. I'll be getting advanced students soon. And, Dr. Landra —"

"Ov, Small Weight. You may call me Ov. And if you could inform the others that the proper way to address me is not Dr. Landra, but Dr. OvLandra, according to the custom of my people."

Ann smiled. "Roger that. Ov, may I please, please play splat? I checked the dodeck, and it's still in great shape, and Sister Quartermaster packed our uniforms, and six of the rockjacks play, and they're really good."

Again, the doctor laughed. "Your side is fine. You will have to invite Commander Orion McVee and Lt. Rose Chan to your games. I will be most interested to see you play. My people invented the game, you know."

"DelKeeva in 2167 introduced a game using a zero gravity dodecahedron-shaped court with a gyroscopic ball in what sports authorities called a cross between basketball, lacrosse, and professional wrestling. That last is hyperbole, since holding is against regulations. Adopted by traders who saw the merit of the zero gravity exercise and skills, the game quickly grew beyond the zerog community and achieved Olympic status in 2196. And KeeKeeva and GalKeeva won the gold just last year. No Landras have competed since the 2224." *The Fifth Joyful Mystery: They find Jesus in the temple. Our Father...*

Several Hail Marys later, Ann realized OvLandra had neither spoken nor moved. She paused in her prayers and looked up. "Ov?"

Ov was watching her with peculiar intensity. "My clan has been in disgrace for over two decades. That is why I am here, to find my uncle's family and rectify the situation."

Ann felt her guardian angel spread his wings over her protectively. She didn't understand why, but thanked him. "Your uncle is missing? Is that why you've been on the *Edwina Taggert*?"

"This ship is special to him, and it holds his secrets, I'm sure. It has been ten long years. I shall be happy to see my family again. I have been alone so long."

"But Ov, how could you be alone? There's Captain Addiman, and he's so nice! So are Commander McVee and Lieutenant Chan and..." She stopped in confusion when Ov's expression hardened.

Then the zerog shook herself. "Of course. They are most kind. But blood is family, and I long to see them again."

"*I hunger for the bread of God, the flesh of Jesus Christ ... I long to drink of his blood, the gift of unending love.* Water, blood and fire; faith, hope and love. Maybe families are blood, but even more, they're love."

OvLandra closed her eyes and took in a deep, slow breath. "Go now, Small Weight. You have duties, I am sure. Another time, you shall come to my quarters. Perhaps we shall discuss families more."

I'll be your family. The words were on Ann's lips, but she felt the feathery softness of angel wings over her mouth, and she slipped off the table and out of the room in silence. Andi wanted to meet for dinner, and she had been Ann's best friend since they were children, like a sister, and the rockjacks were family, too. Oh, she hoped on this mission, she could help Ov understand that families were so much bigger than blood!

* * *

Laughter echoed across the dining hall.

The table seated twelve, but far more crowded around it, sitting shoulder to shoulder, some standing behind, leaning on the seats. Miner, researcher and crewman alike focused on Andi and Ann beside her.

Andi stifled her giggles, took a sip of water, and continued. "So, there we were, two pre-teen kids —"

"You were thirteen. I was nine," Ann corrected.

Andi waved the comment off. "— standing ankle deep in —"

"Oh, don't say it!" Kelley cried. "You'll make me lose my appetite. How did we get on this subject, anyway?"

"Chris asked." Ann cocked her head when he started to blush.

"I just, um, wanted to know what it was like growing up in space," he muttered.

Andi turned to him with eyes shining with mischief. "Glamorous, isn't it? Anyway, the chief engineer said the reclamation system was jammed. He gave us shovels! That's all we did for a week! When we stopped at Rangara station, we went straight to the commissar's office and begged him to let us contact Godmom and arrange passage home. That was the last time we'd ever run away from the convent."

"I didn't run away," Ann amended matter-of-factly. "I went along to make sure you came back."

"Oho!" Commander McVee, who had lately insisted people call him by his first name, Orion, set his foot on Chris' chair and draped an elbow on his knee. Once again he'd put himself between Chris and Andi. Chris tried not to glower. The first officer was everything he wasn't: tall and lean, with holostar good looks. The stupid archaic uniform just made him look even more heroic, and Chris had seen plenty of the women following him with their eyes. If Chris wore a uniform like that, he'd get looks — and snickers, he was sure. Not that he could wear heroism any better. He wondered if the crew had been chosen for their looks as well as their skills. At least the rumor mill had McVee and Rose Chan in a long-term relationship.

McVee leaned closer to Andi, though his focus was on Ann beside her. "And what if she'd decided to stick it out all the way to Earth?"

Ann blinked at him, like a child caught in a lie, then ducked her head. She picked at her food with her fork before answering. "I'd have had to report us. But first, I would have fixed the exit valve on the reclamation unit."

"You could have done that?" Andi shrieked as the group roared.

"Are you angry?" Ann squeaked.

"We shoveled that...for a week! We were both crying! And you kept saying, 'We suffer for the souls in Purgatory.'"

"But that's a good thing!" Ann protested. "Besides, you never ran away again. You stayed and finished your education — and look where you are now."

"Yeah!" George agreed. "A well-respected rockjack who still takes her turn at the shit plant — but at least she knows where the exit valve is!"

"Oh, that's it!" Andi shouted over the laughter. Even Ann clamped down on her lips in an effort not to laugh. Andi glared at her, then slammed her hands on the table and leaned toward George. "When we get done with the mission on 2217RB86 —"

"Hey, that brings up another thing," Ian interrupted. "Could we give this rock a name?"

Chris cleared his throat, "Well, Dr. Thoren was waiting until we reached the Ky-bo."

Ian laughed. "Vac that stale air! I don't want to call it a number for the next month and a half. Twenty-two, seventeen, ar-bee eighty-six! Makes my jaw hurt. How about something simple but stellar, like...Planetlan?" He arched his hand across the air as if picturing it on a marquis.

People around him groaned. One person threw a napkin at him.

"I agree, though," Reg said. "We need to name it before Thoren decides to name it after himself."

A few people rolled their eyes, but Chris added, "Or after our sponsors."

"Like colite?" one of the miners asked archly, and Chris reddened and started to stutter an apology.

Dale piped up. "We could return to the tradition of naming it from a creation myth."

"You know, Chris discovered it. He should name it — and the ship, too," Andi said.

"Okay." Ian twisted toward Chris. "Got any ideas?"

"Well, I had been thinking," he started.

George hollered before he could continue. "Hey, everybody! Come here! Chris is going to finally name that rock we're heading to!"

"Uh," he stammered as the rest of the diners gathered around. Dr. Thoren was nowhere to be seen, but Sister Thomas smiled at him from across the table, and others left their plates to join them. McVee stepped back, giving him the stage. Andi put her hand under his elbow, pushing him up. The simple contact sent a happy jolt through him. He stood, took a deep breath.

"Well, this all started because I was studying some data sent from the last government-sponsored probe to the Kuiper Belt, one of the last probes sent out just for the sake of pure research. It wasn't very popular. The American President, Linda Montero-Fadil, used a lot of political clout to get the program pushed through. The press called it 'Fadil's Folly.' I thought it'd be, you know, fitting if we remembered her."

Behind him, James said, "So 'Fadil's Folly'? That has a nice irony."

Snorts erupted across the room. Ian laughed. "Brilliant! The Folly it is!"

"The Folly!" All around him, people lifted their glasses.

When the cheers died down, Sister Thomas asked, "And the ship?"

He knew that one. It's what they'd been calling it all along.

"The *Discovery*."

Chapter Eleven

Thoren's mouth twisted with distaste. "The Folly?"

Standing at the conference room table, addressing his supervisor, Chris felt his confidence retreat into a tight little knot in his stomach. How did he get elected spokesman? Around the table, the others offered their encouragement: James with a smile; Rita, a gentle nod. Ann had her hands clasped together in an effort not to clap; her happy shrug made her look years younger. He saw why the miners called her "Little Sister." He wasn't quite sure why she was even at the meeting; she'd just followed Andi in. Commander McVee was filling in for Capt. Addiman; he nodded and spread his hands in a 'sounds-good-to-me' gesture.

"I filed the registration first thing after lunch." Andi grinned, slow and self-satisfied, her eyes on Thoren.

Chris gulped. He hadn't thought about that, about it being so...official.

Thoren cleared his throat. "By contract, it is, of course, yours, so you may name it as you please. As for the ship, I believe —"

"*Discovery*!" Ann burst out. When all eyes turned to her, she looked at Chris with eyebrows raised in invitation.

"Well," he stammered, "we were thinking. That is..."

"It's a great name, William," James said easily. "We all refer to it that way, anyhow."

"It is fitting," Rita added.

Thoren nodded. "Very well. We shall use *Discovery* as a working name for the time being."

Although Thoren's voice remained level, Chris caught the look that darkened his eyes. Chris sat down fast. *Take your victories where you can.*

"Anything else, Mr. Davidson?"

He shook his head, and James took up the conversation.

"Ian is asking if there's any way we can open up one of the swimming pools." He glanced at McVee.

The First Officer leaned back in his seat and crossed one ankle over the opposite knee, relaxed, in charge, and comfortable with all eyes on him. "I think we have enough water. The question is if we have the right filters. I'll have Quartermaster check and get back to us. I like the idea. It's good recreation for everyone. Incidentally, Lieutenant Chan is setting up a splat tournament. Doctor OvLandra says you're cleared to play, Ann. You know, you've really impressed her, and that's not an easy thing to do. I heard she invited you to her quarters; do you know the protocols?"

"Oh, yes, I've been studying."

Thoren cleared his throat. "Yes, fascinating."

McVee took the hint. "Sorry, I digress, but OvLandra's been the pride of the *ET* for a long time. Anyway, I'll check on the pool. It'd be good to have some other forms of entertainment around here."

Thoren surprised them with a wry chuckle, "As an alternative to the 'educational movie night'?"

He shared a smirk with McVee, who explained.

"Our Comms officer brought this to me for approval to distribute." He pressed a button on his console, and the large screen lit up.

A gray, skeletal creature with a huge, oblong head snapped its jaws at a woman who cowered and whimpered in fear. Over the hissing and howls came a voice that lilted like all salesmen of any age:

"Don't know what's waiting on that unexplored alien ship? Not anxious to be caught by surprise? Well, neither are we. And, thanks to the cinematographers of old, we don't have to be."

The scene changed to spacesuited figures wandering in a dark cavernous room filled with large, leathery eggs.

"Every Monday night, we'll be analyzing the procedures and tactics of others who have gone the way we dare go now. After each full-length feature presentation — in its extended form remastered exclusively for CruiseGalactic — we will hold analysis and discussion."

The woman, now in a full spacesuit, strapped herself into a chair, then blew open the hatch to blast the alien into space.

"We don't have to operate in a vacuum. Come join us for these life- and-death discussions. Remember: they made the stupid mistakes so we don't have to!"

The last image froze on the screen: a man on a hospital bed with a pale yellow scorpion-like creature with long legs clamped over his face. Over the still appeared a small box that said in bright flashing letters, "First showing: ALIEN, directed by Ridley Scott. Download a reminder into your calendar now! Avoid death by alien intubation!"

"And now we know why Sean and Ian wanted to get the theater working again," McVee pronounced.

Ann leaned toward the screen, her eyes wide. "It looks so real," she marveled.

Chris clamped his hands over his mouth.

"Well," Rita finally managed to say after a few tries. "I think we've exceeded the bounds of tastelessness." She glanced around, caught James' gaze, and pressed her fist against her mouth to keep from laughing. A squeaky balloon sound escaped nonetheless.

Andi's sour expression matched Thoren's. "Was that Ian Hu's voice? What are we going to do with that boy?"

Rita laughed. "He's as old as we are, dear."

Thoren pointed to the invitation on the screen. "The more accurate question is, what shall we do about that?"

Ann looked at them with confusion. "You mean we aren't going?"

* * *

Ann pushed herself off the wall of the dodeck court and smacked the ball flat-handed as she sailed past. It moved with more velocity than she expected — and more than Tommie planned, too. It bounced off the panel before her friend could block it.

"I think I should service the gyroscope," she told Tommie as the older sister twisted herself into a somersault to kill her forward momentum. "The spin is slow, and it's not fighting external forces like it should."

Tommie set a hand on the wall to still herself and caught her breath. "I'm sure the *Edwina Taggert* crew has gotten accustomed to it." Her face twisted into a grin, and she snagged the ball as it rebounded her way. She turned it over in her hands, feeling the angular momentum fighting the change in direction, then slapped it to Ann. "I think they could use the challenge."

"Challenges strengthen the mind, body, and spirit. They should be embraced, not avoided."

"R. Charles Hawkins?" Tommie guessed.

Ann grinned. "You! When I was in seventh grade."

Tommie laughed, and, bracing herself on the junction of three walls, waved one arm in dismissal. "Go! Fix the ball to challenge all of us. I want to work on my Heisman block."

The ball had obviously seen many years of hard play by those who didn't understand the sport; it took Ann some time to smooth out the micro-dents and kinks. When she looked up, she realized it had passed the dinner hour. Nonetheless, she felt a different kind of hunger, and, after returning the ball to its place, made her way to the chapel.

However, when she got there, she found the controls set to "Christian" and the occupied light on. Curious, she eased the door open and slipped into the nearest pew.

Merl stood in front of a dozen of the crew, research and rockjacks alike, speaking about the Codists and how they had abandoned their salvation for the rules of mortal life.

"...my brothers and sisters, we are not bound by the rules of this world, but a higher rule, a rule of mercy! A rule of love! And whose love? Not ours. No, human love cannot save you. Human rules cannot heal your soul! No!"

He speaks with such passion! A shiver of delight ran along her back. *I wonder why he isn't Catholic?*

"It is the love of the one Lord Jesus Christ who does that! Our Lord God, who came to our world as a man, who died and rose again, who has cleansed us of our sins! His love! His mercy! Only God's love is sufficient to rescue our souls. And what does He ask in return? Nothing but that we accept that gift. That's it!"

Ann noticed Cay in the aisle seat, trembling, and she wondered if she should go to him and hold his hand. Then she felt a presence, and the angel sat beside her, his eyes moving with interest from Merl to Cay as his lips murmured Ecclesiastes. Ann sat a little straighter and tried to quell her excitement and listen with all her soul.

There is a time for everything, and a season for every activity under the heavens...

...a time to tear down and a time to build...

...a time to embrace and a time to refrain from embracing...

"No longer do we need to adhere to the code of humans. No more do we need to pray to idols or seek out others to lead us to God. No! For twenty-two centuries, we have had a *direct line* to God's mercy! Jesus paid for that for us with his own life! It's yours, right here, right now! Accept his gift and be free of all your sins, all your doubts..."

Ann looked lovingly at the ring tattooed on her finger.

"Who will come now? Who will approach the banquet of love and accept Jesus as their personal savior?"

Banquet? But the Eucharist remained safe in its tabernacle. She chanced a questioning look at the angel.

That each of them may eat and drink, and find satisfaction in all their toil—this is the gift of God.

"Oh."

Cay leapt to his feet. "Me! Oh, God, please. Let it be me!"

Merl held out his arms. "Of course it's you, Cay! It's all of us. We only have to ask and accept."

The angel continued to whisper to her as Merl led Cay through the Sinner's Prayer.

Afterward, everyone filed out, but the angel kept murmuring. Of faith, of deeds, of sacrifices and danger. *Even though I walk through the valley of the shadow of death, I will fear no evil, for You are with me…*

Merl cleared his throat, and the angel faded away. Ann looked up to smile at him.

"Hello, Merl! That was a very stirring sermon."

He cocked his head as if he hadn't expected that response. "Yet you did not accept God's invitation."

Laughing, she showed him her ring. "Silly! I did that years ago! Thus, I serve the Lord with all my heart, with all my soul, with all my body, and with all my mind."

"The verse is 'Thou shalt love the Lord.'"

"Yes, absolutely! To love, to serve, to adore. You made me think of Plato."

Merl blanched. A couple of others paused at the door to listen. "My sermon made you think of a pagan philosopher?"

She nodded. "Necessary and sufficient conditions. Is accepting God's love sufficient or merely necessary?"

"Merely?"

"As opposed to necessary and sufficient. Certainly accepting His love is merely necessary. *What good is it, my brothers and sisters, if someone claims to have faith but has no deeds? Can such faith save them? The only thing that counts is faith expressing itself through love.*"

"But He who liveth and believeth in me shall have everlasting life."

"Yes, exactly! Liveth and believeth! Necessary and sufficient! So would you like to join me in Adoration?"

Merl cleared his throat and took a step back. "I think not."

Ann stood. "Well, it's neither necessary nor sufficient, but it is loving!"

Merl closed his eyes a moment, then turned to join those who waited for him. Frances gave her a friendly wave, but Cay regarded her with narrow eyes before following Merl out.

She shrugged. *It isn't his season yet,* she thought, as she set the chapel controls to Catholic.

* * *

Chris was deep within the Kuiper Belt, surrounded by dozens of chunks of rocks and ice. With a touch, he could see everything the human race knew about each — their composition, their names, the first time eyes set upon them and someone declared, "There you are!" Still, that didn't excite him as much as what he didn't know. If he used his imagination, he could hear them calling to him, teasing him with their secrets. Like the Folly…

2217RB86, Thoren's voice corrected him in his head. He had not been happy about the name change.

A door chime interrupted his thoughts, and he blinked as the lights came up and the door opened to let Andi in.

"Uh, hi!"

She paused and grinned at the holographic objects surrounding him. "That where we're headed?"

"It's not to scale!"

He winced as she chuckled.

"I'd hope not, or it's the most crowded sector of space I've seen in a long time. What're you doing?"

"Going over more of the information from the Fadil probe."

"*Discovery*'s not enough for you?"

"This is my thesis work." Was her smile approving or patronizing? Oh, how he wished he knew, and why it was so important to him.

Silence stretched.

She shrugged. "Well, how about putting it aside for the evening? I want to show you something, and it has to be now."

"About the mission? 'Cause Dr. Thoren —"

She tossed her head. "Thoren, schmoren! Tell him you had to study for your suit test. You are ready for that, aren't you?"

"Well..."

She strode into the Kuiper belt, took his hand, and dragged him away. The simulation automatically saved and closed as they stepped out of it. "I'll drill you on that, too, then. Come on."

She led him down the halls and to the elevator. They only passed a few people on the way, but everyone seemed to take in that they were holding hands. He caught a couple of people giving them winks and thumbs-ups. In the elevator, she released his hand to press the observation deck button, then leaned against the railing, smiling. He'd dreamed of this moment, feared this moment, and now he had no idea what to say. What kind of fear would Ann say he's experiencing? It all felt like butterflies to him. He swallowed hard.

The observation lounge was done in a beach theme with deck chairs facing a panel that showed a vast and starry sky. Saturn was a small, ringed disk in the upper left. "It's beautiful," he said.

"This? I can see this any day. Give me a minute, and you'll really see something."

She walked up to the panel, pulling a multi-purpose tool from her pocket, and removed the control board from the wall.

"What are you doing?" He tried not to sound as nervous as he felt.

"You wanted to know what it was like to grow up in space. You'll see." She pulled out a couple of wires.

The *zzt!* and small shower of sparks made him flinch. When he opened his eyes again, he gasped and swore. "What is that?"

He pointed to the viewscreen, suddenly alive with streaks of color and bright flashes.

She grinned, a cocky half-smile that made his heart skip. "That is what's really out there, a storm of dust and cosmic rays impacting on and being deflected by the EM shields. Looks like it's slowing down for now, though. I should have brought you earlier. I wonder when the next big wave is?"

"Are we safe?" He felt like an idiot for asking, especially since she was already settling herself into one of the lounge chairs. He forced his legs to move him to the one beside her and sit. He couldn't tear his eyes from the screen. He half-expected that the bright flashes would signal some kind of lethal radiation making its way through the viewscreen to impact on him and give him cancer or mess with his DNA or worse.

"It's as safe as it was before," she reassured. "It's just unsettling, is all. A view like this is worse than useless for navigating, so the newer computers automatically filter out the interference before projecting onto the viewscreen. I haven't gotten to see anything like this since I was a kid. Beautiful, isn't it?"

"You used to see this as a kid?" If she grew up exposed to this and was fine, he guessed he would be, too. He leaned back, settled his feet on the chair, and tried to relax.

"Mmm-hmm." Andi folded her hands behind her head, and the pose made him forget the danger outside the transparent PolySteel and magnetized particle barrier that guarded them from oblivion. "My dad was a trucker out of Arianis, couple of rocks over from St. Joe's. Had a Lock-Mac Sunchaser IV solar sail hauler. I used to love watching the sails unfurl. Mom did accounts, so we mostly stayed on Arianis with her, or went to the convent school, but when each of us kids got old enough, Dad would take us out with him."

"Sounds fun."

"Ha! We had to work for our air. Eight years old, I was doing the dishes and all the laundry, and assisting the engineer, which meant crawling into tight little access tunnels to replace some part that was guar-an-teed never to break." She shook her finger and spoke in a low voice, "'And don't mess up, Missy, or we'll toss you out the airlock. If we all survive, that is...'"

"That's awful."

"Are you spaced? I loved being out there, working with the crew or just standing by my dad while he talked to folks at the stops. He hauled a lot of different stuff — food to construction equipment, whatever needed getting somewhere fast — and he was insatiably curious. I'd learn more on a three-month run with him than I would all year, except when I studied with the sisters, and then I had Ann for competition."

Chris shook his head. "Just seems like a tough life."

"What's wrong with tough? You want to be out here, you have to be tough."

I want to know what's out here. To study it and learn about it and... Aloud, however, he said, "Sister Ann doesn't look so tough."

Andi frowned. "Ann took second degree burns and walked through a fire to save Kelley, and you haven't seen her on the splat court yet. Trust me, she's more rock than dust."

He sat up, rubbed his face. Why couldn't he just talk to this girl? "Right, sorry. I didn't mean to insult your friend or, or any of you."

"Of us?"

"I know this is your life, and if you love it, you love it. I just... I want something more."

"More." Her voice went so flat, it was a statement rather than a question.

"Yes! To explore and learn and study and discover —"

"And you think Thoren's going to go for that? Your thesis is a forty-year-old survey; you just got lucky that no one can ignore an alien ship. If Thoren had his way —"

Suddenly, Chris understood. "That's what this is about, isn't it? Thoren. You just want to recruit me away from him to help in your little power struggle."

"What?" Andi swung her feet to the floor with a stamp.

I'm such an idiot. "Listen, I don't want any part of it. You're right. I got lucky to find the ship."

"That's not what I said!"

"And we're all lucky to even be here! So let's just try to get along for the duration of this mission, okay? I'm going to go study for my suit test."

He stood, and without looking at her, headed to the lift, pushing a button at random so he didn't have to turn around. The last thing he heard as the door shut was her shouting his name in exasperation.

Chapter Twelve

"Welcome to Suits 101 and your first practical." Rita greeted the ten dirtsiders who stood uncomfortably in the spa room they'd cleared for the class. Dr. Thoren was notably absent. He'd insisted that the lessons interfered with his work and that training with the group harmed his status as an authority; after much discussion, Commander McVee had offered to give him private lessons, although he still had to pass the tests with the sisters.

Ian walked in, grinning apologetically and rubbing his hands against his suit to make sure they were dry before putting on his gloves.

Everyone was dressed in skinsuits: thick, form-fitting bodysuits that included socks and gloves and comprised the internal workings of any extended-use spacesuit. The outer workings of the suits were in bags beside each of them. A few of her students seemed to be adapting to the outfit, but the rest fidgeted and pulled at various parts of the fabric trying to adjust the fit, or were self-consciously covering parts of their anatomy.

They'll get used to it in time. I did. In the meantime, let's give them something to focus on. "Andi and Galen will be assisting me today. In this class you will learn to don and remove your suits and to help each other in the same. You'll also learn to read and manipulate the controls. Once you've mastered those skills, you'll begin to work while in your suit. I know some of you have scuba experience —"

"I love to scuba!" Ian raised his hand.

"Wonderful. Then that puts you a step ahead, but remember, there are differences. We'll talk about that later, before Suits 201. First, however, the basics. Let's start with the skinsuits."

"Do they have to be so tight?" Zabrina complained. "They didn't make us wear these during the Luna training."

Rita smiled sympathetically. "That's because the Luna suits are for emergency and recreational use in one-sixth gravity. Your suits are for longer-term work in microgravity, and, unfortunately, yes, they do need to be snug. The material is a nanoweave that reads and interacts with your skin to track your life signs. It contains its own power supply and is partly recharged by kinetic energy. Ian, stop jogging in place; it doesn't use that much power. It can inject medicines and apply pressure to specific areas when necessary: for example, when in microgravity to help prevent your blood from pooling to your head. For that reason, it's important to make sure it isn't wrinkled. Please check that now."

Everyone did so, with varying degrees of shyness. James, Rita noticed, endeavored to check his suit while still keeping his hands modestly in front of him. It was kind of sweet. Still, something didn't look quite right. "James, move your hands."

He looked up as if caught at something. "What?"

Rita demonstrated by putting her hands over her head. "Raise your hands. James, where's your 'pod?"

"My *what*?" His shriek, combined by the way he blushed, made Kelley explode with mirth. Galen and some of the others started to follow, but Rita stopped them with a glare.

"Your medical pod, James." She pointed to the small nanoweave-wrapped black box just in front of her hip, then addressed the class as a whole. "The medpod contains various narcotics to regulate blood pressure and oxygen content, treat pain and handle other emergencies. It docks through the suit to your internal catheter to deliver... James, you do have an internal line?"

When he looked blank, she sighed. "Is there anyone else who does not have an internal line? You would have had a simple outpatient procedure?"

Most people nodded; a few winced at the memory, but two, plus James, shook their heads.

"All right, then. After class, Galen will escort you to Doctor OvLandra. She'll schedule the surgery and see you are excused from duties for a day."

"Do we have to?" Kelley asked. "I mean, our spacesuits are supposed to protect us, right? If we get injured out there, it'll probably tear the suit, and we're goners anyway." She almost sounded as if she preferred that option to the thought of a "simple outpatient procedure."

"Fortunately, that's not how it works. These suits are not like those you see in the old holos. They don't tear easily. You can sustain broken bones and even severe internal injuries without harming your suit. Having said that, the suit has been known to take other kinds of damage, which could affect its — *your* — life-support system. Hence, the redundancy of the skinsuit. You're welcome to ask some of the rockjacks or Ann or Tommie about how the skinsuits saved their lives if you're skeptical.

"For those of you who do have the 'pods, let's review how to properly insert the pod into your dock." Ignoring the couple of giggles, she removed her own medpod and explained its basic workings and how to properly connect and test the device; all information covered in the study materials, and some of her students already had their medpods inserted, but, like a good teacher, she valued redundancy. Once everyone had docked their medpods to her satisfaction, she went on to the suits.

"Most of you have done well on the written tests, which is wonderful, but remember: you must pass the written and practical tests with a ninety percent or better in order to qualify for suit work. For today, however, we're simply going to learn to put it on and to assist each other in putting it on. Under most circumstances, you should have an experienced buddy to help you; however, everyone needs to be proficient, just in case."

Rita led them twice through a suit-up sans helmet, donning hers to demonstrate, then ordered them to remove their suits and try it by themselves a third time while she and her assistants wandered around helping. Andi and Galen both removed their suits before going around, but she kept hers on. She wanted everyone to see how easily someone could move in it once they got the knack. Even more, she saw how James was trying hard not to look at her. Three years of mandatory exercise had nicely toned her muscles, and the skinsuit kept everything in its proper place. *So now I have the model's body I used to pine for at 16,* she thought ruefully. *Just what I don't need now that I'm an "old" sister.*

She knew she wasn't old, and the way James avoided looking at her only served to remind her of the fact.

Doing her best to put such thoughts out of her mind, she went to help Zabrina with her suit.

* * *

Chris snarled as he wrestled with the locking clamp on his glove.

"How's it going?" the voice that, despite everything, still invaded his dreams tickled his ear.

In his dreams, he would have given her a smoldering look and said something mildly witty. Instead, he whined, "I can manipulate a multi-billion dollar telescope. I can interpret data from a dozen different sources. Yet I can't screw on a simple glove?"

"It shouldn't be that hard," Andi said, further squishing his ego.

She sat beside him and took his arm. She settled the glove back on, then twisted the lock. He thought it moved easily enough for her, but nonetheless, she frowned. "Take it off and you try it," she said.

He tried without success.

"Could you do it the first couple of times?"

"Yeah, but it wasn't easy. What'm I missing?"

She pulled off the glove and peered at the ring on it and on his sleeve. "When was the last time this suit was QC'd?"

"I dunno. I didn't use it much."

"And you didn't have it serviced before we left?"

"Well, I didn't use it much."

She sighed. "Sister Rita? We've got a suit problem."

His stomach twisted as he saw his dreams morph into nightmares.

"What? No way! I've got to go down there. That's my discovery!" He rose and grabbed for the glove, determined to shove it on and keep it on if that's what he had to do. No way were they going to keep him from the one thing he'd been hoping for all his life!

Andi, however, tossed the glove to Rita, who examined the ring with a critical eye. Then she took his arm and looked at the wrist of the suit. "If this doesn't fit exactly, you could end up enjoying your discovery with one less limb. But don't worry, Chris. I think the problem is with the glove, and we should have replacements, or Ann might be able to fix it. And if not, we'll find a replacement suit. For now, let's put it on as best you can while we practice with helmets." She handed Andi the glove and went to check on one of the others.

He sank back onto the bench with relief, and Andi knelt beside him and helped him get the glove on. Lines on her forehead formed as she frowned, but he didn't think it had anything to do with the glove. He said, "Sorry. Guess I panicked."

Her grunt didn't sound very forgiving. "Did you really think we're so petty we'd let a little thing like a busted ring keep you from enjoying your moment of triumph?"

Why, why, *why* couldn't he talk to this woman?

* * *

"Well, James, looks like you're getting the hang of it," Rita said. She'd abandoned her earlier idea of avoiding him; it would have been obvious — to him, if no one else. Besides, they worked together fine in other situations. This shouldn't be any different. It's not like they were alone. In fact, Rita made special efforts to make sure they were *never* alone, and James seemed to share her wishes — or at least tacitly agree. "Don't work so hard to lift your feet when you walk, though. They're not ski boots."

"They feel like it." He leaned forward awkwardly to look at his feet.

She laughed. "Look. In fact... Everyone! Look here a moment." When she had their attention, she folded herself forward and touched her toes. Then she straightened, lifted one knee, and rotated her booted foot in easy circles. "Your suit, while not the same grade as mine, is nonetheless quite supple. Another difference between them and the suits you trained in on Luna. You should have a normal range of motion.

"You will, however, need to be aware that you take up more space than normal, especially front-to-back. Your suits are very durable, but who knows what damage you may cause the items on the alien ship if you bump into something while turning around. Go ahead, move around — just be careful of your neighbor."

"You're really natural at this," James said. He opted to set his foot on the bench and rest his arm on his knee.

"It's the result of a lot of hard work and training, believe me." Nonetheless, she couldn't hide a flush of pleasure at the compliment.

"Well, it shows." His voice lowered. "Rita, is there a chance —"

"Sister? We ready for helmets?" Galen's voice rang from across the room.

"Oh, yes! Absolutely. Everybody find a partner. Andi and Galen, come up front and demonstrate, please." With a brief apologetic grin at James, she returned to the front, leaving him to find someone to partner with. For the rest of the class, they were busy with donning and doffing their helmets, and she never found out what he wanted to ask.

Frankly, she wasn't sure she wanted to know.

James, however, didn't seem so eager to let it drop. After the session, she saw him talking to Galen, who nodded and left with Kelley to get her medpod. He lingered while she helped one of the ladies get her gear back into its bag, smiling as the last of the students dragged their stuff into the locker rooms, then headed to her. She started packing her suit and steeled herself.

"Rita, I wanted to ask you…"

"James, I don't have a lot of time to talk right now."

He held up his hands placatingly. "Okay. I just had a couple ideas about how we can use the suit equipment when exploring, and I want to know when you and I, and maybe Ann, can talk about them. Might impact what you teach."

"Oh!" She felt relieved and absolutely stupid.

It must have shown, because the look he gave her was so…what? She couldn't quite tell, but some kind of mix of resigned and annoyed and more closed than she'd ever seen him. It hurt, even more because she deserved it.

He crossed his arms. "You thought I was going to ask you something else, didn't you?"

"I'm sorry, James, I just…" Her voice trailed off, and again, an awkward silence stretched. Her skinsuit, part of the accepted habit of her order, suddenly seemed both too constricting and too revealing. She clutched her helmet tightly in front of her.

When he broke the silence, his voice was gentle, but she could feel the strain in it. "Look, Rita. It's obvious you've made your decision."

"Is it?" She wished it was so obvious to her.

Fortunately, he misinterpreted her question. "Amazingly enough, some things will get through even this thick skull." He knocked on his head.

As he always had, he managed to make her laugh, and it cleared some of the tension between them.

"There's no reason we can't be friends, though, right? Wasn't that what we always were, first and foremost?"

"You're right, James. Friends." She found she was able to breathe again. "Why don't we meet in the dining hall in the afternoon? Oh, wait! Your dock. If Dr. OvLandra does it today, you might not feel up to it."

"Does it hurt?"

"Not much more than getting your wisdom teeth pulled. Mine itched for a week, though."

"Urgh. I hated getting my teeth pulled. Well, I'm going to see if she can get me in today, anyway. It's the anticipation that gets me. I'll keep chanting, 'I'm going to explore an alien ship. I'm going to explore an alien ship.'"

Once again, she felt sheer awe at the thought. "An alien ship. What are the odds we would find one now?"

"Probably on par with my finding you again."

She felt her face redden and knelt to mess with her spacesuit bag to keep him from noticing. It couldn't have been more than a moment's silence, yet it seemed to stretch forever.

"So," he said, dragging out the word, "Ann's getting to be good friends with our ship's surgeon."

"Yes! She's quite excited." She kicked herself. *Quite excited*. She tended to slip into formal speech when she was nervous, and he knew it.

He also knew when to ignore it. "Sean's beside himself with envy. She's the other person who refuses to be V-Rec'd. You should hear the conspiracies he's come up with, like that they only send out assassins and spies to dwell among the humans."

"Oh, please! James, they are human. They've just manipulated their DNA in order to counteract the effects of the microgravity."

"Just," he repeated, his voice tinged, she knew, in disbelief over her cavalier attitude more than the genetic altering.

She shrugged. She'd had to study their differences in case they ever needed to rescue a zerog ship, although St. Joe's had not encountered one since the Ring Wars. "Primarily hormone function for mineral retention, some skeletal-muscular adjustments. And the eyes, of course, to see better in low light."

"And the Church is okay with this?"

"The Zero G Corporation didn't exactly ask the Vatican. It's germ line manipulation, so it's hereditary. Frankly, MuSobla and his associates were geniuses; the traits have been breeding true for generations. Some of the changes are the result of constant living in microgravity, but the actual manipulations were minor."

"But look at them! Plus, according to Sean, they think they're a separate race, and near as I can tell, the Spacers do, too. Isn't that just what *Dignitas Personae* warned against?"

Why is he scolding me? "A century of a strict isolationist policy will do that. The Church has missionaries there, trying to remind them that we're all God's children. In the meantime, we do our best to get along. Code Six."

He barked a laugh. "Did you just invoke *the Code*?"

A flare of anger brought her eyes to his. "They're the rules of space. I live under them now."

"You hated Codism!"

She stood up to yell into his face. "I still do! I don't worship them any more than I'd worship a, a jaywalking injunction. They're not God's laws, but they are Caesar's, and here in the Black, they keep you alive."

"The Black?"

"Space, James! Where not understanding the Code or not having a 'pod can get you killed. Vac! Didn't you have any training outside Loops for LunaTechs before you got here?"

"Do you hear yourself? 'Vac'?" he repeated, and laughed. It sounded ugly to her ears.

He always made jokes when he was trying not to get angry. Well, she didn't want any part of it. Who was he to judge her choice? For that matter...

"Why are you even here — in the Black?" she demanded.

Now, he fiddled with his fingers and refused to meet her eyes.

It didn't matter. She didn't have time to babysit him; too many others needed her.

"Go get your dock," she ordered, and traipsed out.

* * *

"Dr. OvLandra? It's Sister Ann St. Joseph de Cupertino. I have bound my belongings to myself and ask to enter."

"Then enter. The way is clear, and you are welcome."

The door slid open, and she stepped over the threshold carefully. Her stomach gave a slight jump at the change in gravity. It made her smile.

OvLandra returned the grin. "It pleases me to hear the greetings of my people," she said. "Few have my leave to enter here, and those that do seldom remember the formalities."

Despite the fact that she wanted to bounce with glee, Ann kept herself still. "Thank you. I'm honored."

She let her eyes roam the room, taking in the cool green-and-blue padding that lined floor, ceiling and walls, the encased shelves in the corners, the computer mounted near the ceiling with its two VR headsets tucked neatly into webbed chairs.

OvLandra said, "And you perform the Assessment most naturally."

"Do I? Well, Rescue Sisters always assess a situation before going in, so I suppose it's habit."

"Of course. Please, continue."

She turned her head, her body following in a gentle corkscrew. Then she straightened and pushed herself toward the painting on the back wall.

"Oh!"

"It is a hobby of mine. I painted my suit, as well."

"It's lovely. But so traditional."

"Oh?"

She tilted her head slightly to look at the gentle face, backlit by the sun, which haloed the dark brown hair with golden light. The hair, in a classical mid-shoulder straight cut, floated in waves about his head. His hands stretched out, as if to embrace the 'verse. She lowered her head, taking in the long robes, the sandaled feet. Then she laughed.

Four little cherubim, half-hidden in the fabric, held down the hem of Jesus' robes.

OvLandra chuckled with her. "Christ, in his human form, might need a little help with his skirts here, do you not think?"

"I'd think Christ, in whatever form, would know to dress appropriately."

Now OvLandra let out a full laugh. "Perhaps you are wiser than your delicate face reveals."

"And you gave him your eyes!" She looked back to Jesus' face, his eyes far too large and dark for a "regular" human.

"Perhaps He gave me His. Who gave you your eyes, Small Weight?"

"*If we only had the angels' eyes! Seeing our Lord Jesus Christ here, on that altar, and looking at us, how we should love him!* I think I would be content with angels' eyes."

"A beautiful sentiment. Did your father teach you that?"

"My father? Oh, no. Saint John Vianney: *If we only had the angels' eyes! Seeing our Lord Jesus Christ here, on that altar, and looking at us, how we should love Him! We should want to stay always at His feet; it would be a foretaste of heaven; everything else would become insipid to us.* He heard confessions sixteen hours a day. Perhaps he had the ears of Christ."

"The sisters gave you a great love for our faith. How is it that they came to raise you?"

Ann continued to study the painting, her brows knitted in thought. "*If we had faith, we would see God hidden in the priest like a light behind glass, like wine mixed with water.* So certainly Saint John Vianney had Christ's ears, or at least they shared the same space-time. The sisters found me in the wreckage. Everyone else was dead."

OvLandra pushed off from her spot on the ceiling, coming to an easy stop beside Ann so that she could study her profile. "I'm so sorry. And you do not remember your family?"

Ann made a slight shrug. "The sisters have always been my family. They even named me. *Like wine mixed with water.* We only see the wine or the color of the wine. We might taste the water. Taste and see. God comes to us in all our senses. We just don't always notice. I wonder what angels taste?"

"You are both too young and too old for your age, Sister Ann. Have you never felt...apart from the others?"

"*In this new universe, the heavenly Jerusalem, God will have his dwelling among men... This consummation will be the final realization of the unity of the human race, which God willed from creation.* How can I feel apart? I'm reminded of our unity with every Eucharist. What would the Eucharist taste like to angels? *Upon receiving Holy Communion, the Adorable Blood of Jesus Christ really flows in our veins, and His Flesh is really blended with ours.* So perhaps He did give you His eyes, though I think they're yours in the painting!"

OvLandra laughed and touched her shoulder. "You make much of my obsession. Come, let me share another with you."

Chapter Thirteen

Kelley thanked George for her food and paused at the head of the line, scanning the cafeteria for a place to sit. Or rather, people to sit with.

Merl had commandeered one of the bigger tables for his Christian groupies. She grimaced. If she had to deal with another snide comment from them or another religious tract in her email, she was going to do something, no matter how much Andi said to ignore him. Maybe Andi could ignore the "whore of Babylon" messages he sent her, but she had friends around her. Who did Kelley have?

She glanced to where the researchers and a couple of rockjacks were laughing. Ian rested his arm on the back of Zabrina's chair. Kelley frowned. Didn't her friend see through the act? Still, maybe she could sit there; he'd behave as long as Sister Thomas was in the group.

Then again, she didn't feel up to dealing with nuns, either. Sister Thomas was okay, though why she'd chosen to change her name to a man's was beyond her. Did she think it'd give her favor with God to style herself as male? Besides, if she was there and the other two came in, they'd join her. Sister Ann was just weird, the way she talked and always seemed to be having side conversations with someone — something — else. Sometimes, Kelley imagined she could feel that something else looking at her.

She shivered.

Sister Rita was all right, but she didn't always seem happy, and the way she sometimes looked at Dr. Smith when he wasn't looking...Kelley shook her head. *She's not in harmony. I'm not in harmony, either. I miss my own sisters and brothers in the coven. I miss Earth.*

Behind her, George said something to Cay, who grunted in reply. Poor Cay. He didn't exactly feel at home here, either. Andi had told her about the accident, and, while she tried to put a good face on, it was clear she didn't want him on her team, and several of the rockjacks agreed. *Bet he could use some company.*

"Hey, Cay!" She smiled her brightest smile and concentrated positive thoughts toward him as he left the line with tray in hand. "There's an empty table over there. Want to join me?"

He paused just long enough to give her a disdainful look. "Why don't you try that on, Ian? I'm not interested."

As she stood there with jaw dropped, he made a beeline to Merl's table.

The evangelist stood to greet him with a hearty slap. Merl looked past him and gave Kelley a victorious smirk.

She lost her appetite.

* * *

Andi jumped back to keep from crashing into Kelley in the doorway. "Hey, roomie, what's going on?"

"Nothing. Just leave me alone."

Andi gaped at her retreating form, then blew through her teeth. She had no idea what that was about, but she knew it wasn't her fault. Right now, she had to go take care of something that was.

Not that she wanted to. What she wanted to do was spout off to Ann or Godmom, but Ann had caught her on the way to meet OvLandra. Before Andi had started into her complaint, her friend had taken her hands and said, as if giving her a gift, "*You must ask God to give you power to fight against the sin of pride, which is your greatest enemy — the root of all that is evil and the failure of all that is good. For God resists the proud.*" Then she took off, leaving Andi to figure out what she meant.

Was I being so proud? I just wanted to tell him who I am. God, I don't even know why that's so important to me. I don't suppose You'd send me a sign?

She entered the cafeteria and saw Chris alone at a table, studying some readings on the virtual screen before him while trying to eat. He was so caught up in what he was reading, he set his fork down, food still on it, then blinked in surprise when he tried to load it again and found it full. Why'd he have to be so cute?

She sighed and headed to his table. "Hey," she said softly, "can I interrupt?"

He gave a little start at the sound of her voice. "Hi. Uh, yeah. Sure."

She sat in the chair beside him, turning it so she could look at his profile. She resisted the urge to make him turn and face her, as well. A life half-spent in spacesuits made her most comfortable when she could face someone head-on, and she had to remind herself that a dirtsider would not feel the same. "I wanted to apologize for snapping at you earlier. You had every right to be worried. I just wish you had more faith in us. I mean, do you really think we'd leave you?"

Chris shrugged. "I guess I really didn't think. I'm — I don't know — overwhelmed, I guess."

She glanced at the readout on his screen, a comparison of the Ky-boes from the probe. "Is that why you're retreating to this?"

He sighed. "It's not a retreat. This could be important. Look what we found already —"

"— what *you* found, Chris —"

"— just by accident. Listen, I know you probably think this is just a bunch of self-indulgent academia."

She felt her hackles rise, but bit back her anger. "Chris, this is what I was trying to tell you in the observation deck. Just because I'm not at some university doesn't mean I don't appreciate knowledge just for knowledge's sake. My dad was a hauler, sure, but he was also an astronomer. The Vicente-Gaiman telescope is named partly in his honor."

"Really?" But instead of being impressed, he frowned at his food.

"What?"

"It's just... I tried to get time on VG2 to look at the Folly, but they never answered my requests. Just ignored them." He pouted.

"Yeah, well, that's what happens when a drone knocks out your station." Chris sighed. "I suppose. I... Wait! What?"

Didn't he know? "Chris, the telescope itself is on a different rock, thank heavens, but we lost comms and control. It was a couple of weeks before we got it back up, and we lost a lot of requests."

He blinked at her, making the connections but not quite believing them. "You work the telescope? Rocky Flats controls the telescope?"

Andi grinned at his wide-eyed expression. "Which we built from the profits of the colite mine."

"I had no idea! I always thought... Wow." He paused a moment then added, in a voice hushed with sympathy, "That must have been tough, losing the station. I mean, that was your home."

She felt her eyes mist and her arms ache to embrace him. She took in a large breath and tried to shrug nonchalantly. "Well, that is why we're here. We do this little recovery job for Cole, and he rebuilds our station."

"Just like that? A straight across trade?"

"Well, it's more complex than that, and he gets twenty percent of our profits while we get five percent of *Discovery*."

"My ship?" Chris squeaked.

Andi smirked. He was so cute. "Ours, dear."

He opened his mouth to protest, closed it, and got a thoughtful, faraway look. When he spoke again, it was to ask, "Did you call me 'dear'?"

* * *

Ann woke up with the sound of the *Edwina Taggert* crying her name. She lay still, staring into the darkness of the room, hearing her breath panting at one-point-seven times that of her sleeping sisters. Her hands gripped a bunched-up section of the comforter.

Comforter. That which gives comfort. Too much comforter, and no comfort. She sat up and pushed the thick blanket to the foot of her bed. She wiped the sweat off her brow as her gaze wandered around the room.

The darkness comforted her. There were so many colors in the light: reds and browns and golds. Rita loved it. She called them warm colors. Was that why Ann felt too hot?

She shook her head. *We're in a climate-controlled ship. The temperature's a stable 69.8 degrees Fahrenheit, 21 Celsius, 249 degrees Kelvin...but my dream was so cold.*

She slipped out of bed and dressed in the dark. The habit felt comfortable and comforting. She didn't want to wake her sisters, so she ran her fingers through her hair as she eased out of the room.

The lights in the living room came up automatically at her presence, and she squinted against the sudden assault of warm colors and comfortable finery. Before she realized it, she'd succumbed to the urge to flee and hurried from their quarters and down the halls.

She felt at home among the functional grays and the equipment of engineering. Here, the *Edwina Taggert* didn't call names in a worried voice, but purred with the pulsing hum of magnetic fields directing plasma that propelled the ship at six-tenths the speed of light — 179,875,474.4 meters per second — and increasing. As soon as they reached .7C, they'd cut the engines, turn the ship, and fire in the opposite direction to slow down until they matched orbit with the Folly.

With such a small crew, no one manned this control room, trusting instead to the automatic sensors to alert the engineering team of trouble. Ann wandered idly, running her hands over the consoles, musing over the readings. Green, yellow, and red. Red: a warm color. The color of danger, but the color of passion, too. And blood. Christ's blood, Christ's Passion...

Thoroughly comforted now, she went into the engine room itself to admire the VASIMR drive. When the door slid open, she discovered she wasn't alone.

"Oh!"

"Hey, Sister Ann!" Ian twisted around at the sound of her gasp and smiled. "Couldn't sleep, either?"

Without waiting for an answer, he chuckled and resumed leaning on the railing and gazing out at the stories-long electro-magnetic chamber that held the superheated gas and shoved it out the thrusters. "She's a beauty, isn't she?"

Ann stood next to him and set her hands on the railing. She could feel the power of the ship through the metal. That, too, comforted. She shut her eyes, the better to feel it.

"So, what's up with you? Your refined bed too soft?"

"It's fine," she answered automatically, then stopped to consider. "Fine. Refined. Finery. *Solicitude for material things distracts the soul and divides it.* I don't wish to be refined by finery. Here, I feel defined again."

The engineer's brows knitted for a moment with thought. "Meaning...you feel comfortable around engines?"

"They aren't as complex as people."

Ian's face twisted in a way she didn't understand, then he burst out laughing. Still, something sounded...off...about his laughter. If he were an engine, she would know where the problem lay and what she had to do, or learn, to fix it. But not with humans, which really rather proved her point, she thought.

A sweet-faced man in papal robes appeared before her, floating in the gap between the gantry and the VASIMR engine, as if standing in firm ground. He pointed the shepherd's crook he held toward her.

"Robotic sheep don't need shepherds?" she asked, and his smile filled her with such love.

Meanwhile, Ian laughed even harder. "Okay! I have no idea where that came from."

"Why do you laugh?" she asked.

"Because it was kind of funny."

"'Kind of.'" She stopped to think. "But which kind? You laugh a lot. At everything."

He snorted, his mirth dying. "Is that a problem?"

"I don't know. Human psychology lacks accurate diagnostics. There's no gauge."

Nonetheless, his voice took on an edge that clearly signaled "red." "Look, Sister. You can handle life in two ways: laugh or cry. And I'd rather laugh."

"*A time to weep and a time to laugh.* Jesus wept in Gethsemane. Saints and angels weep. Tears and laughter heal, but each in its own time. Sometimes people weep for joy. But you never cry?"

Ian didn't answer. He held himself so tightly, she imagined him vibrating like an overstressed engine, trembling on the urge to laugh or cry. The needle on the gauge moved deeper into red. He scratched at his hands, and she knew that was a signal, but she didn't know of what. She was supposed to do something, but she had no technical specs and no schematic. It hurt to look at him and not know what to do; she turned her face back to the engines.

"*Being in anguish, He prayed more earnestly, and His sweat was like drops of blood.* Blood, sweat, and tears. Body, mind, and soul — the human system, like an engine," she murmured, struggling to understand. She closed her eyes, the better to concentrate. "Not at peak efficiency. Tragedy, sin — they damage the system, create pressure points. Diagnosis and repair — and the pressure needs to be released. Laughter is a release; so are tears. Different release mechanisms, different purposes..."

Sudden conviction clutched at her stomach so hard, her eyes flew open, and she grabbed Ian's wrist. "Ian, don't be afraid. You need release; you need to cry."

He jerked his hand away. "Sister, you really *are* spaced!"

He laughed as he left, but it was an ugly sound.

Chapter Fourteen

"So what's wrong with just putting on our suits and sucking out the air? They should have done that the minute the thing got loose," Gordon Radell said.

About thirty people, including Captain Addiman and the sisters, had shown up for the first Friday Night "seminar." The movie, *ALIEN*, had proven both creepy and campy, and about half the people left afterward to study, work out, or unwind in other ways. A dozen, though, had convened in the dining room for discussion.

"You do not understand the size of the *Edwina Taggert*, my friend," the captain replied. "She is much too big. There would be hundreds of places a creature could hide. I'll give you an example. I was senior navigator for the *Mardi Gras*; she made the Earth/Moon/L5 run. No matter how carefully you scan de luggage, there is always a small problem with pests. So part of her regular maintenance is to expose her to vacuum. Even then, the crew go through after the air is pumped in, and sometimes, we still find a rat. Where they hide, we do not know."

Rita nodded. "When we had a ship infested with snakes, we exposed it to vacuum for a week, and that was a small cargo ship. Even after, we went through with hard suits and opened up every container and exposed them to vacuum, too."

"Snakes?" James asked. Several others gaped.

The three sisters shared creeped-out looks. "Don't ask," Rita said.

Addiman nodded. "My own recommendation: we do not bring aboard anyt'ing that might be alive."

"We're not going to find anything alive!" Zabrina laughed. "We've all seen the scans. That ship is as cold as space."

"On the outside," one of the structural engineers on Reg's team said ominously. "If that's really colite on the hull — or anything sufficiently thick or dense — we can't be sure there isn't something powered or living on the inside."

"Right. For umpteen thousands of years?"

"And do you *know* it's been there that long? Code Three: Don't make assumptions."

"Okay, extremophile life. Maybe. But we haven't found anything more complex than mold outside Earth, and that was deep in the ice on Europa. Complex life can't sustain itself in vacuum."

"Hermit crabs," James said suddenly. When all eyes turned to him, he said, "When necessary, hermit crabs can enter a state of hibernation. You think they're dead. I had one as a kid. It buried itself under the sand. Didn't eat or drink or anything for over a month. I was sure it was dead, but my dad told me to be patient. Sure enough, a couple of weeks later, it dug itself back up, fine as anything. Come to think of it, those things did look kind of like headless hermit crabs." He gave a shudder and drank some coffee.

"Okay. Can we agree then that anything that looks like it might be alive or come alive will not be allowed on the ship?" Galen asked.

"Not unless we're certain it's good and dead," the captain agreed with a grin. "I think we can file that under 'hazardous vermin prohibited.'"

Kelley huffed, "So how am I supposed to study any creatures we find if I can't bring it aboard?"

Ann pulled up a schematic of the ship on her wristcomp and dragged the image to the center of the table. With quick motions, she focused in on the biology lab installed on the outermost deck on the ship. "Mr. Cole's people did a wonderful job designing your and Zabrina's lab. It's already Biosafety Level Five and completely self-contained, and they totally isolated it from the rest of the ship."

She changed the schematic to show the outside of the ship and drew lines with her fingers. "Galen, if we could line charges along here, we could cut the hull and eject the lab if we inadvertently brought something dangerous in."

"With us in it?" Kelley shrieked.

"Your biosuits are spaceworthy for up to ten minutes. That's plenty of time for us to retrieve you."

"If you haven't been implanted by alien eggs," Sean added. He'd wanted to go back and replay that scene to look over the special effects and had been shouted down.

"It's just an extreme measure, Kelley," Rita soothed.

"Absolutely. It would do a lot of damage to the ship," Ann added.

"Oh, yes, the ship!" Kelley grumbled. "Got to think about that."

Galen shrugged. "If Little Sister says they could get to you in time, then I believe it. Besides, that's assuming you didn't already escape first, and I think it goes without saying that if anything looks to be busting containment, you should drop everything and run so we can jettison the lab without you." He leaned forward and studied the schematic. "I'd have to check with Dale and George, but I think we can do it."

"The aliens will be dead, anyway." Annoyance gave Zabrina's voice a sing-song quality.

"What if some are alive?" Ian asked. "What do we do then?"

"Do you think these aliens have eternal souls?" Merl wondered.

Half the group laughed and a few started to kid him about needing something else to evangelize to.

However, Ann replied seriously. "The aliens in the movie didn't seem particularly sentient. More like animals than creatures. And it wasn't their ship, was it? Maybe they were like rats."

"Terrifyingly big space alien rats," Sean pointed out with a smirk.

"With two sets of jaws." Ian made sideways snapping motions with his curled fingers.

"I'm not gonna sleep well tonight," Zabrina whined.

"I think the point Ann is trying to make," Sean said over the din he'd started, "is that there's probably no way of knowing unless we get one awake and alive to talk to, and we've decided to file that under 'Dangerously Stupid Idea.' See how useful this is going to be? What other lessons did we learn?"

"How about the most obvious? No one goes anywhere alone," Rita offered to try to bring some sanity to the discussion. Heads nodded all around.

James spoke up. "We've got better technology than they did. We use it. Before entering a room, scan it first — visual, then IR. Don't touch anything 'hot.' For that matter, don't touch anything at all unless you've got approval. It's not a lesson from this movie, but no one touches buttons, levers, or anything that looks like it activates something. And don't go prodding anything that looks like it was once alive. It's probably not going to open up and attack you, but if it's organic, chances are it might crumble into dust. Get as many readings from it as you can and call in a xenobio team, but don't touch."

They continued on, and Ian took notes (under the heading "Dangerously Stupid Things to Do on an Alien Ship," which everyone soon called the DST). In half an hour, ideas had been exhausted, and folks were getting silly.

Rita stretched. "Well, Sean, Ian, I would not have believed it at first, but this turned out to be a very educational evening."

"Everything I do is educational!" Ian protested while mimicking being stabbed in the heart.

"So I'm learning." She started to rise, as did others.

Sean held up a hand. "Hey! Before we leave, I want to hear about Sister Ann's visit to our mysterious chief medical officer."

Word had gotten around that Ann had been admitted into the zerog's confidences. Folks in the process of leaving sat back down.

"Is she Christian?"

"Merl!" Ian groaned.

"Oh, yes! She painted the most wonderful picture of Jesus on her wall." Ann's mouth budded into a small smile.

"Most zerogs are Christian, Merl," Tommie added.

His face pinched with doubt. "I was led to believe most were heathen Codists." He spat the word.

For an uncomfortable moment, folks looked around to see who he'd offended.

"Where are the Codists, anyway?" Ian asked. "You'd think they'd want to be part of this. See how we should apply the Code to alien encounters." He made a sideways snapping motion with his hands toward Zabrina, "Code One! Code One! Don't panic!"

She swatted his hand away. "I think Thoren scheduled one of his Discussions."

Merl muttered something under his breath.

"Must be where Chris is then," Sean spoke over him.

"No," Ann said. "He's studying with Andi."

"Ooooo!" the group chorused.

"Well, he has to pass his suit test."

"That's right!" Ian declared with over-the-top importance. "He has to pass his suit test." Then he leaned toward Zabrina and wagged his eyebrows at her. "Wanna help me with my suit test?"

Sean rested his hands on the table. "Come on. I want to hear more about OvLandra. What did you talk about, then?"

Ann's eyes got a faraway focus as she thought. "Jesus...and angel eyes. And genetics — lots about genetics. Did you know that zerog chromosomes are seldom dominant? It's one reason they are so isolationistic, to keep from diluting the bloodline and losing the benefits of the manipulations."

Addiman nodded. "To form a liaison with one outside their species is punishable by death for the zerog, his human mate, and their children."

There were gasps all around. Only Sean seemed unsurprised by the news; he wore a thoughtful frown.

Merl snorted. "And they call themselves Christians."

Tommie grunted. "We humans continue to have the death penalty for treason, and shall we discuss the Belt Wars? Yet a significant percentage of non-zerog humans are Christian."

"*Jesus said to them, 'It is not the healthy who need a doctor, but the sick. I have not come to call the righteous, but sinners,'*" Ann added.

"Amen," Merl murmured.

Ann continued, musing. "OvLandra, the doctor who sees not her own illness. Dust motes and staffs. It's a wonder any of us can see. We also talked about Edwina Taggert, the actress. She said maybe next time she'd show me a documentary about the making of the Lola Quintain games. It's very important to her."

"Did she tell you why she was on the ship with humans for so long, then?" Sean asked.

"*Who can map out the various forces at play in one soul? Man is a great depth, O Lord. The hairs of his head are easier by far to count than his feeling, the movements of his heart.* It's enough that she's with us. She's a very good doctor. Sister Lucinda would like her, but I think I might introduce her to Augustine."

"Sorry?" Ian asked, but Ann was studying her ring, her brow furrowed in thought.

"*Physician, heal thyself.* But when there's a staff in your eye, how can you see to diagnose? Staff. Staph infection." She paused to rub the scar on her left hand. "Poison in the body hurts. You can't ignore it. But poison in the soul?"

"Are you saying her soul is poisoned?" Merl asked.

"All souls carry poison. Baptism washes it away, but our fallen natures make us invite it back. *I loved my fall, not the object for which I had fallen, but my fall itself. My depraved soul leaped down from your firmament to ruin. I was seeking not to gain anything by shameful means, but shame for its own sake.*"

"Saint Augustine," James said. "Doctor of the Church."

Ann nodded, but distractedly. "Jesus is the Great Physician. But we skip our appointments, forget our medicine, ignore the illness. When the snake bit me, we cut my hand to release the pressure of the swelling. Tears weren't sufficient. Tears relieve soul pressure, but sometimes we ignore the cause. We let the poisons fester..." Her voice trailed off and she closed her eyes, only to throw them open and pin everyone with her stare. "It's a Dangerously Stupid Thing. Write it down, Ian: 'Ignoring what poisons our souls is a dangerously stupid thing.'"

People traded confused, uncomfortable looks.

James cleared his throat. "Why not? No reason we can't be existential, too."

Sean shrugged and took the console from Ian to type it in.

But Ann shook her head. "Not existential. Practical."

Rita could see the conversation degenerating ahead, and she didn't like the confused, pensive look on Ann's face. She stood. "I'm calling it a night. I need to get a workout in. I'll see most of you in class tomorrow."

There were a couple of moans and shifting eyes. Everyone was supposed to work out every day in a program specially designed for them to build muscles they may need for zero-G work. They anticipated only a week or two of working on the ship, but about a quarter of the research team did not exercise regularly, and it showed in how they handled suit work.

James raised his hand to ear height, one finger pointing upward, the way he always used to when admitting to something. "I haven't been to the gym today. May I join you?"

"Me, too?" mumbled Zabrina, who sounded more resigned than embarrassed.

"All right," Rita said, even though she'd been hoping to have the quiet gym to herself.

Ann stood up, once again bright and smiling. "I'll come, too. I'll help them, and you can do stations. It's good medicine. Blood, sweat, and tears — all relieve pressure."

"What're stations?" Zabrina asked as they headed down the hall. "Some kind of circuit training?"

"Actually, it's a meditation," Rita answered. "Back before the gravity generators were cheap enough for smaller stations and ships, the Rescue Sisters spent a majority of their time in microgravity. In fact, in that first century, any sisters that retired from the OLR usually couldn't return to a gravity well and lived the rest of their lives at the retirement facility on New Vatican."

"Of course, there weren't many who lived to retirement age. Most died in service," Ann added cheerily.

James and Zabrina winced, but Rita was used to the casual way Ann treated the dangers of space life, and merely nodded. "Exercise, however, was very important — to prevent calcium loss and muscular degradation that comes from not having gravity to work against. They spent as much as five hours a day exercising, so Sister Francisca developed a series of meditations associated with particular exercises so that the sisters could pray, as well. Plus, it's a help for those who don't like to work out."

"Like you?" James laughed. "I used to make Rita go jogging with me on campus. I never understood why you loved biking and hated running."

"It wasn't that I loved biking, but at least I was going somewhere. Running in circles was just a waste of time. I like weight training, though, and I do enjoy Sister Francisca's meditations."

"So you two know each other pretty well?" Zabrina asked.

Is that a casual question, or is she fishing for gossip? Rita decided to give the truth as simply as possible. "Yes, James and I were quite good friends when we were teaching at TTUI. Then I, um, felt a need to separate myself from the things of the Earth, so I joined the OLR."

"What? Just like that? Leave everything you've ever known, everyone you've ever cared about?"

"My job, my family, my sisters — I was a Sister of Charity of the Blessed Virgin Mary on Earth — and my friends." Her voice trailed off. The conversation was getting a little heavier than she'd expected.

"Just like that," James repeated, and she couldn't tell if anger or guilt caused his voice to sound so choked.

Rita managed a smile. "I had to go. And I don't regret it. I've been very blessed here."

"Oh, yes!" Ann hugged Rita's arm. "Earth's loss is our gain. It was one of the most blessed days ever when Rita joined Our Lady of the Rescue!"

Rita felt an overflowing of love, and she leaned her head affectionately onto Ann's.

Chapter Fifteen

"More lamps? Just how many lamps do we need?" Chris wondered out loud as he read from the list of items they had to find. It was Day Fifteen of the Great Scavenger Hunt, and Engineering had disabled the lights as an extra challenge.

It had started as an additional duty. A list was posted of things the "Mighty Five" believed the group needed. Quadrant leaders in the dorm wing scheduled scavenger runs throughout the ship. Then, the leader of Quadrant One posted a running list of items they'd acquired with "Eat Our Thrust!" scrawled across the bottom. Soon, all the quadrants had their own running tallies and raced to outdo one another. Items were assigned points based on perceived rarity and value. Leadership permitted it as long as it didn't interfere with work or training. In fact, James had turned it into training by adding procedures that could earn more points. The sisters added one stipulation: that all scavenger squads contain a mix of rockjacks and dataheads and even added obscure items and challenges to make it interesting.

Like today's. Wandering around in the dark creeped Chris out.

"I think Ann's got an idea. Keep your head up and sweep the area with your light, or we're not going to find anything," Galen grumped amiably. Quadrant Three's strategy was to send everyone out in teams of two. They had housekeeping carts to carry small items, and if anyone found anything larger, they called it in for help to reclaim it. As such, they had covered more of the ship, though they had missed some items. Chris was still seething that Quadrant Two had found the hat rack he and Galen had walked right by the day before. That smug look on Andi's face...

He hadn't realized he'd spoken aloud until Galen laughed. "Keep your head up. You'll get another chance to impress her."

He decided the best thing to do was ignore the comment and just be thankful Galen couldn't see him blushing in the dark. "What would Sister Ann want with lamps? She's kind of...different."

"The best kind of different, and don't forget it. Wait until you have her for Suits 201. You'll see. You know, this would be so much easier if we could use our suit comm. Have you aced the suit communications unit yet?"

"No, Thoren's riding me on learning everyone else's job. I'm an astrophysicist, for pity's sake. I'll get it done in a day or two. I got an 85 on the last exam; I just screwed up the override protocols. I mean, why do I need to know that, anyway?"

Galen paused a moment. "Not everyone's getting tested on that; sounds like they expect you to take charge if necessary, and in space, the guy who can talk is the guy who leads."

Chris sighed. "I'm not a leader, not like Andi or James, or… Besides, Thoren's the real leader."

Again the pause. "Listen, I know he's your mentor and all that, but if it comes to him or you, I want you. And I'm not the only one who thinks that way. At any rate, you're the next logical step in leadership on the datahead side, and you know the Code."

"Always have a back-up. And a back-up to the back-up. Who's my back-up?"

"James, I'll bet. Like you said, he's a good leader; he might even be the choice for second with you as his back-up. At any rate, if you want to get on your *Discovery*, you'd better learn those protocols. Besides, you don't want to miss zero-G training. Little Sister's going to teach you the most pulsar stuff, but not until you get that manual down cold."

"Yeah, well until then, what's the problem with letting me use the suit? I mean, I can wear it." He held out suited arms, grateful again that Sister Rita had found a replacement glove. "I can wear the helmet in class. Why not now?"

"Gotta earn it, and they're making it harder for you. The Sisters think pretty highly of you. Bet Andi had something to do with that, too."

He smiled, despite the flip in his stomach. They seemed nice enough, but Thoren had warned many of the researchers about the Catholic Church having an alternate agenda for the mission. He reminded them all that Augustus Cole was Catholic, and that Catholics believed that what they arbitrarily determined as wishes of their God held more weight than the logic of the Code. Even more, the Rescue Sisters had a longstanding relationship with the miners; they would support the rockjacks' agenda. *Be careful and be watchful of them,* he had warned.

Galen was one of *them*. So was Andi. But she'd called him "dear."

All I wanted was to watch pulsars, he thought. He shook his head.

"What's wrong?"

"Nothing." He hoped it stayed that way.

He opened the door and Galen stepped in. Closed boxes lined the storeroom walls from floor to ceiling. Galen started to grab for the first box, but Chris stopped him. "Hold on. First a video sweep. We're going for Smith points, remember?"

He reached into their cart and donned his helmet. Finally, something he could use the suit for!

"Darkside vision," he commanded, and the world became brighter and clearer, though an odd shade of blue. As Galen read from a checklist, he scanned the room: first a general sweep of the horizontal, then the vertical, then focusing at various depths. It seemed rather pointless for a cleaning supply room, but hey, it brought home points for Ol' Quad Three.

"Done," he declared, and Galen shouldered past him with a scanner. He pointed it at the boxes and compared the readings against the manifest and the list. He came to a pile of brooms and picked one up. "You know, I never saw one of these until I came aboard? Push the dirt around. What a concept. What else do you dirtsiders use?" He went to a box marked "dusting mitts" and broke it open.

"Come to Virginia with me, and I'll show you sometime," Chris said as he wandered in, still wearing the helmet and dragging the cart behind.

"Forget it. I was born outside a gravity well, and I'll die outside a gravity well. Catch!" He tossed a mitt at Chris, who ducked reflexively, then dug into another box.

"Quit clowning around. We've only got twenty minutes until we have to head back for dinner. Let's look for duct tape. That's worth twenty-five points each."

"Forget that. I think we just hit the motherload." He held out his prize by the neck. With the helmet on, Chris could read the label.

"Saturan Blue? Vac'in' leak! What else is in there?"

Galen dug through the box carefully, but with the eagerness of a kid at Christmas. "Jack Daniels. About a dozen bottles total. Start checking the other boxes and call in the team!"

* * *

Ann sat at an empty table in the cafeteria, but she wasn't alone. A beautiful man with dark curls and royal robes sat beside her — or made the affectation of sitting. He was talking to her about how shepherding and ruling a nation of strong-minded people weren't all that different, and she picked at her food and did her best to commit his words to memory. He was so excited and so pretty that Ann didn't have the heart to tell King David she didn't understand half of what he was saying.

"Can I join you?" a very live voice said, and she looked up with a start, wondering for one wild moment if the speaker had seen the shepherd king.

Sean smiled at her with calm reassurance. "No cameras, no interviews, I promise. If you sisters want to stay out of the picture, that's just more glory to everyone else."

"Glory belongs to God," she replied.

For some reason, he took that as permission to sit. From the corner of her eye, she saw David raise his brows in amusement and fade from the scene.

"Well, sure," Sean agreed amicably enough, "but don't you think in this case God is willing to share?"

"God's always willing to share. People don't understand that. *His invitation/shared glory; shared suffering/Blessed yin and yang.*"

Sean paused, his fork halfway to his lips. "Wow. That's nova. Did you write that?"

"Oh, no. Father Francis Tran's *Haikus on Martyrdom.*"

"I'll have to look them up. I thought haikus were supposed to be about nature?"

"What's more natural than giving your life for God?"

His mouth pursed a moment, then he nodded. "So what else do you like to read?"

She sighed and again picked at her food. "Right now, I probably should be reading up on sheep."

He laughed. "Thinking of becoming a shepherd?"

She glanced to where King David had sat only moments before. "I'm not sure I get the choice."

His laughter died. "Really?"

She set her fork down and again met his eyes with an earnest gaze. "It depends on what you mean by real. In the 1920s, quantum physics suggested that there was no objective reality, but that observation influenced reality, and they're still experimenting on that today. Dr. Endor Galvin believes that the key to instantaneous interplanetary communications depends on it. *To carry on a conversation between our worlds, we must speak through a different reality.* In 2010, astrophysicists found evidence that even the most basic laws of physics might only be locally applied. Psychology says perceptions equal reality on some level. Yet in Colossians, Saint Paul reminds us that the only reality is Christ."

He chewed on his lip, digesting this. She liked that about the documentarist. He didn't dismiss what she said, even when he didn't understand it. "Okay, but let me rephrase that. Do you mean literal shepherd?"

"David was a shepherd; then he became a king, but in a sense, all he did was change his flock. Jesus, of course, is the Good Shepherd. So do you need domesticated ruminants of the cattle family? Are the skills so different?"

Sean whistled. "You know a lot. Me, I only ever wanted to know about virtual reality and recording. Don't spread it around, but I got this job because my dad's in tight with Cole; usually, I do interactive VR work."

She cocked her head. "Like the Lola games?"

"Well, I'm more about real-life experiences myself. It's kind of what you were saying about perceptions and reality: it's incredibly hard to get the right visceral readings for a gaming situation. Acting isn't enough to fool VR sensors. The actor actually has to feel the experience. That was what made Lola — or more accurately, Edwina — so amazing. Edwina didn't look anything like Lola, but she could make herself believe what she was supposed to be experiencing on a biological level, yet she was completely sane. Plus, she could take a beating. Have you seen the stuff Lola deals with in the games?"

Ann shook her head. "Our order has proscriptions against VR entertainments." She'd been glad of that when OvLandra had invited her to play one of the games; nonetheless, the doctor had pressed a documentary chip on her when she'd left. It still waited in the leg pocket of Ann's pants.

"Okay. I can see that. Take my word for it; it gets pretty intense, and Edwina did her own stunts. Then with KelLandra's recording equipment... It's still cutting-edge technology, incidentally. Hey! KelLandra! Do you suppose?"

Ann nodded. The chip in her pocket called to her. "They're clansmen; that's why she's so interested in the *Edwina Taggert*. She lent me a documentary of him and Edwina. Would you like to see it?"

He leaned forward. "Would I!"

* * *

Across the cafeteria, Merl watched as Sister Ann passed a chip to Sean. So, first, she charms the Captain, then the engineering crew, and now their documentarist? What wiles did she have on them?

Was that why she had come to his service that night — to attempt to sway him, as well? She'd not returned since, which was a relief. Perhaps he'd discouraged her. A pity, that. What a triumph it would have been to bring her to True Faith. Still, at least Cay had been saved. Speaking of...

Merl stood and greeted Cay with a brotherly hug as he set his tray on the table. "And how is the newest member of the flock?"

* * *

Rita waited until the door to Thoren's office had shut before storming off toward the dorm area. McVee called for her to wait, but she didn't slow her stride. She had to get away from the office before she surrendered to her anger, went back, and let the mission commander have it with whatever wrath God might see fit to lend her. Infuriating man!

She and McVee had gone in to discuss Thoren's test scores and determine a plan of study to help him pass the next time, and he'd not only had the gall to suggest Rita's standards were unnecessary and unrealistic, but also took the opportunity to share some "concerns" he'd been hearing about the training. And the sisters. And Ann.

After the things Thoren had said about Ann and her "disruptive, oddball ideas," she was tempted to tell Tommie they should go ahead with her offhand suggestion that they teach him Suits 201 by locking him in the zero-G training room and not letting him out until he passed the course perfectly or they got back to Earth.

I am not a very good shepherd, she thought, remembering the crazy array of information windows on sheep and shepherding that Ann had been poring over last night. Right now, she felt more like a cattle wrangler dealing with a large and stubborn bull.

She rounded a corner and nearly plowed down James. *How big did Ann say this ship was? Why can't I avoid this man?*

"Hey!" James grabbed her elbow before she could stomp past. McVee caught up to them. "You all right?"

She fought to keep her tone neutral. He hadn't done anything, after all. "Why shouldn't I be?"

"I'm not," McVee retorted. "I want to know who decided whining to Thoren was going to get them their way. He's not in charge of the crew. I am."

"Oh, I'm sure this is happening in some of those important Codist discussions," Rita quipped. "How in the 'verse did he get chosen for this mission? I thought the great Augustus Cole was a legendary judge of character."

James grimaced. "That was a university decision. Even Caesar has to play politics sometimes."

"You know Cole that well?" McVee asked. "Fine, what did this 'Legendary Judge of Character' say about the university choice?"

James checked to make sure the halls were empty. "'The man is in desperate need of rope.'"

"How remarkably vague and unhelpful," McVee sneered. "If you'll excuse me, lady, gentleman, I've some business in Engineering."

Once he left, Rita sighed and slumped against the wall, crossing her arms loosely and cocking one foot back. "You know, one thing I have not missed is playing politics."

James chuckled. "Me, neither. Working for ColeCorp, I just turn in my reports and let someone else handle the rest. "

"Mother Superior handles it for our station, and Tommie when we're on mission, if necessary. I wish Tommie would handle it here. She's got the strong will."

He smiled at her. "You underestimate yourself, as always. Sister Thomas is a little too stubborn, too blunt. She and Thoren would have dug in after the second meeting and we'd get nothing done. You've got the right combination of stubbornness and diplomacy. Augustus chose well. Don't underestimate Cole. You wouldn't be here if he didn't think you needed to be here. That goes for Thoren, too. We just need to give him his rope."

Rita frowned. "No chance of you calling him and telling him what Thoren's done so far with his 'rope'?"

His expression soured, but not for the reason she expected. "I'm not Augustus' 'inside man,' if that's what you're thinking. He wasn't even completely honest with me about this mission."

"Meaning what?" When he didn't answer, she asked, "James, you never wanted to be in space. What in the 'verse could he have offered you?"

James grabbed her by the elbow and pulled her into an empty room. She steeled herself. Here it comes. *Go ahead, say it was me,* she begged. *At least then we can get rid of this elephant on the ship. Or would that make things worse? I don't care, anymore. I just want to be done with this.*

He paced away from her, then braced himself on a conference room chair. He looked so...worn...that she regretted her words. "James, I'm sorry. I —"

"My mother," he said. "Augustus is taking care of my mother. And Charlotte."

"Your sister? I don't get it."

He spun the chair around and flopped into it. "Mom has Alzheimer's."

She felt the blood drain from her face. Rachel Smith had been one of the sharpest women she'd ever met. "I'm sorry. I didn't know."

"Well, you left without a forwarding address, didn't you?" he snapped. "It was about six months after that. It's been fast, too. She doesn't recognize me, barely recognizes Charlotte. Cole offered Charlotte a job near Mom, painting murals."

"But only if you agreed to this?"

"I just got back from comms; she sent me her concept. It stretches across three buildings. It's a dream come true for her. And when she's done, you know others are going to hire her. But mostly she can be with Mom."

Rita sat next to him. "But you're here."

He stared at his hands as he bumped his thumbs together. "I had two years with Mom, almost two-and-a-half. I have to think about Charlotte now."

Rita choked back tears. "I wish I'd known."

"Do you?" He rounded on her so fast, she jerked back in surprise. His eyes flashed. "Do you really, *Sister* Rita Aguilar? You didn't just leave. You cut me off totally. 'No messages.' That's what your dad told me. I didn't get even that much from your mother superior — your old mother superior at the BVM, that is. Would it have been so hard to have told me you weren't interested?"

"Would it have made a difference?" she shouted.

"Yes! No! I don't know. But you never gave me that chance, did you?"

"You never asked. You laid one cryptic hint, James, then you left to talk to your order, and I was stuck to draw my own conclusions. So, yeah, I ran, but I did it for you."

He made a disgusted sound. "For me? Well, don't do me any more favors, all right?"

"Fine!" She sprung out of her chair and strode out the door, even more upset than she'd been when she'd left Thoren. Once she turned down another empty hall, she ducked into one of the vacant rooms to get a hold of herself. The last thing she or anyone else needed was for people to see her crying in the halls.

Well, you wanted to address the elephant in the room, she scolded herself. *Didn't expect it to have a whole herd, did you*?

She rubbed at her sore arms. She hadn't realized how tightly she'd held herself. *How do I fix this, Lord?*

She shook her head. *A hot bath*, she decided. As long as *Edwina Taggert* had water and energy to spare, she would indulge herself in a hot bath, relax, maybe even cry, then get herself together and talk to Tommie. She went into the room's bathroom, splashed water on her face, and, when she was sure she looked and could act normal enough, left to go to her room.

When she came to a juncture, she took the turn that led to their quarters. A few minutes later, she heard people yelling. Great. Following the angry voices, she came upon Merl and Kelley screaming into each other's faces while one of the rockjacks tried to calm them down by suggesting they apply the Spacer's Code. Neither listened to him, and, when Kelley brandished a small tube at him, he backed away. Merl took the opportunity to grab at her arm, and the two began to struggle.

Rita ran between them. "Stop this right now! Both of you. What is going on?" They broke apart, and she had a chance to notice the red symbol half-painted on the door of the cabin where they stood.

"Whose room is this?"

Merl stepped forward angrily. "Mine! This foul, evil witch was painting a symbol of indecency —"

"This is the triple goddess, symbol of the three aspects of the moon and the feminine polarity of the universe, and it's no more offensive than the abhorrent garbage you keep mailing to my console!"

"Your immortal soul is in jeopardy! I am called by God to —"

"You mean your judgmental, chauvinistic —"

"Enough!" Rita screeched. She held up her hands, and the two fell silent but seething.

She felt the tension in her arms climb up her neck. She did not want to deal with this right now. She pointed at the door. "Kelley, this is vandalism, and you will remove it as soon as I am done with you. Doesn't your faith say, 'But that you do no harm, do what you will?' Merl has done you no harm. He has done what he will. And he will stop now, as I expect you to."

She turned to the irate linguist. "Merl, the fact that you are called to evangelize does not give you the right to shove your faith down someone's throat — or into their console. If you want to evangelize, do it by your prayers and your example, and if — if! — Kelley comes to ask you about your faith, you speak to her not just of God's love, but *with* God's love."

They started to protest, but she cut them off.

"Both of you listen carefully to me. You are no longer on Earth. There is no room on a spaceship for violent confrontations of any kind. You both have copies of the Spacer's Code of Conduct; I suggest you review the section about what topics will not be discussed unless another invites you to do so. There are rules on this ship. Your certifications — your job — your chance to see that artifact — depend on you following them. Is that clear?" When they lowered their eyes, she gave her attention to the door.

"So what is this stuff?" She ran a finger along the still wet sigil and brought it to her nose then mouth.

Merl yelped, "Sister, no! It's blood—"

"Of a tomato!" Kelley rolled her eyes. "It's just ketchup, Sister."

"I see." Rita felt a grin tug at her lips. "Interesting choice of pigment. Go get some rags and get it scrubbed off, now, please, and then this kind of argument ends."

Kelley took a brief cleansing breath, muttered, "Yeah, okay, Sister," and ducked down the hall. Rita waited until she emerged with damp towels, thanked her, then started again to her room, more intent on a hot bath than ever.

Merl, however, followed her, carrying on a one-sided diatribe and even entering the sisters' quarters uninvited.

"You claim to believe in the One God. You even presume to act as if you serve the Risen Lord! Yet you didn't side with me against a —"

"*Presume*?" Rita closed her eyes and said a silent prayer. "Mr. Pritchard, can you lay hands upon that child and banish her demons?"

"No, but —"

"Neither can I. Yet you think sending her religious tracts is going to change her?"

"Well, I've made her angry."

"Right. As she has made you. Inciting anger is not evangelization, Merl. You truly feel called to spread the Word? Then start studying the methods that work. Go back, read the New Testament, and really pay attention to how, when, and with whom Jesus and the Apostles shared the Word. There have been books on the subject, biographies of famous and successful evangelists of all faiths. Study their methods. I'll forward you a few titles you can get started on."

"Are they of your papist religion?" Merl's lip curled.

Hot anger superseded her tension headache. "What denomination are you?"

"The New Congregation of the Second Generation of the Family of Christ. We formed in 2217 from the Second Generationists when our founder —"

Rita cut him off. "The Catholic Church has stood united and essentially unchanged for nearly 2300 years, because, in part, of our leadership through Peter himself. No other faith can make such a claim." She bit back the diatribe she dearly wanted to deliver. "Merl, I'd be glad to discuss this further with you, but I've other matters that need my attention right now, and I think we both need to cool down. In the meantime, begin with your Bible. And remember what I said about the Spacer's Code. It is Caesar's Law in space, and you must follow it. If you want an example of evangelizing among Spacers, check out *Spreading the Word Across the Stars* by Faith Hawkins. She grew up on Phobos Mirandos and worked on colony transports, so her situations parallel ours. This is not an assignment, Merl, but if you feel the Lord is pushing you toward this, you owe it to Him to learn how to do it well."

He gnawed on his mustache, clearly wanting to argue more. However, after a moment, he sighed. "You're right, Sister. It wouldn't hurt to learn. I'm surprised you mentioned the Bible first. "

"Maybe you should learn more about Catholics, then. Seems you're operating under some false assumptions." When his eyes narrowed suspiciously, she shrugged. "Start with Acts of the Apostles. For space, the Hawkins book, and Corriander's *Tricky Topics and the Code* is another good one. Just don't forget you have a suit test in two days."

At that, he grinned. "Not to worry. That I'm ready for."

She escorted him to the door. After it slid shut behind him, she leaned her forehead against its coolness and sighed. Behind her, she heard Tommie chuckle and turned to see her standing in the doorway of the study. She gave her a wan smile.

Tommie smiled back. "You are devious, Sister Rita. Hawkins' book in itself is a subtle tool for Catholic evangelization."

"We do what we can. 'But that we do no harm.'" She rolled her eyes and flopped onto the couch. "Codists and wiccans and evangelists, oh, my. Maybe I should study shepherding like Ann. Or herding cats."

"They herd cats on Earth?"

Rita chuckled. "Just an expression."

Tommie settled on the chair. "Let's just hope that's the worst mischief we encounter on this trip. You okay?"

"I'll tell you after a long bath."

* * *

Reg Alexander whooped as he pulled a bottle of Saturan Blue out of a box marked "antibacterial agent." He swung it over his head and looked at the rest of the Quad Three team that crowded into the leader's suite. Galen and Chris still had on their suits, as did Zabrina, who with Reg, had pushed them aside and had dug enthusiastically into the box. She caressed a bottle of Jack Daniels, cooing at it.

Reg called out, "All right! Let's start this party!"

From where he reclined on the top bunk, one of the miners said, "Whoa, gravfoot. Let's think this through."

"Oh, I'm sorry," Reg said sarcastically as he started to untwist the wires securing the cap. "I didn't realize you rockjacks were teetotalers."

Galen pulled the bottle from his hands. "Listen, Reg. He's got a point. You can't just get drunk in space. Too many stupid, dangerous things can happen."

"Like we're going to let that happen. We're all adults here. We're not stupid."

"Have we been to different parties? You want to bet everyone's lives on it? Besides, this isn't just our booze. By rights, everyone should get a chance to enjoy it. Plus, we're going to need chaperones and some designated escorts to get people to their quarters, if necessary. This is a luxury liner. They must have had intoxication protocols. I wonder if there are any portable breathalyzers still aboard?" Galen added.

"I dunno, maybe we should save it for after we explore the ship?" Zabrina suggested. "You know, a victory celebration?"

Reg gave the bottle a longing glance. "I think I'll go nuts thinking about all that Saturan Blue."

Galen rolled his eyes. "You'll live. All right: box this up — that one, too, please — and we'll take it over to the sisters. If anybody can be trusted with a stash of booze, it ought to be sisters, right?"

* * *

"Are you sure we should have a drinking party?" Worry gave Ann's sunny blue eyes a stormy tint.

Thoren cleared his throat and cast a "significant look" around the crowded cafeteria. James had suggested they have their meeting there, over lunch. Maybe he hoped that the public setting might make their mission leader consider his words more carefully. They'd taken a long table toward the corner of the room: just Thoren, Addiman, James and all three sisters, along with Galen, whose quad had discovered the contraband booze. Andi had decided that was excuse enough to let him attend the leadership meeting in her stead.

Rita could hear Andi's laugh rise above the conversation of the crowd. The cafeteria had transformed from the quiet den of only a few weeks ago. The training sessions, team activities, and dorm arrangements had bonded the groups. Set dining hours made sure folks took meals together, and Chan indeed had a flair for cooking, ensuring the days they didn't depend on pre-packaged meals were crowded, boisterous affairs.

Today people mixed more than usual, maybe because Sean chose today for some candid V-Recs. Kelley and Merl were even at the same table with the core group of miners and researchers. Everyone seemed happy, relaxed, and comfortable with each other.

Rita wished she felt so comfortable. She had had a long cry in the tub, but couldn't bring herself to talk to Tommie about James, especially after Ann showed up from a suit training session commenting on how he'd been unusually focused. Rita knew that focus. *He focuses on work; I run. Neither of us is very good at confronting a problem.*

"No one's paying us any attention, William," Rita reassured the mission commander.

"Besides, everyone knows about Quad Three's find," James said as he dipped a piece of steak into ketchup. "For all that they swore themselves to secrecy."

Tommie snorted. "If that's how they keep secrets, we'll be lucky not to find other research ships when we get to the Folly. Obviously, someone had a nice little contraband op going, but the real mystery is why it was still on board."

Captain Addiman shrugged. "Person gets fired for another reason. The contact gets cold feet before the deal goes down. CruiseGalactic scrapped the *Edwina* pretty sudden; mebbe there's no time to get it offboard."

Rita took in his thick accent. She'd learned to judge the captain's mood by how deeply he reverted to his Jamaican roots. Right now, she guessed he was more than a little angry that one of his crew had been stealing from the cruise line under his command. She wondered if he had a suspect, and if it might be someone still on board.

"Where did you hide it?" Thoren asked the sisters.

"If we told you, it wouldn't be very well hidden, would it?"

The sheer innocence of Ann's reply combined with the look on Thoren's face was too much for Rita and she burst into laughter. James was second to go, followed by Tommie.

Rita's laughter died when she noticed how James looked at her, however. "What?"

"I'm sorry, what?" he said, as if confused, but she knew better. Still, she didn't know what to say.

"You stare at Rita a lot," Ann said, her voice flat, her eyes on her meal: an offhand observation made while her mind was mulling over some other problem. Rita realized she hadn't joined in the laughter, either.

She was about to ask Ann what was wrong when James said, "Do I? I'm sorry, Rita. It's just..." He turned to the others. "When Rita and I were colleagues together at TerraTech, she was a sister in the Order of the Blessed Virgin Mary. They wore the dress of the day instead of habits. Guess I'm used to seeing her in tailored jackets and long skirts."

"It's been months. This is the approved habit of our order." Rita's voice sounded tight to her ears.

"I know, and I know why it makes sense. I just can't get over you wearing pants. Not just you. Any religious, but I know you and..."

He paused, flustered. Rita knew she should have felt flustered herself, *would* feel flustered, if it weren't for the way Ann was frowning and picking at her meal. She caught Tommie's eye, saw from the slight grimace that the older sister had noticed, too.

"I'm sorry. I don't mean to offend."

"Not at all." Tommie saved him by chiming in. "In space, where gravity is a product of Man rather than the gift of God and can cut out at any time, a skirt is not only impractical, but immodest."

"No cherubim to hold our skirts," Sister Ann murmured. "I had a dress once. It was powdery blue, with flouncy bloomers and lots of lace and layers that fanned out when I spun..."

Thoren cleared his throat. "If we could get back to the subject of the party?"

"A party's a bad idea. People shouldn't drink in space." Ann shut her eyes, her brows slightly knit. She'd abandoned even the pretext of eating, her hand resting, but tense, beside her fork.

Capt. Addiman covered it with his large dark one. "Do not worry, Little Sister. The *Edwina* has hosted many fine parties. She will keep us safe. And my crew knows what to do. We will keep everyone well cared for."

"We'll check with Dr. OvLandra about sober-up pills, too," Tommie said. "You pay for it with the headache later, but you get instant clarity."

James cocked a brow. "And you know this how?"

Tommie returned the expression with a grin. "I wasn't always a sister, you know. Even owned a tight skirt or two."

"Skirts are stupid!" Ann slammed her hands on the table and stood. "Skirts are stupid, and parties and drinking are stupid, and, and something goes wrong and reactions are slowed, and she didn't know what to do!"

The entire room went silent.

"Ann?" Rita started, unsure what to ask.

"Come, Annie." Tommie stood and moved toward her.

Ann flung off Tommie's outstretched arm and fled the room.

Tommie muttered under her breath and followed.

"What was that all about?" James voiced the question Rita didn't dare ask.

She didn't like the smug look on Thoren's face, like he'd been expecting, even wishing for, something like this to happen.

She stood. "Excuse me. I should go find them."

James asked, "Do you know where they are?"

That was a silly question. "She'll be in the chapel."

* * *

Kelley watched the doors close behind Sister Rita before turning to the others at her table. She sneered and smoothed her peasant's skirt. "What's her problem?"

None of the miners answered her, just traded worried looks. By Andi's side, Chris shifted uncomfortably, half afraid to ask the same question, even without the snippy tone.

Ian shrugged. "She doesn't like skirts? Guess it makes sense. Personally, I keep hoping the gravity will cut out." He leered playfully at Kelley.

She stuck out one leg and pulled her skirt to reveal a fabric-covered calf. "You're not seeing anything but skinsuit."

"A guy can dream."

"Something upset Ann," Andi said, ignoring the interchange.

Chris watched Andi chew on the side of her mouth and berated himself.

She'd let Galen take her place at the lunch meeting, since his quad had found the liquor.

My quad, too, Chris thought sullenly. He could have gone to the lunch meeting; then he'd know what was going on. But Andi would have gone too, then, and he didn't want to get caught between her and Thoren, not when things were starting to go so well with her.

Lenny pulled his eyes from the door. "Easy, Andi. It might not mean anything." Still, he didn't sound like he believed his own words.

"So Little Sister's upset. What's the big deal?" Ian asked.

The miners glared at him as if he were stupid.

"I used to spend part of the year in the convent; Ann and I grew up together," Andi said tightly. "Nothing upsets Ann, not unless it's really, really bad."

She shivered and wrapped her arms about herself. She didn't seek comfort from Chris' touch, but didn't pull away, either. He gave her arm a slight squeeze, not sure why. Maybe just to let her know he was there for her?

"Last time I saw her cry, someone died," Lenny added.

Kelley snorted. "Well, vac! I'd cry, too, if someone I'd known had died."

"No, no. Not *had*. *Was going to*. And she knew she couldn't save him."

Kelley chuckled cruelly and leaned back in her chair, crossing her arms. "What? She's *clairvoyant*? Can nuns do that? Thought they'd consider it evil or something."

Sean set down the camera. "I dunno. Didn't saints sometimes have that ability?"

Most of the table chuckled, Ian hardest of all. "You think Sister Ann's a saint?"

"We are all saints," Merl interjected. "It says in the Bible, 'the mystery which hath been hid from ages and from generations, but now is made manifest to His saints. To them God would make known what are the riches of the glory of this mystery among the Gentiles, which is Christ in you, the hope of glory.' Colossians, Chapter One, Verses 26 and 27. You've only to believe."

Ian rounded on him. "Well, I don't believe, okay? I'm no saint, so put me in your List of the Damned and shut up."

Sean shrugged and spread his hands entreatingly. "I'm just saying there's more to her than meets the eye."

Kelley tossed her hair over her shoulder. "Right. Just because someone talks nonsense doesn't make her holy."

"Ann does not talk nonsense!" Andi flared.

"No, she doesn't," Sean agreed. "She doesn't always talk linearly, to be sure, but she makes more sense than most of us realize."

Lenny thumped Sean on the back. "You speak-a Annese!"

Ian burst out laughing. No one joined him.

Andi stood. "I'm going to talk to Rita."

The leadership was also rising from their table. Chris took Andi's hand. "Hold on. Let's go find out what happened first. Maybe it was a misunderstanding or something."

She gave him a terse smile and a slight squeeze of her hand. He felt a happy jolt, and, as he led her to Dr. Thoren's table, he hoped that he could find something to make that smile a little easier.

Before the others could answer, Thoren said to him, "We were having a perfectly rational conversation, and she suddenly became irrationally upset. Certainly this does not surprise you?"

Chris paused, his follow-up question gone. Actually, he wasn't sure if it surprised him or not. Ann seemed a little, well, strange. Flighty even. Yet the miners and most of the ship's crew seemed to think she was the greatest thing since R. Charles Hawkins.

His mentor crossed his arms and raised one brow at Chris, excluding the rest of the group. Back at the university, everyone would have slunk away, leaving Chris to his fate. He wasn't sure if he preferred the rockjacks crowding his back, especially since they all seemed to be waiting to see what he, Chris, would say.

"Well, something must have happened. I mean, she was pretty upset, and the rockjacks think…"

Thoren glanced in their direction and barely avoided rolling his eyes. "Yes. Well. No doubt they believe that such behavior is a sign that she has some kind of special connection to God, and if she's happy, God's love is assured and all will be well. A supernatural good luck charm."

"It's not that…" Chris started to protest, then paused, thinking about what they'd said. *How come no one else is speaking up? They're right there!*

Thoren jumped into his silence. "Even in these post-modern times, when our understanding of the universe is almost complete, so many still insist on the archaic worships and superstitions that nearly ripped our Earth apart. That is why the Code is so liberating."

He placed a friendly hand on Chris' shoulder. "Which do you want? To spend your life in ignorance worrying about why a mentally deficient nun gets upset, or enlightened and enabled by a simple, yet complete, rule of living?"

Chris could feel the tension of the rockjacks that had joined him. Andi's hand squeezed his. Was she holding back the urge to lash out, or telling Chris to do something?

He had to do something, but what?

He gulped. "Sister Ann's quite smart, really, sir, she —"

"Yes, yes. An idiot savant quite adept at parroting back religious writings and technical manuals. I understand that, but —"

"There ain't any 'buts,' Dr. Thoren." Anger thickened Lenny's voice with malice.

A half-dozen torqued-off rockjacks shifted to surround them. Andi let go of his hand. Chris swallowed hard.

James stood from the table and cleared his throat. "Let's all calm down."

Lenny leaned his large bulk toward the professor and spoke again. "You don't have to understand about Little Sister. I'm not wasting air to explain her to you. But you *will* respect her." He pinned Thoren with his stare, so that the professor dropped his arm from Chris' shoulder and backed up a step — right into the rockjacks crowding him from behind.

"Don't underestimate her, Thoren. Or us."

Thoren glanced around him, seemed to realize he was standing slightly hunched, and straightened. "Are you threatening me?" he demanded in his most dignified and authoritative air. He glanced toward Chris' table, as if seeking allies.

Sean, Chris realized. *He's hoping Sean will record this.* But Sean was no longer at the table. Neither was Andi, he noticed. Why did she leave?

"Of course not," Lenny said, leaning back slightly. He started to crack his knuckles one by one. "Just a friendly bit of advice. You know, we've got a saying in the Belt: Don't judge a rock 'till you've seen the insides. Until you understand better what's inside Sister Ann's head, I suggest you secure your opinions. Misunderstandings can be so dangerous. After, all, Code Ten."

"Don't quote Code to one who's dedicated his life to it."

"The Code isn't supposed to be dedicated to, gravfoot. It's supposed to prevent petty arguments and stuperiorities so we can devote ourselves to exploring space. And before you start getting holy about the Code, you'd better remember what it says about respecting others' 'archaic worships and superstitions.'"

James stepped between the two. "All right. You've each had your say. Code Six goes both ways, right?"

Lenny narrowed his eyes at Thoren once more, then turned to the others. "C'mon. Let's see if we can find out what's really upset Little Sister."

Chris started to file out with them until Thoren cleared his throat.

Miserably, he waited, then followed his mentor out.

* * *

Ann ran blindly down the corridors, feeling the emergency bulkhead doors slamming behind her, even though she knew they weren't, and hearing the hiss of escaping air and the screams of people who, moments before, had been laughing and toasting. Someone was yelling for everyone to run.

But no one was there, not even the saints. Saints and prophets, crowding her days since they got on this ship, and now, she was alone. Forsaken. *My God, my God, why have You forsaken me?*

A sob escaped her throat. *Forgive me! I'm so scared and alone!*

"Ann, slow down!" Tommie called from behind.

She couldn't. Not until she was someplace safe.

She reached the chapel, fumbled with the controls, and hurled herself down the aisle. She fell to her knees before the holographic statue of the Virgin holding the Holy Child, her mind too blank to even pray. It didn't matter; after only a moment of gazing at Mary's peaceful face, Ann began to feel herself calming.

"Ann?"

Ann whirled and saw Tommie in the doorway.

"I'm sorry!" Ann whispered as Tommie knelt beside her. "I don't know what came over me. I don't understand. I..."

Tommie wiped the tears from her cheek. Ann felt a rush of love and security.

"Just tell me what happened, Annie."

Ann shook her head. *Screaming, running. Something grabbing her from behind.* "I don't understand."

Tommie caressed her hair, the way she used to when Ann was a child and woke up from nightmares she never remembered. "When we found you, you wore a dress, powder blue with lots of ruffles and a long train."

"I couldn't run in it," she whispered.

Tommie nodded. "Your skirt got caught in a closing bulkhead door. It saved your life."

Again Ann shook her head. "I don't remember," she whispered.

* * *

Rita found Ann and Tommie in the chapel as she'd expected, kneeling before the statue of the Virgin Mary. Ann had buried her head into Tommie's shoulder and was sobbing like a small child while Tommie stroked her cropped hair and whispered reassurances. She couldn't break in on that. If she were someone else, Mother Superior or even Andi, but not her.

Not sure what else to do, Rita closed and locked the door behind her, settled into a pew, and prayed the prayer her mother would ask her and her brother to pray whenever they had done something that made her despair.

> *Look upon us, O Lord,*
> *and let all the darkness of our souls*
> *vanish before the beams of Thy brightness.*
> *Fill us with holy love,*
> *and open to us the treasures of Thy wisdom.*
> *All our desire is known unto Thee,*
> *therefore perfect what Thou hast begun,*
> *and what Thy Spirit has awakened us to ask in prayer.*
> *We seek Thy face,*
> *turn Thy face unto us and show us Thy glory.*
> *Then shall our longing be satisfied,*
> *and our peace shall be perfect.*

She had prayed her newest Novena — to St. Rita — recited a rosary and had started into some free-flowing intentions, when Tommie laid a hand on her shoulder. She looked up and saw Ann behind her, her eyes rabbity and her hair ruffled and pointing in a thousand directions. She sniffled and wiped her red nose on the sleeve of her skinsuit.

"You prayed for me?" she said in a small voice.

Rita felt tears sting her eyes. She nodded.

"I'm never truly alone, am I?"

Rita didn't trust herself to speak; instead, she just embraced her.

They didn't encounter anyone on the walk back, but a quick glance at the comm showed a dozen messages from various Rocky Flats crew, plus James and Chris. Unfortunately, they'd have to wait until she understood what had happened herself, so she quelled her impatience by running a hot bubble bath while Tommie made them tea.

Sister Ann squealed with delight at the layers of bubbles, yet protested. "It's such a waste of water!"

"Nonsense. All the water is purified and recycled and the soap is biodegradable and good for the plants in hydroponics. The *Edwina Taggert* was designed for such luxuries, Ann, and there's no reason you can't enjoy them once in a while."

"Like a party?" she asked.

Rita hugged her. "Let's discuss that later. Right now have a nice long soak, but don't fall asleep." She gave her a kiss on the cheek, felt Ann tremble as she fought back new tears, and hastened out of the room.

In the living room, she sat on the couch, and Tommie handed her a cup. "I've been scanning the messages. Looks like we're going to have some damage control on our hands."

Rita sipped her tea. "Are you surprised? What was that all about?"

Tommie held the teacup as if warming her hands and looked into it as if expecting answers. "We found Annie in some wreckage, the only survivor. Her skirt had caught in the bulkhead door."

"Oh, no. And her parents?"

Tommie shook her head. "We don't know. No one even had a chance to don a suit before the next compartments depressurized. The hull was riddled with holes. Sister Lucinda was an EMT at the time. She didn't think she could revive Ann. It was a miracle. Even so, Annie spent a month in a coma.

"We filed a report with the Belt Patrol, tried to find out if she had any kin. Some of us wanted to go back and check the ship for records or personal effects, but we found it had already been claimed and scuttled. The Patrol wouldn't tell us by whom. About a week later, a gentleman came to the convent by a special shuttle. He insisted on speaking only to Mother Superior — that was Sister Katerina then. She died before you came aboard. She took him to the infirmary to look at Ann, then they went to her office. He spent fifteen minutes talking to Mother Superior, then he left. Mother Superior called us together. She said we would be raising Ann ourselves. That's when we chose her name. Mother Superior never told us if the man had told her her real name.

"When Annie came out of the coma, she didn't remember anything, not even how to talk. We thought she'd sustained brain damage from the lack of oxygen. She didn't speak for a year."

Rita lowered her cup. "You're kidding." She scowled, trying to reconcile that with the brilliant young sister she knew.

Tommie shook her head. "She used to have the most horrible night terrors, but by the time she was speaking again, she was a part of our family."

"She never asked about her real family?"

"Once or twice, but we didn't have any information. Mother Superior took whatever that man had told her to her grave, except for one command: protect Ann from all outsiders. After she died, we received an immense sum of money. We rebuilt the docking bays and the dorm with it. There was also a note reminding us that Ann was never to leave the Sisters."

"But that's horrible!"

"Fortunately, it's never been an issue, but they must have had a reason. I hadn't seen wreckage like that since the Ring Wars." Tommie sipped her tea and said no more. She stared at the far wall, but Rita sensed she was remembering the accident.

Or was she wondering if it was *an accident?* Rita shivered.

"Tommie?"

Tommie shook herself slightly. "Lot of finery on that ship. Like here. Might have triggered some memories."

That wasn't what you were thinking. Rita didn't press the point, despite her suspicions.

Tommie drained her cup. "She'll be fine. She's a strong young woman, and she has God on her side and knows it. Still, we should probably keep a closer eye on her. In the meantime, what do we tell the crew? The rockjacks know her well enough to know that she doesn't get upset unless it's serious."

"Well, can we just say that our conversation stirred up some disturbing memories and leave it at that? But we should probably ask Ann what she'd like us to say."

"We can tell them." Ann surprised them by appearing at the bathroom door wrapped in a large terrycloth robe. "I got sleepy," she said as she came to sit down on the sofa. Although wet and red-cheeked from the heat of the bath, she looked more herself and calmer.

Ann took a cup of tea from Tommie with thanks and sipped. "Let's just tell anyone who asks that I suddenly had a memory of when my parents died, and it upset me. But I'm okay now, because the Mother of God gave me comfort. Plus, I have all of you. And...maybe some folks would like to pray with me for my parents?"

Her eyes misted a little then, and again Rita gave in to the urge to hug her. "Of course, we will," she whispered.

Chapter Sixteen

"Okay, that was the sickest movie yet," Frances declared to the table at large. They'd just finished *Code Fail*, about miners on Jupiter's moon Amalthea who encountered a sludgelike creature that seeped into their suits and took over their minds while it slowly ate them alive. The explosives specialist looked at her coffee as if it might rise from her cup and attack her.

Sean shrugged. "You were the one who wanted something from this century. That was the movie that got Edwina Taggert her start."

"I see why." Frances shivered. So did several others around her.

Ian scratched at his hands. He could still feel the monster crawling on them, thick and viscous, like congealing blood.

He stood abruptly. "I'll catch you all tomorrow."

One of the rockjacks smirked. "Really fissioned you, didn't it? Laugh it off, man. It's just a movie."

He felt so filthy. Why couldn't he get clean?

"Ian?" Kelley asked. "You all right?"

"Yes, I'm fine," he snapped. "I just don't want to tear out this movie, okay? I mean, tear up. Apart. Whatever. Have fun with it. I'm fine, really. I just want to catch a swim before I go to sleep."

On his way to grab his swim trunks, he passed Merl's room, where several folks had gathered for a Bible study. Merl was talking about the ten plagues.

Water that flowed like blood. The firstborn dying, a just punishment (Merl said) for the Pharaoh having killed so many Jewish babies. Ian scratched at his hands and hurried on, trying not to think of dead babies floating in a sea of blood.

On the way to the pool, he ran into Reg and Galen.

"Seen any of the sisters?" Reg asked. "We've got the perfect excuse for the party: Chan told us next week we're going to break the system record for farthest anyone's ever traveled away from Sol."

"Not far enough," Ian muttered, and brushed past.

The cool, chlorinated water of the pool soothed him, and he swam the full length underwater, surfaced long enough for a breath, then back, breathe, and again. He knelt at the shallow end, unwilling to leave the embrace of the water, and caught his breath before doing a neat crawl back to the deep end.

Sister Ann was sitting on the high dive, legs dangling over the edge, but still.

"This is the wrong kind of water," she said while he swiped back his hair and wiped water from his eyes. "It won't cleanse you. Sometimes the salt of tears is better."

This again? "I'd rather swim."

She nodded, but her eyes were dark. He felt a surge of annoyance. What was her obsession about him crying, anyway?

Still, she dropped the subject. "The rules say no one swims alone."

"It's okay. I'm a lifeguard." He treaded water and craned his head to see her. She wore her skin suit, even the socks, and it surprised him how slight of frame she was, like a lanky adolescent. She gripped the side of the board, more for comfort than balance, but nonetheless, she did not look at home.

"Lifeguard," she repeated. "One who guards life. You guard lives from the water?"

"Accidents or carelessness, more accurately."

She tilted her head, pondering. "What about the willful? It's hard to protect the willful. Sometimes you have to protect the innocent against the willful. Lifeguards. Guarding life. Guardians."

Ian paused, confused. A part of his mind groaned. *Now she'll start speaking Annese.*

He decided to try to deflect that. "Listen, I'm sorry about the other night, calling you spaced."

She shrugged. "Water under the bridge. Bridge over troubled waters. Tears are troubled waters, or do they wash away the trouble?"

Back to that again? Maybe this wasn't the best tactic. Still, he said, "I heard you had a good cry. Did it help?"

"It was a scary memory and sad, but I don't remember the details, just the pain and fear. There was pressure I hadn't known about, and I hadn't realized it had been building. I ran to the Blessed Mother for comfort, and Tommie told me what she knew. *Pain and fear motivate, but faith and knowledge direct. Sometimes, you experience all four before you have an epiphany.* When the pressure was relieved, I felt better. But I didn't have an epiphany. At least, I don't think I did." She released her easy grip on the diving board so she could set her elbows on her knees and rest her chin on her fists. Her face screwed up in thought. "I don't always think linearly."

"Really?" He hoped she wouldn't notice his wry tone.

She didn't. "Epiphanies aren't linear. So would I know if I had had one? Or am I being willful in not remembering? It's hard to protect the willful. Sometimes you have to protect the innocent against the willful. Lifeguards.

Guarding life. Guardians. Are you a good lifeguard, Ian?"

He felt his stomach clutch, and suddenly the water seemed too cold.

She continued, oblivious. "*Angel of God, my guardian dear/To whom God's love commits me here,/Ever this day, be at my side,/To light and guard, Rule and guide.* Do you rule and guide, Ian?"

"I'm no angel, Sister Ann. I'm not a psychologist, either. Just an engineer specializing in drive systems and a part-time lifeguard. What are you doing up there in your skinsuit?"

"Sometimes it's easy to be a lifeguard, isn't it? There are rules and procedures. When the rules conflict, it's harder. Code Ten: Know your situation, your priorities, and your orders. Code Ten assumes we can know our situation, our priorities, and our orders. When we don't, we can rely on our guardian angels, but people don't listen to them enough. From the beginning of time, we've refused to listen to the angels, to the prophets, to the rules. We're a willful people. I didn't want to get my habit wet."

He decided not to remind her that there were extra swimsuits. "Are you planning to swim?"

"I'm not sure yet." Her gaze had never left the expanse of the pool, but now, she turned her focus to him. "I don't understand the water."

Finally, something Ian could answer. "It's as close to zero-G as you can get on Earth, and no spacesuit needed."

"Oh!"

Ann pushed herself off the diving board.

"Wait!"

She hit the water with a huge, messy splash and continued to plummet down.

"Vac!" Ian swore and dove in after her.

She didn't struggle as he wrapped his arm under hers and pulled her to the edge. She clung to the side of the pool, coughing up water.

"What did you think you were doing?" he demanded.

"There's still gravity." She sounded more befuddled than angry. "So much water, and there was still gravity. Space is a vacuum, and there's hardly any."

"Well, yeah. I didn't mean to imply —"

She held up a hand, cutting him off. She stared at a puddle on the edge as if it could speak to her. "I'm trying to understand water. Humans are fifty-seven percent water. We need sixty-four ounces of water a day to stay healthy. Six hundred, twenty-two thousand gallons of water in this pool. So much water. Yet, you feel wet, but you never feel clean." Her expression accused.

"What? Ann, you feel all right?"

"I feel very wet. Pool waters; water from the tanks of the *Edwina Taggert*. Baptismal waters; water from Christ's side. Water is a universal solvent, but it can't dissolve sin, not alone."

"Uh, maybe you should go dry off?"

"No." With the ease of a gymnast, she pulled herself up and to a kneeling position on the edge. "I was prideful. I need to say an Act of Contrition and let Saint Adjutor scold me, and then you both can teach me to swim, please?"

"Us both?"

"Well, you, but he'll pray for both of us."

* * *

Chris rubbed his eyes and took another sip of coffee to help bring the numbers on the screen back into focus. Lt. Chan, the navigator, had contacted him after the Codist meeting to tell him they'd gotten some early telemetry from the probe as it approached the Folly. The topic was Code Twelve, forming relationships when the opportunity arises, and a couple of the guys from the research team were griping that not enough of the female rockjacks followed it, which was leading to a heated discussion. Chris was grateful for the excuse to leave.

He'd practically run to his lab to download the data and add it to the wealth he already had. As the computer strove to chart predictions based on the telemetry, he'd fought back the urge to see if Andi wanted to join him. What kind of date would she consider that? Besides, all the talk about Code Twelve had reminded him why he'd sworn off women, especially Spacers and cute co-eds…

What if Andi's different, though? The thought refused to go away, and he'd been relieved when numbers he could work with actually appeared on his screen.

Two hours later, however, he didn't find the results so comforting. He reached for his wristcomp to contact his mentor, then hesitated. Should he wait until the morning?

He looked at the schematic again and shook his head. Even if it was past midnight, he needed to know.

Dr. Thoren let him finish his explanation and send the results to his room's computer. Chris bit his lip and tried not to drum his fingers while his supervisor checked his work.

"This is all the data you have?" Thoren asked.

"Yes, sir. We'll get more in a couple of days. In the meantime?"

"We do nothing. There's too much margin for error."

"But, sir!"

"You could be wrong. To say anything now would be premature. Code Three."

"I know, but —"

"Chris, I've just been informed that researchers and rockjacks alike want to have a party when we break the distance record. We've worked hard to develop this camaraderie. Do you wish to ruin the mood when you could be completely off vector?"

"No, but I..."

"A few more days. More data. More surety. Tell no one, is that understood?"

Chris sighed. "Roger."

He switched off the comms and spun his chair to again look over the projections of Folly and its nearest object. Probabilities or not, he couldn't help feeling that 2217RB87 was heading right toward his discovery.

Chapter Seventeen

"So, Small Weight, it has been many days since you last visited me," OvLandra greeted Ann as she stepped into Sickbay. Rather than have her sit on the examining table, she directed Ann to her office, where the gravity was high enough to hold people to the floor, but low enough that she could remove her exoskeleton.

Ann settled into one of the comfortable chairs. So much comfort on the ship! Still, when she saw Ov's eyes close with relief as the zerog settled into her own comfortable chair, she said a silent prayer of thanks for the well-cushioned seat.

"I'm sorry, Ov. I'm much busier now. I started teams on making lamp lines, and everyone has passed the basic suit course, so I'm teaching, too."

"And, apparently, trying to drown yourself," OvLandra concluded sternly.

"Drown? Oh, no! Ian is very good at protecting lives from the water. But he doesn't understand the water, either. Six hundred twenty-five thousand gallons, and he swims and swims, but he'll never get clean. It's the wrong kind of water. I needed to understand his water."

"Are you sure this isn't about your recent upset?"

"Tears are water, but they aren't enough, either. *Pain motivates; faith directs.* I'm not sure he understood any better after the lesson, but he needed to be a good lifeguard. Saint Adjutor will watch over him, and I learned to swim."

OvLandra folded one of Ann's hands between both of hers. "Ann, as ship's doctor, I'm also responsible for the emotional wellbeing of the crew."

"Oh! Ian washes his hands again and again, but he never feels clean. We have to help him understand why."

Ov's smile strained. "I'm speaking of you, Small Weight."

"Me?" Ann blinked, her focus still on Ian and pools and what he thought he could wash off. It was important, too, maybe even a safety issue. If Ov could talk to him, it might help. Yet Ov hadn't called her to discuss Ian? "Why me?"

"I've been told about the incident in the lunchroom. You remembered the accident that orphaned you, didn't you?"

Ann's eyes clouded, and she shook her head. "It was...visceral. I remembered being afraid, and running, and something dragging at my skirts."

"What about your parents? Did you see them? Did you see your father?"

Already, the memories were hazy. "I didn't see anything. Except the dress. It was a very pretty dress, but no cherubim to help me."

OvLandra hissed. "Try, Ann!"

But the tension in OvLandra's voice distracted Ann from her memories. "This is important to you."

"Of course it is!"

Ann tilted her head. "Why?"

Abruptly, OvLandra backed up. "Ann, this is serious emotional distress. We don't want it to interfere with your duties."

Ann laughed. "Oh, OvLandra! *There is no exercise more profitable and useful to the soul than to suffer.* I was frightened, and it was a very strong feeling, but Holy Mary led me through it, and my guardian angel protected me. Oh! Just like he did then. Tommie held me when I cried, and Rita prayed and drew me a hot bath with lots of bubbles, and I talked to Andi about it, and now you're so concerned, too! *The greatest lie Satan tells is that we are ever alone.*"

* * *

Ian ran, jumped, and dunked the ball through the hoop, hanging onto the net for a beat before dropping back to the ground. "All I know is if I want something, I go for it, no stopping to agonize or debate." He tossed the ball toward Reg.

"Yeah, how's that working for you with the ladies here?" Reg asked. He dribbled the ball and stepped back, making a show of waiting for Chris and Galen to catch their breaths.

Ian threw him a rude gesture. Basketball was the only time he'd scored all trip.

Chris set his hands on his knees and panted. Reg and Ian had invited him and Galen to a game. His body reminded him how much time he spent at a desk. He'd been studying on Luna too long. At least Galen was having a hard time, too.

"Look, guys," Chris said. "I appreciate the advice."

"But will you follow it?" Ian asked.

"It's not that easy."

"Not if you make it so hard," Galen said. He wiped sweat off his brow. "How many more sets of this game?"

Reg gave a maniacal laugh and started toward the basket. Galen moved to intercept.

Chris pushed himself into motion to cover Ian.

"Well?" Ian said as he feinted one direction, then ducked past Chris on the other side.

"What?" Chris asked, then realized Ian was still on the subject of Andi.

Why'd I even bring it up? That's right. I didn't. "Guys, Andi is wonderful. Amazing."

"Gorgeous," Ian added.

"Very intelligent," Galen puffed.

"With eyes like the stars/and hair like the Black," Reg sang, arms swung out theatrically, ball balanced in one hand. Galen took that opportunity to knock the ball away and take control of it. He raced down the court, threw the ball, missed. Ian caught it on the rebound; Chris just managed to pace him back the other direction. At least he did a good enough covering job that Ian was forced to pass.

Yeah, gorgeous and intelligent and strong. And perfectly wrong for me. "Okay! I get it! But the point is — don't take this wrong, Galen — she's a rockjack. When this mission is over, she'll go back to her mining op, and I'm back to Luna, so what's the point?"

"Right here!" Reg said, and threw from the three-point line.

Ian cheered. "The point is, you have right now. We're on this tub for four more months. Make the most of it."

Chris nabbed the ball from Ian. "I've had 'right now.' I don't want right now."

"You sure you know what *she* wants?" Galen asked.

"How would I know?" Chris passed to him, forced his legs to speed down the court in time to get Galen's return, only to find Ian in front of him. He bounced the ball hand to hand, weaving, looking for an opening.

Ian spread his hands in exasperation as much as to block Galen. "You're never going to know until you ask. Vac', Chris, take the shot."

"Fine!" He threw the ball, and it sailed in.

Ian watched it bounce on the floor and shook his head. "Not what I meant, but good one."

"I'm done!" Galen called. "Too long at full gravity for me. Besides, George and I have our first round of splat tomorrow. He'll kill me if I'm not top of my game because I was playing basketball."

"Wimp!" Reg teased, but smacked him on the back. Galen stumbled forward, and, with a dramatic cry of pain, fell prone on the floor.

That looked like a good idea to Chris, so he splayed out on the floor beside him. The others crouched down next to them. Ian handed Chris water, and he pulled himself into a sitting position to drink.

Galen propped himself on one elbow. "Splat is not for wimps," he said, "but it is about defense. Unlike basketball, which is all about scoring, splat is about protecting what's yours. It's a very zerog philosophy, but that's how a lot of us feel here in the Black."

Chris took the hint. "Andi doesn't think I do a very good job of defending her."

Galen laughed. "Andi can take care of herself, and she knows it."

Chris rolled the bottle between his palms. "But I didn't defend you guys against Thoren at lunch the other day. I didn't defend Ann."

"No offense," Ian cut in, "but Ann is a few chips short of a full console, if you ask me."

Galen shook his head. "You haven't known her long enough. Sean pegged it when he said she doesn't speak linearly, but I have never known her to not make sense in the long run. Seriously, if she tells you something, pay attention and remember it."

Fear Andi, if you must, but don't be afraid of her, she told me. Chris sighed. "So what, then? She doesn't think I can defend myself?"

"Can you?" Galen asked. "Can you fight for what's important to you? Do you stand up for what you believe in?"

Chris thought back on his life: all the times he'd walked away from an argument, avoided a conflict, just let things go. Was it really Code Six — live and let live — or was he just afraid to stand his ground?

Galen sighed into his silence. "Listen, Chris. We'll be at *Discovery* soon, and then everything changes. Ian's right that all we have is right now, but if we use this moment right, it leads to more moments. You can't be afraid to try."

Again, Chris heard Ann's voice in his mind. *Be not afraid.*

* * *

Rose Chan sighed with pleasure. "I would be as fat and happy as Buddha if I had unlimited access to these," she said as she took another bite of chocolate.

Rita hummed her agreement. "I was never a big chocolate fan, but after a year without, it's certainly a treat. Where did you ladies find this again?" she asked Andi and Kelley.

The two glanced at each other conspiratorially, but Andi answered. "When we were exploring the Valle Marinaris deck. We only found the one box, so we thought it appropriate to share it just among us ladies."

"Well, I appreciate the invite," Rose said, "and the fact that you scheduled the party after my shift."

"We women have to stick together; besides, men don't appreciate chocolate like we do." Kelley broke off a small piece of her bar and dropped it into her mouth. She closed her eyes in silent bliss as it melted on her tongue, then said, "I don't think I could live without chocolate. In my book, there's only one thing better."

"What's that?" Ann asked. She toyed with her unwrapped bar.

The room erupted into giggles. Ann looked from one lady to another, uncomprehending. Rita rolled her eyes and was about to say something school marm-ish, when Tommie surprised them all by saying, "There were days in my youth I'd have taken chocolate over a man. No egos to feed, no demands..."

"And you know this *how*?" Kelley teased.

Tommie got a faraway look. "His name was Reese. Crazy as a plasma storm, icy as the rings when he had to be. Met him in the war; he was Special Ops, and I was their pilot. He used to call me, 'Taxi.' Drove me to distraction, but oh, he could made me laugh."

"What happened?" Zabrina leaned forward in her cushion.

Tommie shrugged. "Mission. I dropped off twenty; ten returned. Reese wasn't with them."

The room was silent. Then Zabrina whispered, "Oh, I'm so sorry."

Tommie gave her a lopsided grin. "It was a long time ago."

"I didn't think nuns could fall in love," Kelley accused.

"*Sister*. Nuns are cloistered, while sisters are active in the world. At any rate, I wasn't a sister then. Just a pilot and a woman in love. Nor did I join the Order to run from heartbreak; it was several years later when I took vows."

"Then why did you?" Kelley asked.

"Tired of war. Tired of death. Loved the excitement. And I found something more. I'm not sure I can explain any better. It was actually similar to falling in love. You don't plan or expect it to happen, but when it's right, you know it." She looked at her goddaughter, who blushed and ducked her eyes.

"How's it going with you two?" Zabrina asked Andi.

She shrugged. "Wish I knew. He doesn't really talk to me."

"Not about the things she wants to talk about, anyway," Kelley sing-songed.

Andi sighed, and her godmother pulled her close and murmured reassurances.

From the corner of her eye, Rita saw Ann frown thoughtfully.

"What about you, Rita?" Zabrina asked.

Rita gave a guilty start. "Me?"

"Yeah. Why'd you become a nun — I mean, sister?"

"Oh! Um, well, twelve years of Catholic school. When I turned eighteen, I knew it was what I wanted."

"What if you changed your mind?" Zabrina asked.

Rita froze. Had she been so transparent? Had they heard about James' and her argument or noticed how they were avoiding each other now?

But Zabrina was looking at all three sisters, and Tommie answered. "Then you leave the order with our blessings, but you don't get to be a religious sister and a wife. They're separate vocations."

Kelley shook her head. "I don't understand why you'd so willingly submit to such a limited life."

"*Limited*?" Ann exclaimed. "I don't understand." She looked from Tommie to Rita.

Kelley, however, answered, tossing her head in a dismissive gesture. "I wouldn't expect you to. I'm sure the Dalai Lama doesn't feel limited, either."

Ann's brows knit together, trying to find the connection, while Andi looked ready to argue. Tommie spoke first.

"Kelley, don't confuse commitment with limits. Every time we make a choice to have something, we choose against having something else. When I was in the military, I chose to accept the limits set upon me by my superiors. Now I've simply accepted a higher and more loving authority."

"Or marriage," Andi added. "You commit to one person, forsaking all other lovers, but it's not a sacrifice. It's a fulfillment of love."

"Or chocolate!" Ann said. All eyes turned to her.

Rose hummed in agreement. "That makes sense. Eating it all day long could make you fat and happy as a Buddha, but if you want to do other things — like space work, especially Outside work — you have to stay in shape. So you choose not to indulge."

Kelley shook her head. "But if I want to, I can have some chocolate now and then."

Ann shook her head. "I'm allergic. God created us each differently. *You knit me together in my mother's womb...I am fearfully and wonderfully made.* Fearfully — full of fear. Fear of God means reverence and awe. He made us with reverence and awe, full of reverence and awe..." Her voice trailed off in thought.

Rita took up the conversation. "We make our choices based on those differences."

"But that's different. I mean, if you hate chocolate..."

Andi snorted. "You kidding? Ann *loves* chocolate. Remember when my dad brought us that big box, and you and I ate the whole thing in one sitting?"

"I remember that," Tommie said. "Ann's whole face swelled, and she had hives everywhere. You were in Sickbay for days, remember?"

Ann pulled out of her reverie to nod. "And I cried and cried. I thought

God was punishing me because He wouldn't let me have chocolate. But Mother Superior told me that part of being unique was that certain things will be bad for me. I just had to trust that God had other treats for me, and He does. Like key lime pie!" She turned her whole body toward Rita. "You make the best key lime pies."

Rita laughed. Every Christmas, her parents sent her enough ingredients to make her favorite pie for the entire convent. She got to spend days in the kitchen, cooking. The first year, she'd wept with homesickness, but now, she was able to enjoy the memories. Except for those with James.

Ann was still watching her, her eyes bright.

"Wait 'till our lime tree bears fruit. Then you're in for a treat," Rita said.

Rose sat forward, "We have a lime tree in hydroponics!"

Ann gave a squeal of joy.

"Well, I think we're making pies!" Rose stood. "Ann, come with me to pick the limes. Rita, you go to the kitchen and see if we have everything else we need."

"If not, we can put it on the scavenger list," Andi added.

"Have fun," Kelley dismissed them, leaning back on the pillow Rose vacated. "I hate lime. So what are you going to do with that chocolate, Ann?"

"Oh!" Ann looked with surprise at the bar still in her hand. "I thought I'd give it to James when he finishes the intermediate course. Does he like chocolate, Rita?"

"Absolutely. He's a chocoholic. You'll have a friend forever."

"That's settled, then."

"What about OvLandra?" Zabrina suddenly asked. "Did anyone invite her? She's a zerog, but she's a woman, too."

Andi shrugged. "Oh, we did invite her. She declined."

Ann added, "Zerogs can't tolerate chocolate. Something in the genetic manipulations."

Kelley was still reclining, her eyes closed as she let another bite of chocolate melt in her mouth. "So how do zerogs fit into your 'God made us fearfully and wonderfully' assertion?"

Rita's hackles rose, but Tommie set a warning hand on her arm and nodded toward Ann.

The little sister read the wrapper: "'Hershey's Luxe. Grown from the choicest genetically engineered cocoa trees to bring you a poetry of bitter and sweet.' *Poems are made by fools like me/But only God can make a tree.* But together, you get chocolate."

Andi stuck her tongue out at her roommate, and it set the whole room laughing.

* * *

Even after they'd parted ways and Rita was heading toward the kitchen alone, she was still chuckling. *Leave it to Ann to compare vocations to something like food allergies.*

"What's so funny?" said a familiar voice behind her.

She froze. She stifled the urge to take off and waited until James had caught up with her, taking that moment to school her voice into casual calm.

"Nothing, really," she started, then stopped. He was squinting at her. "What?"

He looked both ways to make sure the hall was empty. "Is that chocolate on your face?" he hissed.

Rita wiped at her mouth. "Andi and Kelley found a few bars —"

"— and decided to cut us guys out? Thanks loads. Hope the other ladies are neater than you. You'll start a riot, and I'll be leading the way. Ah! You keep missing it. Hold still." He licked his thumb and wiped along the edge of her lip. The contact sent a shock through her.

He stuck his thumb in his mouth, then frowned at her. "And you didn't save me a piece?"

"Ann has a whole bar for you, once you pass the intermediate course." *Please let my voice sound steadier than I feel!*

James smiled. "Now there's motivation! So, heading to find some milk?"

Rita cleared her throat. "Actually, Rose mentioned they have a lime tree. I thought I'd see if we have the makings for key lime pie."

James shrugged. "They're probably Persian limes."

"It would still work." Her whole body shivered inside, and she was way too aware of how little distance there was between them. *Please don't ask to join me!*

As if hearing her silent plea, he said, "Well, I'll leave you to it. I remember how you liked to cook alone."

As soon as he left, she leaned against the wall and gave in to the shakes.

He didn't mean anything by that, she told herself sternly. *How many times have I seen him treat a child the same way? Besides, after our blow-out, he can't have any hope for... No. This is my problem. It's not fair! Some days, I think I have it all figured out, and then...*

Do I want chocolate or key lime pie?

Chapter Eighteen

Distance Day arrived. Chores were waived, labs were closed; training, which was mostly complete anyway, postponed. The only scheduled events were the finals for the Distance Breaker Splat Tournament and the ensuing party.

In the meantime, Rita luxuriated in sleeping in — or more accurately, going back to bed after morning devotions, but she didn't care to split hairs. She hadn't slept in since Earth, and she enjoyed every minute of it.

When, at last, her back began to ache in complaint of the unaccustomed leisure, she opened her eyes, stretched, and breathed in the silence. Tommie and Ann must have gone off to do their own thing. Andi and a few of the others planned to decorate the Antares Lounge before the splat game, but she still had plenty of time.

She grabbed the paperback copy of *Starlotus* that Quad One had found on a scavenger hunt and went to fill the tub with bubbles and the hottest water she could stand.

By the time *Starlotus* had driven off the invading aliens and Captain Denaire and his crew mourned the loss of their first officer — his wife — the water had grown tepid, and Rita's toes resembled raisins. She turned on the shower to wash away the soap and the tears shed for the brave Commander Mira Denaire while she considered her next move. How long had it been since she felt bored?

It was too early for the decorating, and she was read out for the moment. She didn't want to waste that "just showered" feeling by working out, and no way was she going to go watch Tommie and Ann practice. She'd cringe enough during the actual tournament.

So: lunch, then to the chapel.

The chapel was already set to "Catholic." *Odd.* Rita opened the door from the "narthex" and entered the holographic chapel.

James turned his head from where he sat in a middle pew.

"Oh! I'm sorry!" She took a step back to the door.

He gave her a puzzled look, then indicated the seat beside him. "You'd have never apologized in Indy."

"You're right, I..." Flustered and ashamed, she genuflected and sat in the pew beside him.

In his lap he held the small breviary that had belonged to his grandfather. It looked even more worn than she'd remembered.

"You thought I stopped praying, didn't you?"

"Of course not! I…" Her protest died on her lips. She didn't know what she'd thought. "James, I…I'm sorry."

Tears stung her eyes. She turned her head and blinked them away.

"Rita." Frustration and annoyance filled his voice. "If I really had a calling to the priesthood, would I have left? It's not your fault. It's not anybody's fault."

She glanced at his worried eyes and forced herself to take a breath and release it slowly. "You're right. Guess that was conceited of me." Her nose stung. She pressed her knuckle against it. Her eyes were sure to be red.

"Hey. It's all right. I'm all right with how things turned out. I'm happy. Rita, are you —" He set his hand on hers, and she jumped.

"Am I what?" She pulled her hand away.

He hesitated, and she knew he'd had to change mental gears. Good. She didn't want to know what he'd planned on saying.

"Are you enjoying being a Rescue Sister?"

Her eyes dropped to her hands. "Well, it's certainly been a challenging experience."

He watched his hands turn his breviary. "You know, when I said we should go to the asteroid belt and get you some of that colite, I was kidding. Yet here you are."

She shook her head, and three years of training caused her to face him steadily without realizing it. Nonetheless, her chest tightened. "Here *we* are! I would never have thought of you on a space adventure!"

He twisted his mouth into a grin, and, at last, looked at her. "Yeah, well, I'll be glad to breathe air that isn't recycled, and I'm trying very hard not to think about the water."

For the first time in days, she could breathe easily. "It's cleaner than what you'll find on Earth. I know. I spent three weeks studying the process."

"Oh, the glamorous life of a spacer!"

Her eyes moved over his face, taking in the sadness that hid behind the ironic twist in his expression. Maybe he really was happy, mostly. She wanted to say something to make him fully happy, and she didn't know what to say. What she *wanted* to say. What would *Ann* say?

Something confusing and profound, no doubt. I'm not Ann.

"It has its moments," she replied. "Are you going to the splat finals?"

"Is that one of the moments?" His voice twisted with doubt.

She chuckled. "Not for me, but Tommie and Ann are in the finals, so I have to go. But you might like it. You like hockey."

His brows furrowed. "You realize how incongruous 'Sister Ann' and 'hockey player' are?"

"Come and see."

"Okay. But in the meantime, I'll leave you to your prayers."

She watched the door for a long time after it closed behind him, silent, letting herself feel the ache in her heart.

Back in Indy, they'd never missed an opportunity to pray together.

* * *

The lounge hadn't been touched since *Edwina Taggert* was sold the first time, so it took longer to get ready than the party crew had expected. Rita and Andi ran to the splat court, pausing only long enough to adjust to the change in the direction of the gravity as they entered the stadium. All along the edge of the circular room, people settled into seats facing a transparent dodecahedron made of hexagonal windows outlined in flashing colors. Rita's Earth-born instincts rebelled at seeing people over her head sitting as comfortably as those to her side, and she closed her eyes to let her brain adjust to the fact that the gravity was floorward, no matter which way the floor faced.

Andi jerked her head toward where James was waving and pointing. "Oh, look! James saved us spots. Choice seats, too! Come on."

"Great." Rita pasted on a smile and followed in Andi's wake as she waded through the crowds toward the front row facing a hexagon-shaped window. Perhaps if Andi went first, she'd sit by James, and Rita could sit by Sean.

No such luck. He'd saved one seat, and Sean beside him another, but when they got there, Sean moved, murmuring a shy greeting toward OvLandra as he sat next to her. Rita had never seen him hesitant around anyone, and it distracted her from her own hesitation as she settled between him and James while Andi took the seat on James' other side.

"'Bout time you made it," he said as they settled in. "It's a testimony to how everyone regards you that we kept these seats, but in another minute, I might have been mobbed. Oh, and one of you had better explain this game to me fast."

Rita started to ask why he hadn't just looked it up, then realized that he probably hadn't on purpose. If so, she didn't want to know what that purpose was.

Fortunately, Andi took on the job. "It's really pretty simple — in theory. The court's a dodecahedron, right? So twenty sides, called panels: eight are red, eight are blue. The other four are the mutual panels, or mupes. The goal of the game is to prevent the ball from hitting a mupe or your own panels. If it hits a mupe, both teams lose. In tournaments, they're also eliminated, which is what happened to Galen and Lenny and the team from engineering. Above all else, you protect mutual territory. With me so far?"

She paused as Francis, the announcer, called for attention and introduced the teams. As a name was called, each player came rocketing in, rebounding off each of the four transparent panels in turn. Andi told Chris that was traditional. Tommie and Orion McVee dashed about with military precision. Rose executed her pattern with showy twists. Ann hardly seemed to make an effort, yet soared around the room with as much speed as the others. The *Edwina* team wore red, the Sisters blue.

The crowd hushed as they took their places: Tommie and Rose near their panels for defense, Ann and Orion toward the middle for offense. A small door near one of the windows opened and Capt. Addiman threw in the ball.

"Since it's a small court, there's no central dodeck to launch the ball at random, so it has to bounce three times, then play begins," Andi explained as the ball smacked one window, pinged off the corner of two panels and ricocheted off a third. No sooner had it, than both Ann and Orion flung themselves toward it.

"What happened with the rockjacks and engineering?" Rita asked as Ann reached the ball first and smacked it toward the red side with the back of her hand. The force pushed her back, but, with a twist and a tap of one foot against a panel, she changed her vector to intercept Orion's rebound.

Andi shrugged. "Engineering was too aggressive, and Galen wasn't on his game. Came out griping something about basketball. The game is more about defense."

"So how do you win?" James asked.

"Each team has eight panels to protect. If the ball hits their panel, that panel loses its color. If you've lost five panels before the game ends, you lose."

"And if neither side does?"

With a head-butt, Rose sent the ball hurtling toward her partner, but Ann intercepted him, swooping under his legs and sending him into a spin before he could contact the ball. Tommie easily deflected it. People cheered.

"Depends on the tournament. Sometimes, both teams progress; sometimes, the team with the most panels moves on. Really, that's it, other than you have to strike the ball, but not the players, and there's no parking."

"Meaning," Rita interpreted, "you can hit the ball with any part of your body, but you can't catch, hold, or throw it. You also can't hit, kick, knee or grapple with the players, though body slamming is allowed, and you can't hang onto the panels to hold yourself still."

"Body slamming?" James rubbed his elbow.

Rita couldn't help but chuckle. Her students had done enough body slamming of themselves and each other by accident during training; even more in Suits 201, where Ann had set up an obstacle course. Maybe Thoren was right about taking private lessons, after all; she didn't think he could have taken the blows to his dignity.

"I've treated several minor injuries and one dislocated shoulder — Engineer's Mate Nick Fergusson, fortunately for your mission," OvLandra put in lightly. "It's always interested me that you weighties play more aggressively, even though you are so frail."

"Frail?" James' question turned into a squawk as McVee powered into Ann, preventing her from intercepting the ball and slamming them both into the window. The audience winced and shouted in sympathy. Then a cheer rose as Tommie shoved the ball their way, and Ann hooked it with her foot and sent it spinning to impact the nearest red panel before Rose could block it.

"Do not let my frame fool you," OvLandra continued when the cheering had died down. "We may need supports to move around in your gravity, but my people are designed to be sturdy, and we heal quickly."

The ball rebounded off the panel toward a mupe. Ann twisted free of McVee and deflected it onto a blue panel.

"What was that?" James demanded.

"Wait," Andi warned, her voice tight with anticipation.

The ball bounced off the panel, and Ann was in the perfect position to send it flying at an oblique angle toward red. It smacked the panel and only a desperate move by Orion kept it from hitting a second one. The crowd rose, screaming in its excitement as Ann again took command of the ball and forced Orion into defense, as well.

Only OvLandra stayed sitting.

When everyone had again resumed sitting, Sean said, "Sister Ann's pretty amazing, isn't she?"

Something in the way he said it made Rita glance at him. He was looking directly at OvLandra as if he expected an answer.

OvLandra had been watching the game with narrowed eyes, but Rita watched her face wipe into an expression of general, innocent interest. "Perhaps I am not the only one impressed with her," she replied blandly to Sean.

Sean turned away without answering, but, although he again faced the window, he didn't seem to watch the game. Rita saw him glance once more at the ship's doctor, just a flick of the eyes. He frowned in thought.

What was going on?

* * *

Chris frowned at the readouts on the screen, then snapped off the monitor and slouched back in his seat, jamming the heels of his hands against his eyes.

Why, why, *why* was the universe doing this to him?

He'd gotten more telemetry on 2217RB87. Lots of telemetry. Someone on Massell station had also noticed what he'd suspected and ordered the probe to take more readings. The result: he had hard proof that not only was 2217RB87 going to collide with the Folly, but it would also do so soon, like *before-they-would-get-there* soon.

He'd called Thoren just as the professor was heading to the party, and what had his mentor said? "Run the numbers again. Twice and thrice and yet again. Let's not be hasty," the professor insisted.

Meaning, tell no one and miss the party redoing work he already knew checked out. He'd privately named the Ky-bo "Fate" to suit its behavior and the way actual fate seemed to work on his life.

"No," he told the Ky-boes around him. He had to get Thoren, show him the simulations, and make him understand. Then they needed to call a meeting. Folks would probably need sober-up pills, but they had to figure out what to do.

He ran his fingers through his hair and headed to the lounge.

* * *

"So where's Chris, Andi?" George asked as he poured a finger of Saturan Blue into Frances' cup.

Andi gave a howl of frustration and smacked her cup on the low table. "Why do people keep asking me that? I didn't even see him at the game."

The party was in full swing: Tommie and Ann had been heralded as the victors, while McVee and Chan took a lot of leak for losing to a couple of nuns and were made to distribute the first round of drinks. Folks had settled into groups, nicely mixed between crew, rockjack, and datahead. Even Kelley looked like she was having a good time for once. Of course, it probably helped that she'd offered a beer to Ann, who innocently took a mouthful and promptly spat it back out all over Ian. Ann took it in good humor, declaring it "chocolate" and refusing to explain to the men what she meant.

"You want I should talk to him?" Lenny asked. He was on his second finger of Blue, and it only took a little alcohol to bring out his New York Sicilian accent.

Fortunately, the folks around the table moaned as the last of the Blue was poured, and Andi saw her escape. "Next one's on me."

At the bar, Andi handed the empty bottle to Merl, who was taking a turn as bartender. He checked it against the list, looked up her quota, then handed her another one before going to a table to deliver some glasses of water. As she reached for it, Dr. Thoren set his hand softly on her forearm. He traced little circles on her arm with his fingers.

"So, Andi, tell me: why does such a lovely specimen of the female race bear so masculine a name?"

"It's short for Andromeda." She started to pull away, but he tightened his grip.

"Andromeda! *Now Time's Andromeda on this rock rude/with not her beauty's equal.*"

What in space? "Dr. Thoren, how much have you had to drink?"

"If I am drunk, my dear, it is your boundless beauty that intoxicates me."

She forced herself not to roll her eyes. "Ri-ight. Well, I'm sure you can sleep that off. Now if you'll excuse me." She tried to pull her arm free.

"Andromeda. Andi. It's not just your beauty. It's obvious to me you have hidden intelligence and sophistication."

"Hidden?" She twisted away, hoping he'd take a hint and release her before he embarrassed himself further. Her friends were all facing away from the bar, laughing at something. No one had noticed her and Thoren. She wasn't sure if that was a good thing or not.

"I've noticed your...attempts...with my protégé. My dear, don't settle. There's so much more in store for you — things I can give you. Opportunities. Experiences of intellect and culture. Luxuries to sate all your senses. This life you lead..."

"And what's wrong with the life I lead?" She snarled as she turned back toward him and set the bottle on the bar, lest she decide to waste good drink by smashing it against his head.

When Chris walked into the room and saw Thoren and Andi holding hands at the bar, all thoughts of Ky-boes and alien ships fled as fate dealt him yet another blow.

Thoren leaned a little closer, and Andi could smell the alcohol on his breath. "I'm certain it has had its...interests. But surely a lady of your obvious worth should not be satisfied to surround herself with the laboring rabble of..."

Over in another corner, Ann suddenly looked up toward the bar with keen interest.

The "laboring rabble" were rising as a group to approach the bar.

Andi had noticed, too, and tried to pull her arm out of Thoren's grip without jerking it. The man had more strength than she'd realized. "Dr.

Thoren, you need to secure that leak before there's trouble."

His patronizing smile might have charmed someone with a few more drinks in her, but it grated on Andi's increasingly raw nerves. "Andi, my dear, you don't need to put up a show. After all, Code Twelve. I'm sure even the most — pardon the pun — hardened of rockjacks would understand — nay, *respect* —"

"Understand what, exactly? Andi, this datahead bugging you?" Lenny asked, moving close enough to Thoren to get in his space without outright threatening him. Behind him, five rockjacks had fanned out around them.

At the door, Chris stood frozen, ice stabbing his heart as his mind played out Thoren's coed routine. *Right about now, he's explaining how the Code allows, "nay, respects" a certain promiscuity among Spacers. I waited too long. Oh, what would that matter? It didn't with my ex. Code Twelve, right?*

He wanted to walk away, but he couldn't make his feet move.

Ann glanced Chris' way, then rose and wandered toward the bar.

Thoren, still firmly clutching Andi's arm, leaned against the bar and addressed Lenny. "This is a private conversation."

"Excuse me if that doesn't make it through my hardened rockjack brain, but it seems to me that you didn't understand earlier? You mess with one of us, you mess with all of us."

Thoren smiled at Andi triumphantly. "You see, my dear? That is just the archaic tribal mentality —"

"What did you just call us?"

"Who's going to pray with me?" Ann demanded. Everyone in the group gaped at the small blonde in the black habit, who beamed at them as if oblivious to the growing hostility around her.

"What?" Both Lenny and Thoren replied as one.

"To pray with me!" Ann repeated as if to small children. She took Lenny's hand in hers, then pulled Thoren's off Andi's arm. While Andi had used considerable force yet still hadn't removed it, it slid easily into Ann's grasp.

She bowed her head. "Dear Father in Heaven, we thank you for this time of fellowship and for the great adventure ahead of us. Grant us strength of body and soul, that we be fit instruments for Your purpose. Guide us in wisdom, patience and love so that, while doing good work together, we may also enjoy this time and become good friends. In the name of the Father and of the Son and of the Holy Spirit. Amen."

She released them with a smile, ignoring Lenny's confusion and Thoren's scowl.

"Thank you! But Andi, come pray with me in the chapel, like when we were girls. Please?" She held out one hand to her friend.

"All right. Sure." Andi gave her an I-don't-know-what-you're-playing-at-but-I'll-go-along look, handed the bottle to the miner behind her, and took the proffered hand. They started for the door, swinging their arms like schoolgirls. People stared, but everyone had gotten used to odd behavior from the little sister.

At the door, she grabbed Chris' hand. "You, too!"

"But I'm not Catholic. I can't really pray..."

"Nonsense. Everyone can pray. Even Dr. Thoren was praying just a minute ago. It helps if you remember you are fearfully and wonderfully made. Come on. Andi and I will teach you." She started down the hall, dragging him along.

At the chapel, Ann released their hands and dialed up the correct setting. She gave them a happy smile and bounced on her toes as the door slid open. Her face changed to a deeper joy when she looked in the chapel. She hurried to the altar, Chris and Andi apparently forgotten.

Once again, Chris had time alone with Andi; once again, he found himself tongue-tied and terrified. It didn't help that they were standing in front of a Catholic church with a nun reciting prayers a couple of meters away. His mouth worked but all that came out was, "Um."

Idiot! Just talk to her! Ann told him not to be afraid of Andi, so why couldn't he keep two thoughts together around her?

Ann said I'm fearfully and wonderfully made. Well, she got the fearful part right. Say something! Anything!

He opened his mouth again, but before any sounds worked their way past his vocal cords, Andi spoke up. "Look, she's really expecting us to pray. Let's go in for a few minutes, then we can sneak out and find someplace quiet to talk, okay?"

"Yeah, uh, okay. I mean, that's stellar."

She noted his discomfort. *Like she wouldn't notice? Smooth, that's me. Idiot!* But all that washed away when she took his hand. "Let's just kneel a bit and be with God. We don't have to say a rosary or anything formal."

"Um, okay, but, uh. I don't know what a rosary is."

She laughed, but not at him; the sound played over him, easing some of his nervousness. "Well, there's one more thing we can talk about. Later."

They slid into the last pew and knelt side by side. She leaned her head over folded hands, and her lips moved as she silently recited some long-familiar prayer. He mimicked her posture and the way she held her hands, watching her out of the corner of his eye. Once he'd gotten the pose right, though, he didn't know what to do.

Be with God, she said.

He didn't know what that meant. His parents had never discussed religion, except to say he should make up his own mind. Then Dad died, and Mom never talked about it again. When he'd first arrived at Luna Tech, a pretty brunette had invited him to a Code discussion. He'd been more fascinated by how her hair moved than he had in the topic, but she invited him back again and again. By the time their relationship grew, then dissolved — over Thoren and Code Twelve, ironically enough — he'd become such a part of the group, he didn't dare leave. After all, if he really understood the Code, he'd respect her beliefs on open relationships, right?

It suddenly struck him that that was probably not the best thing to think about in church.

Fortunately, Andi leaned back, touching her head, belly and shoulders. "I'm ready," she whispered. "You?"

He nodded, knowing it was a lie.

As they snuck out, they heard Ann's voice continue its soft litany of prayers.

They walked in silence to the observation deck Chris had come to think of as theirs. The viewscreen, still disabled, sparkled and flashed with impacts, though fewer than before. Chris had gotten over his fright and found he actually missed the earlier frenetic display.

Andi pulled two lounge chairs close together and took one. As she crossed her legs, he realized for the first time that she wore a slinky dress with a split skirt made of a shimmery rainbow fabric.

"You look amazing!" he blurted.

She raised her eyebrows at him, then laughed. "You think the only thing we scavenged for were electric wires and lamps? Come on, sit down."

He was almost afraid to. She *did* look amazing. He didn't know if he could trust himself, and after what he'd just seen with Thoren…

She must have read his mind, for she gave a big sigh. "Thank heavens Ann swooped in when she did. If I'd had to listen to Thoren and any more of that Code Twelve leak!" She ended her sentence with a sound of disgust.

"Leak?"

"Space girls are easy," she sneered, then noticed his confusion. "You *do* know what Code Twelve says?"

"Do not be afraid to form relationships. But that's exactly why…"

He stumbled to a stop as her brows knitted and her face grew stormy.

"Please tell me you don't believe that leak? Do you know why Code Twelve was written?"

"People in space were getting afraid to form attachments."

"Yes! Emotional, interdependent, *committed* attachments. The zerogs had isolated themselves from humankind, and spacers were starting to do the same, even from each other. Everything was business, even the sex. But people started realizing how dangerous that was: no lasting friendships, no families, no lifelong love. Just whatever suits you at the moment? Aiy! We take chances in space — just being in space is a risk — but spacers were taking more and more risks, unnecessary risks, and the only reason that could be found was they didn't have anyone to live for."

"I'd...never heard that."

"Yeah, well maybe your Codist groups aren't as open-minded as you'd like to believe."

He looked out the viewscreen, brooding. His mother wasn't a Codist, but that didn't stop her from going from man to man, dragging him along like extra baggage. Andi didn't realize how good she'd had it, with a mother at home and a father who wanted her around, even on his runs.

He should tell her that. He should even explain that he envied it. But when she set her hand on his arm, all he said was, "You don't have to be a Codist to believe in easy love, you know."

"Oh." Her voice went flat, and she pulled her hand away, and he realized he's screwed up again.

"No, wait! That's not what I meant."

She sighed in exasperation. "Well, what *did* you mean?"

"Well, not that you — or I — or we —" He stopped and shook his head. "Why can't I think around you?"

That should have made her smile. It always had with the other girls he'd dated. But she just sat up and scowled. "Maybe because I'm trying to make you think for yourself?"

"What? What does that mean?" He, too, sat up to face her.

"It means that you never seem to think or do for yourself. You let others do the thinking for you."

"What about you?" he snapped back. "You're a Catholic. You do whatever the Pope says."

Her eyes smoldered, and not in the sexy way. Why, why, *why* did he help fate by sabotaging things himself?

"Listen, Mister. There's a difference between accepting leadership and blindly following. I know why I believe what I believe. But you, you just coast with the group, let Thoren tell you what to think, what to do —"

"Thoren!" In a rush, the whole reason he'd gone to the party crashed to the forefront of his mind. "Vac! I'm an idiot. I have to talk to Thoren!" He got up.

"What? Did you understand anything I just said?" She threw her hands in the air and stood up to leave.

"No, wait!" He leapt after her and spun her around. She ended up in his arms, a moment he'd been dreaming of, but all he could think of was mankind's greatest discovery getting destroyed in an astronomical crash of rock and ice. "You don't understand. This is about the Folly and Fate — I mean, 2217RB87 — I triple-checked the data and —"

"Chris! Slow down." She set her hands on his cheeks, and he stilled. "Start again. What about 2217RB87?"

"It's going to hit the Folly, maybe a week before we get there."

He felt her whole body tense, but she spoke calmly. "And you triple-checked this?"

He nodded. "I have to tell Thoren."

"Vac Thoren! Does Addiman know?"

"Addiman?" Light dawned and with it, fear. He glanced at the screen, imagining it afire with the impacts of debris from two Kuiper Belt Objects. "Oh, vac."

"How long have you known about this?"

"Tonight — I mean, I suspected, but Thoren said to keep quiet until we were sure."

"Thoren again. That man is so invested in his own stuperiorities! Oh, never mind. Go, call the bridge, transfer your data to them and I'll get Godmom, Galen, and Addiman."

"What about Dr. Thoren?"

She looked at him like he was spaced. "Can he fly a ship? Navigate? Did he crunch the numbers or just tell you to do it while he took the opportunity to make advances on me? As far as I'm concerned, he had his chance at a say in this and threw it out the airlock. Besides, if he wasn't already drunk when he hit on me, he was halfway there."

She took a deep breath and released it. "And now I'm thinking for you. Look, you decide. If you want him there, if you think he needs to be there, get him a sober-up pill and meet us on the bridge. But after you transfer that data. Every minute we waste puts us twelve million kilometers closer to disaster."

* * *

"But three burns a hole/and four smacks your soul —"

"Ah! 'Vacs your soul!'" Rita shouted and pointed at the offender.

The song dissolved into laughter and catcalls as James groaned and picked up his shot glass. This late in the party, everyone had had their limit of alcohol, so to add "interest," a couple of the research team concocted a brew that was part soda water, part vegetable juice, and mostly Tabasco.

Cheers rose and again dissolved into laughter as he knocked back the drink and came up sputtering.

"How, how can you even... How can you *mess* this song up?" demanded Zabrina. She was either a lightweight or had been sharing in someone else's ration. "You didn't, didneven — did *not* even know the words until tonight!"

"'Vac'—" James started, then fell into a choking fit to the amusement of all. "'Vac' is not a word on Earth. Not like you use it."

"Well, we have a lady of the preligious ursuasion here," Zabrina continued, totally serious and completely oblivious to the snickers around her. "So it's only fitting we should miner — mind dour — *mind our* vac'in' manners!"

"Vac'in' manners!" came the cheer.

James raised his eyebrow at Rita, his eyes twinkling with mirth.

"Just so! Now, from the top: *In a bar down in Tener/there is a bartender, who's stalwart and stoic and grave...*"

They got to the second verse before someone else fumbled the words and had his taste of "solar flare." Meanwhile, Zabrina had curled herself around Ian, who was looking like his prayers were being answered.

Not on my shift, Rita thought to herself. She looked around: except for a few folks chatting in various corners, only the "singers" remained. Tommie had left earlier with Addiman in tow, but Merl was at the nearby table, talking to Cay and watching the proceedings with distaste.

No matter. She leaned back and caught his sleeve. "Merl, can you keep vector on this rabble while I escort Zabrina to her quarters?"

"I'll help! Buddy system, right?" Ian started to stand.

James clapped a hand on the engineer's shoulder and rose, pushing him down in the process. "I'm calling it a night, anyway. I'll help."

"I don' wanna go!" Zabrina pouted, though she allowed Rita to pull her to her feet. She swayed, and James caught her arm.

"Come on, now. We've got to mind our vac'in' manners in front of Sister, right?"

"Vac'in' leak, we do!" She punched the air with her fist, accidentally knocking Ian in the head, but, before she could stoop over to "kiss his boo-boo," Rita and James pulled her away. Everyone raised their glasses in farewell as they resumed singing.

"Saturan Blue! How I love you/You're always good for a finger or two..."

* * *

"She going to be all right?" James asked as Rita exited Zabrina's quarters.

"She fell asleep as soon as she hit the pillow, and I don't think she'll remember much come the morning. I've set the door to lock. Ian's going to be disappointed, praise the Lord." She chuckled, then realized James had been lounging against the wall the entire time, waiting. "I thought you were going to bed yourself."

"I thought I needed an escort."

"You're not drunk."

"Nah. I drank enough to feel loose, but not stupid." Then he gave a deep sigh and regarded her with a long, wistful look.

"What?" She seemed to say that a lot around him, but she couldn't think past the pounding of her heart.

"Nothing. I'm just really glad we found each other again. I wish..."

"James."

"No." He pushed himself off the wall and pressed his fingers lightly against her lips. "You don't need to say anything. It's...just the alcohol talking. Don't worry about it."

He turned and headed to his own room, but it was several more minutes before Rita could make herself move. She fled to the chapel, the words of an ancient prayer Ann had taught her spinning in her mind:

Steer the ship of my life, good Lord, to Your quiet harbor, where I can be safe from the storms of sin and conflict. Show me the course I should take. Renew in me the gift of discernment, so that I can always see the right direction in which I should go. And give me the strength and the courage to choose the right course, even when the sea is rough and the waves are high, knowing that through enduring hardship and danger in Your name we shall find comfort and peace.

Lord, please, just tell me what You want from me!

She found the chapel already set to "Catholic," and bit back a sigh. Ann must still be praying. She started to head back to the party to relieve Merl when something stopped her, and she spun back to the chapel doors and opened them.

The altar area glowed with a swirling rainbow light that flowed from the holograms of Mary and Jesus of the Sacred Heart. In the middle of it knelt Ann, face upturned, trembling.

Is something wrong? Yet Rita didn't feel any sense of danger, just of lasting peace. She closed her eyes to drink in the peace, wanting it to fill her, but it teased at her instead.

The light faded, and Ann slumped.

"Ann!" Rita ran down the aisle and knelt beside her, taking her by the shoulders.

"Rita!" Ann smiled with delight and embraced her. She shook, and her hair and face were wet.

"Ann, were you crying?"

"Was I?" She pulled back and wiped at her cheeks and forehead, then looked at her hand with curiosity. "Blood, sweat and tears. Water, blood and fire. Father, Son and Holy Spirit. Baptism, Communion, Mercy..." She squeezed her eyes shut, and Rita couldn't tell if it was in concentration or pain.

"Ann?"

"The flames of mercy are burning me, clamoring to be spent. I want to keep pouring them out upon souls, but souls just don't want to believe in My goodness..."

"Saint Faustina. The Divine Mercy. Ann, what is it?"

"Mercy is divine! But people don't want to believe it. They're scared or feel unworthy or think they'll give up too much. Why do some people think forgiveness means losing? So they cling to the illness in their souls and that's a Dangerously Stupid Thing to do. *I loved my fall...* Falls are exciting, aren't they? The rush in your belly..."

Rita struggled to follow the young sister. "Is that why you pushed yourself off the high dive?"

"Ian was there. The lifeguard who didn't guard life, but he saved mine. He's a good lifeguard now, but he doesn't know it. He doesn't know he changed."

She shook her head, making her sweaty blond hair stand on end. Her breath grew fast and hard. "Changing vector is hard. You have to apply thrust in the right direction. Force equals mass times acceleration — $F=ma$ — and sin can be so massive. We forget gravity is variable, yet constant. God's mercy is, too: we fall, but He catches us. In water, in fire. Too many souls don't want to believe!"

She gripped Rita's hands, and again Rita was reminded how strong Ann really was. She pulled them out of her grip and covered Ann's hands instead. "Ann, you need to calm down."

"It's so exciting! But it's going to be dangerous, Rita. To make a proper course correction, you need to know where you are and where you're going. Sheep are stupid, which is why they need a shepherd, but humans! Humans are mind and soul, body and spirit. And will. Too much will. Too many clinging to their fall. Too many are confused by fear, like Kelley in the fire. They lose their vector, refuse to listen to the lifeguard, don't follow the shepherd..."

Ann turned back to the holostatue of the Sacred Heart, listening, her face in a beatific smile.

Rita waited until her breathing had slowed to something closer to normal, then asked, "How about we go back to our room and have some tea?"

Ann gave the last of the smile to Rita. "Faith, hope, and love. It's so good we are here! Yes, let's do go to our room and get some sleep. We have so much to do. It's all going to be different tomorrow!"

Rita had no idea what that meant, or what anything Ann had said meant, when it came down to it. She stood and helped Ann up, and they walked out of the chapel, arm in arm.

"Rita? I still don't understand about sheep."

Rita set Ann's head on her shoulder. "That's okay, dear."

"Or wolves or lions..."

"I'm sure if you need to, you will."

* * *

Early the next morning, sixty of the seventy-five people aboard the *Edwina Taggert*, most still groggy from the night's festivities, assembled in the auditorium. They grumbled and slouched, unaware of the terrible blow fate had planned for them.

Thoren decided that Chris could deliver the blow, since Chris decided to go behind his back and tell Andi and the *ET* crew without consulting him first.

Since in Andi's eyes, Chris had decided to withhold his suspicions until practically the last minute, she not only agreed, but suggested he craft his apology well.

As he pulled up the image of Fate's intercept route and he looked into the shocked and angry faces of the audience, Chris figured he knew pretty well how the Folly felt. He braced himself.

George delivered the first counterblow: "And you just yesterday figured this out? Vac, man! What the f—"

"Belay that!" Sister Thomas came to his rescue before people could start shouting. She rose from her front seat and joined Chris. "The important thing is what we're going to do about it. Chris, if I may?"

Relieved, he handed her the holo controls and stepped to the back, on the other side of the stage from Thoren. His mentor kept his face schooled in neutrality, but Chris could tell he was glowering over Sister Thomas usurping what he believed a just punishment. Andi, however, looked from her godmother to Chris and lowered her eyes in embarrassment.

Lieutenant Rose Chan had joined Sister Thomas and was pointing to the schematic she'd pulled up. The white line showed the curving path of the Folly; the straighter yellow line on intercept from inside the curve marked the path of the *Edwina Taggert*; and a curved red line from outsystem, the

Fate. Graphics of the Ky-boes and ships showed their current position on their path.

Chan pointed to the yellow line. "Right now, we are burning our engines to slow the ship. So what we do is decrease engine burn from here to here. That will increase our velocity, and we'll overtake the Folly's path." She paused as the graphic of the ship moved forward more quickly, crossing the orbit line of the Folly before it got to that point. "Then, we use the Kayfarers for a hard deceleration burn and a course correction."

"When was the last time you used the fusion engines?" Galen asked.

Chan gave him a glance full of mild annoyance. "They were serviced before we left. *Edwina* will be fine. The point is, we can intercept the Folly before 2217RB87, the Fate, does."

"How much before?" James asked.

Sister Thomas cast a you-wanna-get-this-one? glance Chris' way.

Chris steeled himself and stepped back into the light. "We'll have three days, if we want to get away safely."

He winced at the storm of protests that followed.

"Three days? We're going to be lucky if we see even a third of the ship in that time!"

"Obviously, extraction is the priority now!"

"Fast and dirty. Sorry, Chris, might have to blow the ship apart."

"Why are we even talking about this? We should just scrap the mission!"

"Oh, shut up, Cay!" Rockjacks and researchers chorused.

"That's enough!" Sister Thomas' voice cut through everyone's shouts, and folks stilled. "You are professionals, people! Behave like it. The Sisters and I have reviewed the plan, and we believe it's safe to proceed."

George stood up. "Do we have telemetry on the Folly yet? Three days is going to be cutting it vac'ing short if we want to extract it intact."

"It's waiting for you," Andi answered before Chris could.

"Galen and I might have a way to add some time to the mission as well," Tommie said and reset the simulation. Again, the *ET* approached the path of the Folly, but two small dots left the ship as it approached the Ky-bo. "As the *Edwina Taggert* gets close to the Folly's orbit, we launch *Basilica* and *Rockhopper* with a mining team and all the equipment we can carry. We go ahead to the Folly and prepare the site while the *ET* does its turn-around. We return to the *ET*, and a couple of hours later, I can ferry the first research team."

"Can you do that?" Kelley asked.

Galen nodded. "Sure. Both ships are designed for harder deceleration and maneuvering than the *Edwina Taggert*. It's pure checklist, no problem at all."

Finally, Dr. Thoren spoke. "We are losing too much valuable research time as it is. We send a research team, as well."

Andi laughed. "We are going to be working: checking soil and ice, laying charges, installing the generator and an airlock. We don't have the volume to ferry a bunch of dataheads who will then have to sit around and wait on us."

"We can help!" Chris interjected. "You'll have that many more hands to do the grunt work, and then, when the airlock is ready, we will be, too!"

Even though Sister Thomas had taken charge of the briefing, Thoren crossed his arms and raised a brow in Sister Rita's direction. Chris added his own pleading eyes.

"Ten hours of suit work is a lot," she said doubtfully, "but maybe a few..." She turned to Ann.

The little sister had been studying her bracelet tattoo as if she hadn't been paying attention to the conversation, yet she answered readily. "James could do it. And Ian. Gordon. Reg has the stamina, if he passes his suit test." Ann named two others.

Thoren cleared his throat.

"You haven't passed your suit test, either, Dr. Thoren. A shepherd can't let a sheep leave the pen unless she's reasonably sure he'll be safe."

McVee squashed his lips together in a grimace and shook his head at Rita, then shrugged an apology to Thoren. Chris got the feeling the apology was sincere, but not necessarily heartfelt. He shivered at the closed, hard look Thoren gave the three, but neither Rita nor the commander seemed especially concerned. Ann continued to gaze at her tattoo and didn't notice.

"So." Thoren did his best to sound magnanimous. "Only the six then?"

Ann finally pulled her attention from the glowing beads on her skin and pinned Chris with her gaze. "It won't be easy for you."

Chris gulped. He knew that; in his training, Ann had put him in a full suit and made him move items in the zero-G room back and forth for six hours. His muscles ached for days. In fact, he'd discovered new muscles to ache. But no way was he going to lose his chance to be first on his ship. "I want to try."

Ann shook her head. "You can't try."

He pulled himself straighter. "Then I'll do it."

Chapter Nineteen

The *Rockhopper* set down on 2217RB86, the Folly. Galen announced over the suit intercoms that the anchor had set. The engines powered down, and the gravity faded, causing everyone to rise against their restraints. Andi called for the first team to unbuckle, check suits, and make their way to the cargo hatch.

Chris felt her hand on his shoulder. "Come on, Datahead. Time to see what you got us into."

Chris opened his eyes. Across from him, Ian slapped at the buckle release and shrugged out of the harness. "You're not going to throw up, are you?"

"No!" *Vac!* He sounded like a twelve-year-old. He was so glad Sean had decided to go with James on the other ship. At least Sean had made him recite a little "First Landing" speech the day before. He planned to use it as a voiceover for what he V-Rec'd today. Now, Chris couldn't even remember the words he'd spent hours crafting.

"I'm fine," he said to no one in particular and shook off his own restraints, physical and psychological.

In the less-cramped space of the cargo bay — "less" loosely used in this case, as the bay was filled with equipment intended for at least two missions — they checked each other's suits, careful not to bump into the many rolls of wire, generators, or tanks of stickie and explosives that lined the walls or piled up around the MiGR. The microgravity rover itself filled a good third of the space. The vehicle looked like a child's toy made of piping and tanks, with two rows of seats behind the driver, and skids and railings for carrying personnel or equipment. Andi had told him it was more durable than it looked. He hoped so; still, he avoided bumping into it.

"Everyone, activate your boots," Andi instructed.

He issued the command and felt the reassuring pull of his magnetic soles toward the floor.

When she had everyone's confirmation that their boots were functioning, she directed Galen to depressurize the hold. "Dataheads, get in front on either side. You get to be first to see, but we'll go out ahead to set up drag lines. Copy?"

"Works for me," Gordon's jovial reply sounded over the others' responses of "copy." Chris wished he could be so relaxed.

Galen's voice sounded over the suit comms. "Depressurization complete. Opening the bay doors."

The door opened to a black velvet sky, sprinkled with stars. The Milky Way cut a great swath across the sky, clearer and brighter than anything Chris had ever seen, yet he barely noticed it.

Looming over the horizon, the dim, malformed shape of the Fate dominated the view.

"It looks bigger in person," Reg tried to joke. His voice sounded dry, and he cleared his throat.

"Check your eleven o'clock, about fifty degrees from the horizon," Andi suggested.

There, the *Edwina Taggert* traced a fiery path away from them. With the ship turned around and the fusion engines burning to brake the ship, it looked like it was flying into its own plasma.

"I'm so glad I hadn't seen that before." Even Ian sounded weak.

George's voice, however, boomed even through the comms. "Okay, enough sightseeing! We have nine hours until we head home. Let's get some work done! Team Two is ready with the drag lines. Andi, do we have your permission to go?"

There was a pause while Andi confirmed with Galen and the *Basilica* team. "*Basilica's* down, and Ann is bringing a line to our ship. Team Two, proceed to the *Discovery*. Everyone else, grab your stuff. No one makes a trip empty-handed."

Chris watched as rockjacks in teams of two filed ahead, carrying long spools of cable. One team anchored the main line to the *Rockhopper*; the others attached their lines to it. They double- and triple-checked the connection, then pushed themselves gently off the ramp. Even that small force sent them flying, and Chris watched, heart pounding in his chest, while, as a team, they twisted, activated their hand maneuvering units, and shot off toward the dark shadow that Chris realized, with a start, was the alien ship.

"Rita to Chris." The Rescue Sister's voice sounded over his suit. "You okay?"

He noticed his suit display had issued a gentle warning about elevated metabolism and realized he was having a hard time catching his breath. He inhaled deeply, held it, then released it slowly. "I'm fine," he told her, "just...overwhelmed for a moment."

Her warm chuckle reassured him. "Trust me, I know the feeling. I hate when the door first opens. It'll get easier. Just concentrate on the job."

Team Two reported that they had the first three drag lines in place and were ready for supplies.

"Andi to *Rockhopper* teams. All right people, time to get to work.

Research, remember your training: at all times stay anchored to a line or to a ship. Both safety lines. Move slowly and deliberately. If you push yourself off this rock, there is not enough gravity to pull you back."

George added, "And for shit's sake, don't toss anything! At best, it'll break orbit. At worst case, it'll come back around and smack someone in the back of the head."

"Oh, I want to try now!" Ian burst out.

"That'll be a good way to get grounded," Andi warned. "Rockjacks, make sure the dataheads are anchored when you send them on an errand. Let's move."

They had just piled into the MiGR, the magnets making the boots even clunkier than ski boots, when Sister Ann did a graceful roll over their heads and hovered in front of them. Her feet connected to the deck as the magnets in her boots engaged.

"Not Chris," she said. "He's coming with me."

"I am?"

Her smile shone brighter than the stars or Fate. "Roger. It's your discovery, and we decided you need to be the first to touch it."

"You did? I will?" His heart raced for a new reason.

"Surprise," Andi murmured in a low mezzo, and the warmth in her voice filled him. He followed Ann to the end of the ramp in a happy daze.

Ann made him attach one line to the drag line while she attached his other safety line to herself. She positioned herself so that she faced him, her back to the *Discovery*. "We're going to fly, like we did in 201 in the shuttle bay, but faster. We want to beat the Meeger there! Ready?"

"Yes. Ready."

She didn't move, but waited for him expectantly, brows raised. He realized her feet no longer touched the deck.

"Oh! Right. Releasing magnetic boots." He held himself still as the magnets died.

"Wonderful! Hang on!"

"To what?" he started to ask, but she grabbed him by the arm. She hit the jets of her hand-maneuvering unit, and his question ended as a squawk as the ground fell from under his feet and rushed below him.

Ann laughed with a free delight he'd not heard from her before.

"Ian to Ann! I wanna be next!" Ian whined over the intercom.

"Ian, vacuum is not like water."

"Copy, Little Sister. I promise not to jump."

"How fast are we going?" Chris asked, and his heads-up display gave him the answer. Even if it wasn't faster than a good run, he gulped.

"Chris, look up. Look with fear and not fright!"

He tilted his head up and gasped.

Before them, stretching at least as long as the *Edwina Taggert* and cutting a huge, dark swatch out of the horizon, the alien ship rested. The space-suited forms of the mining crew swarmed around her like insects, a few overflying her, carrying equipment and scanning the hull for microfractures or stress points, others digging under her to set the charges that would free her; one team working to set up the generator for power and lights. He especially wanted the lights, so he could see the ship better.

He must have spoken aloud, because Ann laughed. "We can't see the ship, but our suits can!"

"You're right!" He called up the head's-up display and extended the spectrum and translated it to the visual field. Suddenly, the *Discovery* lit up with color and design.

Ann changed direction, and soon they hovered above the ship, so he could see it from above. The six arms curved from a central sphere like a pinwheel, each bearing its own unique design.

"Wow," he breathed. They couldn't destroy it! It would be like defiling a museum.

"Isn't it pretty? Merl and Gordon and James will have such fun figuring out what it means."

"If it means anything." The swirls and lines moved in beautiful and complex patterns, like the Celtic scrollwork in the offices of DihydrogenMonoxide, Inc. back on Drake.

"We may never know exactly what they mean, but they mean something. We just have to have a common reference to work from. It's a rosary tattoo."

"Pardon?"

"On my arm. *The Rosary is the most beautiful and the most rich in graces of all prayers; it is the prayer that touches most the Heart of the Mother of God. Storehouse of blessings, most probable sign of eternal salvation.* The tattoo itself guides me in prayer."

"Oh, I didn't know."

"Of course not; you lacked a frame of reference, so you thought it was a decoration."

He switched to a private line. "So, Ann, is this important to Catholics — the Rosary?"

"*Reference and knowledge do not always impart understanding or appreciation.* But if you ask Andi, she'll teach you."

Then she was on the mission line. "Time to go back down and touch your ship."

She brought them to a spot between the first and sixth arms, where a group of miners from *Basilica*, plus Sister Rita, James, and Sean, waited with the equipment to set up a permanent airlock. Several U-shaped hoops had been anchored to the ground nearby, and she easily slipped her boot into one. Chris aimed for the nearest and missed. She tugged smoothly at the line and pulled him back, steadying him until he managed to get his toes secured.

They stood before the *Discovery* at a large, blank spot in the fabulous decorations.

"The airlock's going here," Frances said. "We just couldn't ruin all the design work."

"Thank you," he whispered, knowing it was silly, yet unable to resist the rush of joy and kinship he felt for the recovery crew at that moment. He pressed his gloved hand against the mysterious hull. It resisted like any other surface, yet tears misted his eyes.

"From now on, everything is different," he whispered.

Of course, the next few hours weren't quite the "different" he'd hoped for. While the miners and sisters installed the generator and airlock, Reg, Ian and Frances took readings of the ship. Meanwhile, Lenny and George examined the crash site to determine the best way to free the *Discovery*.

Chris and the other dataheads were put to work hauling cable, pre-staging equipment and all the little tasks that didn't require knowledge or skill. Despite the light duty, a few hours of hard work had Chris panting from the effort of keeping his body oriented to the Folly, and his eyes strained from seeing everything through the enhancements of his heads-up display. He felt a headache coming on and ordered his medpod to give him an analgesic.

"Sister Ann to Chris. How are you doing?"

He groaned inwardly. *She must be checking my vitals along with everything else she does.* "It's not as difficult as Suits 201, but it's harder, if that makes sense."

"*From the fruit of their lips, people are filled with good things, and the work of their hands brings them reward.* The airlock is up, and they're cutting the hull now. You should return to the Meeger and rest."

"No, I'm fine, really." Was Andi listening? He did not want to look like a weak dirtsider.

"Chris, that was an order. Please acknowledge."

He held his breath until he could reply without sounding surly. "Roger. Returning now."

"Take the others, Ian. Be their lifeguard, please."

"Roger that. Come on, guys. Time to get out of the pool!"

The other researchers didn't seem to mind having a break, so Chris held his tongue and made his way back to the MiGR, strapped himself to the rover, and tried to find a way to rest and stay upright.

Ian laughed at him. "Let go of the gravity paradigm. Pretend you're in a pool, and just let yourself float." He crossed his arms over his torso and let his body float until he was in a reclined position.

Chris followed suit, though he turned his body away from Fate. Even though his mind knew it was four days away from their maximum safety window, his gut kept telling him that any minute it would crash down upon them all. In the other direction, however, the Milky Way spread its starry arm, and he distracted himself with trying to determine which star would likely have held the planet from which the ship came.

He fell asleep listening to the chatter of the rockjacks.

Chris floated among the stars, free and calm as they swirled around him, calling his name and teasing him with their secrets. Then Sister Ann stepped out of a black hole with a frame in her hands. Laughing, she placed it over him, and the whole universe accelerated. The stars moved faster, some racing away, the rest coming together until they formed a pattern: ten Class Gs and one red dwarf, five groups in a chain held by a blue giant, a red dwarf, then three Class Gs and another red dwarf, then the Southern Cross. The chain encircled him and spun and Ann pointed to each in turn, chanting "Blessing, blessing, blessing..." Then Andi was calling his name...

"Andi to Chris. Come on, sleepyhead! Wake up."

"What?" He awoke with a start that sent him spinning. He grabbed the MiGR to halt himself. He noticed everyone else had gone, and Ian was waiting, already tied to the drag line.

"What happened?" he asked, still disoriented. Then he realized he'd been sleeping and moaned. Way to impress the girl of — literally — his dreams.

Andi, however, didn't sound the least perturbed. "Don't worry about it. Best thing you can do is nap when you can, but we're about ready to knock the hole in your ship, so if you want to go..."

"Yes! I mean, roger that. I'll be right there." He pulled himself along the rover to the drag line and carefully attached first one line, then the second. Only after he'd finished did he realize he hadn't tried to force his feet Follyward. Maybe the nap had helped.

"*We'll* be right there, Ian says," Ian cut in. "I traveled three-and-a-half billion miles to see this, too, you know."

Ian checked the lines and gave Chris a thumbs-up, and they headed to their next adventure.

* * *

Ann shivered with excitement as Andi again reviewed the mission for everyone. She could feel herself grinning as wide as during any rescue, but she thought Mother Superior would not disapprove this time. Besides, surely everyone felt the same thrill? Like falling off the high dive, only better! Maybe she would share that thought with Ian later.

The prep group consisted of teams of two, with the simple objectives of following halls, setting up lights, and checking for stress or any damages that might cause a problem with extraction. They had six portable fusion generators to provide electricity; one would be stationed by each arm.

Since Ann had the most experience with dangerous situations, she would go first, accompanied by Ian, who'd done best in suits training. Reg would join Dale in examining the first arm. The rest would start around the main sphere, hopefully circumnavigating the ship and reaching intersections to each arm. Of course, that assumed the interior had some kind of logic humans followed, an assumption they didn't want to make.

"Which is all the more reason I should go first," Ann had insisted in the planning meeting. She still didn't understand why everyone — even Rita — had chuckled at that.

It didn't matter; they had agreed, and her guardian angel would lead the way, whether they knew it or not.

Eight suited people crowded the airlock. The rolls of cables of lights and a small generator made it a tight fit, so Ann and Ian had the honor of shoving the cut-out panel. They attached two grips to the door, magnetized their boots to give them a stable base to push against, and leaned against the metal.

It barely resisted, but moved away from them and floated down and off in the direction they'd pushed. Ian caught the door by one of the grips, dragging it to a stop, then attached it to the floor with some stickie. Then he looked around the first room.

"Whoa." Ian's voice was hushed with awe. "*Edwina Taggert*, do you see this?"

"Thoren to Research. No. We're getting static. Can you describe?"

Bless Dr. Thoren! He sounds so disappointed and annoyed. "Sister Ann to *ET*. The Rescue Sisters' suits have stronger transmitters. Standby."

Ann squeezed past Ian and twisted to get a good view of the area above them. Ian's large spotlight illuminated a tangled mess of metal above them. Ann had never seen a real jungle, but, if someone were to create one out of rebar, cable and scaffolding, she imagined it might look something like this. The vibrations caused by their break-in had set the cables to swaying. She could almost imagine creatures roaming through it, swinging off the cables, clambering around the rods.

"What fun!" she exclaimed.

"Fun?" Ian interrupted his own, more mundane description to exclaim. "Are you sure that won't come crashing down on us?"

Addiman added his own doubts. "*Edwina Taggert* to Ann. We are seeing this clearly, but it does not look so safe."

"Chris to Ian. Come on. Let us see. Is it damaged?"

"I don't think so," Ann said. "Just not what we were expecting, but Ian is right. We should make sure it's stable. Hold positions, please." She pulled her grapple from her utility belt and made sure the wire was set to flow freely. Then she pushed off, using the slightest burst of her HMU to slow herself so that she stopped at one of the bars with a feather-light touch. She wrapped the grapple around the bar, then headed back to the airlock.

With boots again magnetized, she pulled on the cable gently, then with increasing force. Ian joined in, but the tangle held firm.

"I think it's supposed to be this way," Ann concluded. "I see what looks like a door, a hexagon-shaped iris. I'll fly across with a drag line and a prier. Ian, wait here until I give the clear."

"Thought we agreed on teams of two?"

"I'm lifeguard; I need to test the waters."

"Copy. Standing on the shore. Can I dip my toe in the water?"

Gordon cleared his throat loudly. "Would you stop bantering and get on with it? We have, what, four hours left?"

"Three hours, forty-five minutes until we have to return to the shuttles. *Have patience with all things. Never be in a hurry, but do everything quietly and in a calm spirit*," Ann replied. "I'm retrieving my grapple now. Thank you, Ian!" she said as he leaned out into the ship and used his piton gun to shoot a hook into the floor and attached a new drag line to it.

"Just putting my toe in," he quipped.

The prier, a spidery machine of pistons and magnetic feet, worked as well opening the alien door as it did human ones. They had already agreed to cut open most of the doors, but a few should be preserved so they could close for transport. This door was the only line of defense should the airlock fail.

Ann shot a piton into the wall on the other side of the door, then peeked around the doorway to see if the anchor went through. It did not, praise God. She stared down the hall with her naked eyes, but she only made out vague shadows and a sense of curves. She whispered a prayer of thanks to St. Clare, anyway, and switched first to infrared, then cycled up to ultraviolet, recording both directions of the hallway before pulling a double-light lamp from where it was attached to her belt and applying it above the door with stickie. Again, she saw nothing but curving hall, intersections and doors. "We're green! Come on over!"

Ian's shout of joy almost drowned out Chris'.

* * *

The first teams came in, everyone pulling themselves along the drag line because the boots did not adhere to the floor — or the ceiling; Ian tried. Reg and Dale set up the first generator, and Ann and Ian took one long string of lights down the hall in one direction, while Andi and Chris took the other. Soon the hallway was, if not bright, at least no longer a void of blackness.

"Okay, I thought it was crazy at the time, but making these light lines turned out to be a good idea," Ian admitted.

The second team arrived, James especially exclaiming over the unusual first room. "I have no idea what that could be," he said. "Is there a chance the ship landed upside-down?"

Reg grunted. "We won't know until we crack open some doors, I suspect."

"Even then, we might not know," Ann added. "What if their need for gravity differs from ours?"

"Remember our mission," Andi said. "This is survey and prep. That's it."

"What if we see an alien?" Gordon asked.

"Mark where it is; we'll bag it and bring it if we can?" James asked.

"As long as I don't have to touch it."

They split then: two teams to go clockwise, two counterclockwise. The coils of lights and the generators made things awkward, but at least the halls were wide and clear, if oddly shaped.

"Six sides again." James stated as much for recording as to voice his thoughts to the others. "Just like six arms. So maybe six is an important number?"

"Six is a great mathematical number," Reg cut in. "That's why our clock and compass are divided into multiples of six. But I can't say I'm happy about these doors. How weird to go crawling up and down at angles."

Gordon asked, "Does this mean they always operate without gravity? I mean, if you set an object on a slanted floor, it'll slide, right?"

"Or the gravity is toward the outside, like the old stations that used spin to generate force."

Reg answered. "If that were the case, it'd have to keep spinning even after landing. Otherwise, everything would fall once it stopped. Not the best use of power."

Andi made a verbal wince. "If so, nothing will be in its proper place. Even with the microgravity of the asteroid, things will have been pulled Follyward until they settled on a surface. Could be a mess."

James sighed. "Deal with that when it comes, I guess."

Ann's group reached the first arm quickly, a long corridor curving gently, again hexagonal in shape. Reg and Dale attached a piton to the floor and started a new drag line. Before heading off, James pulled out a thin sheet bearing the number one, tore off the cover to the adhesive backing, and stuck it to the wall beside the junction. Then they moved on, marking junctions in the pattern James had trained them in, recording (though there didn't seem to be much more than hall at the moment), and setting up pitons to take more drag lines and stringing lights between the generators.

"You've been awfully quiet," Ian said when James and Gordon split to go down the second wing.

"I'm listening," Ann replied. She hoped he didn't ask for elaboration, because she didn't want to lie, yet she didn't think he'd understand if she told him that she heard angels whispering and couldn't make out what they were saying. It was like that with angels sometimes; when they needed to be a heavenly choir, they could fill the skies, as with Jesus' birth. Other times, they appeared, sometimes in human form, as with Abraham, and sometimes in angelic form, as with Mary, but more often than not, they would speak just outside the range of human hearing.

It's not the ears, she thought. *It's the faith. Or is it? Guardian angel, I know you are ever with me, but why can't you speak up?*

She wanted to ask everyone to be quiet so she could listen, but she knew that would lead to questions she didn't know how to answer, not in a way they'd understand, anyway. *Hmm, maybe it is a lack of faith. Mea culpa. Jesus, I trust in thee.*

"This is Sister Ann. We've found another junction. Again, corridors leading up and down." She marked the upward-leading one, while Ian took the downward.

"This is Andi. We copy. We have one, too. Looks like they kept a nice symmetrical pattern. Want to bet there's a junction between the third and fourth arms?"

"Agreed. Can you mark it? There's something in the third arm I need to check."

Ian laughed. "And you know this, how? We're not even at the arm."

Mother Superior used to say, "Sometimes, a hunch is just your angel talking to you." "A hunch, Ian. Like knowing we'd need the extra lights."

"Copy."

"Andi to Ann. Anything we need to know?"

"When I know, I'll tell you, promise."

When they got to the third arm, Ann dolloped a blob of stickie on the floor and Ian placed the generator on it, then started setting it. Her angel spoke clearly: *Come hither. Come alone.*

"I'll get the lights and the drag line," she said. "When you finish, wait here. I shouldn't be long."

"Oh? What happened to going alone being a DST?" he demanded.

Ann laughed. "I'm never alone. I'll keep in constant contact."

Before he could protest further, she'd pushed herself off the opposite wall and soared into the hallway.

"This hall sounds like Arm Five," she reported as she twisted to shine her light in a full 360 degrees. "Very short compared to the others. I wonder if there's a large room filling the rest of the arm. No side doors, but colors on the walls. Ian, leave the lights off, please; I want to get some full spectrum readings."

"Roger. Awaiting your signal."

She turned off her helmet lamp and called up the heads-up display. Outside and in the halls, they had seen beautiful and intricate designs they didn't understand, but here, she knew. She could feel the reference as much as see it; even without the angels guiding her, she would have known. She started to open her mouth to call to James, to tell him to come and see, but she felt the feathery touch of angel wings on her lips, and she swallowed back her words.

"Ian to Ann, you promised chatter. Heck of a time for you to get shy."

Called back to herself, she pushed forward again. "I'm sorry, Ian. I'm fine, just...awed. It's definitely artwork. Approaching the door now."

An angel with a flaming sword stood before the door!

Ann gasped and drew back so sharply that she had to put out a hand to keep from traveling backward.

"Ann? What is it?"

The angel brought one finger to his lips, then faded.

"Ann? Come on; what's going on?" Andi added her own request on top of Ian's.

She managed to catch her breath enough to answer. "Stand by."

The door irised open.

Ann peered in. Upon the floor and all the flat surfaces lay the deceased inhabitants of *Discovery*, while the angel, now without his sword, spread his arms and rays of mercy shone from him.

"O Great Father! Wondrous God of Ages. Your mercy extends beyond worlds!"

And the angels were there, in many forms, like they had come to Ezekiel, and they sang of glory irised and warning.

"Ann? Are you all right?"

"Rita to Ann. Report, Sister!"

"I'm fine!" she snapped. Why couldn't they be quiet for just one minute so she could listen? It was too late. The angels had fled. But two things she knew: This was holy ground, dangerous to those who didn't understand, and...

"Tommie! Rita! They didn't die alone. They didn't die alone!"

* * *

"Wait a minute! You found the aliens?" Ian exclaimed.

Over the suit comms, Ann babbled nonsense about something being scary and wonderful, and fire and water, while Rita tried to get her to slow down. Obviously she'd spaced over something she saw.

"Ann, just go back to Ian and finish the prep. We'll come back to it later."

"No, Rita. No one can go in here. I need ten minutes to listen, to assess the danger. To be still. *Be still and know I am God.* Let me be still!" And then she started whispering about being sorry for her sins.

Yep. Spaced. Ian released himself from the safety line and pushed down the corridor. "Ian to Rita. I'm going to get her."

"This is Rita. Belay that. Stay where you are."

He bumped against the curving wall and used it to change his vector as Ann had taught them. He saw her folded into a kneeling position before the open door. "It's okay. I'm just going to make sure. Hey! That door's open."

Faster than he'd thought possible, Ann unfolded herself and shot straight at him. She slammed him into the wall, then pushed and maneuvered so they were both heading back to the main corridor. He just caught sight of the doors closing.

"Ian, you can't go in there! Not you, of all people."

"Were there aliens in there?"

"That's not the point! It's the high dive, and the water is more dangerous than you are able to swim!"

They came to the entrance, and, with the same decisive skill she'd used to drive him out of the wing, she now caught the edge of the junction and his suit and stopped them both. He got a good look in her faceplate and saw that her eyes were wide and rabbity with unshed tears. Over the comms, everyone was asking about the aliens. Rita called for them all to be quiet.

"Ann, would you please make sense?" he demanded.

"Listen to me, everyone," Ann said instead. "The third arm is off-limits to all personnel. No one enters the third arm until I can assess the threat."

"And only you can do that? Of all the ridiculous —"

"Belay that, Ian," Rita cut in. "Ann is safety officer on this mission. Her word stands, whether you understand or agree with it or not. We have an hour and fifty minutes until we have to pack up and head to the shuttles. Continue prepping the other levels. Acknowledge."

Ian looked past Ann down the corridor, then back to her face, challenge in his expression. But her eyes were closed and her lips moving — in prayer, no doubt. When she opened them, her face held its usual serenity.

"This is Ann. Roger. We'll set a drag line to meet Andi and Chris at the 3A junction, then take it up to the next level."

She let him go, but frowned. "You released your safety lines. Come on." She grabbed his trailing cords and re-hooked them to the drag lines along with her own.

Definitely a few chips short of a console, Ian thought as he trailed after her, craning his neck to look at the third arm, still dark from the unlit lights, until the curve of the ship obscured it from view. *And we trust our lives to her?*

Chapter Twenty

Rita looked around the conference table and couldn't shake the feeling that Thoren had assembled a tribunal rather than a debriefing. Even the seating reflected it. Thoren had chosen a spot in the middle of one side, with Chris and Ian flanking him. James and Andi took the heads of the table, while Tommie and Rita sat beside their sister. They had run through the verbal recordings of the incident and had just played back the visual — or what there was of it.

Ann didn't seem to understand she was in the hot seat, or if she did, she was too preoccupied with other things to notice. "I did not turn off my suit recorders," Ann repeated. Her eyes were bright, as if with tears, but Rita got the idea she wasn't flustered over the accusations so much as the thought that no one seemed to be listening to her. Even when she looked at Rita, her expression seemed to say, "Why are you all being so dense?" It didn't help that every time she tried to explain, Thoren would cut her off, or Ian would complain that she was speaking nonsense.

Andi held herself so tightly she was stuck in a half-standing position, and, even though she seemed as confused as everyone else, only a stern word from her godmother had kept her from standing and shouting in defense of her best friend.

Ian glowered; Chris looked torn and betrayed; James wore that pensive wrinkle between his brows that never signaled anything good. Even Tommie, who, of all people, understood Ann's unusual behaviors, seemed at a loss. She had set her jaw against the urge to yell, and Rita got the impression she hadn't decided who she wanted to yell at more.

Ann's tattoo was flashing through the Sorrowful Mysteries. Not a good sign.

And Thoren? Rita clasped her hands tightly to keep herself from slapping that smug look off his face. *Lord, protect us from stuperiorities!*

Rita forced herself to take a deep breath and keep calm and focused. For the first time, she wished she'd gotten tattooed; the small tingles of the beads working through the Divine Mercy Chaplet would have been comforting right then.

"And yet your suit camera shows nothing from the time you came within sight of the door to the time you threw yourself toward Ian," Thoren concluded. "Can you explain that?"

"No! Yes! I —"

"Will you stop accusing her?" Andi flared. "It's not like Ian's cams showed anything more." Ian's recording only showed the closing of the door, with a frustrating glimpse of a blurry room beyond that even Sean's computer enhancements couldn't clarify.

"Hey! Mine were just on visual spectrum. I wasn't expecting to get tackled by Sister Splat."

Andi snapped at him. "Give it a rest, Ian. Sister Rita told you to stay where you were, and, you not only disobeyed her, but released both your safety lines. For all you know, she saved your life."

"No," Ann muttered, not to contradict her friend so much as thinking aloud. "Not life. Saved? Maybe, but not physical danger. *To light and guard; to rule and guide.* Lifeguards guard life, but sometimes, it's not life that needs guarding..."

Thoren cleared his throat. Ian shifted in his chair and tried, for once, not to mutter "spaced" as he had several times already. Chris glanced from Andi to Thoren, then hunched like a turtle retreating into its shell.

Rita set her hand on Ann's arm. "Ann, just try. We're listening."

She shook her head, then looked Thoren straight in the face. "You won't believe me, Dr. Thoren, and, Chris, I don't think you would, either. Maybe later. Maybe after... but not now."

"After what?" Chris asked.

Again the change in moods, this time from conviction back to frustration. "I don't know! No one gave me the chance to find out! I just know that it's going to be wonderful and terrible and...and dangerous..." She shook her head, eyes focused away from them.

However, she'd said the one word to roust Tommie from her own anger. "Danger? What kind of danger?"

"I don't know. They didn't tell me — and it's not dangerous for everybody, just the ones who aren't ready. And for some people it's going to be so wonderful, but others on this ship can't go!"

"*Who* didn't tell you?" Thoren asked, and the "gotcha!" tone made Rita's hackles rise.

"Can't go? To the *Discovery*?" Chris exclaimed.

"To the third arm," she answered, encouragement and exasperation warring in her voice.

At last, James spoke. "You think anyone can go into *Discovery*, but some people need to avoid the third arm?"

"Yes!" She bounced in her chair.

Thoren pinched the bridge of his nose as if to stave off a headache, while James asked, "Why not?"

"Because! It's, it's the eye of the needle. You have to remove your shoes.

You have to know how to hide your face and bare your soul. Some will dance while others will be consumed." Her voice trailed off, and she shook her head. "Please, I know not everyone understands what that means. It's bigger than language, and too many in the crew lack the frame of reference for interpretation. That's why I have to go in first, so I can explain better. Being outside the room wasn't enough. Outside the box, we don't know the state of the cat. *There is a difference between a shaky or out-of-focus photograph and a snapshot of clouds and fog banks.* We can't know if there is life or death until I have looked in the box. I need to see what's in that room. Then I can know what we are dealing with."

"But your suit cams?" Chris started.

Ann shook her head. "Inadequate. It's just a camera — limited spectrum, clouded perceptions. Interference. *Wisdom enters through love, silence, and mortification.* I have to go to the third arm, alone and in quiet. A guide should know the territory. Lifeguards need to understand the waters."

Thoren's voice dripped with sarcasm. "And you're our guide?"

"I didn't ask to be!" Ann flared. "I never asked to be a shepherd. That's just how it is. Moses didn't ask to lead. Jonah ran away at first. But I don't run from my Lord, Dr. Thoren."

"Wait a minute," Chris cut in. "Are you saying *God* told you all this?"

Ann did a very uncharacteristic thing. She rolled her eyes at him.

Thoren's voice turned cold. "May I speak to you outside, James, Chris, Ian?"

As they left, Tommie and Andi exchanged determined looks and went after them.

I should go, Rita thought. *I'm the leader. But we can't leave Ann alone.*

When the door closed, Ann wrapped her arms around herself. She started to shiver.

Rita put her hands on Ann's shoulders. "Annie, calm down. It'll be all right." She wasn't sure she believed her own words. She had no idea what was going on, and she'd never seen Ann like this: reckless, overwrought...

Ann muttered, "Why couldn't I just talk to you and Tommie?"

"Ann." She waited until the younger sister focused. "It's just you and me. Tell me what you saw that makes you think that arm is so dangerous."

"I think it was Michael."

"Michael?"

Ann shrugged. "He held a flaming sword. Rita, I didn't touch the door. You don't presume upon the gates of Eden, and I know it's not Eden, but..."

Something clicked. "You mean the Archangel Michael?" She kept her voice level.

"Tradition isn't clear. There could be other angels. And it wasn't Eden, but it was fearfully and wonderfully made. I don't have to understand," Ann whispered to herself. "I just have to have faith that this will work out."

Still, when Thoren walked back in with the others in tow and flatly announced that Rita would accompany the research team while Ann remained on the *Edwina Taggert*, Ann burst into tears.

Chapter Twenty-One

Once again, Chris crowded into the airlock with seven other people. This time, they had a bit more moving room. Rather than huge coils of wire and electric cabling and generators, they only carried door openers: priers, small tanks of explosive stickie, and the firing mechanisms. George had trained them last week on using the cut-away compound, not that it was that hard to use: the putty applied like bathroom caulk and remained completely inert until a current was sent down its length. It also didn't explode so much as burn through whatever it came in contact with. Pretty idiot-proof, actually, yet several of them (Chris included) had tiptoed around as if expecting their tanks to explode with the slightest impact. In the end, George had actually pounded two tanks together to prove his point.

Some folks still tried to protect their tank, but Chris had too much else on his mind to worry about it.

Ann. Andi had been so flamed about Thoren taking Ann off site duty, and he was sure the other rockjacks felt the same way. Someone — Sister Rita or Sister Thomas, probably — must have warned them to keep their opinions to themselves, because all of them had done nothing more than give the research team the cold shoulder. They'd sent one representative to the prep meeting, Dale, who had kept abnormally silent.

Ann, however, had been her usual boisterous, chatty, difficult-to-understand self. When Thoren commented on how well she was taking her grounding, she'd replied, "Obedience is part of the life of a religious," with all the neutrality of describing a well-functioning machine. She'd even compromised so far as to agree to a team exploring the third arm, as long as it was Sister Rita and James.

"They have the proper frame of reference," was all she said, and glanced at Chris as if he should understand what she meant.

He didn't, but he was glad Sister Rita was going to be on the team. All the researchers felt more comfortable with her than Sister Ann. Ann had a scary brilliance he didn't think he could trust. Yet she seemed to trust his "brilliance" implicitly, and that scared him, too. Stable Sister Rita just made more sense.

"Remember," James told everyone before they opened the inner door, "this is a basic survey: mark rooms and turns, open doors and take readings. Record, catalog, and report."

"Stay with your buddy," Rita added. "Keep your lines connected to each other, as well as to the drag line. If you need to go farther than a safety line permits, start a new drag line. Report in before going to a side corridor. If you run into trouble of any kind, report in immediately. Even if you're doing the right thing, we need to know what's happening, got it?"

A litany of acknowledgments, and she directed Chris to open the airlock. Sean excused himself and rose to the ceiling to get a better angle as Chris pressed the door code, hooked himself to the drag line, and pulled himself across the first room.

Everyone had seen the footage of the metallic chaos that hung from the ceiling during the prep meeting, but it hadn't prepared them for the reality.

"I don't like it," Zabrina said. "What can do that kind of damage and not hurt the hull?"

"I was thinking about that," Ian said, as he floated across, on his back so he could look up. "It doesn't look like an explosion or anything. Sabotage, maybe?"

Rita, however, surprised them all. "I don't think there's anything wrong with it. Looks like one of Ann's challenge courts to me."

Once everyone had gathered in the hall, Reg and his partner broke off to further examine the first arm. The rest fanned out for their first objectives. James had chosen some doors leading to the interior, and each team would open one and see where it led.

As Chris and Kelley headed off to find their door, between the fifth and sixth arm, Kelley asked over a private line, "So, you didn't see any aliens?"

"No. I mean, other than the first room and the third arm, all we saw were halls and doors."

"Well, here's hoping we run into something more interesting. Because if that spacey sister forbids us from the only exciting thing on this ship because 'her God told her so,' I am going to mutiny, and I won't be the only one. You'd be with us, right?"

Chris sighed. Mutiny. Just what he needed.

* * *

Rita paused at the door and made adjustments to the prying equipment. Fortunately, several human designs also employed iris-style doors, so she was able to set the magnetic grips into place, activate the switch and program it to open to peephole size, just in case there was atmosphere in the room. When her instrument showed negative, she removed the prier. The door closed, and she took one of her large grips and placed its round, flat surface in the center of the iris. She described a five-foot circle with the cut-away, set the igniter, and pushed back.

The smoke from the burning chemicals and dissolving metals dissipated quickly in the vacuum.

She pulled on the grip, half expecting the individual pieces of the door to slip apart, but they held. She pushed instead, and the entire circle slid free.

James whistled. "Well done."

"I've had practice. Rita to *ET*. We've got our door open and are looking in."

James moved up but did not enter, instead using one hand to hold himself steady while he swept the area with his camera and described the scene. She couldn't help but admire the business-like tone in his voice, as if he'd routinely explored alien ships. Or was this part not so different from what he'd done in the past?

"Right," he answered over the mission line. "You splat players will love this. The room is a dodecahedron, I think. Poles or columns stretching from one side to another, meeting a sphere in the center. Along the sides... controls, equipment of some type. I think this might be Ian's bailiwick. Otherwise, it's empty. I don't see anything that looks like a life form. Just equipment."

"Anything on the ground?" Reg asked. "Something that might be an android of some kind?"

A pause. Rita noted him shaking his head before he caught himself. "No. No loose equipment at all."

"That's spooky," Zabrina said, her voice nearly a whine. Again moving to another line, Rita asked Ann to check Zabrina's status.

"Increased heart rate, and her breathing's a little shallow, but she's not near hyperventilating yet. Shall I ask Ian to flirt with her? That should distract her some," Ann replied.

Rita laughed. "Ann Marie! You are developing a devious mind."

"Copy, Rita," Ann replied blandly. "I'm learning."

So she was. Rita heard her ask Ian to turn on some charm and calm his teammate. Rita snorted. "Is that a good thing?"

"Oh, I hope so! King David suggested it," she added, making Rita glad they were on a private line.

"Zabrina's pulse is slowing. Everyone else looks fine. George reports that they're satisfied with the integrity of the first arm, as far as they can see, and are going to set melting charges on the ice below it." Ann then repeated the last over the mission line.

Chris and Kelley were reporting that they had ignited their own cut-away.

James laughed. "Hey! I think I see it. Looks like we found an important area, then! So, Rita, ladies first?"

"Chicken," she teased, but taking the end of the lines, she pushed off gently and made her way toward the central column. One line was a simple safety line; the other was the monstrosity of extension cords and duct tape Ann had had folks working on during the trip to the Folly. She reached the central column, pleased that she was slow enough to stop herself with the lightest touch. She sprayed some stickie and affixed the end of the safety line. She wondered briefly if they'd run out of the spray-on glue-goop and reminded everyone to use it judiciously.

"And don't confuse it with cut-away!" Reg just had to add.

One hand on the drag line, she called for James to give it a tug. He confirmed it secure and pulled himself in, rubber-necking so much he couldn't keep his vector. In the meantime, she started another drag line and met Chris and Kelley at their door, then did the same for Ian and Zabrina. The other teams had reported finding rooms of equipment and consoles, and, like here, no aliens or tools lying free.

James directed folks to set lights and each record a different area. She focused on her section, running her suit cameras through ranges from infrared to x-rays and relaying them to Ann. The combination of the familiar and the alien perplexed her. Buttons, dials, levers, even what she could imagine might be viewscreens, clustered together in differing combinations that suggested workstations of some sort. But for what? Each grouping, placed along the outer edge of the sphere, centered around a circular depression.

"Gravity didn't affect them, not like it does us. They could hang upside-down for hours. If they understood upside-down. So many colors," Ann said. "More than we can see."

"It's not a dodeck, either," Ian added. "Too many sides, and each has six sides itself."

"Hexagons again," Kelley said. "Do you think it's a sacred symbol for them?"

Ian snorted. "More likely it has some kind of practical use. I think we're on the bridge. Or maybe engineering."

"I think maybe they had six arms," Chris said, his voice sounding strangled over the suit comms.

James, sounding more like a professor than an explorer, said, "Okay. That's a plausible hypothesis. What gave you the idea?"

"Look."

Everyone followed Chris' flashlight beam to where it illuminated the transparent bubble above where the columns met.

Rita shrieked.

A large, crablike creature with six appendages was pressed against the bottom.

Everyone started talking at once — gasps and curses, hoots of awe and excitement — but it wasn't until Rita heard Ian shout, "Zabrina, no!" that she was jarred from her own surprise. She tore her gaze from the creature to see the young woman trying to disengage her second line while Ian held tight to her first one.

Letting out her own line, Rita pushed toward her, snagging her from behind. Again Zabrina screamed. It cut off mid-stream, and Rita knew Ann had cut her out of the general comms. A moment later, she heard Ann telling everyone to remain calm, that Zabrina was all right.

Rita switched to a private channel. "Zabrina. Zabrina, you have to calm down. It's okay, honey. It's dead. It can't hurt you."

"How do you know? How do you know? Anything could hurt us here!"

Rather than argue, Rita made shushing sounds and repeated her reassurances until the frightened girl stopped her struggling. Then she said, "It's all right. We've taken every precaution we can — and then some, right? It's been dead for probably hundreds of years. You'd said so yourself on movie nights, right? Trust me: you have more to fear from Ian."

At that, Zabrina laughed. "Him, I can handle. Oh, vac! I'm sorry. I just...I hate things like that, like crabs and spiders and, and that thing is so big!"

Rita pressed her helmet against Zabrina's so she could see her face. "I know the feeling. But I promise you: it's dead. It's just a shell."

"You're right. You're right. Oh, no! Did everyone hear me?"

Zabrina's back was to the group, and over her shoulder Rita could see everyone poised, waiting to rush in if necessary. Rita let go with one hand to give them a thumbs-up, and they relaxed.

Meanwhile, Ann cut in. "I cut you out of the general comms while you talked to Rita. You tell me when you're ready, and I'll reconnect you."

"I'm sorry. I'm just scared. I don't even know what I'm doing here." She sniffled.

Ann replied, "No one does! Isn't it exciting?"

Something in Ann's earnest tone made Rita want to laugh, and she saw Zabrina react the same. The girl blinked and looked up and away, torn between a smile and a frown. "Vac! I can't wipe my eyes," she said.

Rita squeezed her arms reassuringly. "They'll dry. Are you good? Can you continue?"

She took a deep breath, let it out slowly. It fogged her faceplate momentarily. "I'm fine. Ann? I'm ready to talk to the others."

"Copy. Go ahead."

"Guys? I'm sorry. I sort of freaked out there..." She looked on the verge of tears again until Ian cut in.

"Don't worry about it. But can we get a move on? Bet Reg needs to get back to the ship to change his diaper."

"I resemble that remark!"

Rita allowed herself to chuckle before taking on a stern tone. "All right, people. Back to work."

Kelley had launched herself at the sphere and was braced on one of the columns leading to it as she circled the alien. "James? I want to get it out of here."

"Let's not!" Zabrina cut in. "I mean, is the sphere whole? There might be atmosphere in there. I'd rather we save it until we get the ship back and have the right equipment."

"Sure you're not just scared?"

"Thoren to Research. We should assume that the ship will not make it intact."

"Andi to *ET*! Thoren, we can do *our* job."

James cut across the chatter before it could erupt into a fight. "We know it's here. We have two more days to explore. If we don't find another...specimen...by then, we can take this one on our last mission. Copy?"

"All right, that makes sense, but I'd like to stay here and study it some more."

James said. "That's fine. There's a lot in this room to record. Chris, why don't you do a top-to-bottom to complement the individual readings we got? Everyone else can move on to their second assignments."

"Thoren to Research. That sounds like a wise decision, James. You have a Go."

Oh, well, thank you. Rita looked at James and saw he was thinking the same thing. But he placidly acknowledged along with everyone else, and folks split again.

She suppressed a shiver. She and James were to check the third arm. With Ann's talk of removing shoes and hiding their faces, she couldn't help wondering if she'd find a burning bush.

What if she did? What if she saw the Archangel Michael?

Adam and Eve were thrown out of Eden. She didn't feel too sanguine about confronting an archangel with the one man she might be in love with at her side.

* * *

James and Rita entered the short hallway. As Rita floated past him, he paused to admire the ease with which she went about her business assembling the unit to tackle the next door. While she worked, he took recordings of the walls, thinking how much he'd love to share this with his sister, then stationed himself next to her. Over the comms, each team was reporting their progress. No one had found any other aliens yet, which wasn't surprising in the empty halls, but Ian and Zabrina's door opened into another spherical chamber, and, near as they could tell from the entrance, it was empty.

Rita had the prier secure but hadn't activated it yet. She was still, her lips moving, though he could not hear her. "James to Rita. What's up?"

She continued to speak silently a minute, then her voice sounded in his suit. "Talking to Ann. She's very nervous."

"Yeah, well, she's got me nervous, too. What did she mean yesterday that we should go because we've both been to Confession?"

"I wish I knew. I don't think she's worried we're going to die."

Thoren's call interrupted her. "*Edwina Taggert* to James and Rita. Have you entered the next room yet?"

"James to *ET*. Not yet. Rita's locking the prier in place right now."

"Please do not dally."

Dally? He bit his lip.

Rita, however, replied with deceptive cheeriness, "If a little dallying improves our safety, I'm all for it. Code Nine, William."

James chuckled. Rita had changed so much since Indy.

Ann's voice whispered over his intercom. "James, Rita, this is very important: *Stop entertaining those vain fears. Remember it is not feeling which constitutes guilt but the consent to such feelings. Only the free will is capable of good or evil. But when the will sighs under the trial of the tempter and does not will what is presented to it, there is not only no fault, but there is also virtue.* Before you enter, you need to say the Act of Contrition."

What? He understood why she seemed to be whispering. He could only imagine what Thoren would do if he heard her directive. "You know, Merl said a prayer for all of us before we entered."

"It's not the same, and you know it. You're not asking for a blessing. You can't remove your boots, and there's no water. The veil is torn; we're saved but not sinless, and it's on the DST list: *Ignoring the poison in our souls.* I wish I could explain better, James, I really do. Maybe we'll all understand once you're in the room, but please, do this?"

James turned to Rita, intending to ask with his expression if she understood Ann's odd request, but Rita floated, still, head bowed, eyes shut. Praying.

"Roger, Ann. Complying now."

"Thank you!"

He paused then, reciting the words, trying to mean them, his mind split between the prayer, the suit chatter of folks reporting what they'd found (empty halls, chamber of baffling equipment, still no aliens), and the nagging feeling that the little sister had gone nuts. And Rita. He'd thought after their argument and reconciliation that he'd come to accept her choice, but that day he'd seen her with the chocolate had brought his feelings back. How could one simple touch affect him so strongly? *God, show me what to do.* He finished as he saw Rita cross herself. The motion seemed so fluid and natural, despite the suit. He mimicked her.

Thoren called in, demanding an update.

"Hold your horses, William. We're looking in now." He waited for Rita to press the button to activate the prier. Again, she opened it enough to check for atmosphere, even though Ann had seen the door wide open earlier. Finding none, she let the prier continue its task. James leaned forward, sweeping the room with his light.

The first thing he noticed was the sheer size. "Rita, you've got to transmit this! I think this chamber goes down for the rest of the arm. There are doors along the walls, and more of those columns everywhere. I can make out shapes on the columns. Kelley, Zabrina, I think we can get you a specimen. Whoa!"

Littered across the floor were the large, spider/crab bodies lying in various poses. Hundreds, maybe as many as a thousand.

James' mouth worked, but nothing came out.

Rita cleared her throat with difficulty and said, "Rita to everyone, I think we found the crew."

Chapter Twenty-Two

The *Edwina Taggert* actually had two bridges. The small one, where the crew normally did all its work, was a sparse businesslike affair with seats and virtual consoles all facing the captain. The large bridge, done in a traditional cinema design, had the captain's seat in the middle with actual counter-type button-pushing consoles spread in a horseshoe pattern facing a huge main screen. Built specifically for tourists, the oversized bridge had a large observation theater in the back. Normally, the crew of the *Edwina Taggert* only used this bridge to roleplay adventures for the entertainment of its passengers, although, in an emergency, the prop consoles would lower, and working virtual consoles would replace them. On this mission, of course, they used it to accommodate all the people not busy with other duties who wanted to observe the exploration.

Everyone gaped at the images on the viewscreen. Rita had set up several lamps along the walls of the chamber, and the room was awash with color and design...and dead alien bodies.

"There must be hundreds of them," McVee's voice was hushed with awe. "Look how they're lying: some are upside-down, some on their side."

"How would you know it's upside-down?" Thoren asked.

"Well, one side's got to be the up side. The point is, why are they all helter-skelter that way?"

Ann replied, "They died in free-fall. Eventually, the microgravity of the Folly pulled them down to the floor in whatever position they died in. If we got the mass of one, we could find out how long the ship has been here. A minimum time, anyway."

"They look like those...things in that movie," Rose added from the nav console. "They're disgusting! Are we sure those are the aliens? I mean, the actual crew, and not their pets or food or whatever?"

"They're the people," Ann said. The lights played across the columns, reflecting in moving iridescent colors, like light through bubbles. She directed Rita on where to turn her head as her mind played over the patterns on the walls, overlaying them with the pattern she'd seen from the outside. They were the same, even to the location of the portholes. She reported this back to James and Rita.

Rita reached up and grabbed one of the columns, squeezing gently in case the material was brittle. Instead of it breaking, she pulled herself up slightly. "I think these may have been walkways for them; significantly fewer bodies lay directly under the pillars."

"Kelley to *ET*. I should be in there," Kelley complained.

Ann closed her eyes against the clutch in her stomach. *Angel of God...*

Thoren pulled himself away from the view. "*Edwina Taggert* to Team Two. Kelley, I want you and Chris in that third arm chamber." Then he turned toward Ann. "Provided that's all right by our safety coordinator? Rita, I take it you've found no otherworldly dangers."

Is it okay? Ann prayed. *I'm scared for them.*

Rita ignored Thoren's tone. "Everything seems safe. Ann, what if they came in and bagged one of the aliens and took some measurements? They can stay close to the door."

She felt reassurance, but not necessarily comfort. She could give them Padre Pio's words, but they wouldn't understand.

"Ann to Team Two. Go ahead, just as Rita said. Stay in the main chamber, near the door. Do not go into the side rooms, roger? And no one else."

James added his agreement. "Finish recording the central chamber first, though. Let's keep things methodical. That'll give us some time to check out a couple of these side chambers."

"We have thirty or forty doors. Some of them are open," Rita said. "Shall we mark them?"

"How about if we just record two for now. You take the high road, and I'll take the low."

Ann felt a stab of fear and took a breath to contradict James' order, but Thoren glared at her. Flanking him, King David gave her a nod that said, "patience," while Ezekiel rolled his eyes at the mission commander and sneered with impatience. Nonetheless, he, too, seemed content with the idea of James and Rita entering the side chambers.

Jesus, I trust in you. "*ET* to James and Rita. Proceed, but tread lightly."

"I'm ready to duck my face and prostrate, if necessary," Rita said, on a private line for her benefit. She hoped James was prepared, as well.

In the meantime, she prayed for some words to arm Kelley and Chris, just in case.

* * *

"Uh, copy," Chris told Ann, though he wasn't sure he really understood. *"Remember that you are fearfully and wonderfully made"? What did that mean?*

Kelley, too, seemed to have trouble understanding her 'advice.' "*We are only as alone as we choose to be?* What kind of leak is that?" she demanded over their private line. "And why are we recording this room?" Kelley demanded. "It's not like anything in here will get shuffled in transport."

Chris had to agree and thought that maybe James was stalling them, but all he said was, "We're being methodical."

"Methodical!" Kelley spat the word. "We're wasting valuable time."

"Thoren to Kelley." Thoren's voice came quietly over the intercom, and Chris noted it was not on the mission channel. "Discontinue your current task and proceed to the third arm."

"Roger that!" Kelley disengaged her safety line, pushed herself off the main column, and shot toward the exit nearest the third arm, dragging Chris by the line connecting them. Then they came to the piton and Chris' line caught, she unhooked his, too, and shot off.

"Kelley, slow down. We have to attach our safety lines!"

Kelley came to an intersection and pushed off to change direction, and only Ann's training kept Chris from floundering into the wall. He fervently hoped Ann or Rita was listening and would back him up, but he saw he was still on the private line with her and Thoren.

"Come on, Chris! We're inside a ship. What could happen?"

He didn't have a good answer for that, but at least she slowed down.

* * *

"*Edwina Taggert*, this is Rita. I'm entering a side chamber now."

The room was small and empty, save for some controls. Opposite the door, a small window gave a view of the black sky. She saw the subtle edges of a well-sealed enclosure. She turned back and pasted the lamp above the door she'd entered. Her can of stickie, near the last of its contents, gave a weak foam, but it was enough for her last lamp.

The light filled the small room and reflected off the glass, shattering into a rainbow, each color so vibrant they seemed to glow from within. Rita caught her breath. How long had it been since she'd seen a rainbow, a real rainbow? Since she'd left Earth behind. Left James behind.

As a child, she'd dreamed about dancing in the light of a rainbow. She remembered crying when her father had told her no one could catch one. "The best you can hope to do is dance in the rain with someone you love," he'd said.

But she'd seen Ann surrounded by a rainbow in the chapel.

Rita reached out, caressing one line of color, then another. She stepped forward and stood in the rainbow, surrounded by the light. Today, millions of miles from home, a rainbow had caught her.

* * *

At the entrance to the chamber, Kelley paused, grasping the edge, her breath loud in the mic. "It's amazing!"

Chris caught the edge, stopping himself with a jerk and looked across the long deck. Rather than awe, he felt vaguely nauseated.

Kelley said, "All my life, I've dreamed about aliens. I never thought I'd see anything beyond a microbe." Her hand moved up, as if to brush back her hair, and bumped the side of her helmet. She laughed.

Ann's voice came over the comms. "*Edwina Taggert* to Team Two. What's your status?"

Kelley twisted to face Chris and brought a single finger to her helmet.

Still looking at Kelley, Chris mouthed, "You sure?"

She rolled her eyes at him and pushed herself hard toward the ceiling, again forgetting the line that still connected her to Chris. He had only a second to shout, "Hey, wait!" before the line went taut and he got yanked with her.

He saw one of the pillars coming directly for him — or him to it — and put out his hands. The impact sent him off on a different direction, toward the wall, this time pulling Kelley with him.

"Chris!" Kelley shouted.

"Sorry!"

"Ann to Team Two. Are you all right?"

Kelley laughed, "Fine! We just — whoops! Look out!"

Two open hatches leading to side chambers gaped at them like open mouths. Chris flailed, trying to change his direction, but too late.

They each sailed into one.

Chris bumped his legs on the threshold, sending him into a forward spin, straight toward a pair of aliens locked in a six-legged embrace. He gave a shout and flung up his arms, just as the line connecting him to Kelley caught on the wall between them and halted his progress.

The world spun. He had a hard time catching his breath, and all he could think of was how inadequate he was to this task and how he'd let Kelley disobey safety rules, break the Code, and get them in trouble. Thoren would be leaked, and the Sisters, and Andi. If he didn't die right there like those horrifying aliens. Why, why, why didn't he do anything right?

Then Ann's words returned to him: *You are fearfully and wonderfully made.* And there were two kinds of fear: fright and awe. He wanted to look with awe. Why didn't he look with awe?

Fear, if necessary, but do not be afraid.

He forced his eyes open.

He was still floating prone, face toward the floor. Below him lay the aliens, curled around each other. Comfort or passion? He wondered if they even had such feelings. He looked up, saw a small window. He thought he saw a single star.

Suddenly, he felt Andi there beside him, her suited hand in his, their helmets touching so that they didn't need the radios to hear each other. Not that they needed to talk; it was enough to share that moment.

Distantly, he heard Dr. Thoren's voice, demanding he report. Demanding he perform. Demanding. Then dismissing his responses, "rewarding" his accomplishments with new demands. Suddenly, his approval meant so little compared to that star, the woman beside him, or the moment they shared.

Other potential moments flashed through his mind: on a station together, launching their own probes, studying the scans, laughing, gasping, embracing each other in joy at some new discovery. Embracing and discovering each other...

We are all fearfully and wonderfully made.

"*Edwina Taggert* to Chris, come in, please! This is Sister Ann, please respond."

Chris blinked and found himself in the small chamber on *Discovery*, a little window in front of him, a couple of dead aliens below. "Chris here. I'm fine. I'm okay." He wondered at how breathless he sounded.

Ann's voice rang with relief. "Thanks be to God. Chris, I can't reach Kelley. Where are you?"

"Kelley here!" the xenobiologist cut in. "Sorry! I was...disoriented for a moment."

Chris gave a very gentle push and floated out of the chamber toward her. "Are you okay? Ann, we're in the main chamber in the third arm." He gave Kelley a challenging look, and she nodded her assent.

"Right. I'm fine. A little shaken is all. I'm sorry. I guess I pushed off too hard, forgot we were still tied together. That was an amateurish thing to do. Guess I need Remedial Suits 201." She gave a great shiver, as if her suit had gone cold. He wasn't sure he liked it, but she waved him away, sending herself spinning in the process. He hooked his foot on the open door and grabbed her.

Where are Rita and James? Why hadn't they come to check on us?

"You were just excited, but go slower next time," Ann said. "Your heart rate is a little fast. Take some deep breaths."

"I'm good. Really. Shall we try for the ceiling again, together?"

Chris nodded before he realized she couldn't see it. "Gently and on three."

He reached out and took her hand, but he felt acutely aware that it wasn't the hand he wanted to hold. He was going to do something about that as soon as they returned to the *Edwina Taggert*.

* * *

Rita danced in a rainbow. The colors swirled with her, and they were more than colors. They were warmth and soothing music and love. She twirled and didn't ever want to leave.

Her upraised arm blocked the light. The rainbow disappeared, and she blinked, then laughed at herself.

"Rita?" Ann called.

"I'm fine, just a momentary flight of fancy. The light from the lamp reflected — or I guess I should say refracted — against the wall. It was just...very lovely in here for a moment. The lamp shifted slightly, though, so the effect is gone. I'm starting the measurements."

She thought she finished her work quickly, but when she exited, she found James floating outside her door, arms crossed over his chest, boots crossed at the ankles. He even leaned back slightly, though no wall supported him.

She couldn't help it; she laughed. "Was I so long you had time to loiter?"

"Not really." He unfolded himself, slowly so that he wouldn't set himself in motion. He had a self-satisfied grin on his face that compelled her to grin back. Maybe later, back on the *ET*, she'd ask him if he'd felt that same peace she had.

"What?" she asked, and didn't even mind that she was using that same question again.

He chewed on the inside of his cheek, biting back a secret wanting to be told. "You'll see. I think I've figured out what this place is."

"Ann to Research. Almost time, everyone. You have twenty minutes to complete whatever task you are on and return to the Meeger."

"Already?" Chris blurted out, and Rita felt the same way. Where had the time gone?

Others echoed his sentiment. Zabrina, however, sighed with relief. Rita thought she might talk to her about switching out with someone; she didn't think she'd mind. Kelley might want to stay on *ET*, as well, and study the alien.

"Copy *ET*. Chris, Kelley, got an alien?"

"We do indeed! Got some measurements, too, so if they did fall from the walkway, we can figure out an approximate age for their crash."

"Excellent. Reg, status on Arm One?"

"All green, so far. There aren't as many doors here. If I had to guess, this is the storage arm. We sealed a couple of microfractures. I want to check out the engineering room Ian thinks he found."

"Zabrina and Ian, sir, Zabrina and Ian," Ian corrected.

Merl spoke. "We also found what looks like living quarters, perhaps for their version of a quartermaster. While interesting, I think I'd be more use in the control room or engineering next time."

"What's the matter, Merl? Didn't find a copy of their Bible in the dresser drawer?" Ian asked.

For a miracle, Merl replied with equal teasing, "Should I find one and translate it, I'll get you one of the first copies, Ian."

James chuckled. "I think we'll be doing some reassignments, anyway. In the meantime, pack up and let's head out."

Chapter Twenty-Three

"Escape pods? Really, James?" Despite her best efforts, she could not hide her skepticism — or the fact that she was fighting back giggles.

James frowned at Rita. "Granted, this is a preliminary hypothesis."

Oh, James, why didn't you mention this to me on the trip back? I could have saved you some embarrassment. Instead, all he'd done was grin at her in a way that had made her uncomfortable. Now, she kicked herself for thinking it had been about her. He'd just been excited about his hypothesis. If he'd told her, she could have explained then why whatever those rooms had been, they could not have been for escape. Instead, he'd just given her smug, starry-eyed smiles.

He wasn't grinning now. "Let me just explain my reasoning."

He cast the rest of his dark look at Dr. Thoren. The euphoria of their successful first mission had worn off on the trip back, yet Thoren had insisted the research team debrief immediately; to lock the rockjacks out of it, Rita guessed. The result was a tired and punchy crew, some of whom had had perhaps four hours' straight sleep in the last twenty-four. Chris kept shifting in his seat, half paying attention, his eyes on the door; Kelley brooded more than usual. Ian was yawning, though that might have been an excuse to lay his head on Zabrina's shoulder. Tommie seemed fine, though she admitted to catnapping in *Basilica* while she waited. Ann seemed impatient, moody impatient, and Rita had never seen her like that.

Thoren spread his hands. "I hardly think there's a need. It seems a sound hypothesis worth investigating."

"No!" Ann started from her chair, but Rita took her arm and eased her back down.

"Dr. Thoren," Rita said, hoping to calm the rising emotions, "there's really no reason for that. I saw one of those rooms. I was in it. It's not designed for escape."

James turned toward her. His face was intent, but at least he didn't scowl. "Every one of those rooms is outward facing. There's no furniture, no discernable function."

"No communications equipment, no supplies."

"You're thinking like a human, Rita. How do we know? Maybe they grab the supplies from the bay en route to their assigned pods. "

Thoren started forward. "Another reason to investigate that area further."

Ann dropped her head into her hands — another uncharacteristic behavior. "*You foolish and senseless people, who have eyes but do not see.* It's not an escape room or a docking bay for escape pods. It can't be. Nobody escaped!"

Despite her scolding tone, her statement caused the room to explode into giggles.

"I considered that," James said over the chuckles. "I'm postulating that there was some kind of failure, and that the alien we found in the central sphere was trying to work an override."

Chris cleared his throat, and James fell silent. Thoren, however, turned toward his protégé with crossed arms. Under his expectant glare, Chris started to wither, but then, with a glance toward Ann, he pulled himself straight in his seat.

"I'm sorry, James, but I have to agree with Ann. There are too many aliens. Thirty pods that could fit perhaps six aliens, maybe ten in a crunch. But from the photos, the computer estimated over six hundred in that room."

James spread his hands, unconvinced. "That's assuming this is the only such chamber."

"If it weren't, why would they all be crowded in that one?"

Ann gave Chris a small proud smile. "If this was a chamber holding escape pods and if there were others, we should have found some clues. Like similar markings on one of the arms, but none of the other arms had the doors and swirls pattern like that."

Kelley jumped into the conversation. "It could be a survival-of-the-fittest thing. Only the strong get the escape pod. You can't assume they think like we do."

Ann turned in her seat to face her. "Yes! Exactly! So why assume they intended to escape?"

"Yeah." Ian half-yawned his agreement. "If they were supposed to be fighting for the right to survive, wouldn't you have seen signs of fighting? Were there, like, severed limbs or stuff?"

"We didn't look that closely," Kelley started, though with less assurance than earlier.

Chris spoke up. "There were a few that were, uh, stuck together." While some folks snickered, he held up his hands and clasped the palms together, fingers intertwined. "Like the ones I saw in the escape pod."

Rita's stomach turned over. *When had they done that? How did I not know?*

She again reached for Ann's arm, but the little sister had stood and was bearing down on Chris like the avenging angel she claimed guarded the chamber. "You went into a pod? Knowing it was a direct violation of orders?"

Chris shrugged, shoulders half-hunched, like a kid caught breaking a rule he didn't necessarily agree with.

Ann spun toward Kelley, but rather than yell, her voice filled with emotion.

"Are you all right?" Ann whispered.

Rita saw Kelley's eyes widen, and she ached with the other woman's sudden vulnerability. Then the moment passed, and Kelley tossed her head and blew out her lips, dismissing Ann's concern.

Thoren cleared his throat and strode to James' side. "For the moment, let us table such side issues and continue with the briefing, shall we?" He pinned Ann with his gaze.

She met it with narrowed eyes and squared shoulders. The tension in the room again rose.

Chris broke in. "Ann, we didn't mean to do it. Kelley moved too fast, and I didn't have my vector, then I hit a pole, and we ricocheted. It was careless, and I'm sorry. If you want to ground me, I understand, but I promise I'm not going to let myself or someone I'm with get careless again."

Ann turned her back on Thoren and crossed her arms at Chris. "How are you made?"

Around him, people shifted in confusion, but Chris seemed to understand the question. He gave her one of the most confident smiles Rita had ever seen him wear. "Fearfully and wonderfully."

Apparently that was the right answer, for Ann's scowl transformed into a brilliant smile.

In the third row, Kelley made a disparaging sound. "I don't need your forgiveness — or your permission. I'm going to be studying that alien, anyway."

Ann sighed, but nodded. "It's not my forgiveness that can heal you, Kelley."

She sat herself back beside Rita and faced Thoren and James with all the primness of a Catholic schoolgirl and all the authority of a Mother Superior.

"But you, James Malloy Smith. What staff is in your eye? You, of all people, had the necessary references, but you refuse to apply them. They didn't go there to escape. They gathered there to die."

* * *

How had this briefing gotten away from me? James wondered. His idea had seemed so brilliant, so logical, but, caught under Ann's expectant stare, he felt his doubts rising. He was an archaeologist, after all. And a greenfoot. It's not like anyone on Earth needed an escape pod. Aside from a safety briefing on the way to the moon and the training on the *Edwina Taggert*, the closest he'd ever come to escape pods were the lifeboats on *ColeMiner*. Was he trying too hard to think high-tech? Was that the staff in his eye?

I should have thought this through, instead of thinking about...whatever was in the pod. The vision he'd experienced had been so real. He just wanted to go to his quarters, shut his eyes and relive the best parts of it, and maybe figure out the rest. Why did Thoren have to call for an immediate debriefing?

Beside him, Thoren glowered, and James put aside his woolgathering. He had to regain control of the discussion at hand. Besides, he felt pretty confident where Ann was going with this. "You think it's their chapel?"

"Too far from home. No way to get help in time. Where would you want to spend your last minutes of life?"

A few folks looked away, caught in their own thoughts.

Kelley shifted in her seat and half-raised her hand. "Well, I wasn't going to say anything, but I did get this real feeling of spirituality while I was there, especially in the 'pod,' if that's what we're going to keep calling them. It was almost tangible. I've never felt like that outside of nature. It was like —"

Merl cut off her statement with a loud harrumph, and she fell silent.

Ann turned and reached across the second row to touch her arm. "God's everywhere. Otherwise we couldn't be."

Nonetheless, Kelley gave Merl a dark look and excused herself.

"Great job, Merl," Ian snarled as the door closed behind her.

"Spirituality! What would she know of the True Spirit? Tell me: were there any crosses, any sign that they knew the Risen Christ?"

"Oh, let's not get into that right now, shall we?" Ian groaned. It ended in a yawn.

Ann was still half-turned in her seat, assessing Merl with a frown. "Your shoulders are too narrow, Merl," she said. "The sheep slip off."

Merl stopped cold in his rant. "What?"

Ann just shut her eyes and shook her head. "Luke understood." Then she turned around, and, as if nothing had happened, said, "James, I will find you a real escape pod. Then we can discard this silly theory."

"And how do you intend to do that? From here on the *Edwina Taggert*?" Thoren laughed, a snide sound that made James' hackles rise.

Nonetheless, Ann tilted her head and pursed her lips, as if she didn't understand why he would ask such a question. "Faith, hope, and love - and epiphany."

"Of course," Thoren snorted.

"Of course. Why do epiphanies scare you so? Is it because you can't control them?"

"What?"

Rita slapped her knees and stood. "Dr. Thoren, with all due respect, this has been a long debrief after a very long mission. People are tired, nerves are frayed, and no one is operating at full intellectual capacity."

"You can say that again!" Reg called out, pointing at Ian, who had succeeded in resting against Zabrina, though he hardly enjoyed it in his unconscious state.

Rita raised her brows at Thoren in a see-what-I-mean? gesture. For some reason, James felt his heart skip. He'd been so annoyed at her earlier; his nerves had frazzled, as well.

"Maybe we could put this off until after everyone's had a meal and a nap?" he suggested.

"And the *Rockhopper* is docking soon!" Chris blushed when amused glances turned to him. "I just think we should welcome them back. Tensions were kind of thick this morning."

"That's a wonderful idea!" Ann bounded out of her seat and reached for Chris' hand as she had at the party.

"Sir?" Chris asked, though he stood up and took her hand.

Thoren chewed on his lip. James wondered if he'd realized he would lose this fight, but the senior researcher nodded magnanimously. "We shall reconvene in eight hours in order to cover any other issues, like Sister Rita's rainbows."

"That?" Rita laughed. "It was just an optical illusion, I'm sure."

"Except that there was no indication of rainbows or any other refractive activity on your recordings, but there was about five minutes of nothing."

Rita froze. "What? That's not possible."

She turned to Ann, who nodded in unconcerned confirmation.

Thoren's mouth twisted into a half-grin, which he shared with James. "Yes, the both of you were incommunicado — as were Chris and Kelley — for the majority of the time you were in the pods."

* * *

Chris lay on the examination table with a large dome over his head, while, at the control panel, Dr. OvLandra took readings while relaying a litany of questions and instructions to him over a small mic: "Think about how coffee tastes. When was the last time you stubbed your toe? Remember your first kiss."

On the beds opposite him, the other three who had been in the pods, plus Ann, sat and waited.

Kelley fidgeted and hugged herself. "We could have brain damage, and no one thought to mention that until the *end* of that stupid meeting?"

Rita agreed completely. The thought that what had been only a few seconds of whimsy to her had been five minutes thirty-two seconds on tape — a tape that showed no rainbows, nothing outside a simple empty room with some floor cushions and a small window, in fact — had her wanting to shiver as much as their xenobiologist. For Kelley's sake, however, she kept a calm demeanor. She set her hand on Kelley's knee. "I'm sure we're fine."

"No, you're not. How could you know?"

OvLandra hefted Marley, Captain Addiman's large and lazy tomcat, off his perch and set him under Chris' hand. Rita grinned. She'd direct him to stroke Marley's silky fur while playing a recording of his purr.

James caught her gaze and leaned toward her. "Second best part of the test," he murmured.

Something in his tone made her skin prickle. Was he flirting with her? Ridiculous. She must be tired. She leaned away, nonetheless.

"You don't have brain damage." Ann spoke with surety rather than reassurance. "At least not from alien technology. That's why I wasn't concerned."

"How would you know? *God* tell you?"

"The only damage was what you took in with you."

"Ann," Rita tried to keep the impatience from her voice. "We don't remember five minutes of our lives."

"Seventeen-twenty to seventeen-twenty-five yesterday," Ann challenged. "What were you doing?"

"What?"

"Five minutes of your lives. What were you doing from 5:20 to 5:25 p.m. yesterday?"

"I don't remember exactly," James replied while Kelley scoffed. "But I was working in my lab. I remember that much."

"And you remember being in the pod. And you remember what you were thinking and feeling in the pod, too, whether you want to share it or not."

James ducked his head.

"Praying," Rita said into the silence. "You and Tommie and I were in the chapel, and I was praying."

"No, you weren't," Ann said. "We were supposed to be praying, but you weren't. You —" Then she stopped, as if saying more would break a confidence.

It would have, too. Rita didn't know the exact time, but she did remember for a while she'd just felt overwhelmed by the change in plans and being responsible for the crew on the alien ship and Ann's crazy warnings... Even about working so closely with James, alone. She'd been remembering how calm and stable her life on Earth was, and wondering how she'd gotten herself mixed up in such insanity. No, she hadn't been praying. She'd been crying.

At the exam table, Dr. OvLandra asked Chris if he'd ever seen rain.

"Rita?" Again, James leaned toward her, but this time with concern.

Ann hopped off the examination table and went to take her hands. *"When things fall apart, faith tells us to look to the broken pieces. Out of them a new whole may emerge."*

"I'm fine," she reassured them both, though she could not meet their eyes. "You're right; I wasn't completely aware of myself or my surroundings, but I wasn't on a mission."

"Yes, you were. A personal one — and that's the point."

Before she could elaborate, however, Kelley demanded to know how Ann knew what Rita was doing between 5:20 and 5:25. Meanwhile, Dr. OvLandra had removed the scanner from over Chris' head and told him he could join the others.

"I was watching her. God told me to. The difference between a fuzzy picture and one of clouds and fog. Observation imparts information, collapses the system. The only reason you are worried is because we recorded the time. Our observation collapsed that system. But we were outside the box, collapsing a different system, and it's not the one you need to worry about."

Kelley groaned and lay back on the bed. "I am too tired to translate Annese! Can I please just go to my room and take a nap?"

OvLandra looked up from studying their results. "I see nothing untoward in your scans, Kelley Riggens. You may leave, but if you feel anything out of the ordinary, please return."

"Oh, trust me. Everything I'm feeling is very ordinary." She jumped off the bed and made a beeline for the door, bumping into Andi.

"Kelley! You okay?" Andi asked.

Kelley tossed up one hand in a brusque affirmative as she stormed out, shoving past the other rockjacks and researchers that crowded the doorway.

Andi didn't even bother to shrug at her roommate's curt behavior, but ran to Chris. The others followed, a half-dozen or more, rockjacks still in their suits. "What happened? They said you were getting brain scans!"

Chris didn't let her finish her sentence, but didn't bother to reassure her, either. Instead, he took her face in his hands and kissed her. After a startled moment, she wrapped her hands around his waist and kissed him back.

While most folks gaped, George howled his approval, and soon others joined in. Rather than shrinking away in embarrassment, however, Chris just pulled her in closer. The neck ring of her spacesuit made it a little awkward, but that didn't stop him, either. When he pulled away, both were a little breathless.

"We need to talk," he said, ignoring or oblivious to the sarcastic comments of their audience.

"Ya think?" Andi replied, but she let him take her by the hand and lead her away.

At the door, he stopped, looked at their interwoven fingers and turned back to the group.

"The aliens I saw in the pod? It wasn't an attack. It was an embrace."

Then they were gone.

"What got into him?" Rita asked.

"An epiphany," Ann replied.

* * *

James smiled. About time that boy got some confidence.

What would have happened if he'd been more confident in his own feelings three years ago? His own vision returned to him: he and Rita, dancing in the rain. He'd held her, not in the intimate embrace Chris had had on Andi, of course, but a loose hold as they moved through the fast steps of a country techno-swing, out on the lawn, the grass soft and wet on their bare feet. He'd told her how incredible she was, and she'd blown him off with a laugh, but he insisted it was true. She was amazing.

He could have held her like that, all those years ago at TerraTech. If he'd just told her. Instead, he'd let her go, not intentionally, but by leaving her with half-dropped hints and unspoken convictions, and never taking the chance to find out how she'd felt. Now, they sat, side-by-side, yet on opposite sides of a vow, and he felt such a loss.

Rita caught him staring. She furrowed her brows at him in question. To cover, he jerked his head toward the Sickbay door. She acknowledged his unspoken statement with a wry grin. It made him want to cling to that vision and make it real.

Ann, however, regarded him with a disappointment he didn't understand.

* * *

No sooner had Chris and Andi started down the hall to her quarters than Chris' wristcomp sounded. "Mr. Davidson, if you are done in Sickbay, I'd like to discuss some mission assignments for the next run."

Andi scowled, and he felt her tense; anticipating, no doubt, that he'd drop everything to go running to tend his mentor's bidding. That was another thing he needed to change. "Sir? I'm occupied at the moment, but can we meet in the cafeteria in half an hour and talk over lunch? Eight hours of suit snacks didn't really cut it."

In the silence, he smiled at Andi over his wristcomp. Her own grin grew in mischief the longer Thoren paused.

Chris was about to hang up and damn the consequences when Thoren said, "Of course. We need to keep our strength up for the next mission. I'll meet you in half an hour."

"That should be enough time, right?" he asked as he logged off. "I mean, you need to get food and sleep even more than I do, and we have this whole mission to talk."

"Talk about what?" Andi demanded, though the tone in her voice said she knew. She was sharp, maybe even brilliant. He didn't know for certain, and he kicked himself for having wasted three months not finding out.

"Do you want to change first?"

"I think I want to know first."

They had started down the Starlight and Saturn hall, and Chris stopped at one of the empty cabins, the door of which had been jury- rigged in the scavenger hunt to earn extra DST points. He pulled her in.

In the dim light, she wrapped her arms around him to kiss him, and he let her, once; but he knew he had to say what he needed to say, now, before the vision faded and he lost his nerve.

He kept his eyes on their hands. Somehow, it was easier that way. "Andi. You're the most incredi—"

That was lame. Inadequate. He tried again. "I thought, the Folly, the ship... They'd be the most awe-inspiring, life-changing things I'd ever encounter. But then I met you. I know I've not shown it well, but talking with you, learning from you — being with you — I found something I didn't even know I was looking for. And it's not even just you. Finding you, I've found myself."

Conviction gave him courage, and as he lifted his gaze, the words of his heart tumbled out. "Andi, I love you. And I want to be the kind of man who can stand up for you and stand up for myself. I'm not very good at that; I'll need some help, but I want to do it. When this mission is over, I want us to find a way to be together. I mean, if you feel the same?"

"It's about time!" she said and kissed him.

* * *

OvLandra asked to see James for a few minutes, but ordered everyone else out of her Sickbay. "You should all get food and rest. You do not wish to be fatigued on your second or third missions.

"You, as well, Small Weight," she told Ann, and Ann felt a rush of love for her friend.

Once in the corridor, Ann's thoughts turned to Kelley, and she asked the Bridge to check her location.

Rita overheard. "Do you want to go check on her?"

Ann shook her head. "She's probably sleeping. It's all right."

"All right?" Cay repeated, his voice rising with hysteria. "How can you think any part of this is 'all right'? Something in that ship is active enough to make humans hallucinate; it's swarming with aliens —"

"Dead aliens," the rockjacks chorused. From their droning tone, they must have already heard this before.

"Remember what James said about hermit crabs? How can we be sure? And we invited one aboard."

"It's secure in Kelley and Zabrina's lab," Ann reassured, but Cay just threw his hands in the air, declared them all "spaced" and stormed down the next corridor they came to. Aside from some sighs, the group fell silent in his wake.

Sean broke the silence. "Ann, why does Dr. OvLandra call you 'Small Weight'? Did you know that's usually reserved for family and friends, you know, other zerogs?"

"She did say once that I've picked up the customs of her people quickly," Ann offered, but she remembered that Ov had called her that before she'd visited her in her quarters. Her guardian angel urged her to listen and be watchful, but she wasn't sure why.

"You can't be the only person who's adopted her customs around her. I've talked to the crew. She's taken an unusual interest in you. I don't know. It's just odd."

Almost as one, the rockjacks around them stopped and turned their attention to Sean. "You think this is a problem?" Lenny asked.

Sean blushed, but replied, "I just think you need to be careful, Ann."

Since her guardian angel had advised the same thing, Ann took Sean's hand and promised she would.

In their room, Tommie had left a loaf of bread, a soup tureen, and a large carafe of tea on the living room table before going to sleep.

Rita gave a happy moan. "Bless that Tommie. I so did not want to have to walk to the cafeteria." She flopped onto the couch and hit the warming buttons on the trays. Then she put her feet up on the couch and sighed.

Ann took the duty of serving them both. Rita had gone through a complete decontamination, along with the other three who had been in the temple arm. She was definitely cleaner than if she'd had a bath and wore a fresh skinsuit and habit. Ann was glad; she thought Rita would fall asleep in the tub, and that was the wrong kind of water for immersion.

"I never should have suggested Chris and Kelley bag the alien," Rita said after she'd had some bread and cup of tea. "I'm sorry, Ann. You should have been there today, not me. You understand this better than I do."

Ann ladled the thick stew into a bowl and passed it to her. "*Man proposes; God disposes.* I'm not sure I was supposed to be there. Even if things have gone wrong, we just have to look at the pieces with faith and find the better whole. Rita, you were so blessed! You found rainbows. Chris found his heart. But Kelley and James..." She shook her head. "James doesn't understand. Why doesn't he understand? He was a priest."

"Seminarian, Ann. He wasn't ordained. Maybe that's it?"

"He should still understand the frame of reference. He's being willful. Kelley is scared. And sad. It's good she's not going back tomorrow; she'll be closer to the fold. Fold, is that the word? Lost sheep sometimes need time to know they are lost. That's what Merl doesn't understand. Merl!" Her eyes went wide. "Merl can't go into the pods, Rita. His shoulders are too narrow, and he confuses sheep and wolves, and he refuses to see rainbows, because he only wants to see empty crosses."

"Ann!" Rita snapped. "Slow down. You're not making sense."

"I'm sorry. Too many parables," she lamented. "The Pharisees didn't understand. Even the disciples didn't always understand. How can I explain? I've never even seen a herd of sheep! Please, please listen, even if you don't understand."

Rita set her bowl down and pulled Ann close, resting her head on her shoulder. "It's all right," she murmured. "I think after today, even Thoren has to agree that the third arm is off limits. Shhh, Annie. It'll be all right."

Ann rocked slightly, murmuring, "A priest. I wish we had a real priest. James didn't see rainbows, and he doesn't see a temple. Oh, Rita, you're so lucky."

* * *

Rita didn't feel lucky, just worried.

That night, she dreamed of Merl pulling the wool off sheep and screaming about the fur underneath, while Ann talked to David about the challenges of shepherding.

And she dreamed of rainbows only she could see.

Chapter Twenty-Four

For all her nightmares of earlier, the next shift on *Discovery* seemed to be going according to routine. Rita applied the cut-away compound in a smooth circle on the door of their next room. She had the toe of one boot anchored in the suction handle outside it; another handle was attached to the center. Over the headset, she heard the chatter of the teams as they went about their own assignments. Ian and Reg were in the engineering arm, hoping to find the engines themselves, but so far reporting control room after control room. Chris and Sean had just finished exploring a supply room and were working on their second door. Thoren had cut a deal to get on the exploration team and was working with Merl in the control room to try to match some of the symbols and perhaps get some idea of what the instruments were for. In Engineering, Gordon and his teammate were doing the same. She and James had decided to start along the second level of the central sphere. So far, they'd found what looked like a meeting room and a broom closet.

We got the exciting section, Rita thought.

James watched her from where he floated, anchored by one of the many handholds in the hall. "You're really good at that," he said over their private line.

"Lots of practice. It helps that I'm not worrying about the injured people on the other side."

A small snort, then silence. She imagined him shaking his head, but couldn't turn to look. "What?"

"You. In space. Saving lives, working with explosives."

"It's not an explosive, really. More like an acidic compound. See? There are two stripes separated by a chemical barrier. I actually 'ignite' it by dissolving the barrier."

"Do you hear yourself?"

Is that disbelief or admiration? Actually, I don't want to know. "James, thanks for agreeing to make the pods off limits for now."

"It's not a problem. Like I said, a find like this will take decades — lifetimes! — of study with teams of experts. We're here to survey."

"Ah, yes. To seek and record the broom closets." The circle complete, she put the application gun away and pulled out a second tube with a needle. She programmed the activator voltage into its controls, then pressed the needle into the compound. She reported the action to Ann on the *ET*.

"You can learn a lot from a broom closet. Seriously, I'm having the time of my life. Do you know what kind of archaeology I usually work? Sift through buckets of dirt looking for evidence of anything that might stop some building from being constructed. The only time I've gotten to explore an intact site — well, relatively intact — was when Cole took me to Egypt as his pet archaeologist. And, I suppose, when he had me searching a sunken ship for evidence of his great-grandparents."

The current raced along the barrier, creating a spitting, smoking trail as the two chemicals interacted. Slowly, the compound ate into the door, leaving a darkened circle.

James continued. "Never mind that this is an alien race. Do you have any idea how thrilling just finding an intact site is? We're seeing it just as they left it who-knows-how-long ago? Broom closets or not, I'm excited to see what's behind each door, and to see it first with my own eyes."

"Well, here's your next chance. *Edwina Taggert*, this is Rita. We're about to open our door."

"Copy, Rita. Be very careful. It's not a closet this time."

Rita didn't bother to ask how Ann knew that; she'd just say "hunch," anyway, in deference to Thoren listening to the mission channel. Ann did, however, whisper a Hail Mary. Rita knew she did that for every open door, a small ritual of the Rescue Sisters to pray for the souls in need behind it, but now she prayed for the explorers instead.

"Sean to everybody! Guess what! I think we just found the medical bay!"

"Still feeling excited about that broom closet?" she asked James with a tease in her voice.

"Oh, just open the door!"

The circle had stopped smoking. Bracing both feet against the wall, she took hold of the handle on the freed disk. She tugged, and the door moved, but it seemed to take longer than the others. "Rita to *ET*. I think you're right, Ann. The door seems thicker than the others."

"Copy, Rita."

"See? Maybe not a broom closet this time," James said.

"Thoren to James. Should we join you?"

Rita paused in her work to let James get a good look at her face — or rather, the annoyed grimace on her face. His expression said he shared her feelings, but he replied jovially enough, "We're fine right now, William. Keep working with Merl. Can you imagine the coup if we could identify some of these systems and maybe get a hint at their language?"

"Copy. We'll continue here, then. Thoren out."

James acknowledged his reply, then switched to their private line.

"Dodged that bullet. I still don't see how Tommie could have agreed to pass him on his suit test."

"He got an 89. Besides, it was the price we're paying for his agreeing to make the third arm off limits. Even Ann agreed that was more important. Plus, Tommie wants us to take your advice. We're giving him rope, and I think she's hoping he'll hang himself."

"There's an attitude for a sister!" James laughed.

"Don't forget, she's a hardened veteran of the Ring Wars. If she taught school, she'd probably have a ruler."

"Yeah, well, I'm pretty certain that Cole's hoping he'll slip up enough on this mission that he can get him taken off directing the long-term research."

Rita grunted. In deference to Ann's "hunch," she was trying to pull the door out instead of push it in, in case there was something important near the doorway, but it wasn't cooperating as easily. She directed James to get another handle, and they tried again together.

"And if he succeeds? Would you take the spot if he offered it?" Rita asked. The door was moving more easily now that they worked together, but it still resisted. They went slowly, anyway, to keep the pull smooth and even.

"I...don't know. It depends on a lot of things."

"Like your mother?"

"That's one. Her Alzheimer's is moving fast, even with treatments. She waited too long to get diagnosed."

"James, I am so sorry."

"Well, that's the second thing. Dr. OvLandra found something in the scans yesterday. Looks like I'll need to get treatments myself when we return."

"What?" In her shock, she let go of the door and spun. He grabbed her shoulder and stopped her.

"Easy! She said it's so early, it'd have been years before anyone would have noticed, but as it is, now, it's 99 percent curable. That brain scan might just have saved my mind. Going into that pod's probably the best thing that could have happened to me."

"Are you sure?" Rita asked. Why was this so important to her? Why did her heart ache so?

Maybe he saw it. "I'm sure." His voice was low but warm.

She turned her gaze back to the door before the moment could get more intimate. "All right, then. Let's see what other surprises this ship holds."

* * *

From the central area of the *Discovery*, Thoren listened as the exploration teams bantered back and forth about their finds. Satisfied everyone was occupied with their jobs, Thoren switched to the private channel he shared with his shift partner, Merl.

"I think they're all sufficiently occupied."

"Agreed." Merl had suggested to Gordon that he find some symbols in engineering to match the ones on his console and sent the visual. "That should take a while. Shall we?"

Thoren watched Merl pull himself back to the main line, then switch his safety line to the one leading into the third arm. He smiled to himself. Yes, he'd chosen wisely. He and Merl didn't see eye-to-eye on a number of issues, but the man did understand authority, and Thoren understood how to speak to his fears. They already shared a certain contempt for the three sisters who seemed to think the authority of their Church applied to everyone. When he'd seen Merl storming back to his quarters, muttering under his breath about rainbows and false miracles, he'd invited him to his office and let him rant as he made a few careful suggestions. A mere fifteen minutes later, they not only had a plan to his liking, but Merl believed it was his own idea.

The sisters may think they're in charge, but no one tells me where to go on my ship. Bad enough they denied me the chance to make that historic first step. Which reminds me... As he and Merl floated over the throng of dead aliens on their way to Rita's mysterious pod, he made a mental note to talk to Kelley Riggens again about the creatures. His aberrant protégé may have named the ship without his approval, but he'd already succeeded in making an agreement with the xenobiologist that one of the life forms they found would bear his name. *Of course, we were expecting microbes. A full life form like this. Perhaps the Thoren-Riggens life forms...*

"There it is!" Merl's voice broke through his musings. He reached out and touched off a long walkway pole to change his direction. Thoren moved to mimic his gesture, but pushed too hard and ended up sending himself spinning instead. Despite himself, he gasped and flailed.

Merl, however, anchored himself on a toehold and pulled him in. "Easy, doctor. Are you all right?"

Red-faced, he nodded as he grasped the handhold near the open door of the pod. He cleared his throat, strove for a self-depreciating tone. "Fine, thank you, just overestimated the force. I didn't have quite as much time to practice as others."

"You're a busy man. I've found that the more I let go and let the Holy Spirit guide me, the easier it is."

Glad he was still facing away, Thoren replied neutrally. "I'll keep that in mind. Perhaps you should continue your task?" Even though they were on a private channel, they avoided speaking of their current mission directly.

"This shouldn't take more than a minute."

"Excellent."

Merl entered the pod.

One minute stretched to five. The *Edwina Taggert* called the three-hour mark.

What was taking Merl so long? Or was he so inaccurate in his estimates? Quelling a sigh, Thoren pushed himself toward the opening.

Merl hovered in the center of the pod, motionless.

"Dr. Pritchard, how's your progress?"

No answer.

If he's injured, I'll have to pull him into the central sphere before calling for help, or risk another bothersome argument with the Safety Sisters. Grumbling at the inconvenience, he braced against the edge of the opening and steadied himself before pushing in.

* * *

The disk slid free, and Rita and James wrestled it to the hallway floor. He held it in place while she secured it.

As soon as she gave the clear, James all but bounded to the open door, although his drag line caught him before he could pull Rita by their safety line. She hurried to join him as he described the long, deep chamber.

"Obviously a storage room. We have lines and lines of small containers, twenty or thirty deep, in some kind of storage cabinets — transparent doors, obviously. *ET*, are you seeing this?"

"I have Rita's feed on the main screen, James," Ann said, her voice breathy with excitement. "And I'm relaying it to the biolab."

"Okay." Rita could tell from James' voice he didn't see the connection, but Ann's words had made her heart skip.

She played her own hunch. "*ET*, I'm going to extended spectrum."

The room dimmed, then filled with symbols and designs. Unlike most of the ones they'd seen so far, however, these ones were readily identifiable as animals and plants, albeit as odd as the aliens themselves. Even better, each row had its own illustrations, clearly labels.

Is this why I saw rainbows? Rita wondered.

Kelley's and Zabrina's squeals of delight overrode hers.

"*Two of every kind of bird, of every kind of animal and of every kind of creature that moves along the ground will come to you to be kept alive,*" Ann whispered.

"What?" James asked, then he must have switched his visuals, because he, too, whistled. "I don't believe it."

"Rita to everyone. We found the ark!"

* * *

Thoren stood on a cliff's edge, so high he was staring down into a chasm of clouds and rainbows. He pulled in a strong breath in surprise, but didn't jerk away. He didn't need to fear. The ground beneath him was firm. Solid. He wouldn't fall.

So, jump.

The urge startled him. Jump into that chaos of fluff and color? He glanced at the cultivated landscape behind him. Orderly. Familiar. Safe and under his control. He snorted. *Jump? Right.*

Yet the urge continued, gently beguiling, promising joy. He leaned just a bit out, momentarily tempted to just let go...

Let go? Like Merl lets go? Like Sister Ann probably lets go?

"Thank you, no." He pulled back and crossed his arms. His lip curled into a sneer.

As he watched, the rainbows faded from the clouds. The sky turned gray.

Then he was back on the threshold of the pod, blinking at the glare of the artificial light as it reflected off Merl's faceplate. The other researcher shook him urgently.

"Thoren! Thoren! Did you see? Did you see?"

"I saw." He didn't necessarily see what the linguist had, but that hardly mattered at the moment. Of greater concern was how to make best use of this discovery.

Merl's face, however, was wild with panic. "What do we do?"

Before he could come up with an answer that would calm the agitated man, James' voice sounded over the suit comms. "Thoren, did you hear us? We found the aliens' ark. If we're interpreting these symbols right, we might have the genetic material of thousands of species! Merl, do you want to see these markings for yourself?"

The thought seemed to terrify Merl.

"Sister Ann to Team Two. Merl, are you all right? Your blood pressure is up and your pulse is racing."

Thoren replied quickly. "This is Thoren. Dr. Pritchard is fine, just...startled by the news. However, perhaps we should finish our task in the central chamber. You will be recording the ark, of course? Symbols of possible life forms will not assist us in determining how to move this ship. It might be better use of our time if he studies those symbols later."

Then he switched to the private channel. "Get a hold of yourself, doctor, or we will not be able to do anything." He resisted the urge to quote the Code.

"You're right. You're right." Merl took a deep breath and began murmuring nonsense.

Thoren shook him, sending them both swaying. "You will speak of this to no one. I will determine the best course of action." When he saw the doubt in his partner's eyes, he put on his most winning smile. "Trust me, Merl. I knew you were the right person to bring here, didn't I?"

"God led us here."

"Of course." He brushed off the comment. Code Six. It didn't matter, as long as Merl let him take control. "Now we must bide our time and avoid suspicion. Agreed?"

Merl nodded, but his lips never stopped moving.

"And do calm down before you alert that specious Sister Ann and ruin any chance of our taking action!" Thoren led the still-blithering man out of the third arm.

* * *

When Cay heard the announcement about the ark, he dropped the charges he was setting.

He heard the witch scream with joy, and even Sister Rita seemed excited. For that matter, everyone did. *Are they all spaced? Isn't anyone thinking about what the ark means? The aliens didn't just intend to explore. They planned to colonize. To invade!*

And they were heading toward our system!

Fred interrupted his panic with a slap on the helmet. "Get moving, Cay. We've only got a couple of hours left."

Cay snatched the timer from where it floated in front of him and got back to the job, ignoring the trembling of his hands. *Obviously no one understands this like I do. Question is — what do I do about it? Merl had said that God had a purpose planned for each of those who followed Him. Maybe this is my purpose. Maybe I've come here to save humankind.*

He paused, next charge in his hand, an idea forming in his mind. He could do this. He *would* do this.

Vac humankind! Just as long as Mars was safe — Mars and Dove.

Chapter Twenty-Five

James bit back his exasperation. The debrief was shaping up to be as big of a disaster as the impending crash of the Fate and Folly.

In addition to the research team, Captain Addiman and Commander McVee were there to represent the *Edwina Taggert*. Andi and George also returned on *Basilica* to be part of the meeting at Thoren's insistence.

"The discovery of the ark has changed our priorities," he announced. "Effective immediately, Research will put all its efforts into transferring the ark contents to the *Edwina Taggert*. Meanwhile, the Recovery team will find a way to disengage one of the pods from the ship. Captain, I will need your crew to prepare one of the landing bays for storage."

The room erupted.

"The third arm is off limits." Ann's voice was twisted with confusion. "Why do you think we'd bring a piece of it aboard?"

"We're not abandoning the *Discovery*," Andi stated, and the rockjacks cheered. Chris, James noted, was among them.

Thoren pinned his protégé with his glare. "We are running out of time. Further, we have no guarantee that your demolitions won't damage the ark, causing us to lose the most important discovery of mankind's history. I am the mission commander."

"Listen, Thoren," George hollered, and Andi made no move to restrain him. "You may not understand our 'simple tribal ways,' and you sure as hell don't know nothing about mining. But Cole trusts us to do our job."

"Why are we discussing this?" Reg exclaimed with disbelief. "Isn't this, oh, Number One on the Dangerously Stupid List? We don't bring biomaterial on board, especially if it might be alive and just waiting to be revived."

"I agree!" Zabrina stood to be heard. "Kelley and I can be fat, dumb, and happy the rest of the trip studying just the one alien we brought on board. And that's spooky enough in that lab without piling in hundreds more frozen samples that could do who-knows-what."

And so it went, with Thoren stressing the limited time, the importance of the ark, and his own authority while everyone else piled on more objections. Finally, Rita stood. "All right! This is getting us nowhere! Captain Addiman, this is your ship."

He nodded. "We bring nothing else aboard. If the samples survived so violent a landing, they should survive the extraction of their ship and the trip to the research station."

"There! That's settled," Rita said before Thoren could re-assert his authority. "Andi, we'll need a couple of rockjacks with welding experience to replace the door and reseal it tomorrow to protect the room further. We have one mission left, folks. Removing the ark or a pod is off the docket. What's our priority?" She nodded to Thoren, returning control of the meeting to him, and sat back down, seemingly oblivious to his glower.

Ian stood up. "You know, everybody was so excited about the freeze-dried animals, that we're overlooking the true find of the century. Warp drive!"

"Warp drive? Is that even possible?" Chris' voice broke with excitement.

"Sure, just fiscally unpopular. Scientists have been playing around with the idea since the early twenty-first century, but we didn't have the technology to make it work. Then, with the Great Expansion, commercial interests focused on near space, and with it, the money. Bending space so near the planets comes under the Dangerously Stupid List. Anyway, now only a few of us actually study it. I may be a theorist, but I think I know enough to recognize a warp engine. That is our ticket to the stars, people!"

"And what is it you need?" Thoren asked.

"Every bugbot we have, and anyone who knows how to program them — and delay our next mission until they're all programmed."

"We've only got one mission left!" people around him protested.

He spread his arms askance. "Which is why we need to concentrate on those engines. Look, Thoren: the third arm is a mystery, and the ark is supernova — if it is the ark and not their idea of a snack bar — but the most useful thing for the human race is that engine."

Thoren pursed his lips, but nodded. "Agreed. Andi will have a couple of her rockjacks seal the ark; Ian, you will release the bugbots. How many people will you need to assist?"

Ian shrugged. "Actually, once they're programmed, Reg and I can do it easily enough on our own."

"Then everyone else will resume their usual missions. *Basilica* will take the next shift down, while *Rockhopper* waits to ferry you and Reg with the Recovery crew."

Before the rockjacks could scream their protests, Tommie cleared her throat. "*Rockhopper* should go first with the recovery team. As you said, time is of the essence. Therefore, we should give them every available minute to free *Discovery*. That way there will be more time in-system to study it."

Even the researchers seemed to agree it was worth the risk. Thoren growled in his throat. "Fine. But I want every possible researcher to go down with *Rockhopper*. Settled. Now, there is one more important announcement that must be made."

Thoren cleared his throat, and James noticed Merl look up from his Bible as if caught at something.

"I have," Thoren started, and he smirked as his gaze settled on the sisters, "a confession to make. Three hours ago, I entered one of the mysterious third arm pods."

"What?" Rita exclaimed. Gasps and shuffling echoed her outrage.

Andi chided, "You know, Thoren, for a Codist, you sure have a hard time following orders," and James couldn't help but agree.

"Code Eleven: when dealing with the unknown, knowledge is your most important tool. I made a considered decision," he spoke over the hullabaloo, "because I needed more information about the cause of Sister Rita's hallucinations."

"Her what?" James found himself shouting and half rising from his seat. *How dare he!*

Rita set a restraining hand on his arm. Her other hand held back Ann. "The rainbows that didn't show up on the recording."

Thoren nodded regally. "Indeed. I must commend Sister Rita on her honesty. At least she was forthright in reporting of her experience. I believe it's time all of us who were in one of the so-called 'pods' explain what we saw. Chris?"

Rather than jump, as he might have done, Chris smiled at his mentor and held up his hand, still clasping Andi's. "I saw what my future could be."

Andi leaned her head on his shoulder. Behind them, James could hear a chorus of sighs, accompanied by someone's teasing retching sounds. Ian or Reg, probably. The happy couple just gazed into each other's eyes, only the twinkle of mischief in Andi's said she recognized the attention they'd drawn. Chris was oblivious in his joy.

Oh, to feel joy like that!

"Dr. Smith?"

James gave a guilty start. "I'd rather..."

Thoren interrupted. "I think it's important we all answer honestly here. Your hallucination, please?"

He shifted in his chair, suddenly aware of the eyes on him.

He forced his voice to stay neutral. "I...was dancing with someone. In the rain."

He felt Rita's hand tense on his arm. He stared at his lap.

"And did you indulge in this fantasy?"

Pulling her back, wanting to slow the music down, turn dance into embrace...

"No. I did not indulge." Despite his best efforts to stay calm, he snapped his reply.

Thoren nodded approvingly.

"And what was your 'hallucination?'" Rita asked.

"I was standing on a cliff's edge as someone urged me to jump. Now, I propose —"

"And did you?" Ann asked eagerly.

"What?" Thoren snapped.

But Ann shook her head. "Of course you didn't jump. You stayed where you were safe. Gravity kept you safe. Gravity brings the rainfall."

The little sister leaned forward, rubbing her temples with her fingers. "Power of gravity. Safety in power. But personal power won't make you safe..."

"What are you going on about?" Thoren demanded.

Ann hissed. "Quiet. Daniel's helping me read. Wrapping power like a cloak, like the rain...but that's a different vision. Different vision, same theme...you stubborn and willful people who look and do not see..."

Thoren gaped at her, then glared at the other two sisters. Rita, intent on Ann, ignored him, but James could tell Tommie had met his gaze. He could almost feel the clashing forces. After a moment, Thoren cleared his throat and continued.

"Now, while I do not propose to know the significance of rainbows, I think we can all agree that Chris has acted upon his vision."

"For the better!" Andi exclaimed.

Thoren gave her an indulgent wave of his hand. James found himself suddenly too warm for the room. *He's certainly enjoying himself. Wish he'd just get to the point so we can get on with preparing for the next mission.*

"I've no doubt he agrees. However, it is my assertion that we have stumbled onto some kind of alien mind-control device."

"What?" James gasped. Once again, the room erupted into bedlam.

* * *

Ann squinted her eyes shut and tried to concentrate past the babbling of the chief magician — no, head researcher. Babbling. Babylon. *Might as well be in Babylon, for all these people understand.*

The prophet Daniel crouched before her, showing her beautiful things, scary things, things she didn't understand, but knew the others would if she could just explain them right. It didn't help that she only saw snatches, hints...

These are not your visions to see. Only to interpret rightly.

"How can I interpret what I don't understand?" She moaned softly. In the chaos around her, not even Rita heard. Thoren was saying something about the effect spreading.

How did Joseph understand the seven skinny cows? How did I understand the writing on the wall?

Tears of shame dampened her lashes. She prayed for the Holy Spirit to fill her. Daniel, a Daniel she knew only she could see and could never explain, covered her hands with his and added his prayers to hers.

Around her, in the room, a true babbling Babylon, people argued and panicked. She heard someone crying. A strong, powerful king presided, feeding on their fear. David didn't think he was much of a king; and he, of all people, should know.

They need a shepherd. Even if you've never seen a real sheep.

"All right! That is enough!" Ann stood and stepped in front of Thoren, interposing herself between the king and his subjects. "Listen to me! Don't be afraid! There are no mind-control devices. And they're not escape pods, either."

"Young lady, sit down," Thoren commanded.

"No! I will not sit down and let you drive this mission by fear." She turned her back to him, Thoren the king. Thoren the wolf. She had to think about the sheep. "Please, calm down! The only fear is *your* fear. Your fear is the fear you bring, each of you. The aliens didn't gather in fear. They gathered there in reverence. They died enveloped in love and peace."

"Is this your studied opinion?" the king sneered.

Ann rounded on him. "Of course not. If I had gone first through that door like I should have, I might have a studied opinion. Maybe I could explain better then." Then she turned back to the quieting but frightened flock, confused now about who to follow. *Help me make them understand.* She felt Daniel beside her and her angel behind her.

"But that doesn't mean I don't understand. The Lord has helped me understand. You have to listen to me!"

"We're listening," Tommie said.

Bless her! Bless how she folded her arms and stared the King down. St. Joan of Arc would have used that look to quell the French king.

"Okay." Ann took a breath. She felt her body quiver with adrenalin and the Holy Spirit. "There's no mind control. No one has had hallucinations. They're, they're visions. Communication. Invitations! You don't indulge! You accept!"

Ann caught Chris' glance toward Andi and took a step toward them. "Yes, Chris! You understood! Of course, you did; you're used to epiphanies! You accepted. And it's so beautiful."

She turned to Rita: dear, sweet, conflicted Rita. "It's not always fun, and it's not always easy, but it is exciting, and it is beautiful. I promise you: these are only invitations to joy."

In the back of the room, Kelley stood and dashed out a side door.

Later, Daniel said. *Your place is here.*

Rita stood up and, with a glance at Thoren and Ann, went after the distraught xenobiologist.

"What about me?" James asked — or was it a challenge? Either way, she knew he knew the answer better than she did; he just didn't want to consider it.

"You had the correct frame of reference, then you shrunk it to fit the piece that suited you. You have to accept the whole vision, not just the parts you like."

James paled, and sweat broke out on his brow. As he wiped his face, Ann felt Daniel's hand on her shoulder. *Well done.*

Thoren laughed, an ugly sound. "So these are invitations? Meaning, I should have jumped?"

"Yes! Why are you so afraid?" Was he a wolf in sheep's clothing or a sheep in a wolf's?

"I hardly think the cliff was in a microgravity environment."

She rolled her eyes. Infuriating man! Beside him, David mimed knocking sense into him with a shepherd's staff.

"Gravity! Gravity held you to the ground, and you think it keeps you grounded. But you don't care about the gravity. You care about the power. Gravity isn't a power. It isn't even a force. It's the bending of space-time around matter. And you matter, William! And not because of your own power. If I were there, I'd have pushed you. You need a push." She bit her lip, suddenly seeing the king as a small and scared child. "Don't you see? They would have caught you."

"Who?" Thoren began, but Merl leapt to his feet.

"Thou shalt not put the Lord thy God to the test!"

"God is not being tested!" she roared back. "This is not a test. The aliens understood that. It's communication. Communion. They went there to die, because that's where they were closest to God."

Thoren gaped at her, red-faced. "Oh, for the love of —"

"—God! Yes, that's it exactly. Are you starting to understand?"

"Hold on." James perched on the edge of his chair. Why was he afraid to stand? To take a stand? Understand. Stand under. If only he'd stand under God, maybe he'd understand God's gift. "I know you believe this is their chapel."

She ignored the angry exclamations and sounds of disbelief, but Daniel murmured to her that many were listening.

"There was no altar," Merl objected.

"Do you know what an alien altar would look like?" Ann countered.

"So, then, what are the pods?" James challenged.

"This discussion is ridiculous. We were subjected to hallucinations and subliminal messages," Thoren asserted. He raised his hand to push Ann aside, but it froze, and he lowered it just as fast. Ann bit back a smile. She'd thank Daniel for defending her later.

In the meantime, she needed to stop the impact his words would have on the others. "Not hallucinations. Visions. Not subliminal messages. Sublime suggestions. They don't control your actions; they are meant to guide you."

James leaned forward. His eyes gleamed. Closer to understanding, but he still would not stand. *Why are you so afraid? Or are you just being willful?*

King David appeared beside him, resplendent in his royal robes. He grinned at James. "Bathsheba," he mouthed and patted James on the shoulder.

James didn't even flick his glance in the great king's direction. "So you're saying it's a spiritual reflection chamber?"

Before Ann could answer, Merl again let out a roar. "Blasphemy! God does not need human technology to communicate with us."

Someone laughed. "It's alien tech, Merl!"

Ann jumped in, "And we don't know for certain how it works for the aliens."

"Then how do you know what the pods are for? How do you know this was a sacred place?" James pushed.

Claiming a hunch wouldn't work, not here. Ann thought an apology to Mother Superior and braced herself. "Because I had a vision."

Thoren snorted. "So you disobeyed your own directive?" Emboldened by his accusation, he stepped forward, but again, Daniel stopped him from overshadowing her. Rather, he blocked the head researcher, so that he stood where Ann could address him and the flock.

"Of course not. I never even entered the chamber. Didn't Merl just say God does not need technology? *Pain and fear motivate, but faith and knowledge direct. Sometimes you experience all four before you have an epiphany.* And sometimes you just need faith. Sometimes faith can be sufficient, but always faith is necessary. "

Thoren made a disparaging sound. He probably thought he sounded regal, but to Ann's ears, it was the growl of a cornered wolf. "So your god told you to stay out?"

How could she get him to understand? If only he would understand, then he could stand beside her and they could finish the mission in safety. "Our God, William. He is yours whether you accept Him or not. There's a reason it's called a leap of faith."

"Can we table the whole 'God' thing for a moment?" Sean asked. "Divine vision or tapping into the subconscious, what's the big deal? Other than the fact that we don't have time to be playing with it right now, what's the danger if someone has a 'pod experience'?"

Ann looked at Ian, praying he'd understand. "Six hundred, twenty-two thousand gallons of water. It can buoy you up or drown you. Truth is the same, and too many people don't understand the water. We don't have a qualified lifeguard."

Ian crossed his arms. "You almost drowned in the pool."

"Exactly! I didn't understand your water. But I had a lifeguard, and you saved me. Now listen to me when I tell you we don't have a lifeguard."

"Yet everyone is fine." Thoren crossed his arms and smirked. The king become a spoiled prince.

"Are they?"

People gave uncomfortable glances at Kelley's empty seat. Rita was with Kelley, and Ann knew she'd be all right. Kelley felt the pain and fear; she just needed to accept the faith. Rita could teach her, at least until Ann could go to them.

She turned her eyes to Merl. "Are you all right? Visions aren't always rainbows."

"Rainbows!" Thoren scoffed. "Visions. We are wasting time. What Merl saw is his own business. Sister Thomas, get this child out of here so we can return to productive work."

"Wait," Sean said, "I thought you wanted everyone to share their vision. I thought you were afraid their minds had been altered."

Anger flashed across Thoren's face, but so quickly that Ann didn't think anyone caught it. Still it caught her by surprise. Daniel, too, for he didn't move to slow the mission commander until he'd overshadowed Ann. Even from behind him, Ann could tell he was treating Sean to a condescending smile. "I wished to illustrate the need to further investigate the device. Shall we reopen that discussion? Having experienced the pod personally now, it is my studied opinion..."

Ann gaped.

He sees writing on the wall, but refuses to accept the message, Daniel told her. Beside Thoren, David threw his hands in the air, then tore his own shirt.

A quick scan of the rest of the team showed she wasn't alone in her shock. Yet no one rose to contradict the king. Like sheep they were milling, confused, and too easy prey for the man who pretended to have their best interests at heart. And there was another sheep, too, lost and desperate to re-enter the fold. The time was nearing, and she had to get to Kelley, but leaving the rest with this wolf was just as dangerous.

Tommie was watching Thoren with stoic calm, but when she caught Ann's glance, she raised one eloquent brow. From the seat beside James, David, his tunic torn and his hair wild, gave her an expectant look.

Ann felt the air around her harden, like a strongsuit. Like armor. Her eyes narrowed until the king became a blur. She heard her voice, sharp and hard as titanium: "By the authority invested to the Order of Our Lady of the Rescue under Standard Contract, section 2, paragraph A, I remove you, William Thoren, from your status as mission commander for exploration of the *Discovery*. You may continue to oversee the research taking place within the confines of the *Edwina Taggert*. Sister Thomas Aquinas Kruger?"

Tommie stood and turned to the crowd. "I concur."

Thoren started to sputter his protest, but Ann no longer cared. She'd done what she could. The king wouldn't listen, and he needed to be removed before he hurt anyone else. It might even be too late. Something awful was going to happen, she just knew it. He had ropes around other people, and the cliff was crumbling under his feet, and he'd never notice the real abyss until he was spilled in.

All he needs to do is cry out, Daniel told her. *Someone else is crying now.*

"I have to rescue Kelley," she told the room and hurried out.

* * *

Rita dashed out the door, but found the corridor empty nonetheless. A snarl of frustration escaped her throat. She ran toward Kelley's quarters, figuring that was her most likely place to go.

What was wrong with that man? The last thing we need is wild accusations of hallucinations and alien mind control. He didn't even watch that movie. Lord, give me patience and make it quick, or I may do something I'll have to confess later.

So intent was she on the corridor ahead, she didn't even see Rose Chan rushing down the side aisle. They collided.

"Oh, Sister! I'm so glad I found you! What's wrong with Kelley?"

"You've seen her?"

"Yeah, she was running down the hall crying. I tried to ask her what was wrong, and she just shouted, 'Like you care!' and rushed past me. What happened?"

"Which way?" Rita asked, and when Rose pointed toward the labs, Rita took her shoulders. "Thank you. Now listen — Dr. Thoren has proposed some rather wild and upsetting theories about *Discovery*. There are bound to be rumors soon. Just remember they are theories, and not well-substantiated at that, all right?"

Rose's brows knit together. "Uh, okay. But what...?"

Rita shared a smile she did not feel. "I don't want to make it worse by suggesting anything. Ann is trying to set him straight, and believe me, when it comes to understanding technology, alien or otherwise, Ann is the person I'd trust."

Rose nodded. "We're not in any danger?"

"Of course not. Now excuse me. I really need to check on Kelley."

"Yes! Right. Sorry. Hey!" she called as Rita rushed away. "Tell her I care, okay?"

Rita searched the laboratory wing, poking her head in each office and calling. She paused at the end. This was ridiculous. She called up to the bridge. "This is Sister Rita. Can you give me Kelley's location?"

She made him repeat it twice, then turned down the side corridor. Sure enough, the chapel light showed "Occupied."

Inside, she found the room transformed into a grassy hill, large rock formations to one side, a full moon bathing the blues and grays of evening in its silvery light. The restful scene nonetheless made her shiver.

In the center of a circle of stones, each bearing a holographic candle, Kelley sat, cross-legged, her arms around her stomach, still sobbing.

Rita walked into the room and sat next to her. She could feel the individual blades of grass pressing against her suit. "Kelley, honey?"

"I want to go home!" she burst out. "I want to go back to my home and my coven and my sisters, back where I belong!"

Rita wiped tears off her cheek, brushed back a wayward strand of hair. "You belong here, Kelley. You're an important part of the team."

Kelley laughed, angry. "Team? Some team. I went into one of those pods. When Chris did. I was the first. Did anyone think of that? Thoren sure didn't remember."

"I remembered." Rita squeezed her arm. "Want to tell me about it?"

"At first, I felt this peace, and it was so lovely. Then...nothing! I was just...alone. A-abandoned. Uncared about. And it hurt!" She buried her face into Rita's shoulder. "If everyone else got an invitation, I got a rejection!"

Rita wrapped her arms around her and caressed her hair. "No. Honey, that's not true."

"Of course it's not." Ann spoke from the doorway, and both ladies turned toward her. The bright light of the corridor should have silhouetted her, yet Rita could easily see her face, alight with compassion. Just...alight.

"I'm sorry you're upset, Kelley. You weren't rejected. Of course not! Everyone else got an invitation, but you, you were given the greatest invitation of all."

Kelley pulled away to pin Ann with an angry closed glare. "Invitation? Really? Why should I get the invitation to pain? Is this your God's twisted idea of justice?"

Ann's face twisted in perplexity. "Justice? No, no, not like you're thinking. No thinking. No thoughts. Feelings. Impressions. Emotion. Empathy! Padre Pio, Eleanor of Europa, St. Teresa of Avila... *Pain so sharp that it made me utter several moans, and so excessive the sweetness caused me by this intense pain that one can never wish to lose it.* To be invited to see into a man's heart is such a gift — but you! You didn't see the heart of just a man. You are so blessed!"

Suddenly Ann looked around, noticing the chapel décor for the first time. "This is pretty, but you're focusing on the wrong light. You're not seeing His light, His heart...His precious, precious heart..." She turned to the holographic controls, fingers flying over the keyboard.

Calmer now, Kelley gave a sigh bordering on exasperation. "Ann, I don't understand. Whose heart?"

As if waiting for that question, golden light bathed the room, the grass a vibrant green, the stones stark and strong against a clear blue sky. The smaller stones surrounding them were in turn surrounded by wildflowers. But on a far hill, partly shrouded by a building storm, a man slumped on the cross.

Ann walked to Kelley. Taking both her hands, she pulled the tear-stained woman up.

"His heart," she whispered, and her voice broke. She took a breath. "You weren't the one abandoned."

Kelley shook her head. "I, I'm not sure I understand."

"You have to want to," Ann urged. "You have such empathy. You feel so deeply. He has invited you to share in His heart."

Kelley shook her head, small, jerky motions that echoed her trembling. She glanced behind her and gasped.

"Don't be afraid. *The sweetness caused me by this intense pain that one can never wish to lose it.* Accept this invitation. He who gives it loves you so much."

Ann released her, then backed away. As she neared Rita, Ann held out her hand to pull her back out of the ring. Together, they stood, watching as

Kelley closed her eyes and hugged herself.

Ann squeezed Rita's hand. "The bay doors are opening," she whispered. "She's only seeing the aloneness. The barrenness."

"But *that barrenness is the pause of the tree before putting out its fruit*," Rita whispered back. She knew what a first look into the unknown felt like. Rita's eyes stung. She longed to go to Kelley, but forced herself to still. This was an invitation she had to accept herself.

Kelley spun around, once, twice, then turned back and forth, like a compass needle regaining its bearings. She made a hesitant step, and another, each growing in confidence, until her last step out of the circle was a stride. The candles, though holographic, flickered out as she stepped past. Only afterward did she open her eyes and gaze upon the cross toward which she'd moved.

Her hands flew to her face. Her legs buckled, and she fell kneeling on the thick grass.

"I'm sorry. Oh, God, I'm so sorry!"

Ann's smile came out full force. Then her eyes widened. "Not appropriate yet," she muttered to herself and schooled her face into sympathetic neutrality. She gave a small nod to Rita, and they went to Kelley.

"All this time," Kelley whispered as she leaned into Rita's embrace. "All this time, I felt so alone and rejected, and going in that pod just made it worse. But I wasn't being rejected; *I* was rejecting *Him*. What do I do? How can I make amends? "

Ann shushed her. "Just feel. That's what the pod was showing you to do. God wants you to know how much your soul was cherished and missed. Just feel that now. "

Rita stroked her hair and murmured reassurances until Kelley's trembling ceased, and she pulled away to gaze at the crosses. For the next several minutes, they sat beside her. Ann watched intently and tried not to smile or talk. Rita had a moment of fancy, seeing herself as a sentinel standing guard over someone's vigil; she began to pray the Divine Mercy chaplet. Their comms beeped once, but Ann typed in a quick answer, and no one else bothered them after that.

Finally, Kelley heaved a sigh and shook herself. "I am so sorry," she repeated, but this time factually and with a confidence in her voice. "I had no idea that God could love so much. Really, I just..."

Ann's brows knit at the thought of someone not understanding God, but a moment later, the expression cleared and she hugged Kelley's shoulders. "It's atmo out of the airlock. You've brought Him consolation, a single beautiful drop of consolation in a sea of bitterness. Just wait — He'll immerse you in His peace."

"Actually." Kelley's gaze turned inward, her face perplexed. "I do feel peaceful. Like I've never felt before, except for that one moment in the pod. I...wow. I mean all those years of meditating, I thought... but no. Do you always feel like this?"

She glanced from Ann to Rita, but before Rita could answer, Ann said, "Of course! And when I don't, it's because I've forgotten I can."

Kelley turned back to Rita.

Rita gave her what she hoped was a reassuring smile. "I have. Not all the time, but enough. Some people never do. "

"St. Mother Teresa of Calcutta. Some fires never feel the warmth of their own flames," Ann said.

Rita gave her a small nod. "*Yet blessed are they who do not see and still believe,* Jesus said. It's the same for feelings. Everyone experiences faith differently. Enjoy that you have, but don't expect to feel like this all the time. Faith is more than emotion." She prayed that wouldn't discourage her, but she didn't want her basing her faith on what she was feeling now.

Kelley laughed. "That's probably a good thing, because I am limp! And famished. I think I'm done feeling for a while. What do I do now?"

"Eat!" Ann said. "Go study the alien. Rest. Then, when Rita gets back from Outside, come to our quarters. We'll talk and give you some things to read. It'll be time to think and to understand. It's so exciting!" Ann gazed at her, then gave a happy squeal and hugged her.

"I don't know," Kelley hedged as Ann pulled her to her feet. "I made such a scene, and I've been so rude to everyone."

"You've been feeling unwanted," Rita said, "but that's not the case. People are worried about you. Rose even stopped me in the hall to ask if you were okay. "

"Our Lord's is not the only invitation you've been rejecting," Ann said. "But it's okay. You've felt the depth of God's love. Go feel the love others have for you. "

"And as for scenes," Ann added, "you are not alone in that this trip. In fact, I'm sorry, but Rita and I need to get back to our quarters. Tommie wants to talk to us and James ASAP."

Something in Ann's tone made Rita sigh. "Oh, Ann, what did you do?"

* * *

"And I am telling you, my brothers and sisters! I am telling you that they do not know the danger God has led us from, nor do they understand the warning He, in His Divine Mercy, has sent to us!"

In the small conference room off the living quarters, the twelve people of Merl's Bible group shifted in their seats, most with unease, but Cay with impatience. Merl had texted each of them to meet him as soon as the rockjacks had cleaned up from their mission. Cay hadn't even wanted to bother with that. As he'd set his blast charge into the rock beneath the ice of the Folly, a plan, brilliant and bold, had appeared in his mind, like a vision, like a message from God. Instead of securing the charge, he had eased it out of its hold, pocketed the charge in his suit, and pretended to finish the job. He'd done the same with the next one he was assigned to lay. He figured he might have to do this alone, but when Merl called, he realized that his brother in Christ had sensed the same danger he did. He'd wanted to run to him, to ask his blessing.

To his surprise, Merl dismissed the ark. The crew was dead; the ship crashed; the threat of invasion gone. Instead, he worried about that stupid third arm and the supposed mind-control devices within.

"The devices tempt you with beautiful visions — the joys of heaven on Earth. But God allowed me to see the truth beyond their lies! The fires of Hell await those who give in to its false promises!"

Cay clenched his fists in his lap and prayed that the sermon would end. It didn't matter, anyway. Physical invasion or attacks upon the soul, he had the solution.

No one debated. Merl never gave anyone a chance, but sent them off to ponder his words and pray. As folks filtered out, Cay held back until only he and Merl remained.

Not noticing, Merl flopped into a seat, dazed and spent. He closed his eyes, and a tear traced a line down his cheek. The sight filled Cay with anger. Would he just sit and play the victim? He strode to him, intending to shake him into action, but stopped himself halfway there. No. Merl was scared; anyone could see that. He didn't need belligerence; he needed reassurance. How many times in Cay's life had he needed reassurance only to be slapped and told to buck up?

Dove had understood. Dove had given him support and love. For her, he would do the same for Merl.

He approached more slowly, and knelt before his spiritual mentor. He looked so old.

"Merl, my brother, please don't despair."

"But I do." Merl spoke without energy, without passion. "You can't know, Cay. The things I saw in store for Man. We stand on the cliff's edge."

He shook his head. He cried no more tears, but didn't seem aware of the ones already spilled.

Cay squeezed his arm. "It's all right. The ship will never make it in-system. I can — I will! — make sure of that. You told me God had a reason for my being here. I understand it now. He needed someone who had access to the explosives and the foresight to realize the danger we faced. He needed me!"

* * *

Once again, Ann awoke to the sound of Edwina Taggert yelling for her to run. This time, however, she didn't feel the wild urge to give in to the command. Instead, she eased out of her too-comfortable bed and knelt beside it, praying the prayer Sr. Lucinda had taught her: *Steer the ship of our souls...*

When at last she felt calmer, she gave into a different compulsion, and went in search of Ian. He should have finished with the bugbots by now, so she checked the pool. Swimming wasn't a sufficient cure for what troubled him, but he might think it necessary. Instead, she found the pool room empty, the waters still but for gentle waves caused by the filtration system. It felt very peaceful. No wonder Ian loved it. If only that peace could enter his heart, but it was the wrong peace and the wrong water.

His lab, then. She decided against asking the Bridge to locate him. It might raise questions she didn't have answers for, and after yesterday, Tommie and Rita told her to keep a low profile and try not to cause any more disruption. Perhaps that's why, when Thoren exited from Ian's lab, her guardian angel pushed her into the shadows until he passed.

When he'd turned the corner, she hastened to Ian's lab. He was hunched over a lab sink. The rising steam and frantic splashing sounded like an alarm in her mind.

"Why are you washing your hands?"

Ian yelped and spun, flicking water in an arc around him. It missed the bugbots that stood like sentinels on the shelf across from the sink, but did track a line across Ann's T-shirt.

Rather than apologizing, Ian swore. "Vac, Little Sister! What are you doing here?"

Ann wiped her shirt. "You weren't in the pool. Why are you washing your hands?"

"To get them clean, of course. Is there something wrong with liking the feel of clean hands?"

"But they never feel clean, do they? You wash and you wash and you never feel clean. You swim — six hundred, twenty-two thousand gallons of water, chemically treated to kill bacteria, and you don't feel cleansed. It's the wrong water, Ian!"

"What? Is this that crying thing again? I should cry over my hands?"

His hands were red from the heat and scrubbing. Why didn't he understand? Ann prayed for the right words, but all that came out of her mouth was, "It would be a start."

"I have a mission to prep for, if you don't mind."

But she did mind. She couldn't let him go, not like that, with his red hands signaling the danger to his soul and his diagnostics incomplete. She stepped between him and the table holding the bugbots. "I do mind, Ian. I have a mission, too, and it's more important than the *Discovery*. I must mind it. So I need you to mind me. I know you don't always understand what I'm saying, but I need you to mind my words. Please."

He gaped at her but didn't laugh. She felt a surge of hope. Then his expression closed. "Get out of my way."

He started past her.

"Ian, you have to listen to me!" Ann grabbed his hands.

Dozens of tiny souls ripped from their mortal homes before they had the chance to scream. Ian's hands slick with blood and gore. It didn't matter that he wore gloves, the blood was there.

Ann shrieked and jerked away, slamming into the table. The bugbots rattled as they toppled over. With a growl, Ian scooped them into a carrying pouch, then pinned her with an ugly glare.

"Sister, you really are spaced!"

As the door closed behind him, she sank to the floor, shivering and rocking.

Chapter Twenty-Six

Reg reached into the pouch hanging off his spacesuit, and, after a couple of false starts, managed to get his gloved hand around the pillbox-shaped prize and set it near a narrow opening between two conduits. With a careful tap, he turned it on. Small legs unfolded from around it, and the bugbot raised itself on its four spindly legs. As it ran through its mechanical systems check, he called for a heads-up display on his faceplate and ran a diagnostic of its sensors and data transmissions. At another cavity in the warp drive, Ian was doing the same.

He chuckled at the acrobatics of the bugbot. "I could watch these things all day."

"Well, don't. We've got stuff to do," Ian replied, then switched to a private channel. "I saw some openings in the next arm. I want to take a couple of these beauties there and set them roaming. You stay here with the rest."

"What about teams of two?"

Ian made a disparaging sound. "Come on. It's down the corridor. Nothing but dead machinery. Much as I trust the rockjacks, I want to get as much data as I can just in case they break something in transit. It's not like we have a repair manual."

Reg paused, thinking. Ian made an effort to breathe normally and even spoke to mission control to report another bot on its way.

Thoren replied, "Excellent. Do keep in mind our schedule, Mr. Hu, Mr. Alexander."

Ian gave Reg a theatrical shrug. Thoren might not be mission commander, but he was still in charge of the entire project. They both knew they had to keep him happy if they wanted to study the ship when they got back to the inner system. In this case, that worked in Ian's favor.

Reg frowned, but made a shooing motion.

"Copy that, Thoren!" Ian said. "Not too much longer now."

He headed to the next arm and dutifully dumped his last bugbot in the nearest maintenance tube. Then he headed to his real assignment.

Much as he wanted to like Sister Ann, she was spaced. Unbalanced or something. All this talk of the pods being some kind of holy chamber, like God would communicate to people if they entered the right room. Then she tells everyone they're too dangerous? You'd think a nun would want God to talk to people. And what was that all about in his lab earlier?

A familiar itch irritated his palms. Why now? He bit back a grunt of annoyance and forced his mind back to the special assignment Thoren had given him.

Of course, Thoren had it wrong, too. Mind control. Seriously? Mind control made Chris take a chance with Andi? Mind control would make James fantasize about dancing in the rain? Oh, yeah, and what about Kelley and her experiencing "agony, and sweetness beyond the agony" that she never wants to forget?

Ian turned down the third arm. His suit cameras were on full spectrum, so that the designs of the walls played on his heads-up display in blues and purples, but his mind was on the blissful look Kelley had worn when she'd told him that. He had never seen her so relaxed. And the fact that she was actually talking to him and the other guys after being so cold before? He knew what that meant, even if no one else wanted to believe it.

Suddenly, he laughed, thinking of Thoren's fantasy. And Ann told him to jump! He should have. What fun might he have found in his fall? But then again, he had said he felt pretty powerful. And power was the ultimate aphrodisiac.

He paused at the door and took in the aliens scattered about. Naked, all. Some embracing. Yeah, there was no fighting going on. They'd known they were going to die and had chosen the best way to go.

Earth had had its own fertility cults. Maybe "Little Sister" was right. Maybe it was a temple, after all.

As if his thoughts summoned her, Sister Ann's voice came over his headset. "Reg, Ian, status please."

"Last bots are in and mapping. Everything looks green," Reg said.

"All good here," Ian replied, but his voice sounded off even to him. Damn it, his hands were itching again!

"Ian, are you all right?" Ann pressed. "What are you doing?"

Distraction made him careless. "Just checking out something for Thoren. Only take a minute, then I want to get out of this damn suit and wash up."

"What did Dr. Thoren ask you to do?"

Vac! What had he just done?

"Just take a minute!" he called and pushed off to the nearest pod. "Be not afraid," Ann had said. If there was one thing Ian did not fear, it was a good fantasy.

But Ann's voice held panic. "Ian, get out of there!"

* * *

Rita stood with one foot hooked into a toehold and both hands on the edge of an open rescue balloon. Inside the bag floated bits of material and wrapped-up bottles and curios they could only guess at: things to keep James busy on the long ride home.

She was not looking forward to the long ride and having to find ways to keep James from talking to her about his vision. Dancing in the rain! Her stomach clutched at the thought, and she didn't know if that was a good or bad thing. Thank heavens she'd been busy until it was time to suit up. With the research team spooked over Thoren's mind control device theory and Thoren and Ann at odds, she had enough to think about.

James, his arms full of artifacts, floated over and placed more in the bag. One bumped against another and started to spin away. Rita snagged it and gave it a gentle push back among the others.

"Thanks. I know the tech and the ark are probably our most important finds from a scientific point of view, but this is the stuff that's going to give us our cultural framework." He stopped to give a derisive laugh.

"What?"

"Oh, just Ann and her frameworks. You really missed a show when you took off after Kelley."

"I heard all about it." Rita sighed.

Rita had wanted to shriek and kick something when Tommie related what happened in the meeting after she'd gone seeking Kelley. Instead, she'd contented herself with a sigh. "Oh, Ann!"

"I know. I shouldn't have yelled at Dr. Thoren," Ann had sighed back.

She and Tommie had traded exasperated looks.

Tommie said, "Threatening to push him off the cliff probably did more harm than good." Still, the older sister's mouth had twitched in a suppressed grin.

It's not like we all don't have that fantasy, Rita had thought, but since that kind of empathy would not have helped matters then — or been a very Christian attitude — she asked, "Couldn't you have found a better way to explain yourself?"

"Of course not."

Of course not. Do I really want to know? Rita had braced herself. "And why not?"

"Capacitors!"

"What?"

The look Ann gave her said she was as exasperated as Rita felt. "*Make yourself a capacity, and I will make myself a torrent.* Information — like energy. Information flows, information collects, information distributes. But there's too much resistance, too many resistors. The circuit can't complete; information backflows, fills the capacitor, fills the capacity. Fills past capacity. Resistance, torrent, backflow — the capacitor blows, and I'm sorry, but I really tried!"

"Capacitors?" James said when Rita had related the story. "That girl is a piece of work."

"A piece of God's work, James," Rita scolded. "I admit, her thinking is unorthodox, but I've seldom known her to be wrong about anything."

"*Edwina Taggert* to Ian." Ann's voice came over the mission line and interrupted Rita. "What did Dr. Thoren ask you to check out?"

"Just a quick favor. Nothing to get fired up about. We'll just be —"

Ann cut him off: "Ian! Get out of there! The third arm is off limits. I repeat, Ian, stay out of the pods! The water is too deep for you! Stay away from the third arm! Reg!"

Rita and James exchanged startled looks. "Reg, Ian? This is Rita. What's your location?" She hoped that their knowing someone onboard was onto them would be enough to stop their mischief, but she unhooked herself from the drag line just in case she was wrong.

Reg's tight voice confirmed her suspicions. "I'm so sorry. He said he was going to the fourth arm to drop off some bots. I had no idea he planned... I'm heading there now. "

"Reg, be careful, but be fast. Ian can't be in there. He can't cry so he only laughs, and he doesn't understand tears can wash..."

Rita had never heard Ann like this, not over the headsets.

Tommie cut in. "Ann, protocols! Discipline."

"Reg here. Ian's in a pod. What do you want me to do?" Reg's voice was tense. Was he thinking of Thoren's theories or Ann's warnings?

"This is Rita, Reg. Stay where you are. I'm on my way." She unhooked herself from the safety line that connected her to James. "James, stay here. I'll be faster without you."

"But I can help," James started, when suddenly, they heard Reg yelp.

"Ian! Ian, what's wrong?" Reg called.

Rita grabbed the edge of the hole in the door and shoved hard, flinging herself out of the room. She twisted so that she hit the opposite wall feet first, and kicked off hard, grabbing the drag line just enough to change her vector so that she rocketed down the long corridor of the fifth arm. In her helmet, she could hear Ann directing Tommie to land as close to *Discovery* as possible and calling for everyone to prepare to evacuate the ship. She also heard Zabrina in the background, murmuring reassurances to Ian and Reg's frantic shouts to Ian to keep his suit on. She did not hear Ian's replies. She switched to their private channel.

"Get it off me! Get it off me!"

"Ian, stop it! There's nothing there! You have to keep your suit on! Reg to anybody—help me!"

"Ian, this is Ann. Listen to me. You're a lifeguard. Guard yourself. Calm down. If you flail in the water, you drown."

"It's everywhere! Oh, God, it's alive! Get it off!"

"No! Stop it! Ian!" Reg's words degenerated into grunts of a struggle.

Rita reached the curve in the arm, twisted and kicked off the wall. Why was this corridor so long? She could hear a frantic Reg begging Ian to calm down. He must be trying to physically restrain him, without much success. She called up her suit controls, spoke the code to override Ian's suit, and ordered it to administer a sedative.

"Reg, it's Rita. I'm almost there. Ian, listen to me: we'll get whatever it is off when we're in the ship. Do you hear me?"

"It's all over my hands, I can't stand it. I have to!"

"Ian, no!" Reg shouted.

Rita caught the opening to the central bubble and used it to align herself for her push toward the third arm. As she rounded the curve, she paused. Through the open doorway, she could see the two men struggling, a crazy tangle of arms and legs floating free near the center. Their safety lines, no longer connected, writhed like snakes around them. Even with a sedative, Ian fought like a crazed man. She wouldn't be able to stop him. She reached down and pulled one of the rescue balloons from her belt.

"Reg, keep Ian still!" Neither acknowledged. She ordered Ian's suit to give him another sedative.

Ian swung his head back, banging the helmet against Reg's, who jerked in surprise and let go. In that moment, Ian got his hand free. He twisted desperately at his opposite wrist.

Despite everything, Rita felt a wave of relief. He could remove a glove and survive; the pressure cuff below his elbow would seal off the suit. That would give her time to envelop him in the balloon before he did something worse, like remove his helmet. She lined herself up, tensed her legs for a big push. She'd have to move fast. He was at least thirty meters away, but it was a straight shot. She could do this if Ian just stayed still.

Reg again moved in on Ian.

"Reg, stay back!"

He collided with Ian, and the two floated from her view.

With a snarl of frustration, she pushed to the chamber entrance.

"Let Ian go! I've got him. Just back away!"

No response, and again they were tangled together like zero-G wrestlers in a grudge match. The balloon could hold two, just barely. If they'd cooperate enough to let her get it around them. She grit her teeth. *Saint Gillian, a little help here!*

Reg grabbed Ian's wrist. Momentum brought Ian against the central column, and he grabbed a walkway with his free hand, got his feet between himself and his friend, and pushed. Reg went sailing to the side. Ian, sobbing, clawed frantically at his glove.

Rita launched herself toward Ian. She pressed the button on the balloon, and it began to inflate itself. The rush of air slowed her, but she'd expected that, and if the balloon wasn't at least partially inflated, she'd never get it around him without help.

"It's disgusting! I have to get it off! Yes!" Ian twisted the ring.

Just another meter. She began counting seconds. *One, two...*

Over the headset, she heard Ann directing everyone to pack up and head back to the MiGR, her voice calm but without the usual serenity she had during a rescue. In the background, she caught angry voices. She ignored them and concentrated on counting.

Six, seven...

A stream of mist spewed from the opening in Ian's suit, and all other sounds in her helmet were drowned out by his scream. Reflexively, he curled up around his glove, causing him to spin instead of move in a twisted line.

Thank you, St. Gillian! Ten...

Rita caught him in the bag and sealed it. She adjusted the atmospheric controls. At thirteen seconds, the light showed a low but comfortable atmospheric pressure. "Ian! Ian, can you hear me?"

Raspy breathing interrupted by sobbing.

Rita sighed. Her own breath sounded heavy. She felt like she'd run a marathon. Latching Ian's balloon to her belt, Rita pushed gently to where Reg held himself steady on a bar as he tilted his head back. His visor was spattered with blood, but it seemed to have come from his nose and not a head injury. Even so, he had his eyes tightly shut, and his mouth grimaced.

"Did I ever mention I get sick at the sight of blood?" he asked through clenched teeth. "That's why I'm an engineer. Please don't make me open my eyes."

Rita hooked his line to her suit and placed his hands on her arm. "Just hold on, and I'll guide you. It's going to be okay. Ann, tell Dr. OvLandra."

"Already on it. OvLandra will meet you in the landing bay." Over the private line, Ann added, "He shouldn't have gone. Laugh or cry, he always said, and he couldn't cry. He shouldn't have gone."

Chapter Twenty-Seven

Crouched below the first arm of *Discovery*, Cay checked to make sure Frances had her back to him and was intent on placing her own charges. Thus assured, he moved the suction grip he'd attached to the hull of the *Discovery*, revealing a shallow start of a hole he was drilling with his laser. He fought back curses. If he had to keep doing little bits on the sly, he'd never have time to drill enough holes and set the charges. He needed a miracle.

Frances shifted position, and he hastily hid the hole with his grip and covered the action by making it look like a stretch. He looked around at the crisscross of safety lines along the dug-out ditch below the ship: thin, neon yellow lines marking the progress of the recovery team as they planted the explosive charges to release *Discovery* from her prison of stone and ice. He needed to reach at least two more spots for explosives — preferably under the third arm. That would send a message to rescue teams — or invasion ships.

"How you doing?" Frances asked.

"Going slow. Tired, I guess." He wished he could just share his plan with her. She was his sister in Christ, right? But no, she had thought Merl was overreacting. She was as blind as the rest. Even Merl had reacted to his plan with doubt, though he promised to say nothing, but instead to pray on it. Pray? Would prayer protect them if more aliens came?

God made men of prayer and men of action. Cay was a man of action. And he was on his own.

God will provide. Didn't Merl say that? I just have to trust.

Even so, he was surprised when Ann's voice came over their headsets. "*Edwina Taggert* to Recovery Team. Two people on the research team are injured. We're evacuating the research team, but Rita needs to be free to care for the injured. We need someone to drive the Meeger to *Basilica*."

"This is Frances. I can see both the Meeger and *Basilica* from here. We're almost done. I can go. I'd be a lot faster if I could leave Cay here and use my jets, and he could finish laying the charges. Cay?"

"Roger that! Go!" *Praise the Lord!*

"Andi here. Frances, you have permission to detach and head to the Meeger. Cay, when you finish, move to your next position, but keep in contact with George. Five minute intervals. We don't want anyone else hurt."

"Roger — five minute check-ins."

"Roger, Andi." Frances passed him her charges, unhooked the line from the ship, aligned herself on the target, and pushed off. She wobbled a bit when she fired her jets, but quickly steadied herself and made straight for the vehicle.

Cay twisted himself so he could watch her go. When he was certain she was out of sight, he set his laser cutter to a higher setting and drilled a deep, but narrow, hole into the opening of *Discovery's* hull. If his calculations were correct, the explosives in his case would be enough to rip the ship from the asteroid and send it flying into space.

* * *

James pulled himself hand-over-hand in quick, hard strokes that set him bobbing. Over his suit comms, the rest of the research team reported their own progress toward the MiGR. Everyone wanted to know how Ian and Reg were doing and what they were doing in the forbidden arm in the first place, but Rita had demanded an end to all chatter, except reporting their progress, and, like professionals, they complied.

James held back his own questions, stewing instead over the cause of all this chaos. Thoren!

Augustus, what were you thinking? "Give him rope." He's hung two of his own people with his "rope," and he'll find a way to make it look like he had nothing to do with it. If that doesn't work, he'll hide behind the Almighty Code to keep any of the blame off himself. He'll try to pin this on Ann for interfering with his authority. Might even make it stick with the university. Rope! Oh, Augustus, you and I are going to have words when I get back to Earth!

He arrived at the airlock, the last of the team and just in time to join Gordon and the others. They opened the door, transferred the lines one at a time, double-checking each time, closed the door, then pulled themselves quickly to where the MiGR sat idling on its jets, one silver rescue balloon floating behind it.

Everyone else waited in the MiGR, held rigidly in place with their straps. Rita, however, had harnessed herself to the side, where she could face Reg. Reg sat in a seat with his head tilted back. His helmet was darkened; Rita's doing, James guessed. Bloody noses were relatively harmless, but the sisters had told them in training that, stuck inside a helmet, any kind of bleeding injury to the face made a frightening mess. He'd want to keep his eyes shut, too. Ian must be in the balloon bobbing behind them.

"Strap yourselves down fast but tight," Frances told the new arrivals. "We're going to break some speed limits. When we get there, stay in your seats until we tell you to move. Rita will fill us in when she can."

Behind faceplates, James could see wide eyes and tense expressions as everyone buckled down and tested each others' straps.

"Brace, Rita!" Frances called as she swung the hovercraft around and sped toward the *Basilica*. In less than half the time it had taken them before, they crossed the distance and bounded into *Basilica's* hold. James imagined he felt a rush of air even as the ramp was closing behind them. Frances snapped off her restraints and swung herself over everyone's heads in a move that would have made any Earthbound gymnast jealous. Moments later, she was heading back to the MiGR with a first-aid kit.

The ship shook as Tommie took off, but the two ladies barely staggered. Despite everything, James couldn't help but admire Rita's strength and grace. The slight glow in her helmet told him she was looking at a display. Then it darkened, and she reached for the neck lock.

"Sister Thomas to Research. The hold is pressurized, and gravity is engaged. You can take your helmets off now and unbuckle, but please stay with the Meeger."

"What about Ian?" Gordon asked. The balloon holding Ian had settled gently to the ground. "Has he got his helmet? Should we—"

Rita answered. "Ian is fine for right now. It's going to be all right."

They could only sit and mutter among themselves as Rita and Frances removed Reg's helmet and helped him clean up. Already his nose had stopped bleeding, but that hadn't prevented him from needing a vomit bag. Sean started to get up, but Chris grabbed his sleeve, and he reluctantly sank back down. The murmuring faded into the stillness of a waiting room in a surgery ward.

They remained in silence, save for the two women reassuring Reg. Finally, Frances stowed the dirty rags in a biohazard bin. Reg, calmer, assured everyone he was okay.

Sean burst out, "What about Ian?"

"Ian is unconscious. Sedated. He tried to rip off his spacesuit."

Gasps and shouts filled the cargo hold with sound. Rita raised her hands and her voice.

"He'll be all right! He only got his glove off. His suit, like all of your suits, has safeguards, remember? Plus, I got him in the bag before any serious damage was done. I need to tend to him next, but first, does anyone know if he was taking medication of any kind?"

"What are you getting at?" Sean asked.

Rita's gaze turned to him and her eyes flashed. "Dr. Thoren convinced him to investigate a pod. Ian panicked. Whatever happened to him, he was not prepared to handle it."

Sean gaped. "So it *is* a mind-control device?"

"We don't know that, and everyone else who has entered a pod has come away fine, but we do know that that area is potentially dangerous, which is why we declared it off limits." She set her jaw, and James knew she was biting back some disparaging words about their former mission commander.

Around them, he saw the team's worry grow. "People, the only reason this happened is because they disobeyed orders and went into the pods. We're not in any danger."

He turned to Rita. "You, Chris and I each experienced the pods, and we're fine. So what happened with Ian?"

"That's what I'd like to know," she replied before raising her voice to the group. "Something was different about how Ian handled his experience, which is why I ask: does anyone know if he was on medication or drugs of any kind that he did not report?"

Sean bit his lip. "You said he took off his glove? Did anyone ever notice how Ian was always scratching at his hands? Washing them, too."

Rita nodded. "And he was talking about something being on his hands. Okay. Good observations. All right. We'll be at the *Edwina Taggert* in a couple of minutes. I'd like to get Ian out of the bag and onto a stretcher. James, will you help me? Sean, get the stretcher from that wall, please?"

Rita knelt beside the balloon. She pierced the seal and released the air slowly, then pulled the seal apart to reveal the unconscious man, curled in a fetal position on the floor, the bottom of the bag and his suit spattered in blood. The glove, its strap ripped, lay near his feet, along with the skinsuit glove. The other skinsuit glove lay beside his head, while the suit glove itself hung loose from the suit. His hands were raw from deep scratches and his nails thick with blood.

"Oh, Ian, what did you do?" Rita murmured as she knelt over him.

James set his hand on her shoulder. "Wait a minute. He pulled off his glove? Are you sure he doesn't have decompression sickness?"

"Of course I am. The first-aid kit is right there. I need gauze." Gently, she rolled Ian onto his back. He was clutching one hand with the other. He moaned.

James didn't move. "Look, Rita, I'm a diver. I know about the bends. Sudden depressurization —"

She hissed in annoyance. "James! Remember Suits 101? We're in space, not the ocean, and spacesuits have safeguards. A compression cuff inflated and sealed the leak just below his wrist in less than a second. And I got him into a pressurized bag in under fifteen."

Sean knelt next to her, the stretcher under one arm and the kit in his hands. She took the kit and, after thanking him, instructed him on where to lay the stretcher and how to lock it to the deck. She pulled on medical gloves, then rubbed antibiotic cream on her hands to the pulled-up cuffs of her sleeves, then reached gently for Ian's.

James stepped out of the way, but still hovered near her shoulder. "But Rita!"

"Trust me. He did more damage to himself than space did." One finger at a time, she pried his nails out from where he had dug them into the back of his hand. When she pulled them away, James saw the torn skin underneath. Not just torn. Flayed. One nail had dug out a chunk of skin and meat; even with stitches, he'd have a scar.

"Tommie, time?" Rita called loudly.

"Four minutes. We're approaching the magnetic barrier now."

"Thanks. Everyone, settle in for landing. James, I want to clean and wrap this fast, but first, let's strap him into the stretcher. Can you get his head and, Sean, his feet?"

"Of course." He squatted at Ian's head and did as directed while Rita held Ian's hands. Ian moaned and thrashed his head, but weakly.

Rita murmured reassurances while also warning him to stay still so she wouldn't have to sedate him again. Once he was loosely strapped in, she returned to treating his hands.

"I don't understand. Why would he do that?"

"I don't know." Rita sighed. "But I'm certain Ann will have a guess."

* * *

Ann left the bridge as Commander McVee handled the docking procedures. She ran to the bay, turning right and left with the unconscious ease of familiarity and practice. At one point, she pulled open a maintenance panel and squeezed through the narrow confines, cutting two decks off her path. She got there slightly out of breath and just behind OvLandra and the two crewmen she'd drafted to help her.

"Reg Alexander's injuries are superficial, and he is ambulatory. I shall escort him to Sickbay and prepare the scanning equipment for Ian Hu. He can wait quietly," Ov was telling the others. "Lieutenant Rose Chan, you and Sister Rita Aguilar will care for Ian Hu in the shuttle. Get him stitched up, check for deeper injuries, and bring him to Sickbay for scanning. It is fortunate we have his earlier tests."

"He's not injured, aside from his hands. That's not the problem," Ann said.

Ov met her statement with a slow blink, an acknowledgement, but not an agreement. "We don't know that. The device might have damaged his mind." Then they were heading down the hall, Ann forgotten.

Ann leaned against the wall, hooking her foot in the steady bar out of habit and tried to make sense of the messages in her heart and mind. "He's not injured. He's sick. So sick. Soul sick. And he ignored the illness of his soul, even though it was on the DST list." She looked at the medical team and felt her stomach clutch so hard, she had to close her eyes. Was this fear?

He's so soul sick. I'm not a healer. I'm not! People don't confide in me. That's for Father, or Mother Superior — but me? I don't know if I can do this. I don't know what to do.

The saints were around her, watching. Waiting. Expecting.

The door opened. The medical team hurried through, pushing the stretcher between them. She saw the doors of *Basilica* opening, people pouring out.

Ann glanced around her. Where had the prophets gone? David and Daniel, even Ezekiel? They'd led her this far. Why did they go now?

The medical team took the stretchers into the ship. The rest of the researchers gathered to the side, a tight group, so scared for their friend. Too much fear.

I didn't make them understand. I think I'm explaining, but I'm not making sense to them. What do I do?

Ann's feet didn't move. Ian needed her help, but she felt so help-less.

Rita. Did Rita feel like this before a rescue? Ann had seen her hesitate at the airlock, eyes shut. She'd always thought it was the first step out of the ship. Lots of people had trouble with that. But was that it? Or did she just feel overwhelmed and inadequate? Stepping into the unknown, feeling so small against a need so large.

But she does it. Every time. She doesn't know how brave she is. I didn't know, either. Now I have to be brave, just like her. Faith, hope, and love. They will make me brave.

She pushed off the wall and strode into the bay.

OvLandra stepped out of the shuttle, one hand on Reg's elbow to steady him, even though he protested that he was fine. He was pressing gauze against his nose, which had started bleeding again in the change of gravity and air pressure.

When he saw Ann, his face twisted in the pain of guilt. "I'm sorry," he told her. "I should never have let him go alone. Buddy system, always, you told us. I deserve to be grounded."

She shushed him. *"When things fall apart, faith tells us to look to the broken pieces. Out of them a new whole may emerge.* Ian has been broken for a long time. We have to help Ian become whole again."

Reg's brows knit in confusion, but before he could ask his question, there was a crash, and she ran to the *Basilica* and the person she needed to help rescue.

She found the stretcher overturned and Rita leaning over Rose, who slumped against the MiGR, holding the back of her head and breathing fast against pain and dizziness. Ian had scooted against a far wall, hands in front of his face in a defensive gesture. Torn gauze hung in bloody strips off them, but he hardly noticed as he tried to focus both on Tommie and James as they inched toward him.

"Go away!" he moaned. "Don't touch me. I have death on my hands. Stay back!"

"Ian, we just want to help," Tommie said. She glanced at James, and he circled to the right as she spoke to the delirious man. "We need to get you to the infirmary and take care of those hands."

"No! Don't touch them! Don't touch me!"

"Ian, it's all right." Tommie moved to the left, making sure Ian tracked her.

"No, it's not!"

Ann spoke. "You're right. It's not." She stepped through the open space and knelt down beside Ian. "It's not all right. But you can be."

"You don't understand," he moaned. "You can't know."

Yet she did. Tiny lives, torn from the protection of the womb, torn from this life, as Ian stood by, a willing accomplice.

"The lifeguard who didn't guard life. A doctor who wouldn't heal," she whispered. "A clinic where life ended. And you. You were pre-med?"

She closed her eyes as the world slipped out. "Dreams destroyed to make room for other dreams. Lesser, greater, it didn't matter, but you thought it did then. So much blood. You wash and wash, and it never comes off..."

Ann opened her eyes, but the world was blurry through her tears.

"Please! Don't touch me." Ian pulled his knees close to his chest, his hands sandwiched between them.

Then the horror vanished. A warmth of compassion flowed over her, mixed with the low-key adrenalin rush of a rescue. Her vision cleared, and she met his frightened, remorseful eyes with a steady gaze. Faith, hope, and love. She reached out and set her hands on his knees.

"Don't protect your pain. You've done that too long. There's nothing noble about suffering without hope."

She pushed his knees down. Ian, face slack, his gaze captured by her, let his feet slide. His breath quickened as she took one of his hands between hers.

"You have to have faith that you can make this right. God forgives. His mercy extends beyond time, space, or life. Even the taking of life. That's what He was telling you in the pod. You didn't listen then. You protected your pain, guarded your guilt. It's time to stop."

Gently, she removed the torn bandages, rolling them, easing the gauze where it stuck, careful not to start the bleeding again. He moaned a protest, yet didn't move. She held his mangled hand before him.

"God hates what you did even more than you do, but He loves you. That's what you have to understand. This won't make things right. You just make more pain. Pain upon pain. Blood upon blood. Hate upon hate. Let it go, Ian. Faith, hope, and love — and you are loved."

She kissed his hand lightly and pressed it against her cheek.

He stared at her a moment, then his features went slack.

James leapt forward and caught him as he finally gave in to the sedatives and relaxed back into sleep. With a grunt of effort, he lifted the young man and carried him to the stretcher. Rose had stood up, insisting she was fine, and she and Rita strapped Ian firmly to the bed.

James studied Ian's peaceful face, then turned to Ann. "What was that?" he asked.

"A rescue." Ann smiled, her eyes still on Ian. Then she shook herself. "But we're not finished yet. Rita, do you need James to help with the stretcher?"

"I'm fine," Rose reiterated. "Rita and I can handle it."

Rita, buckling a last strap, looked up long enough to nod.

Ann took James by the wrist and pulled him to the ramp. "Come with me. We need to talk."

When she got outside the shuttle, however, she saw the research team still bunched together to one side of the bay, talking amongst each other, waiting for instructions. One of the researchers was sobbing against Gordon's shoulder. Dr. Thoren stood before them, his eyes on the ship, unreadable.

Sheep without a shepherd. Chris isn't ready yet. Now James can't stay. So they huddle in a pasture too scared to move while the wolf makes his plans.

Ann shook her head. She needed to understand about shepherding. No time now. On-the-job training.

"Go change. I'll meet you outside the suit room." She gave James' hand a squeeze and went to the group.

Everyone asked questions at once: Was it a mind-control device? Would Ian be okay? How badly was he hurt? Had he gone mad? What if others were going to go *couritza*, and it was just taking longer? Was it contagious?

Fear, and behind the fear, blame. Thoren was no shepherd now; he was the wolf. They knew it, but for how long? They went against her to follow him once. Would they do it again? People forget wolves more easily than sheep did. That's why people are harder to shepherd.

"Is that Ian's blood on your face?" Sean exclaimed, and everyone fell into shocked silence.

"Listen to me," she said. "Ian will be all right. This isn't a weapon. It's a gift. Ian didn't understand how to use the gift, and it hurt him. If you misuse it —"

"And I suppose you know how to use it?" Thoren demanded.

Wolf in shepherd's clothing. Shepherd leading his lambs to the slaughter, but there's no wedding feast. No celebration. No reason. Just sheep in his way.

Too many sheep analogies, Lord! I've never even seen a sheep!

"What?" Thoren asked, and she realized she'd spoken aloud. Mother Superior would be angry.

She squared her shoulders. "Dr. Thoren, I do understand the pod devices, and I could know how to use them if I got to study them. I am certain of this. But this is not the time for that discussion."

"I agree." Captain Addiman appeared at the door, followed closely by two large crewmen. They surrounded the head researcher. Addiman seemed to have grown larger in his anger, and he loomed over Thoren.

Thank you for sending another shepherd! Ann prayed.

"We have gone over the recordings in Dr. Hu's lab," Addiman said. "And we know that you encouraged him to violate a prohibition of de Safety Officers of this mission for no better reason than your own curiosity. We have sent a message to Luna Technological Institute and ColeCorp notifying them of this. Until we receive a reply, you are relieved of all duties and prohibited from de alien ship and research areas."

"I beg your pardon?" the king responded, haughty in his power. "My own curiosity? Obviously, no one else is taking the Third Arm Problem as seriously as I am. Since our Safety Officer preferred to hide the problem away rather than confront it."

Ann felt her hackles rise, but a sudden impression of ropes uncoiling from his mouth distracted her into silence.

"I merely employed Code Four — improvise intelligently — and took the effort to assign a covert team to further study the problem. Code Two: double and triple check everything; Code Eleven: knowledge..."

"Oh, can that leak!" one of the researchers and his most ardent follower, cried out. "That could have been me in Sickbay if I'd listened to you! I told you I thought it was a bad idea. Maybe no one else was hurt, but no one's been exactly the same, either. You said you thought it was a mind-control device, but you wanted more people to go in? When we are out here, alone, months from help? What happened to Code Nine, Dr. Thoren? What happened to safety?"

"I was considering the safety of the human race."

But his follower had again buried her head in Gordon's shoulder, and the rest of the researchers crowded around her.

Addiman leaned in toward Thoren. "Do not give me cause to confine you to quarters for de duration of de trip. *Edwina* has dealt with troublemakers before; we can do so again."

As the Chief Researcher gaped, Addiman nodded to his men, who, albeit politely, took Thoren by the arms and escorted him out. The captain watched until the doors closed, then turned back to the group. "Listen to me. You cannot help anyone standing 'ere. Get out of your suits. Eat, rest. And pray for Ian. I promise to tell you more when we know more."

Ann gripped his arm. "Thank you," she whispered. Then, secure in the knowledge that this part of the flock was cared for, she went to find another shepherd.

Chapter Twenty-Eight

James peeled off the skinsuit with a sigh of relief that quickly turned into a gasp of disgust. He needed a shower. And a cold drink. And for someone to explain just what in the world was going on. He tossed the sweat-soiled suit into the laundry and reached for the clothes he'd stuffed into his locker seven long hours ago. He inhaled and decided he wasn't good to anyone, reeking like this. Ann could wait for five minutes.

The warm water felt wonderful, and James turned his face to the spray. He ran his fingers over his hair, allowing himself a moment to relax. It felt so good. Like rain. Warm rain on a spring evening...

He jerked the water settings to cold and grabbed the soap.

Get a grip, James. Two men — two friends — are in the infirmary, we're millions of miles from help, and no one knows what happened to Ian. Ann would have a guess about what happened to Ian, Rita had said. So why is she wasting time with me? She needs to talk to Dr. OvLandra. Or Rita. Rita would understand her better, especially if she starts talking nonsense. Yet...

He saw it again: Ann kneeling in front of Ian, kissing his bloodied hand. Ian sinking into peaceful sleep, when sedatives had failed to calm him. And she...glowed. Maybe she did know what she was doing.

Or she was wise enough to let the One who would know work through her.

If so, I shouldn't waste her time. He dried off in hurried, rough strokes, tossed on his T-shirt and jeans, slid on shoes, and dashed to the exit. The others were starting to come in. Sean tried to grab his arm to get his attention, but James brushed him off, saying he had to find Ann.

"Get her a washcloth!" Sean called to his retreating back, and he paused at the sinks long enough to wet one.

He found Ann in the corridor, leaning against the wall, one leg bent and anchored in the steady bar along the floor. She gave him a brilliant smile as he handed her the damp cloth. "Oh, thank you!"

She wiped her face, then ducked into the women's locker room to toss the dirty washcloth into the laundry. No sooner had she emerged than she asked, "Do you have your *Rituale Romanum*?"

"My what?"

She looked at him as if surprised to discover him so stupid. Then she grabbed his wrist and started pulling him down the corridor. "We'll download it if you need it."

They rounded another corner and stopped at a maintenance hatchway. She pulled it open. "Shortcut," she said. "No one will look for us this way."

He glanced at the narrow aisle. *In for a penny.* He followed her in. He could walk upright, and stick his elbows out some, but not much more. After the wide hallways of the *Edwina Taggert*, he felt claustrophobic.

"On some ships you have to crawl, but these are so roomy," Ann said, and James didn't know if she'd read his thoughts or was oblivious to his discomfort. "Either way, they still call them Jeffries tubes. See? Electrical and computer wiring and plumbing. We hide them away to protect them from damage, but build accessways to get to them if they get damaged, anyway. If we went back that direction, we'd end up near the landing bay. See that door? That takes you to the quartermaster. There's a small cabinet further down that holds diagnostic equipment. Maps are good; diagnosis is important, but without understanding, it's only so much information."

Ann took him through a maze of turns, and up and down ladders, chatting about the machinery and circuits, until he lost track of their location and the conversation. As they passed one of the doors, Ann ran her hand along it lovingly. "We're right behind the labs now, you know. Access tunnels are so cozy and useful. You should always know them — and always know all the escapes from a room."

"Ann, why do I need a *Rituale*?"

"Well, you don't if you remember it, of course. Do you?" They came to another ladder, and she grabbed the rungs.

James stopped and glared at her with arms crossed. "Just what has Rita told you about me?"

"Come up here. There's room to sit."

He joined her in a wide, square area. The walls had empty bolt holes and cables that were sealed with electrical tape. Ann held one of the cables with the same tenderness with which she'd held Ian's hand. For a moment, James thought she might press it to her face. Instead, she lowered it gently, then sat down cross-legged in front of him.

"They ripped a piece of her out," Ann explained. "A virtual reality room was on the other side, and the controls were here. But it interfered with some of the research equipment, and Cole ordered it ripped out. Captain Addiman said the salvage yard owner would sell it. That doesn't matter, though. It's still the *Edwina Taggert*, right? Humans can do that to their creations — change things, alter purpose, rip out what doesn't work. But when we do that to ourselves..." She paused, waiting for his reply.

He rubbed his eyes. "Ann, what are you asking of me? And what did Rita tell you?"

Ann's gaze dropped to the empty space between them. "Rita doesn't talk about you, but I think she thinks about you a lot. She has this picture of you. A real photo. I saw it when I was servicing her suit. It fell out of her pocket, and I put it back. You were very handsome in your cassock."

"That was another life."

"That's what I'm trying to tell you!" She spread her hands, indicating the room. "You can't just tear a part of yourself out when it interferes. Only God can do that."

"Does this have to do with my vision?" The volume of his question startled him.

Ann blinked, thrown off track. "What? No. Well, maybe, but you don't need rescuing right now! Ian needs our help. He tried to rip out pieces of himself, create bypasses. Bypass the past. But no one taught him how, and the connections were faulty, and it made him sick. Soul-sick. His life shattered, and he needs to look at the pieces and find a new whole."

"Ann!" James grabbed her shoulders. "You're..." He started to say she wasn't making sense, but stopped himself. She probably made perfect sense — if you spoke Annese. "I don't understand. Be slow and direct. What is wrong with Ian, and why are you telling me and not Dr. OvLandra?"

Ann took a deep, shuddering breath. Her focus turned inwards. "I'm trying," she murmured. "The soul, like a ship. Sometimes we damage them. Sometimes, we make...modifications. Choices in our lives. Wrong choices. Damaging choices. Diagnostics point out the problems, but you have to recognize them and want to effect repairs. Recognition, regret, desire to change: they're necessary conditions, but not sufficient. You know that. I know that. Ian doesn't."

Recognition, regret, desire to change? "Ann, are you saying Ian needs to go to Confession?"

In hushed tones, she told him how Ian assisted at an abortion clinic. "All those little souls set free of their bodies too soon. He tried to justify his participation, but how do you justify something so unjust? You can't modify that deeply without swapping the core, and at the core, Ian is a good man.

"His soul is damaged. The device showed him. It's not mind control. It's a diagnostic tool. But he doesn't know how to fix the damage. He's an engineer. He wants to rip out the damaged equipment, but he's targeting the wrong systems. I tried to make him understand, but I couldn't. He needs a better shepherd."

James felt himself grow cold. "Ann, he's not Catholic. And I'm not a priest."

"You almost were. And you can't cut that part of you out any more than he can his past. The *Edwina Taggert* is retooled for a new mission, but she's still the *Edwina Taggert*."

"I'm not a machine." He wanted to shake her. He wanted to shake himself. The rain had turned cold, the sky dark.

Ann gripped his arms and smiled, a light shining through the clouds. "Of course not! You're a caring, compassionate man, who loved God enough to try to dedicate your life to Him. You're not a priest, I understand that. There won't be a sacrament. But there can be healing, and you have to bring it to him."

"Why me? I'm no psychologist."

"He doesn't need psychology. Dr. OvLandra wants a physical cure. He won't talk to me or Tommie, and Rita...Rita picks at scabs, tweaks things and is never satisfied. Humans aren't like machines. They resist retrofitting. She needs to attend to her own diagnostics. Maybe later, but now...James, you have to try."

She stood up and walked to one of the hatches. She pushed and held it open. "Time to come in out of the rain."

* * *

Rita applied a medicinal adhesive gel to the deepest of Ian's scratches, being careful not to overfill the wounds. The glue would protect the wound and hold the skin in place while the genetically adaptive compound became skin and filled in the hole. She ran the wand over his hands to activate the mutations, taking extra care over areas where he'd dug the deepest.

Across the room, Dr. OvLandra tended to Reg's nose while looking over the results of Ian's brain scan. No one complained; zerogs had the uncanny ability to multitask far more effectively than humans. One hand moved with expert tenderness over Reg's nose, checking for breaks, while the other manipulated her tablet.

Rita handed the wand to Rose to put away while she re-wrapped Ian's hand in clean gauze. Then, she secured his arm in wrist straps and started on the other. Even unconscious, she didn't trust him not to tear at his skin.

"You did that really well," Rose said as she stuck the gel and the activator in a drawer.

"I've had lots of practice." She shivered, remembering that rescue — the ship of snakes. She'd gotten the antivenin in time to save Ann and the shuttle pilot, but not before their wounds had swelled so badly that their skin had torn around the bites. Ann had needed a complete tube to cure her hand; the pilot took the balance of their supply and had still needed a skin graft. Rita had had to excuse herself once — no, twice — to throw up while working on him. They'd opened the infested ship to vacuum and left it for three weeks before Mother Superior let anyone into it.

Snake-infested ships, rockets crashing into space stations, now alien devices that cause hallucinations. I can't even imagine what's next. Rita snorted to herself.

"What?" her assistant asked.

"Just remembering what my father said when I told him I was joining the Rescue Sisters: 'But, *Ritita*, you aren't the adventurous type.'"

Rose didn't join her in laughter. "Well, I'm glad you're here — your order, I mean. I grew up in 4Q3S. When the Dolorosa convent was started, people fought them all the way, even the grunt rockjacks, not just corporate management. Yet fatalities and injuries got cut by half. You guys saved my brother's life. I can't even tell you how important you sisters are."

"I... thank you," Rita stammered, feeling warmed and embarrassed and completely undeserving of the praise — or of her fellow sisters. *For pity's sake! I thought I was done feeling like that!*

"And you saved their lives today."

"Well, I wouldn't go that far." She finished taping Ian's wound and passed the rest of the materials to Rose.

The commander took them, moving them from one hand to the other. "Maybe not. I don't know. But I do know that I'm really glad ColeCorp hired you three to protect us." With a small nod, she left to put the supplies in the room cabinet.

Rita watched her a moment, then turned back to Ian, who lay still, his breathing too regular for normal sleep. Rita's smile disappeared. She brushed back his dark hair. *How do I best protect you?*

The door hissed open, making her jump. Ann strode in with a breathless James in tow.

"Sorry we're late," she announced to the room without slowing her stride. She held James' hand and all but dragged him with her. "It was easier to explain things in the Jeffries tubes."

She led James to Ian's side, set his hand on Ian's arm and settled James next to the unconscious man. Smiling with satisfaction, she looked at the monitors.

"I'm glad you didn't sedate him again. Now he'll wake up soon, and he and James can talk."

"Why James?" Rita blurted, still reeling from the whirlwind of her partner's activity.

Ann beamed at her. "You know!"

No, I don't. Rita looked past her to James. With an embarrassed grimace, he made a small sign of the cross with his flattened hand.

She turned her attention back to Ann. "Do you know what you're doing?"

"Mostly. God knows better than me, which is a great comfort."

Dr. OvLandra spoke up from where she tended Reg. "Then perhaps you can help us figure this out. Please, join me in my office." She gave Reg's shoulder a squeeze and instructed him to lie quietly for the time being. She headed to the door on the far side of the room. Ann followed.

Rita hesitated.

"Go on," James said. "We can holler if there's trouble, and Doctor OvLandra might need an interpreter."

Rita felt the change in gravity in her stomach and her hair. OvLandra's office was smaller than the one Thoren had claimed for himself, but had enough room for a tidy desk and two comfortable chairs. One wall had a screen for viewing large scans, while the other wall held a glass case full of replicas of antique medical equipment.

"They came with the ship," OvLandra explained when she saw Rita's interest, "along with a manual I had to memorize explaining their history and functions in order to keep up an image. I prefer modern equipment to such barbarisms."

"IVs aren't modern," Ann pointed out.

OvLandra nodded in surrender. "All right, Sister Ann Marie St. Joseph de Cupertino. You seem to have the best idea of anyone what's going on. What happened to Ian Hu?"

Ann turned toward the door, as if looking through it to the patient beyond. Her gaze softened in compassion, and her head tilted as if listening to someone. "He damaged his soul. Deep, too deep to claw out no matter how he may have tried today. For so long, he tried. He tried to convince himself it was okay, but it's not, and somewhere inside, he knows it. That's why he laughs so much. 'Laugh or cry,' he said. But he's forgotten how to cry. He shouldn't have gone to the third arm. He wasn't ready. He had no guide. People need guides, instructions."

"To the device?" OvLandra asked.

"To the soul."

OvLandra took a deep breath, accepting this odd statement for now. "And Ian Hu didn't have this guide?"

"The device showed him the damage. That's what it does. Like your equipment. He couldn't handle seeing his own wounds. He tried to tear out the damaged systems, but he chose the wrong ones. He doesn't want to examine the problem closely. That would add pressure to the system, and it's already overtaxed. And he can't cry."

OvLandra pressed a button on her wrist control, and a colored image of a brain appeared in a hologram before them. Rita didn't know a lot about brain function, but the dim colors suggested this one was not working at normal levels.

OvLandra confirmed her suspicions. "I am not sure Ian Hu will awaken. He has entered a fugue state. How do we help him? I can't fix his soul."

Ann closed her eyes. "He has to wake up. We can't help him if he doesn't wake up."

"Ann," OvLandra tried again. "What if we calibrate the device to the human brain? Could it return him to normal?"

"I don't know."

"Could it...show him the proper systems to repair?"

"I don't know." She shook her head.

"If you saw the device yourself, truly studied it, could you know?"

"I don't know!" Ann opened her eyes. "This isn't a matter of brainwaves and technology. This is a matter of the soul!"

"Ann." Rita stepped forward and set her hands on Ann's arms. She imagined she felt goosebumps under the skinsuit. She rubbed them. "We can't help Ian unless we can talk to him, drive him from his stupor. If we can get the device to do that, we can help him through the rest, right?"

Ann nodded. "True. Maybe."

"You understand the device better than anyone. Possibly better than anyone ever will. Besides, you haven't even seen it, not really. And if anyone can do miracles, I believe it's you."

OvLandra pushed herself forward. "I'll go with you. We'll figure it out together."

Ann glanced at her, then looked down. Mumbling.

"What, Annie?" Rita asked. She leaned down, trying to catch her gaze.

"I don't know zoology. How many lions in a den? Does it have to be more than one?"

"Uh." Rita paused. Ann never asked a question without reason, but sometimes, she was hard-pressed to understand them. "I don't think so. Why?"

"Too many animal metaphors!" Ann pushed away from Rita and raked her fingers through her hair. The uncharacteristic gesture threw Rita more than any of her off-the-wall questions could. Rita gaped, frozen into inaction as Ann bowed her head and muttered to herself.

After a moment, Ann looked up, her expression calm but lacking its usual joy. "All right. We'll try."

"Excellent!" OvLandra immediately went to her computer and typed in some commands. A series of readings showed up on the screens: Ian's vital signs, including an extensive brainwave analysis.

"We were very fortunate that I scanned Ian earlier even though he did not enter the pods then. We have a baseline to work with. Here are his readings from before the mission, and here from just a few minutes ago. See how active this area of the brain is? In a normal catatonic patient, you'd expect this." She called up a new image.

"I propose first that we scan you, Small Weight, then you and I shall return to the ship together."

"And Rita," Ann insisted. "She should understand what's going on, too, in case she needs to assist you."

OvLandra hesitated. "Of course. It is a good idea."

Brain surgery? Is that what you have planned for me next, Lord? Hey, why not? But Rita caught sight of Ann, and her sarcastic thoughts died. Although the young sister appeared to be studying the screen with her usual calm intensity, years working and living together let Rita see just how tightly she held herself.

She'd never seen Ann so frightened.

Chapter Twenty-Nine

Rita fought against the nightmare.

Aliens bowing on six legs and bleating like sheep as Ann walked into the pod, dressed in a light blue dress and glowing. OvLandra watching with greedy eyes, marking time, then turning into a snake and biting Rita in the stomach.

No, not the stomach. Her medpod.

Rita's eyes flew open as her stomach flipped, but she pressed a hand to her mouth to stifle a scream. She was in the chapel, kneeling next to Ann. Ann remained perfectly still, her eyes focused on Jesus, her rosary tattoo flashing.

Meanwhile, I fall asleep?

She wanted to berate herself, but the impressions of the dream didn't let her. Her medpod dock tingled like it hadn't since she'd first gotten it. She could still envision Ann's face, twisted in pain and fear as the snake also bit through her medpod and sent its poison coursing through her bloodstream.

Rita shook her head hard. She managed to banish the image, but not the feeling of impending danger. Without quite realizing she was doing it, she crossed herself swiftly and headed to the suit-up room.

She called out once and heard only her voice echo back. Nonetheless, after she made sure no one was in the room or adjoining bathrooms, she locked all the doors before using her override key to open OvLandra's locker. She pulled out her suit and breathed a sigh of relief when she saw the zerog's Mark IV. Over the past three years, Ann had made her memorize every circuit, configuration, and, more to the point, override in the suit's manual — and a few more besides. Even though they'd upgraded their own suits four months ago, Rita remembered well enough to do what she needed.

She called up the virtual keyboard on her wristcomp, established a connection with OvLandra's suit, and started typing in commands.

I'm being stupid. If anyone catches me, what do I tell them?

Her hand paused a moment over the keys. She clenched it into a fist. *They'll think I'm nuts, that the device has affected me but took longer to show. That I'm getting paranoid. It won't matter if the argument doesn't make logical sense. Thoren would use it. Besides, what I'm doing doesn't make logical sense, either. She's the chief medical officer. We've trusted her with our lives. Ann trusts her.*

She felt her short fingernails dig into her skin. With a sudden movement, she flung open her hand and finished typing in commands.

She didn't care. Half the people who had entered the pods had entered by accident, and half of them had come away...disturbed.

If that happened to OvLandra, by purpose or accident, Rita was not trusting her with command of their suits.

* * *

Ann hovered at the entrance to one of the "devices," as OvLandra called it. It was still the wrong word, but better than pod. They'd decided to use the one Ian had entered, and OvLandra suggested if they had time, she might have Ann enter a different one as well. Perhaps Ann might see the same things? Different things? The same, but in more detail?

She thought Ov was being ridiculous and had told her that; the only things she would find in the visions were what God had already given to her. It didn't matter. They had to see this through. Everything had its procedures, steps you follow, because bypassing them skews the results. Even the Resurrection had to have the Via Dolorosa.

Lust may lie, and the heart misgive — but God make your feet point forward where you must go.

She'd felt the third arm's pull at her since they'd first orbited Folly. Now it called her more strongly than ever; but with that pull, a warning.

"Ann?" OvLandra's voice, musical despite the suit speakers, intruded on her thoughts. "What's wrong? Are you frightened?"

"Yes, but not of the device." Warmth and welcome touched her where she faced the device, but along her back, like proximity sensors picking up an object it couldn't identify or target, a crawling sensation warned, "It's there. Beware."

"It's all right, Ann," Rita said. "I'm here."

"We're here," James added.

"Copy, James." He had insisted on making the last mission, and others had been glad to keep watch over the sleeping Ian in the meantime. She hadn't liked it, but in her prayers, she'd received a message, not from the saints and not in words, but a conviction so strong, she knew the source, and He wanted Rita and James together for the last of the mission. They needed to know where their feet pointed.

Then, God graced her with just enough time before departure for the epiphany she'd promised James.

Swallowing down her nervousness, she said, "God is with me. Now, go check the room I told you about."

"We will be fine," OvLandra added. "Go ahead, Small Weight. I'll be monitoring you the whole time. I'll take care of you."

Ann couldn't make herself face her friend. She and Rita had gone to the chapel to pray, and instead, she'd dreamed. *Daniel leaning against a hillside, near a cave, a throng of holy martyrs seated before him. He'd said not all lions live in dens, and they'd laughed.*

"Ann?"

"Do what you have to do," she whispered.

OvLandra chuckled. "What does that mean?"

"I'm sorry. I don't understand." Ann shook her head. She felt phantom scratches along her back.

OvLandra urged. "Go. We'll talk once you're done."

The martyrs had all laughed, and St. Ignatius of Antioch said, "Sometimes, you have to toss them in the den yourself!" The earth had shaken around them, and they had toppled into each other laughing with joy. Why should they fear? God was with them.

Why should *she* fear? God was with her, too!

She felt a surge of adrenalin and joy. A smile pulled at her face. This time, she didn't try to stop it.

"You're right," she told OvLandra, and pushed herself in. If she was going to be grappling with lions, she needed to know the procedures. And there was only one place to learn.

God make your feet point forward where you must go.

* * *

Despite Ann's direction, Rita lingered as Ann entered the pod. Once in, she hovered, completely still. Rita called up the readings on OvLandra's equipment and found they didn't differ much from REM sleep.

"This could be awhile," OvLandra said. "Go. Check the room Ann was so excited for you to see. I'll continue to send you readings; you can rush back at any time."

It's not the pod I'm worried about, she found herself thinking. She scolded herself. Bad enough she'd disabled OvLandra's suit; how far was she going to go in her paranoia? Maybe the pod *had* affected her.

"Let's be quick," she told James, and they headed to the third level of the sphere, between the second and first arms, where Ann had promised an epiphany for James.

* * *

The whites and grays of the device room gave way to warm reds and oranges and real wood furniture. The small viewscreen showed a pair of asteroids before a starry landscape; Ann recognized Gamma Eriadne, a useless rock that marked the outer edges of the section patrolled by St.

Joseph de Cupertino convent. The actual view, too. This ship was at rest, floating at the edge of colonized space.

She turned to look at the room again. Textured walls to rival the *Edwina Taggert*, so pretty and so familiar. She looked down to find bamboo mats beneath her bare feet — and above her ankles, the skirt of a pretty blue dress with lots of frills and petticoats and a long train of fabric flowing behind her.

She had just a moment for her eyes to fill with tears before the memory swept over her and she was again Anilou Taggert-Landra, daughter of Edwina Taggert and KelLandra, celebrating her fourth birthday.

* * *

OvLandra watched the two weighties leave with relief. Bad enough the half-breed in the pod had given Sean Ostrand the documentary she'd been told to watch — now that nosey documentarist's suspicions were forcing her to move up her schedule. Everything had to look like an accident if she ever hoped to return alive, mission fulfilled, to the comfort of her home and her people.

Oh, to be home again and outside the harshness of human gravity! To no longer look at eyes too small, observe movements too clumsy, deal with attitudes too permissive.

Although the crew had been kind.

No, she scolded herself. She had been chosen by her clan for this mission not just because of her ability to hide her true feelings, but of her particular disdain for the weighties. The honor of their tribe, of their bloodline, rested with her. Would she betray them? Of course not; she was no Judas.

Do what you have to do, indeed.

* * *

"She told you that?" Rita squawked. Her hand slipped on the grip of the prier, but the magnets held it to the door of the room Ann had told them to investigate. OvLandra had reported that Ann was still in the device, her vital signs normal. Rita had called up a small window on her heads-up display, and her gaze flicked toward it as she worked. The stats remained a reassuring green, yet somehow failed to ease the crawling sensation along her back. She kept thinking of snakes poised to strike. Now James had to toss this at her? "'Lust may lie?'"

"Yes! Then she said we had to work together to resolve this. Listen, Rita. If I gave anyone the impression that I was lusting after you..."

I don't need this! She set the last arm into place, glanced at Ann's vitals. Still dreaming, but normal. *What was she experiencing? I wish I had a way to scan her thoughts. 'Course that's not a new wish.* "James, tell me exactly what she said before you jump to conclusions, please."

"She said that—"

"Verbatim, James!"

He paused, and when he spoke it was slowly, as if dredging up the words. "Lust may lie, and the heart misgive — but God make your feet point forward, where you must go."

Rita groaned. "James, she's quoting someone. Brother Jubal, probably. She's focused on a big problem. Big, like 'the crew' big."

"There are different kinds of lust. Thoren lusts for power," James mused.

"Exactly! I'm betting she wasn't referring to just you. I mean, not you specifically. As far as us resolving anything, she seemed to think part of the answer lies in what we'd find in this chamber. And, no; I don't know why this one or how she found it. Let's just figure out what it is so we can get back to her." Anxious to be done with the conversation, she switched to the mission channel. "This is Team Two to *Edwina Taggert*. We are ready to open the chamber."

Addiman's voice sounded in her helmet. "Very good. Doctor OvLandra reports Ann's readings are much like someone in a deep lucid dreaming state, and she is otherwise fine."

I hope so. Rita stole another glance at Ann's vitals as she activated the prier. She didn't bother to move to one side as the door irised open.

A sudden force pushed her back, and an alien flew out of the opening and slammed against her faceplate. Shrieking and clawing at her helmet, she bumped into James, sending the both of them spinning.

"What is it? Sister Rita, are you all right?"

"Rita!" James yelled. "Calm down. It's dead. It's dead."

He reached to pull it off, but it bounced off his suit and ricocheted back toward her. She screamed again and twisted to avoid it, which sent them both tumbling toward it again. She raised her arm.

"Tommie to Rita, what is going on? Do you need help?"

"Get that away from me!" she screeched as she flung the corpse away. The reaction knocked them against the partially open door, but at least this time, the alien sailed down the corridor.

"Sister, report!"

"We're fine, Tommie!" Rita called, then forced herself to calm. "We're fine. Just...startled. There was an alien near the door we opened, and it blew out right at me and — oh, vac! Vac, vac, vac'ing leak!"

"What?" James asked.

"There was atmosphere in that room! It's all sublimated now. Oh! Tell Kelley and Zabrina I'm sorry." Rita groaned. *Was that what Ann had wanted us to discover? I've ruined that now.*

"It's okay," James said. "There might be other rooms that still have air. We know to be more careful now, right? Besides, we might get lucky and find some airtight containers. You all right?"

"I'm fine. Just...not an experience I want to repeat."

Zabrina's voice came over the helmet. "Zabrina to Rita. Better you than me! Welcome to the club." In the background, she heard Kelley laugh.

"The Shrieking Spacers Club?" Rita giggled. It had just a hint of hysteria in it. She forced herself to take another deep breath. Her suit flashed a warning on her physical state. *First snakes, now aliens? Vac'ing leak, I hate things coming at my faceplate.*

"Better than not having the helmet," James said, and she realized she'd spoken her thought aloud.

Her breathing had returned to normal, though she still felt a bit shaky. *What else could happen today?* "Well, I'm mortified enough to last the mission. C'mon, James. Let's look inside this thing. You can even go first."

"I don't think we're going anywhere just yet," James said. "Look."

Their wild tumbling had tangled them in the safety lines.

* * *

Merl lowered the straw from Ian's lips, and the young man fell back against the pillows with a sigh.

"Thanks."

"I was hungry and you gave me food. I was thirsty and you gave me drink." *You were sick, and I healed you.* Merl bit back a surge of pride. When he had heard about the zerog doctor's dire prognosis for Ian, he'd felt called to rush to the man's bedside to pray over him. No sooner had he laid hands upon the wayward child of God, than Ian's eyes had opened and he'd asked for water.

If only he were as successful at expelling the young man's demons.

"That from the Bible?" Ian asked, breaking him from his reverie.

"Of course. It sustains me, gives me strength and direction."

Ian stared at his bandaged hands. "Know what else is in the Bible? If your right hand keeps you from God, you should cut if off. What does that mean?"

Merl felt the blood drain from his face. After Cay had told him his plans, he'd prayed, yet not found firm direction. After all, there was so much they could learn from *Discovery.* So much good they might do. He'd almost relented. But now this man, this...

Merl grasped Ian's arm tightly. "Ian, do you accept Jesus as your personal savior?"

"I don't deserve to be saved," Ian muttered. "My hands."

...this *unbeliever* had given him just the advice he needed to remain true to his God-given purpose.

"What does it mean?" Ian repeated.

Merl patted his shoulder. "You must accept Jesus into your heart. Only then can you have the promise of life eternal. I must go. You, my brother, have given me words to strengthen me in my purpose."

He walked out, Ian still demanding to know the meaning of the words he himself had spoken. Perhaps they would have meaning for him later. In the meantime, Merl needed to give Cay his blessings and prayers. They could not let this evil continue to spread.

The *Discovery* must not come into the hands of Man.

* * *

Anilou leaned against her father, full, sleepy, and content. She'd finally met her Aunt Dee and Uncle Elrond; they'd brought her birthday presents, including a stuffed animal from her grandmother on Earth. She hugged the lamb more tightly and rubbed her cheek against the soft fur. She'd been disappointed that it wasn't real wool, but she loved it anyway.

"I think someone's ready to count sheep," Uncle Elrond commented as he poured himself another glass of wine. His voice had taken on a lazy slur, and she wondered if he was as tired as she was. He'd said their location had been hard to find. As always.

"Are there more?" she asked, and they all laughed.

"A long time ago, people used to pretend to count sheep in order to get to sleep. The expression has stayed with us even today," her mother explained.

"Oh," she murmured, drawing more inexplicable laughter.

"Now you've disappointed her!"

"No! No, I truly love my one lamb!"

Somehow, that just made them laugh more. She looked from one smiling face to the other, eyes starting to fill. She bit her lip and tried again.

"Hush, Small Weight," her father whispered and pulled her close. "They are just being silly. Pretend with me: six months from now, your little lamb has two babies. Each of them has two babies. Every six months, each lamb has two babies. How many lambs would you have when you are six?"

"And none die?"

He kissed her head. "None die. Ever."

"Thirty-one," she answered immediately. "I'd need a bigger room."

A moment of stunned silence from her aunt and uncle, then a burst of proud laughter and applause. Her father hugged her, and her mother hugged them both. She looked from one face to another, basking in the warmth of their love, then looked back across the table to her aunt and uncle. A movement in the viewscreen behind them caught her attention.

"What's that?" She wiggled her arm out from where it pressed against her father and pointed.

Her mother screamed.

* * *

Outside the pod, OvLandra watched the readings on her helmet display with increasing impatience. No one else had been in the device for so long! Would she never come out?

Patience. Every minute in there is a minute more air she's used up. You've sought this child for more than a decade. A few minutes more, and you will rid your family of its shame. Then you can go home.

She bit her lip as anticipation and homesickness washed over her.

A few more minutes, she promised herself. A few more liters of air expended. She contented herself that no one had noticed her sabotage of the other suits. The more time she waited, the less chance they had of rescue. They would die, and OvLandra would blame Ann. Poor Ann, driven mad by the device and tearing the hoses off everyone's suits before destroying her own.

It'd be easier to fake if they were already dead. Yes, patience would pay. She could wait.

* * *

"I really hate this idea," James told Rita as he unhooked his safety line. Rita, meanwhile, had managed to twist, wriggle, and pull herself out of the tangle of cable. She floated free and easy, while he had a death grip on the nearest handhold. Even then, he didn't feel so secure. He kept imagining his glove slipping.

"Are you sure?" he asked as she hooked her foot on another handhold and pulled the cables off his legs. With a gentle push, she sent the mess floating away. He tightened his grip.

"Relax, James. We normally operate indoors without a cable, anyway. It's just an extra precaution for inexperienced dirtsiders." She spoke with brisk confidence, and it made him smile, especially after the way she'd been shrieking just a few minutes ago. "I'm using my extra line to hook us together. I won't let you go anywhere, all right?"

"What about when we're outside, though? Getting back to the *Basilica*?"

"You also have a second safety line; we'll hook that to the drag line going to the Meeger. It's just too short for us to explore this room, and you want to do that, right?"

She clipped her line to a ring at the side of his suit. As much as he wanted to turn and see her face, he even more wanted to stay still and anchored. "Actually, I was thinking we could go check on Ann and OvLandra instead."

"I'm monitoring her vitals. She's fine for now. But I agree; let's peek in, then go. That's what she wanted us to do, to see this room. Then, if you want, I'll hook you to the drag line, and you head back to the exit while I go check on her."

"No way! You're not leaving me. Teams of two, right?"

"James, I'll be fine. This is my job."

"I'm not letting you go alone," he said, and his heart repeated: *I'm not letting you go.*

"All right. Then let's be fast. All things considered, I think I get to go in first after all."

"Ladies first, of course. Just don't shriek if you see a mouse."

"Mice I can handle. Freaky aliens? No promises. Rita to *Edwina Taggert*, I'm heading in."

"Copy, Rita. Hoping you not see anyt'ing once alive."

James held himself still and watched as she gripped the edges of the open door and pulled herself up slowly. When her shoulders reached the threshold, she stopped and sighed. "Oh, Ann!"

"What? What do you see?"

"I think she found the real escape pods."

* * *

Cay was just finishing plugging the hole with the last of his explosives when Andi called for a status report. He waited as each team called their ready status in turn, then said, "Cay here. Need two minutes."

"Seriously? Good work, rockjack. We'll make a spacer of you yet! Finish up and head back to *Rockhopper*."

"I'll go check Cay's work and meet you there," George cut in, and Cay froze, his heart pounding.

Andi, however, saved the day. "Negative, George. We've been out here eight hours already, and this is our last chance. Return to *Rockhopper* and take an hour break. Then you and I will check the entire ship together."

God is good! Cay set the charges. Twenty minutes — that would be plenty of time to have everyone settled in the shuttle, comfortable. Unaware.

He'd take a lot of fusion when it happened, but they'd understand in time. He'd be a hero.

* * *

Anilou's aunt cried and screamed as her uncle dragged her out the door. "Quick! To my ship!" he shouted. He dashed ahead of them all to start the pre-flight.

Ann's mother grabbed her hand and pushed off after their father. "How'd they find us?" she demanded.

Her father answered, "I don't know. It doesn't matter now. We just have to get away."

"You're right. Go. Elrond's too drunk. Help him!"

"I love you both!" He gave each a quick kiss and rushed down the corridor, skimming past Aunt Dee with the grace of his kind. Her mother hurried after them, pulling Ann along.

Ann looked back at the screen as the door started to close behind them. The small object she'd seen only moments before now filled half the screen. Her mind automatically guessed at its speed and force, and realized the shields would not stop it. She screamed.

"Don't look, Anilou. Just run!"

She buried her head into the fuzzy comfort of the lamb as her mother pulled her along. They made it through one short hall and to the next. Aunt Dee waited near the blast doors, shouting for them to hurry. They sped past it. The ship shook, struck by something they hadn't seen. The gravity cut out. Aunt Dee grabbed her mother's hand, but she was larger, slower, and unused to the lower g. Her mother had to drag her. Ann did her best to help.

Finally her mother shoved Ann forward. "Go, Ana! Go to Uncle's ship. We'll catch up!"

The shove took her past the next blast doors just as something else impacted the ship. She went tumbling, the pretty train of her dress swirling around her, her lamb flying away from her. The ship groaned with a thunderous roar, then a rush of air pulled her back toward the blast doors.

"Mommy!"

"Handholds, Ana! When the door closes, push off with your legs! Go!"

Sirens wailed. Her mother's voice over the ship intercom calmly stated a hull breach and called for evacuation. Ann scrambled for a handhold. She caught one just before blowing through the door and held on for dear life. Her dress dragged at her, the train stretching across the threshold. She glanced back to see her mother holding onto a bar with both hands, pulling herself forward. Her aunt flew, flailing toward the doors.

The blast door slammed shut on her aunt, almost, but not quite slicing her in half. Ann screamed and did not stop screaming. Air continued to leak out.

"Ana, baby! Hand over hand. Go!"

"No. I won't leave you! Hurry. Grab my dress and push with your legs! I'll anchor you."

Her mother reached for the fabric. The doors started to close.

"Hurry, Mommy!"

Her mother laughed. It was the saddest sound Ann had ever heard. "Brave baby! Go to Father, quickly! I love you!"

The door snagged on the train and yanked Ann to the floor. Her head smacked against the hard plating. The world flared white, and, in the brightness, she saw a face, beautiful and compassionate, and she knew that angel would take care of her.

God would care for her parents.

* * *

OvLandra checked her timer. Almost ten minutes. Close enough. She prepared her suit to order Rita's and James' medpods to inject them with the lethal cocktail of medications. She would convince the crew that Ann, under the influence of her "vision," thought she was saving their lives, and that, alas, she, OvLandra, could not help them in time because of the struggle.

Then, when they were back in near-time communications with her people, she would send a message home reporting her success and restoring her family's honor. And if the weighties discovered the truth, she would go to the nearest airlock and give herself to the freedom of vacuum. Either way, her own exile would end.

She set a timer on the command. Thirty seconds should be enough. Then she schooled her voice to move from concern to panic. "Ann? It's OvLandra. Come out now. Ann? I'm pulling you out. What are you doing? No!"

* * *

"No! Cay, you can't do this. Not now!" Merl fought back panic at Cay's text message: *Timers set 5 min. Praise God.*

Stop them! he typed back. *There are people aboard.*

He prayed in the interminable minute that passed.

Too late. Collateral damage. God rest their souls.

"Merl to the Bridge! Bridge? Get everyone off *Discovery*! Bridge! Please, someone respond?"

Only silence met his plea.

"Dear God, what have I done?" He tore off to the bridge, trying while he ran to contact the *Rockhopper* or *Basilica* on his wristcomp. He had to warn them.

* * *

Ann stayed still for several minutes after the vision ended. Tears trickled down her cheeks, yet her heart felt so full. God had returned her parents to her: the memories of their laughter, their love and pride in her. Their sacrifice, not just during the attack that killed them. They'd spent her entire life in hiding, constantly on the move, trying to protect their forbidden love for each other and to keep the product of that love, Anilou, secret from her father's people.

The angel had protected her, too, keeping her alive as the air slowly leaked out around the folds of her dress, until the sisters of St. Joseph de Cupertino convent found her, half-frozen and barely breathing. Then the angel took her memory, making it easy for the sisters to keep her identity secret as they raised her as their own. They'd held her closely and safely, with love so complete she'd never wanted to be anywhere else, never thought about her family.

Now she had discovered her family. Still, no one was with her: St. Joseph convent millions of miles away, Tommie in *Basilica*, Rita on her own mission. Even the prophets that had spoken to her or hovered at the edge of vision were absent. Yet she was not alone.

She blinked the last of the tears from her eyes. She wasn't a child to be hidden and protected, and she was not a martyr — at least, not this way. She was a Rescue Sister.

She couldn't rescue her parents, but she would do her best to rescue her cousin.

* * *

How do I play this? Cay wondered. *Act innocent until the bedlam passes or stand up and proclaim my heroic deed? Proclaim. Got to be bold to impress Dove's father.* He leaned back against the jump seat, feigning sleep while mulling over his announcement speech. They'd be panicked, confused. He'd bound onto a piece of equipment. *My friends! The human race faced its greatest danger to mind, body, and soul. A brave man had to take measures!*

Galen's urgent voice broke his thoughts. "Everybody, strap in now! We're taking off!"

Everyone sprang into action, dashing to seats if they were standing, throwing on harnesses if seated. Already the engines were whining through their warm-up.

Andi shouted out as she buckled in. "Galen, what in the 'verse is going on?"

"Merl says Cay's set *Discovery* to blow."

As outrage stormed around him, all he could think was, *Damn that Merl!*

* * *

James pulled himself up into the small room and looked around. He saw pads, controls and cabinets, but not much else.

"Okay, so tell me why this is an escape pod and the others aren't?"

"You mean other than the fact that neither of us seems to be caught in some vision?" Rita spoke in a rush. "It kept its atmosphere where the other pods had eventually leaked. See the benches? Good size for several creatures to sit if they pulled in their legs, and they're thick, maybe with acceleration padding. The third arm pods had a single simple pallet in a corner. See these? Storage areas for supplies. We can check them out later. And this console? I think it's similar to the one in the main bridge. No windows—"

"Wouldn't an escape pod have windows?"

"Windows are a luxury, James. More practical is a digital display to help you maneuver or land. What do you think? Have you seen enough?"

"Yeah, I'm good. What's wrong? I mean, I know you wanted to be fast, but..."

"I don't know. I just have this really bad feeling all of a sudden."

OvLandra's voice came over the mission comms: "Ann? What are you doing? No!"

Rita felt her heart clutch and a rush of adrenalin sear through her. "Heads-up!"

The display showed that OvLandra had just tried to override their suit systems — to kill them. She checked her suit, James' and Ann's. None had recognized the command. *Thank you, God, for nightmares!* She checked OvLandra's. Her own counter-command had been issued, the sedative administered, but OvLandra's vitals remained strong and active. How?

No time to wonder.

"Rita to Ann! Ann, watch out! OvLandra's gone mad!"

"Ann to Rita." Ann's voice sounded excited and joyous. "I know. It's all right."

"What? Ann!" Rita heard her over the mission frequency, speaking in that reasonable tone of hers about family and redemption, lions and wolves. OvLandra spat back epithets and insults.

"*ET* to Rita! Rita, you have to help her!" Sean's voice sounded over the radio. "She's going to kill her for her family's honor! She thinks Ann's part zerog!"

"What? Never mind. We're on our way." She grabbed James' hand and twisted to brace her feet against the wall.

"Hang on, James. We're going to fly!"

She shoved off just as a series of explosions rocked the ship.

Her trajectory should have taken her and James out the door, but the entire ship shifted so that she crashed helmet first into a wall and was thrown back. James shot partway out the door before being pulled back like a yo-yo on its return. His foot snagged against one of the cables of the prier. It pulled at the prier that Rita, in her distraction, had not double-checked. The magnetic grips sprung free and the door started to close.

Rita yelped and yanked at the safety line, dragging James in just before the door closed on him. A second door closed after that one.

Another strong force shoved them back against the closed door as the escape pod jettisoned.

* * *

"So which do you think you are? Lion or wolf?" Ann asked. She hovered just inside the pod. She was safer inside the den. Around her, she imagined smoke, fire. Demons. She couldn't stay there for long; hiding in the bathtub only worked for awhile. Didn't she tell Kelley that?

"What are you going on about?" OvLandra spat. Her mouth moved, and Ann knew she was trying to get her suit to do something, but it was not responding to commands.

Ann's heart surged with love. Bless Rita! She'd saved her again.

OvLandra snarled in frustration and tore at the machine she carried, trying to make a sharp edge to use as a weapon. "Once again, you're making no sense! Just like my cousin. Abandoning everything his people stood for. Working with the gravbound. Loving a weighty. Then, instead of repenting, running away."

She slammed the scanner against a pillar, and finally the casing ripped.

Ann didn't look at the ruined, yet dangerous, implement in her hand. She'd know when to duck; someone would tell her. Over the comms, she could hear Captain Addiman trying to talk to OvLandra, but he was too far away to shepherd this time. She concentrated on her cousin. "Tell me what my father did."

"As if I never tried! You wouldn't watch the vids I so carefully suggested. Your mother — the great Edwina Taggert! And your father — the VR tech who made her famous. I should have made you watch them. Made myself watch them with you. Maybe if I'd been stronger, you would understand what you have done to my family."

"Our family."

"Shut up! You are not family. You are an abomination! Short and gross and strong. Yet you dare to have your father's eyes." She threw a piece of the scanner at Ann.

Before Ann could duck, the ship shook and heaved. The scanner smacked into a wall, bounded back toward OvLandra. Ann braced herself on the door and kicked it. It sailed away from them both, joining the floating detritus of dead aliens now set into motion by the movement of the ship. It collided with one, breaking its arm off.

OvLandra moved with ease, despite the confusion of the ship, spinning so that she and Ann no longer aligned face-to-face. Nonetheless, Ann held onto the doorway. She couldn't move yet.

"God gave me my eyes," Ann countered. "Just like He gave you yours. And you gave Him your eyes! Why?"

"Shut up! My family has borne the shame for two generations because of your father's folly!" OvLandra grabbed a pillar.

"I think you wanted Him to see like you do. But that's not how it works. We have to see with God's eyes. We have to love with God's heart! We are family, Ov. I love you."

OvLandra roared and shoved herself at Ann, holding the jagged edge of the other half of the scanner before her.

Ann waited until the last minute, then released one side of the doorway and twisted. OvLandra's arm shot past her, and Ann slammed her foot on the zerog's elbow, forcing her to release the device. Then Ann pushed away, twisting to avoid a floating alien in her path and batting aside another she couldn't avoid, murmuring a quick apology as she did. She grabbed one of the narrow bar walkways and pulled herself around like a gymnast.

OvLandra shot just underneath her legs and twisted to come back for another pass.

"Love? If you loved me — if you cared anything about our people — you'd do your duty, stay still, and die!"

"Wolf or lion?" Ann demanded. St. Francis talked to the wolf, and the wolf made peace with the town of Gubbio. Lions were harder. Angels had to talk to them inside their dens. Ann swung hand-over-hand to another walkway, closer to an open pod.

OvLandra paused, perhaps catching her breath, following Ann's every move with her eyes.

"For a decade, I have lived among the gravbound searching for you, stuck on this ship where my cousin forsook his people. It was my only lead, but I knew you'd return to it! I will not let my family face shame for another generation. I will not let you live!" OvLandra shot herself toward Ann.

"Lion, then!" Again, Ann pulled herself around the bar, but this time, as OvLandra sped under her, she swung back down and kicked her into the open device.

"Stay in there!" Ann commanded. "Stay in there and look at yourself through God's eyes until you understand."

She clung to the bar a moment, ready to kick her back in if needed. When OvLandra didn't emerge, she relaxed and tried to contact the ship she now knew was named for her mother.

"Ann to *Edwina Taggert*. It's okay. We're fine. Or we can be. It depends on OvLandra's vision. *Discovery* is moving, though, and I don't think we did that. What's going on?"

No one answered.

"Ann to *Edwina Taggert*, please respond. Ann to Rita, can you hear me? Ann to *Basilica*. Tommie?"

"*Basilica* here. Ann, what happened? Are you all right?"

"We're fine. OvLandra's just looking through the wrong eyes." She glanced back at the den where she'd tossed her cousin the lion. All was quiet.

"Explain that later. Will you be all right for now? How much suit air do you have?"

Ann did a quick check. "Eight hours, fifteen minutes, unless Ov comes out of the device still a lion. Lions are hard work."

"Can you contact Rita?"

"No. Nor the *Edwina Taggert*. Can't you?"

"Vac. A piece of the ship jettisoned. I'm guessing they found your escape pod and got stuck in it. I'm going after it. In the meantime, I need you to make sure they aren't still on *Discovery* but injured."

Ann twisted so she could see inside the device. OvLandra rested motionless, her arms wrapped around herself. She called up her cousin's vitals: slow, but steady. Lucid sleep. She pushed off toward the exit. "Roger. Be there in two."

"Go easy. Conserve your air. I've lost contact with the *ET*, and if Rita and James are in that pod, I have to go after them before they're beyond our ability to catch them. It might be awhile."

"Go! We'll be fine."

"Copy. God be with you." Tommie clicked off.

Ann paused as she reached the door and glanced back toward the arm that had drawn her with its mystery just days ago. Now it drew her for a different reason. "I'm sorry, cousin," she said. "But I have a duty to my sister."

She pushed away to the next arm.

* * *

Aboard the *Edwina Taggert*, the bridge crew and a few of the researchers who had come to observe listened with confusion at the exchange between Ann and OvLandra. Chris, as the new temporary Head of

Research, sat beside Addiman. He felt like he should be doing something, but he was as in the dark as the rest.

"Cousins? Lion or wolf?" Chris said. "What's she talking about? Did the device affect her mind?"

Zabrina's voice trembled with tension. "She's in trouble. But she's just talking Annese. Listen to OvLandra. She's the one raving! Did she go into the device?"

"I don't think so," Rose replied. Her fingers flew over the controls of her virtual console. "But I've not been getting clear readings for the last minute-thirty."

"You mean right when OvLandra said she was going to pull Ann out?" Behind them, Sean's voice grew in alarm. "Captain, we have to stop OvLandra! I think she wants to kill Ann!"

"What?" McVee twisted in his seat to give the documentarist an incredulous look.

Sean had already dashed from the observation console to Rose's station. "*ET* to Rita! Rita, you have to help her! She's going to kill her for her family's honor! She thinks Ann's part zerog."

Addiman called to OvLandra in firm gentle tones. "OvLandra. Stop this madness."

"There!" Rose cried in triumph. "I've got visual from Ann."

They watched in horror as Ann's camera showed the zerog smashing the brainwave scanner and throwing a piece at Ann.

They heard Rita tell James to hang on. The view from her helmet wiggled for a moment, then steadied, focused on the open door. The opening grew...

The view jerked crazily until the camera smacked against a wall. Then it went to static.

"What happened?" Chris demanded.

Ann's images also jerked and tumbled, but the two continued to argue.

McVee pointed. "Look! Everything's tumbling. Aliens. Everything."

"But how could that happen?" Chris felt the blood leave his face. "Quick! Show us the Folly!"

Rose typed some commands, and the camera shots from the researchers shrunk and moved to an upper corner. The main screen showed the asteroid, but the smooth pool of black that had been *Discovery* was now replaced by a billowing cloud of dust and debris.

"The ship!" McVee exclaimed. "The explosives went off."

Just then the bridge doors opened, and Merl ran into the room. His eyes went straight to the scene. "Oh, God, have mercy!"

* * *

"Galen!" Andi commanded as *Rockhopper* steadied. "Show us the ship!"

A virtual screen appeared between the rows of rockjacks, showing the *Discovery* tilting, its first arm still caught in the ice and rock.

"George!"

"On it!" George was typing in commands through his wristcomp.

The series of charges blasted rock and vaporized the ice, shrouding the *Discovery* in debris. They waited.

A single shadow pierced through the cloud, and everyone cheered.

Andi, however, was fighting back a sob. "Galen! Galen, please tell me Merl warned everyone else in time. Tell me no one was on that ship."

An interminable pause, then: "I'm sorry, Andi. They were still in there, but that doesn't mean they're lost. I'm charging the grappler gun. Everyone, sit tight!"

Andi pinned Cay with her glare. "You'd better hope nothing happened to them."

She felt a grim satisfaction in seeing that Cay had the good sense to gulp.

* * *

The escape hatch door slammed shut just past James' foot, neatly slicing the heavy cable of the prier. In a panic, he jerked his leg. The cable flew loose, but he twisted and banged against the wall. The helmet protected his head, but his neck jerked with the force of whiplash. The world continued to spin.

Rita shrieked.

"I'm okay! I'm okay!" he reassured, then stopped. *Am I?*

"Suit check!" he commanded, and gasped a sigh as the indicators all continued to show green. "Rita, I'm fine, I'm just —"

"James, shut up and help me!"

Grabbing at the wall to steady himself, he turned to face her.

Rita was clutching at a tear in the right arm of her suit. He thought he saw small wisps of fog from the leaking air. Rita's face twisted in pain.

"Rita!" He started to push toward her.

"Stop!" she commanded, and he froze. She hissed through her teeth. "Listen to me. There's a broken cable floating around. It tore my suit. It can tear yours. Find it and secure it somewhere."

"But you're losing air. You'll die!"

"James! Think! There're pressure cuffs. It's squeezing the life out of my arm, but I'm not losing air any longer. Secure that cable before it does any more damage!" Her voice rose, and he saw her face was wet with tears.

He had to be strong for her. "Right. Okay. Do you know where it is?"

"Behind me, I think. Go slow. Stay anchored. We're still tied together."

"I know."

While she tried without success to contact the *Edwina Taggert*, *Rockhopper* or *Basilica*, he made his way around her. He looked for a handhold, grabbed it, moved. Then another, trying to circle her. He didn't want to lose sight of her face, though. He banished the vision of her turning blue. As long as she was talking, she had to be okay, right?

"No one's answering," she said.

"I know."

"I don't think we're on the ship."

"I know. That second door — you saved my life."

"Part of the job. Just...return the favor."

He almost laughed, until he saw the cable, poised behind her like a cobra waiting to strike. "I see it. Stay still. It's right behind your leg."

Rita moaned. "This is worse than the broomstick. James, go slow. There's no gravity. Action-reaction. Don't let the edge whip back toward your suit."

"Understood. Broomstick?" He reached for it slowly, just below the knife-edge end, wary of making any move that might cause it to move in turn. He felt like he was grabbing a snake.

"Long story. Vac! This pressure cuff hurts! No wonder Ian tried to claw through his. Got it?"

James' gloved hand closed around the metal. He imagined he could feel its coolness through the fabric. "Got it. Where do I put it?"

"I don't care. Pick a cabinet. Open it slowly. We don't need more debris." She gave a little gasp.

"Are you sure you're okay?"

"Of course I'm not okay! My arm is getting numb. But I'll survive. Just hurry so you can help me. No, wait! Don't hurry. Be careful."

"Make haste slowly. Got it, mother." He found a door, managed to crack it open enough to thread the prier cable in, and slammed it shut. He turned back to her. "Done. Now what?"

She'd reached with her left hand for a can of stickie. The tear in her suit floated free, and James nearly choked when he saw the size of the flap of fabric. "How much air did you lose?"

"I'll worry about that after we fix this. Here, take the stickie. I'll hold the fabric in place."

"We're going to glue it together? Will that work?"

"I've seen it done — by Ann, in fact. My arm is really getting numb. Ow. Here. Now listen: first, just a small burst in the middle to hold it in place, so I can remove my hand and you won't get any on my glove. No, better idea: You put one hand on each side of the tear to hold it in place. Keep the middle clear, and I'll spray. I've had more practice with this stuff."

"I could do it," he protested, but did as he was told. "It's like operating the can of whipped cream."

"Yeah, I've seen you with whipped cream." She tried to smile.

"Hey! That was a long time ago, and it was on a triple-scoop banana split." He pulled the fabric over the tear, overlapping it slightly.

"Is that what was under all that whipped cream? Ready? Stay still."

She gave the nozzle a quick tap. He was about to protest that it wasn't enough, when the long bead of stickie touched the suit and expanded slightly in the vacuum. "Okay. You were right."

"Lots of practice, believe me. Back off and I'll get the rest." She slathered the gooey substance all over the tear and a few inches around it, this time piling it on like he did whipped cream. She handed the bottle back to him. "Secure this onto my belt."

While he did that, she ordered her suit to run an integrity check. He heard her utter a prayer of thanks, then hiss in pain.

"Rita?"

"I'm all right. Just the prickles from the cuff loosening up and the blood returning to my arm. Oh, I hate that! The stickie worked. It's recalibrating my air supply now. What? Twenty minutes?"

"That's not so bad. I was afraid you'd lost a lot more."

"No, James!" She gulped hard, and ordered her suit diagnostics to reset, recalibrate and check again. A sob escaped her throat. "I have twenty minutes left."

"What?" James yelled. "What do we do? James to *Edwina Taggert*! James to *Basilica*! We have an emergency, please respond!"

* * *

As James continued to call for help, Rita forced herself to think. There was no way she should have lost nine hours of air. Unless... Did OvLandra sabotage the suits, draining most of the O2 and fixing the diagnostics to not notice? Why didn't she check that? Idiot!

"James. James! Listen to me. I need you to reset the diagnostics on your suit. Just do what I say." She led him through the procedure while she tried to work feeling back into her right arm. It felt heavy and hot and clumsy. She fumbled for the rescue balloon on her belt. "What's your air gauge say now?"

"That can't be right! Thirty-five minutes. How could that be?"

"Never mind that now. Here's what we're going to do. I'm going to set up the bag. Then I need you to hold your breath while I remove your tank. As soon as you are in the bag and it's sealed, open your helmet..."

"Are you crazy? You have less air than me, and your suit is damaged. You're going into the balloon."

"James!" Rita's voice rose and cracked. She took a shuddering breath. "Look at your suit. You have half an hour of air left. We don't know where we are or how long it will take for rescue to come. I need to put you in the balloon and keep you safe until rescue comes."

"No! You have less air than me."

"I can use your tank. I also know how to slow my metabolism. I know how to change tanks on the bags. I will last longer on the outside than you."

"No! I won't let you!" He was shouting now. He grabbed the bag, fumbling at the controls. Rita snatched at it one-handed, and he yanked it out of her reach. He spun toward a wall.

"James, stop being stupid! I'm trained at this. You're not. It'll be all right."

"I'm not letting you do this!"

Rita grabbed him with one hand and spun him so that their faceplates nearly touched. "James. You're using up air. You have to calm down. Be reasonable."

"No! I lost you once. I'm not losing you again!"

Suddenly lights began to flare in the escape pod, and a high-pitched buzzing penetrated their suits and clamored in their ears.

* * *

Cay bristled under the glare of a dozen rockjacks. Lenny cracked his knuckles, hoping to menace, no doubt; Cay didn't care. Only Andi seemed worried — and she, for the wrong reasons. They were all being stupid. He was going to have to be the hero. Again.

But hadn't he expected that? He still had his laser cutter in his pocket, still with plenty of charge despite the extra work. He'd expected to use it to hold them off while he explained his plan, but in this case, he might need a little more insurance than that.

Good thing they hadn't restrained him, except to strap him into his seat. On Mars, he'd have been bound hand and foot, but here? They didn't expect him to do anything. After all, where would he go? For once, being hundreds of thousands of clicks from the nearest gravity well was going to work in his favor.

"What are you smiling about?" Lenny sneered.

"Nothing." Cay curled his lip at him and crossed his arms. Behind his arm, however, he undid his restraint.

The opportunity would present itself, and he'd be ready to spring into action.

                                    * * *

Ann finished checking the open rooms in the section where Rita and James would have been. *Seek and you will find; knock and the door will be opened to you.* Should she knock? No, they weren't there. She needed to seek elsewhere. When she reported her findings to Tommie, the older sister swore.

"They have to be in that pod, then."

Ann curled herself into a fetal position to rest. She spun with a lazy fluidity. It felt nice. She was tired and a little dizzy, in a familiar way. Snatches of quotes and conversations made a lovely buzz in her ears.

"Ann, are you all right?"

"Heads-up," she ordered her suit and studied the readings. The suit was all lovely shades of green. Lovely, lovely, green. Her blood oxygen levels on her skinsuit indicator, however, showed yellow edging toward red. Belatedly, an alert popped up: Oxyboost?

That's right! She had felt this way before, in training, anyway. All sisters had to know the signs of oxygen deprivation. She ordered the shot, then reset her diagnostics and checked her suit air. Rita had kept OvLandra from poisoning her, but no one had thought to doubt the suits.

Rita! Had she brought Rita into danger — and James, too?

No, that wasn't my call. Faith, hope, and love...and communication.

"Tommie? OvLandra tried to kill me. I'm an insult to the pride."

"Say again?"

Lions and prides and laughing martyrs. Lusts that lie, loves that lie like myrrh. A strong, living scent to drive back the breath of death. She shook her head. Tommie needed her to speak simply. "I think she may have sabotaged James' and Rita's suits, too. If so, they may not have much air left."

"How do you know that? Ann, are you all right?"

"I'm fine," she lied. Lied like myrrh, driving back the stench of death. "Get them first. I'm fine."

Tommie didn't sound convinced. "Ann, stay calm. Breathe slow. Ration that oxyboost. Get close to the airlock. Keep calling *ET*. I think they're receiving, just not responding. Tell them to get *Rockhopper* to you. I'm sure Galen's up to the challenge. I'll keep trying, too."

"Copy, but I have to go to OvLandra."

"Ann! OvLandra tried to kill you. Don't trust her. Go to the airlock. We can get OvLandra later. She would not have sabotaged her own suit. Acknowledge."

"Copy," she replied. That wasn't a lie, was it? She had heard. She just didn't intend to obey.

She pushed off a wall and made her way back to the third arm. Even if her cousin hadn't been there, she had to go. After all, the aliens had gone to die where they felt closest to God. Shouldn't she, too?

* * *

"Make it stop!" James screamed. He pressed his hands against his helmet.

Although she knew he was yelling, his voice sounded muffled against the chainsaw-against-metal screeching assailing her ears. Even if she thought covering her helmet with her arms would help, she couldn't do it. Her right arm burned as feeling returned. The textbooks had not mentioned how much it hurt! The painkiller she ordered barely took the edge off.

"How?" she demanded.

"Push a button!"

"And accidentally open a hatch?" Her suit flashed a warning on her vital signs. She told it to disregard and squeezed her eyes shut. She tried not to sob, failed.

"Do something!"

Suddenly, everything went silent. If it weren't for her own ragged breathing, Rita would have thought the noise had driven her deaf. She felt herself getting heavier, too. They both sank slowly to the ground. "James."

"Thank God! That is so much better. Good work, Rita."

"I didn't do anything. James, there's gravity. This pod has powered up."

"What does that mean? What's it going to do?" he demanded.

"How should I know? I'm not Ann! I don't have phenomenal technical skill or superhuman intuition or a host of saints telling me things. I don't know what this alien pod is doing. I don't even know what I'm doing with my own life!" She flopped onto a seat and stomped her foot on the deck.

"Easy." His voice gentled as he sat down beside her. "I'm sorry. I'm scared, too. You're more an expert than me, right?"

She shifted away from him and closed her eyes against the tears, but fought the urge to curl in on herself. *Expert! Would an expert have gotten us into this mess? Everything is falling apart. I'm falling apart. I don't know what to do!*

When things fall apart, faith tells us to look to the broken pieces — out of them a new whole may emerge. That's probably Brother Jubal, too. Faith, hope, and love. God, help me to look at the pieces with faith!

She tried to swallow back the sobs. "We're going to hold to the hope that they can catch us. We have to get you into that bag."

She opened her eyes. The entire pod seemed shrouded in fog. "This is ridiculous! I can't even see anything — my faceplate is all fogged, and that shouldn't happen."

"Mine, too. Just now. Could the gravity...?"

"Just now?" Her sobs died away with a sudden insight, and she ran her fingers on her faceplate. Moisture beaded and made streaks.

"James. It's not just gravity. There's atmosphere!"

* * *

Cay's opportunity came sooner than he could have hoped for.

"I can't stand this!" Andi declared. "Galen, where are we?"

"Patience, Andi. I do this wrong, we lose the ship. In fact, why don't you get up here and lend me a hand?"

She gave Cay a dark look, and he curled his lip at her. *Go already!*

"Yes! Thank you. I'm on my way."

She unbuckled, and he tensed.

As she passed him, he shrugged out of his shoulder harnesses and lunged into her. They staggered, but he didn't let her fall into Lenny. He whipped out his laser cutter and pressed it against her neck. People around him shouted, but he screamed for them to be quiet. They obeyed, of course. He was in command now. He was the hero.

"Galen!" he shouted so the pilot could hear. "Turn this ship around. We will not retrieve *Discovery*. Do what I say — or Andi dies!"

* * *

Rita read the results on the sampling equipment and laughed. "Oxygen/Nitrogen! Praise God! It's a little thinner, but no more so than say, Tibet. Have you ever been to Tibet, James?"

"Rita, you're babbling. Hey! Wait! What are you doing?"

Rita reached for her helmet to release the seal. Her hands, however, refused to carry out her commands. She paused. *Do this smart.* "Come here, James. We're going to do this one at a time."

Although he stood to face her, he looked as frightened as she felt. "Are you out of your mind? What if there's something the scanner didn't pick up?"

"Then you'd better be ready to slam this helmet back on me. Then we pray the skinsuit medpod can keep me alive and lucid enough to stick you in the bag and bleed your air into my suit. James, we don't have a lot of choice. We should have been rescued by now. Something else is wrong. I know they will get to us. We have to give them as much time as possible.

"So, what we're going to do is this: I'm taking this helmet off. Don't fight with me, James. I'm the expert. You just said so. I'm taking this helmet off and testing the air. I'll hand the helmet to you. You'll be ready to put it back on. If I'm not sick or turning blue in two minutes, you take yours off, too. Got it?"

"Are you sure?"

"Yes," she lied. "Ready?"

He held out his hands. "Ready."

She took a deep breath. *Come on. Make your hands move!*

"You remember how to put the helmet on?"

"You trained me," he said, then added, "You want me to go first?"

"No. My idea. I'm first. Start the timer." Despite the oxygen she'd use up, she took some deep breaths as if steeling herself for a plunge into a deep lake. Then, with a sudden yank, she twisted the seal and removed her helmet.

The frigid thin air hit her like icy water, and she gasped, then coughed.

"Rita!"

"I'm okay! I'm okay! It's just cold!" Her breath came out in clouds, and she could feel the sweat in her hair turn to ice. "It's about eight degrees — below!" She stopped to cough as the sharp chill seared her lungs. Her teeth chattered.

"Are you sure?"

"Look at the monitors on my chest. How do they read?"

He frowned at the readings. "Everything's good. Heart rate's a little fast. Body temperature's a little low."

"Imagine that." She laughed then coughed. "Oh! I'd forgotten what it's like to breathe such cold air! It actually smells very clean, though. There's kind of a...raisin scent..."

"Should I?" He reached for his own helmet.

"Not yet. Hey, I think it's warming up."

The next minute stretched. James stood over her, helmet angled toward her so he could put it over her at any indication of trouble, his eyes scanning her face anxiously. She kept her face tilted up toward his, repeating, "I'm fine," as she made herself take slow easy breaths and tried not to notice how very blue his eyes were.

"That's two minutes."

"All right. I'm okay. Your turn. Sit down." They traded places. A cough rose from deep in her lungs, and she bent over.

"It's okay. Just the cold. Get ready for it."

As he buckled over and coughed, she had to fight back the urge to slam his helmet back on. Was she doing the right thing? What if there was some poison the scanners weren't made to detect? Then again, with less than forty minutes of air between them, they didn't have a lot of choice.

"Cup your hands and breathe through them," she told him. "You taught me that trick, remember? Why didn't you remind me of it?"

"Didn't want your hands near your face," he said. The gloves muffled his words. "Definitely warmer now, though. Maybe 40 Fahrenheit?"

His color looked good; his suit indicators showed green. Rita set his helmet in front of him where he could grab and don it easily, then sat back down. She watched him, elbows on his knees, face in his hands, breathing alien air in an alien lifepod millions of miles from home. And it was all her fault.

She sniffled.

He turned to look at her. "Rita?"

"I'm sorry," she whispered. "You shouldn't be here. And it's my fault. I ran."

He opened his mouth, a protest on his lips, then mashed them shut and took her hand. She wanted to lean against him and cry.

"So you did have feelings for me?" he asked.

She turned her head away but nodded. Her tears felt hot against her cold skin. "I couldn't come between you and your vocation. You would have been such a good priest."

He spoke slowly, as if discovering the thoughts as he spoke them. "I think that if I would have been such a good priest, I wouldn't have given in to the temptation to love you. After all, you have a vocation, too. Look how far you went to protect it — halfway across the solar system."

"More like six-tenths," she retorted, then gave a rueful chuckle. Ann was rubbing off on her. Her laugh became a sob. "I should have just said something. I thought I was protecting our vocations, but I was just running. And now you're here, and we're going to —" She bit her lip, hard. She would not say it. *Faith and hope, right?*

And love.

"Hey," he said, and cupped her face in his hand. He'd removed his glove, but she couldn't find herself protesting. She leaned into the warmth as his thumb wiped the tears from her cheek.

"We're not going to die," he told her. "And I'm the one who chose to leave. If I hadn't been such a coward, I'd have talked with you first. We'd have made our decisions together. Rita, in my vision, it was you I was dancing with."

"I know. In the rain, like my parents used to do." Static buzzed in her earpiece — or was it the memory of rain? She wanted to reject him, to push away, but where could she run? Besides, it was so comforting with his hand warm on her cheek and his blue eyes gazing so frankly into hers.

He smiled. "I remember that. It was beautiful. Rita, I need to know: five minutes or fifty years, will you dance with me?"

His image blurred, and she blinked away fresh tears. It would be so easy to say yes to him right now, to draw comfort from his arms. She could die happy that way, oh, so happy. And fifty years? They would live happily. Surely God would understand.

Of course, God would understand. Even forgive.

And she suddenly knew that's why she couldn't — wouldn't — do it.

"I'm sorry," she whispered. "If we'd met before...but I promised Him. I promised Him, and as much as I love you, I already chose."

And suddenly, the ache in her heart faded.

He brushed his hand over her hair, just once, then withdrew it. "Okay," he said, drawing a deep breath. "Let's face it: compared to the Almighty, what kind of competition am I, right?"

She laughed, and peace flowed over her: the peace of the chapel, of dancing in rainbows. Still, she was relieved to see him smiling as well.

"So," he said. "What do we do now?"

"Put your glove on. It's still cold. Just because we have atmosphere now doesn't mean we will later. Plus, I want us to be ready to evac when Tommie catches us."

"If."

"When. And in the meantime, we do the only thing we can. Pray." She made the sign of the cross, then held out her hands.

He also signed himself, and took them. "We believe in God, the Father Almighty..."

Their voices drowned out the hiss of static coming from their earpieces.

* * *

Ann ordered a schedule of Oxyboost and thinned her air. Nonetheless, by the time she'd gotten back to the central sphere, her newly calibrated suit was declaring only minutes left. She wheezed as her oxygen-hungry lungs insisted on pulling in large gulps of air. She tried to recall the schematics of the suit for some kind of miracle work-around, but it kept getting mixed up with Proverbs and Brother Jubal's "Darkness on the Bright Path," and little sheep kept frolicking over the diagrams.

She shook her head, felt the room spin. She rolled in the opposite direction to counter it. Panic gave way to delight, and she laughed and spun.

Her suit dosed her with oxyboost, and clarity returned enough for her to realize what she'd done — and the time and air she'd wasted. *I have to get to OvLandra. OvLandra has air. Oh, please let OvLandra have air!*

She pushed off and entered the third arm, but floated to a stop.

Everything looked different, out of proportion and blurred on the edges; the white markings of the pods were just light smudges. Aliens filled the air, and they didn't look like sheep at all.

"Ann to OvLandra. I'm almost out of air. Please, help me?"

Silence.

One of the aliens brushed against her suit. She reached for it and gently hugged it against her chest. "Pray with me, lamb," she told it.

* * *

Finally, the *Edwina Taggert* contacted the *Basilica* and the *Rockhopper*, but that didn't give anyone relief.

Chris almost jumped out of his chair when Galen told them what Cay had done.

"He's outnumbered; can't they jump him?" McVee asked.

"Negative. He's got a laser cutter right on Andi's throat. He just needs to turn it on." On the viewscreen, Galen caught Chris' anguished expression and winced. "Sorry, Chris. I've cut acceleration; we're still pointed at *Discovery*, but drifting, and Sister Thomas says Ann doesn't have much time."

"Can she get them?" Addiman asked.

"She's too far, and closer to the escape pod. Even if she could, it would probably set Cay off to know someone else rescued the ship."

"Forget the ship!" Chris yelled. "Who cares about the stupid ship?"

Addiman laid a large hand on his arm. "Let me talk to Cay."

"Wait. Did he say what he wants?" McVee asked. "I mean, why does he want us to leave *Discovery* floating out in space?"

"I don't know, exactly, something about leaving a message to the invaders. He's calm, but *couritza*, if you know what I mean."

"He thinks he's saving humankind," Merl said. "He thinks God has sent him on this mission for this reason."

"Understood," the captain replied grimly.

Chris understood, too. Cay was calm, but crazy enough to put people in danger. To kill his Andi.

* * *

James announced the Mystery of the Scourging, but Rita found herself thinking about the Wedding at Cana.

That marked the beginning of something new in Jesus' ministry. He was no longer just a man in people's eyes. He could work miracles, and now people saw that he was the Son of God. Suddenly, he was God's son. No longer yours. Oh, Mary, did you know? Did you understand that that simple request, offered for friendship, would start the path that would lead to your son being beaten? To his death? How, how did you bear it? You, born without sin, made the greatest sacrifice of all humankind.

Because God asked it of you. It was your calling, wasn't it? And you gave yourself to it. Knowing there would be sorrows, you embraced the joys. You trusted God.

She thought then of her life as a religious: her exciting years as a young BVM, her friends, her sisters, always ready with their love. And now with the Rescue Sisters. Sister Lucinda. Tommie. Ann, full of joy, willing to share her joy. *Why had I insisted on clinging to the sorrow?*

"The Crowning of Thorns. Our Father..."

Did I think there was greater glory in wearing my own crown of thorns and dwelling on my sacrifice? Her mind flickered to the Birth of Our Lord. *There was pain then, too, but good pain. The pain of life. And when the Holy Spirit rested upon you with tongues of fire, was there pain then, too? Yet, after the pain, joy...*

She remembered praying the rosary with James in the university chapel, how his voice was so strong, so sure as they flowed over the prayers. So right. She thought about his saying "I love you" earlier. Had that been what she wanted? Had that been so right?

"The Carrying of the Cross. Our Father..."

She listened to James' voice now, noted how it had become steadier and calmer as the succession of prayers continued. Yes, this is what he needed.

This is what I needed.

* * *

A crown of thorns — a helmet of thorns — pierced into Ann's skull as the fire in her lungs grew. Her body clamored for her to do something! She flung the alien away from her before she crushed it in her embrace. Her arms begged to rip off her helmet while her mind told her again and again there was no air out there.

There's no air!

She flailed wildly, scrambled at the controls of her suit, but her hands shook too hard to obey her commands. She didn't know what she wanted them to do, anyway. She tried to scream, but it only came out a hoarse sob.

It's hard to be a martyr! she cried in her mind.

Then they were there: the prophets, the saints, especially the martyrs. They held her hands, so that they stilled in their wild fumbling. They spoke encouraging words, prayed. St. Lawrence lifted the back of his shirt to show her the crisscross of scars and burns. "They got both sides pretty well done, didn't they?" he joked, making her laugh.

And the One she loved most held her close to His chest and promised her His love, until the panic gave way to calm, and the path turned dark but not lonely.

* * *

Chris gripped the arms of his chair so hard he could feel the metal supports under the thick gel. Still, he kept his face in an expression he hoped looked calm and composed. It wouldn't help anyone to see him freaking out. But Cay had that tool against his beloved's neck, and it was all he could do to keep from standing up and shouting, "Leave her alone!" even if it would only make things worse.

Addiman had listened stoically as Cay outlined his glorious plan: He'd planted charges in *Discovery* and blasted her. He'd hoped to shear off the first arm and send the damaged hull tumbling into space, where any second-wave invasion force would see it and know to stay away from the system.

"They'll know we can protect ourselves," Cay concluded.

But we can't protect ourselves, Chris thought hopelessly. *I can't protect anybody, not even the woman I love. How could we stand up against an alien invasion? We can't do it.*

"No, we can't," he whispered, then he realized that was the answer. "No, Cay. We can't protect ourselves. This will only make it worse!"

"Oh, shut up, Chris, or your girlfriend's going to have holes in her."

Chris stood up. "No, seriously, listen to me! The physics is all wrong!"

"Mr. Davidson," Addiman warned, but Chris hushed him with a wave of his hand.

"Cay, think this through with me, okay? We get one chance to do this correctly. We're doing this for the human race, right?"

"Don't patronize me!"

"I'm not, all right? I am absolutely, stark-raving, scared out of my mind, but I can see that your plan is going to backfire, so just listen to me!"

On the viewscreen, Cay's expression went from pleasure at his own power to doubt to consideration. "Fine. I'm listening."

"Okay, first off, space is big! Huge! The chances that the alien ship will even see *Discovery* are astronomical! Second, they had warp drive. We don't know what happened to this ship, but we have to assume the others will work. Worst case scenario for us: they'll drop out of warp somewhere *in-system* and never see *Discovery*, even if it was on their path. With me?"

"We have to try!"

"I got that!" Chris said, thinking and talking fast. "But we have to try in the right way. Let's assume they do find the ship damaged and drifting. Worst case scenario: they'll investigate."

Cay's face lit up with triumph. "And they'll see the damage I inflicted!"

"With a few localized charges you had to drill into the hull. The aliens came all this distance. They had to have had awesome shielding, and who knows what kind of weapons they carry? Are they really going to believe that anyone could have gotten through their defenses and planted a couple of bombs — or that those bombs destroyed the ship?"

He saw doubt slacken Cay's confident features. Without moving, Andi directed her eyes to the side and down, and he saw that Cay's grip on the laser tool had also loosened. He gulped hard and forged ahead.

"Worst case, Cay — thinking worst case — they board the ship to investigate. They're going to know something else caused their ship to crash, and that all our paltry human charges did was send it tumbling. Even worse, there are humans aboard."

"So?"

"So! Cay, if they get that ship, they will know exactly what they're up against in this system."

Cay's attention turned inward as he considered Chris' logic. Chris tried not to bite his lip or look at Andi too much, nothing that would give his true objective away.

Fortunately, McVee took up the argument. "Cay, he's making sense. Anybody with military experience can tell you, intelligence is vital to winning the war. And, thinking further along those lines, the *Discovery* is our greatest source of intelligence on these creatures."

"Our only source!" Chris added.

McVee pressed on. "If we want to have any chance of defending ourselves, we have got to have that ship."

Cay shook his head, confused, not ready to believe.

"Cay?" Zabrina called from where she monitored the safety console. "Remember that movie Sean showed us? *Lola Quintain and the War of the Worlds*? We couldn't defeat the aliens with technology. We needed a biological weapon. The only way we can find it is by studying that ship. One corpse isn't enough."

"What will you do to me?" he whispered.

Now, Addiman spoke. "You have done some terrible things, Mr. Littlefield, but you've not killed anyone yet. Stop this now, and it will go easier for you."

Merl stepped forward. "And you had the best interests of humanity at heart. God will forgive you, but you need to let Andi go."

"I'm sorry." He didn't just remove the cutting tool from Andi's neck; he dropped it entirely. Andi shoved away fast, and Lenny caught him and shoved him against the bulkhead. He held him in a restraining hold, while the others roughly tied his hands. Cay submitted docilely.

"I'm heading to the con," Andi said. "Galen, let's get that ship! Chris, I love you!"

Chris sank back into his seat, weak with relief, the post-adrenalin rush giving him the shakes, yet wrapped in joy over the words she'd spoken.

"Good work, hero," McVee said.

* * *

They had started the Mystery of the Crucifixion, and Rita found herself wanting to hurry through it to the Glorious Mystery of the Resurrection, when suddenly the pod jerked.

James stopped mid-Hail Mary. "What happened?"

"How would I know? How's the air?" Rita asked. Had they run out of power?

"Fine, near as I can tell."

They paused, silent and listening. Then she heard the tiny hissing over her earpiece.

"James, do you hear that? Stand by and pray!" Without waiting for his answer, she put her helmet back on and used its heads-up controls to adjust the gain on her receiver.

"*Basilica* to Rita. *Basilica* to James. Please respond."

"Tommie!" Her reply came out more like a shriek, and she started trembling. "Tommie! I have never been so glad to hear anyone in my life!"

She gave James a thumbs-up and heard his cheer.

* * *

"OvLandra to *Edwina Taggert*, do you read?"

On the *Rockhopper*, Andi swapped glances with Galen, then stabbed the comms panel. "This is *Rockhopper*, OvLandra. Stay away from Ann!"

"No, please. It's all right. I'm sorry, so very sorry. I...it does not matter now. I have Ann and am sharing air with her, but I need to get her to the infirmary, stat. I am heading to the airlock. Everything here is moving. Is the ship in motion?"

Galen chimed in. "Affirmative. *Basilica* went after a jettisoned escape pod. Sister Rita and James are in it. We've captured *Discovery*, but can't get to the airlock. *Rockhopper* is just too big."

"Then I shall have to come to you. Steady yourself and clear your airlock."

"The grapple is too far from the airlock, OvLandra."

She laughed. "I understand, *Rockhopper*, but it matters not. My people were born for this. Prepare to receive us, and stand by with any emergency supplies you have."

"Copy. Good luck and Godspeed. *Rockhopper* out."

Andi hailed the passengers. "George! Lenny! Get the first aid kit and the emergency oxygen and stand by the airlock. They're coming over. They're alive!"

* * *

Rita spoke into her headset. "Tommie, where are you?"

"Off your stern, or whatever side you want to call it. I'm pulling you in. What's your air situation?"

"About five-and-a-half minutes. James has about five more than that. But that's suit air. The pod has life support!"

Silence. "Repeat that, please?"

Rita laughed. "I'm not kidding, Tommie. Breathable air, sufficient gravity. It's a little cold, but it's liveable."

"Can I tow you into the cargo bay?"

"Are you spaced? Do you have any idea how many protocols that violates? Not to mention the Dangerously Stupid Things list. But you could bring us to the ship, then set up a decontamination chamber. Tommie, how's Ann?"

"I don't know. *Rockhopper's* gone after them. I had to get you before we lost you for good. Stand by. It's *Rockhopper*. Galen says OvLandra is sharing air."

"OvLandra? But she tried to kill Ann!"

"She tried to kill you all. But she's helping now. She's pulling Ann aboard the *Rockhopper*. Hang on in there. I'm bringing you home."

"Copy! Oh, thank God, Tommie! Rita out."

James whooped to hear the news, making Rita laugh. It felt so good to laugh.

"I think as long as we're breathing fine, we save our suit air. You're going to have to go into the balloon when it's time to move."

"Just tell me what I have to do."

She took his hand and pulled him to his knees. "Right now, you have to lead us in the Glorious Mysteries."

Chapter Thirty

Rita heard the chapel doors swish open and hurried to finish the last of her prayers. Instead of praying with desperation in her heart, she whispered the words with thanksgiving. She hadn't felt this comfortable with prayer, with her calling — with herself — in a long time. She wondered how long it would last.

James cleared his throat as he slid into the pew beside her.

Not long, apparently, she thought, but found herself laughing.

"What?" he demanded, a grin spreading on his face.

She shook her head and sat back. "Did I lose track of time?" She checked her watch. No, she still had ten minutes until suit-up.

"You're fine," he said. "I just happened to pass by Chris and Andi. He was hovering over her like a mother hen, begging her to be careful. She was teasing him mercilessly about it."

Rita snorted. "An old married couple already?"

"Anyway, it got me thinking. What we said in the escape pod...you do love me?"

"Of course I do, James." How easily the words came from her mouth now.

"But not enough."

She twisted to face him. "It's not a matter of quantity. God presented me with two wonderful alternatives, but I have to choose."

"And you're choosing to remain a sister?"

She smiled. "A Rescue Sister, in particular." She said that without desperation, too. Could it really have been that easy?

"Accepted the retrofit, then," James muttered.

"What?"

He shrugged. "Something Ann said earlier. It stuck with me, is all. Never mind."

"She has that way." What had Ann been murmuring in her sleep? *The darkness on the bright path makes us appreciate the light.*

James studied his hands, bumping the thumbs together the way he always did when nervous or thinking.

"What?" How long had it been since she could ask that question without worrying about the answer?

"You know, even after I'd given up finding you, there was never anyone else. It always felt like I'd be cheating." He paused, tapping his thumbs, building his courage.

Rita felt her heart hammering in her chest.

"Maybe, maybe it wasn't you I felt I'd be cheating on? Ann was right when she said I was ignoring part of my vision."

"Okay." She hoped her voice would encourage him. She didn't feel comfortable asking outright, but if he needed to talk, she wanted to listen for him.

He licked his lips nervously. "We were dancing, but we weren't alone, really. There were faces all around us, watching. I..." He laughed. "It's ridiculous, but I felt like they were jealous, and I was kind of proud of that. You spun away from me. Into a rainbow. You beckoned me to join you."

"But you didn't? Why not?"

"Because everyone was flocking to the rainbow, and they were all calling to me. So many people, so much pressure. So, I called to you... and that's when the vision ended. Now I feel like William Thoren, too afraid to jump. You seemed so happy dancing in that rainbow."

Despite herself, Rita smiled. "I am."

He nodded. "In the escape pod, when we were praying, I felt something, you know? I felt...touched. It's been a long time since I felt that way."

"What are you going to do about it?"

"I don't know yet."

She covered his hands with hers. "Take some advice: Don't run from your decision. It's hard, but it's the most important discovery you'll ever make."

He nodded, then made himself look at her face-on. "What do we do now?"

She gave him a little shove. "You let me out of here so I can go suit up and do my job. Then get yourself to the bridge. Latching *Discovery* onto the *ET* is going to be quite a show, and I'm betting Chris is going to need some moral support!"

* * *

Ann woke up to find herself lying on a bed. In her own body, and from the feeling of it, not a perfect body, either.

"That's weird," she murmured. Her eyes slid shut.

One of her favorite Earthly voices said, "Hey, none of that. Come on, Ann. Talk to me, just for a minute. We thought we'd lost you, you know. Come on, how are you feeling?"

"Rita!" Ann opened her eyes — Yes, it was her sister! — then let them slide shut. Smiling didn't seem like too much effort, though. "You saved me!"

"Actually, OvLandra did that. She found you, hooked her tank to yours and got the two of you to *Rockhopper*. You should be all right, but we're keeping you here for a few days."

"Mmm." Lying in bed sounded very good right now. "Where's OvLandra?"

"Checking on Ian. Do you remember what happened with Ian?"

"James should talk to him." She knew that, but she didn't quite remember why. Oh, well, it would come to her later. Thinking hurt too much. The Holy Spirit would tell her what to say. Or when to say nothing.

After a few moments, Rita squeezed, then released, her hand. She heard her retreating footsteps.

"Rita?"

Her hand was back on Ann's. "What is it, Annie?"

"Are you staying?" She wondered if she should explain what she meant. Did Rita understand? Talking just seemed like too much effort.

But Rita leaned over and kissed her forehead. "Yes, my sister. Of course, I'm staying. I promised to go where God leads me, and whether it's green pastures or alien ships, I'll follow."

The words wrapped around her like a blanket, and she drifted into a comfortable sleep.

* * *

James stepped into the Sickbay and took a breath to steady his nerves. Beside him, Sean did the same. Ann was talking to OvLandra, and he watched as the zerog tenderly caressed her hair while checking over the readings. By the head of her bed, ignored but watchful, Lenny stood guard over Little Sister. By one of the counters, Merl kept a close eye on OvLandra. No one was trusting the zerog, despite Ann's assurances that her cousin's pod experience had healed her of her murderous intentions.

Cousins. He shook his head in disbelief. Yet Sean had seen it, he said, almost from the beginning.

"It was the eyes, you know? They're just a little too large, and did you notice that she didn't like bright lights? Zerogs have more rods to see better in low light. And her fingers were so narrow and long. I dismissed it at first, because zerogs never take humans — well, standard humans — for mates. But Ann told us about OvLandra's mission, and then when I saw the documentary of Edwina Taggert..."

He'd felt terrible about not having said anything sooner and had asked James to stand by him while he apologized to Ann. So the two had come to Sickbay together.

OvLandra left Ann and disappeared into her office, Merl trailing behind her.

"Ready?" James asked, and Sean nodded.

Ann was sitting up, looking wan but well enough, as she took one of the many tests OvLandra had assigned her to check her memory. When she saw them approach, she put it away and held a hand out to Sean.

He took it and pressed it to his forehead, and his shoulders shook.

"It's all right," she said. "God allowed this to happen. The zerogs have tried to remove themselves from humanity; it's time to come back to the fold, and He needed a shepherd. There are so many shepherds on this ship! And lifeguards. You were like a lifeguard, watching over me."

"But I didn't! I didn't tell anyone my suspicions. I hesitated, and you could have died."

"I thought I might," she mused. "It was very weird, dying. Not what I expected, and I was scared. I think I need more practice."

James resisted the urge to slap his forehead at that statement, but Sean quoted a haiku that made her smile. He left them to talk seriously about death and martyrdom. Lenny would keep them safe. Be the sheepdog, if they were going to keep the analogy. Right now, James had someone else to shepherd.

It'd been a long time since he'd done this kind of thing — too long, maybe — but Ann was right. Ian needed someone to help him understand himself, and he, James, had the best frame of reference.

James pulled up a chair beside Ian's bed. "How are you feeling?"

Ian regarded him with dark and bloodshot eyes. His easy smile had vanished. "I heard what Cay tried to do."

"Cay's troubled. Dr. OvLandra ran a psych profile and found he had a tendency toward xenophobia, but not strongly enough to affect his ability to adapt to the usual rigors of space life. It probably wouldn't have mattered except for the mission. With counseling, he should be fine. For now, he's confined to quarters."

"But *Discovery*'s all right? And Little Sister?"

James nodded. "She'll recover fully, they think. She might lose some memory, but they doubt there's any brain damage. Rita's told me your hands will heal. But what about you?"

He held up his hands. "There's this verse. I think about it a lot. Have for years. 'If your right hand will keep you from God, cut it off.' Guess that is what I tried to do."

James leaned forward. "You know Jesus wasn't speaking literally, don't you?"

Ian shook his head, a denial of James' words. "I tried."

"Ian, our hands don't keep us from God. What we do with them does. Sin keeps us from God. And if we choose to use our right hands in sin, would cutting them off really matter?"

Tears filled Ian's eyes and dripped down his cheeks. "I kept telling myself it wasn't wrong. They weren't really humans yet. I needed the money. It wasn't my choice, anyway, right? I was just, just the right hand. I was the right hand."

His fingers dug into the bandages of his hand.

James gently pulled them apart. "How long?"

"Two years. Then I left. I couldn't do it anymore. So much blood. Blood all over my hands."

"You were the right hand, but now you're not. You removed yourself from the situation. Like the verse said, you cut yourself off from the body of sin. That's your first step. Ian, look at me. God doesn't want you to hurt yourself. He just wants you to return to Him."

Ian held his gaze, then his eyes fell back to his bandaged hands. He nodded.

* * *

Ann stared at the screen before her, lips parted in wonder. Ian had put together the data from the bugbots into a rough schematic of the alien warp drive and had given it to her to study while she was on bed rest.

Around her, quiet sounds of infirmary equipment played soothing music to her ears. It had been so noisy when Ian was still in the bed across from her. He and James had talked a lot, and Zabrina often visited. Kelley, too. She'd come to see both Ian and Ann, but she laughed more when she was with Ian. That was okay. His laugh had changed, grown lighter, though Ann still didn't always get why he laughed. Like when Kelley mentioned the sweetness she'd felt in the chapel, and he'd said, "Oh, is that what you meant?" Kelley had smacked his arm, but she'd laughed, too. Ann still didn't understand, but she wasn't in the conversation.

Maybe I could have confessed overhearing them, and then I could have asked. She filed the thought away. The important thing was that Ian and Kelley were both healing.

Ann was healing, too, albeit more slowly. Not only had she suffered hypoxemia, but sometime in her panic before the saints had comforted her, she'd managed to break a rib. It had taken surgery to put it in place; not an easy thing when the only surgeon was the woman who had hours before tried to kill her. James had told her how everyone had argued to put her in stasis until they reached Saturn, even though Ov insisted that after so much oxygen loss, she would have suffered irreparable brain damage. It was Rita, dear Rita, who had sided with Ov and assisted in the surgery.

Ann shifted slightly and changed the position on the hospital bed. She could have spent her recovery in her room. In fact, most people wanted that. Despite OvLandra's confession and her explanation of how her own experience in the pod had shown her the hellishness of her people's purity program, no one trusted her. But Ov and Rita wanted her under observation, and she still needed oxygen and follow-up treatments with the bone knitter several times a day.

Besides, Ann preferred the infirmary. The beds were not as soft; the comforter did not smother; and even though she now understood why the opulence of the *ET's* decor had bothered her, she still preferred the cool colors and utilitarian furnishings of the Sickbay.

Besides, her cousin had told her that once they were in-system, she would return to her family, share her vision, and make them see reason. Ann was already asking the saints to go with her. She had a dangerous mission ahead. *Surely the righteous will praise your name, and the upright will live.* She trusted OvLandra's change of heart.

A compromise was made. Both Ann and Ov were each under constant watch. Rockjacks and Research supplemented the crew. Ov took it with grace, letting her example convince the others of her sincerity. In fact, Rose had mentioned to Ann that she and Ov had talked more in the past few days than the two had in their entire tenure serving together. Despite the circumstances, the zerog seemed to enjoy the company.

Ann, meanwhile, would have been glad to talk less. It was so much quieter in the convent. She'd never known small talk could be exhausting. *Small. Such a misnomer. St. Charles Borromeo said, "Stay quiet with God. Do not spend your time in useless chatter. "*

But St. Francis de Sales said, "While I am busy with little things, I am not required to do greater things." Both ships are safe. The crew is healing, body and soul. We are bringing the most exciting discovery in history home to study. Perhaps this is my time for little things.

Even so, she'd been glad when this morning, Ian had brought her the schematics as a gift. The real gift was to see him becoming something better than his old self. She hadn't always liked him calling her "Little Sister" before, but now she did.

Which didn't mean she wasn't enjoying the gift of the files, of course! There was so much to learn! She turned her attention back to the schematics. She didn't understand half of it, though she could figure out more if she got the chance to tinker with it. Still, it was such a relief to turn her mind to a puzzle of mechanics and not have to think about people or sheep or lions or wolves.

The wolf stepped up beside her and cleared his throat.

She didn't take her eyes off the screen. "You know, Dr. Thoren, I think they lived in a lighter gravity than we do. Their need to orient things by 'up' and 'down' isn't as strong as ours. OvLandra said it reminds her a little of our people, too."

Out of the corner of her eye, she saw OvLandra turn at the sound of her name and smile. Gordon straightened from where he leaned against a counter, just a tad more alert. Of course, the miners were having the hardest time trusting her cousin's change of heart, but even they had come a long way in a short time.

Or was it Thoren that had made Gordon tense up?

"That does correspond with xenobiology's assessment," Thoren replied, then cleared his throat again. "Sister Ann, I wished to know..."

"It was your vision, but if I'd been there, of course I'd have pushed you off the cliff." Her eyes danced over the graphics as they twisted to show the engine from another angle. Arrows waiting for labels pointed to different areas. So much to learn! So exciting!

"And into the abyss?" he pressed.

"Mercy is an abyss, Dr. Thoren."

"I...see. Well, Lieutenant Chan mentioned that the butterflies are hatching from their cocoons." He paused to clear his throat. "I thought perhaps you might be tired of the same view..."

Suddenly the schematics held no interest. "Do you like butterflies, William?"

Although she could sense his discomfort gauge edging toward the red line, he answered with dignity. "I've always been fond of the creatures. As a child, I was a budding lepidopterist."

Delight fluttered through her like a kaleidoscope of butterflies. "Sister Quartermaster packed a net in *Basilica*."

He raised a brow. A grin tugged at his lips. "Shall we retrieve it?"

"Oh, yes, please!"

He helped her into the wheelchair and pushed her out of the infirmary.

Wolves aren't so bad, are they, St. Francis? You just have to know how to talk to them. You saved the town of Gubbio, but you saved the wolf, too. Maybe, now that the crew is safe, we can save this wolf, too? Ann sighed, a happy sound.

It really is the best job in the 'verse.

Appendix A: Spacer's Code of Conduct

1. A Spacer never panics.
2. Double check everything: Twice and thrice and yet again.
3. Assumptions kill. Do not make them.
4. Improvise intelligently.
5. Spacers survive first, feel second.
6. If it's irrelevant to survival, respect others' beliefs.
7. (unofficial) Trust in St. Gillian.
8. Do not talk about controversial subjects, except in friendly, invited discussions.
9. Those who don't know when to put safety over mission fail at both.
10. Know your situation, your priorities, and your orders.
11. When dealing with the unknown, knowledge is your best tool.
12. Do not be afraid to form relationships.

Appendix B: The Discovery Cast

Augustus Cole: Trillionaire businessman and entrepreneur, bankrolling and overall controller of the Discovery mission

Rescue Sisters
> Rita Aguilar: EMT of Team Basilica; Safety Team Lead for Discovery Mission
> Ann St. Joseph de Cupertino: Engineering, Extra-Vehicular Rescue Specialist; Safety
> > Officer for Discovery mission
> Thomas (Tommie) Aquinas Krueger: Pilot

Rocky Flats Miners "Rockjacks"
> Kevin Hayden: General Supervisor (GenSup) of Rocky Flats Mining Station
> Andromeda ("Andi") Vicente de Chavez: Operations Supervisor of Rocky Flats Mining
> > Station; Mission Lead for Discovery extraction mission
> Cay Littlefield: Rockblaster, intern from Mars
> Dale Michaels: Rockblaster and admin
> Galen Keegan: Pilot, rockjack quartermaster
> George Powers: Iceblaster
> Lenny Marina: Rockblaster, engineering
> Frances Baker: Structural engineer, iceblaster

Researchers "Dataheads"
> Dr. William Thoren: Astrophysicist, Dean of Astrophysics at Luna Technological University, Discovery Mission Leader; from Luna
> Chris Davidson: PhD candidate in astrophysics at LTI; discovered the alien ship; from Virginia
> Dr. James Smith: Archaeologist; from Indiana
> Sean Ostrand: Documentarist; from LEO-York space station
> Dr. Merl Pritchard: Linguist; from Nebraska
> Kelley Riggens: Xenobiologist, zoologist; from California
> Dr. Ian Hu: Aerospace engineering, warp drive specialist; from Hawaii
> Gordon Radell: Cryptographer; from Germany
> Zabrina Muha: Microbiologist, xenobiologist; from Mars
> Reg Alexander: Civil engineering; from LEO-Surat

Edwina Taggert Crew

      Captain Jamaal Addiman: Captain
      Commander Orion McVee: First Officer
      Lieutenant Rose Chan: Navigator, chef
      Dr. OvLandra: Chief Medical Officer, zerog

Extras

      Sister Lucinda: Convent Chief Medical Officer
      Sister Quartermaster
      Mother Superior
      Dove: Cay's girlfriend on Mars
      Boat Man 1: Drove the dingy to pick up James from the dive site
      Cory: Overexcited boy on trip to the moon
      Cory's Mom: Yep, sometimes, we really are just someone's mom
      Distraught Researcher: Yells at Thoren

Appendix C: Glossary of Terms

Assessment: a zerog ritual. Whenever entering a new environment, they carefully examine the entire room to know where things are so they can avoid them while moving about.

Black: outer space.

Couritza: Scared enough to endanger himself or others (from movie *2010*)

Codist: Someone who treats the Spacer's Code of Conduct as a religion

Colite: a new metal discovered in space that humans are just beginning to study.

"I greet you under the auspices of the Code, which promises safety and demands obedience. For the Code is Life.": standard ceremonial Codist greeting

Copy: I hear you

Dirtsider: someone who lives on a planet of moon

Dihydrogen Monoxide: water (H_2O)

Dock: a small (incision?) that connects the medical pod to the body. Through here, a medpod can inject medications.

Dodeck: the field for playing the zero-gravity sport, splat. A dodecahedron-shaped court with four clear panels, eight panels of one team color and eight panels of the other team's color. The panels lose their color when hit by the ball.

"Eat our thrust!": Like "Eat our dust!"

EVA: Extra-vehicular activity. Also called "Outside work."

Extra-solar: really crazy; out of their mind

Go nova: explode with emotion. It can be good or bad, depending on context.

Gravfoot: someone who lives where there is significant gravity

Green: safe, okay to proceed

Greenfoot: Someone from Earth

Hologame: virtual reality games played in an arena--kind of like the holodecks in Star Trek

Iceblaster: demolitions expert with specific expertise in working with ice rather than dirt

Kuiper Belt: The **KUIPER BELT** is a disc-shaped region of icy objects beyond the orbit of Neptune

Ky-bo (pronounced Kie-boe): A Kuiper Belt Object

Leak: a Spacer swear word for something that should be left unsaid; similar to bullshit.

Medpod: Medical pod, or 'pod. A small box containing some common medications that a skinsuit can inject to medicate the wearer

MiGR: Microgravity Rover--hovercraft specifically for extremely low gravity environments

Nova: cool, amazing

Old COOT: CoOperative Optical Telescope. One of two telescopes located at L5 Station between Earth and the moon. It actually records more than the optical spectrum. There is a second, newer telescope, called New COOT.

Order of Our Lady of the Rescue: a religious order founded by St. Gillian of L5 with the mission of performing search and rescue operations in space

Pulsar: amazing, awesome

Pure checklist: easy to understand or accomplish

Rockjack: asteroid miner

Roger: I hear and will comply with the order.

Secure that leak: Shut up; you're talking nonsense, or Shut up; you're talking our of turn/saying something irrelevant.

Skinsuit: a formfitting outfit worn on the inside the spacesuit itself. It has a weave of fabric and semi-intelligent nanites that can respond to the body's needs, including rudimentary medical diagnosis and first aid. For those who wear spacesuits in a long term.

Spaced: crazy

Spacer: someone who lives and works in space, but usually used with the impression of approval, as if to say the person is worthy or *belongs* in space

Stellar: amazing, cool, awesome

Stuperiority: foolishly thinking you are better than someone else

TTUI: Terra Technological University, Indiana

V-Rec: record for virtual reality

Vac: a Spacer swear word, brining connotations of the cold death of space or the removal of something unwanted

Vac that stale air: shut up or forget about that nonsense

VASIMR engines: Variable Specific Impulse Magnetoplasma Rocket (**VASIMR**) is an electro-magnetic thruster for spacecraft propulsion. Real technology being studied for interplanetary travel.

Vectored: cool, neat, on target

Vent air: get upset

Zerog: humans genetically designed to live in zero-gravity environment

Acknowledgements

This book was one of the toughest I've ever written. It started as a National Novel Writing Month project, as an exploration of the relationship between James, a seminarian, and Sister Rita, a professed sister. However, the book demanded — DE-Manded! — to be so much more than that. I have so many people to thank for helping me build this book to what it was meant to be.

Chris Speakman was the one who helped me with crafting the focus. I had as one of the narrating protagonists Chris Davidson, but in the early draft she looked at, she told me to find a real man. Chris Davidson does start out whiny. So if you like the second chapter, which is James' point of view, thank Chris Speakman.

Even with much sculpting and rewrites, I got very frustrated about the plot. At one point, I complained to my friend Ann Lewis that I was writing *Love Boat in Space.* She gave me the perfect advice, which was obvious once she brought it to my attention. I had an alien ship with a mysterious artifact. Why wasn't I utilizing the awesome sci-fi power of that? This book would have been a shallow, trite sort-of romance if not for her. Thanks, Ann!

One of my annoyances about a lot of science fiction is that their literature seems to stop with our century. I did not want to do that, so I made up my own movies, saints, etc., to go along with some readers would already know. I have to thank Timothy Meyers for the Brother Jubal quotes. I adore Tim's story, "Brother Jubal and the Womb of Silence" in *Infinite Space, Infinite God I,* and am honored that he let me bring Brother Jubal and Drake Lunar Base into my world.

As always, I have to thank my husband, who is my idea man, my first source for any question and an inspiration. In particular for this novel, I was at a loss to make Chris be a hero in the end — and no one was in more need of being a hero. I had had a great scene all figured out for him, but then in the rewrite, I changed the final conflict and his chance at heroism. I griped to Rob about this as we were nearly asleep, and, of course, with a single question, he pointed out the logic flaw in the villain's plan that Chris would latch onto and use to become a hero.

I am not a scientist, so it's great I know some. Rob, of course, is my spaceman. Mike Hays gave me some biological info. Simon Morden helped with the astrophysics. If there are any mistakes, they are all mine.

Many, many, many thanks to the following folks who proofread and gave me some great critiques:

Fred Warren, who also writes terrific stories in the Rescue Sisters' universe. It's a pleasure to share my world with him.

Walt Staples, a great writer with a quirky humor and an eagle eye. I hope to meet him again in Heaven.

John Konecsni, who is a very visual thinker where I am not and helped me see (pun intended) where I needed more description.

Carol Ann Chybowski, who had some good insights into OvLandra and Dr. Thoren.

Lisa Mladinich, who, like John, made me see where my character description was lacking. (With thirty-one named characters that I know intimately but readers don't, this was an important issue!)

Jane Lebak, who gave me some fabulous advice on drilling down to the theme of the novel even before I got to the rewrite.

Sue Frievald, who gave it one more sanity check.

Many thanks to Cheryl Thompson and the proofreaders for giving this book its final polish. It's very shiny!

Finally, I owe a great debt of gratitude to James Hrkach of Full Quiver Publishing. As many people had pointed out, my cast of characters is especially huge, and it can make for a confusing novel. James, however, didn't just point this out, he took the extra time to demonstrate where, how, and why it was hurting the book. With his help, I killed some of my darlings (and not in the JJ Abrams sense!). The book is stronger and hopefully a little less confusing. After all, I didn't aim to write *Lost in Space*.

About the Author

Karina Fabian is a cradle Catholic, a geek and a family woman. Her three great loves came together in 1996, when she and her husband went on a date and came up with the idea of an order of spacefaring nuns. The ladies Order of Our Lady of the Rescue (the "Rescue Sisters") work throughout the colonized solar system, doing search and rescue and training. The Rescue Sisters stories have appeared in anthologies, sparked fan fiction, and now have their own novel in *Discovery*.

Karina also writes about a dragon detective working under the direction of the Faerie Catholic Church, a psychic who fought his way back to sanity to save two worlds, and a zombie exterminator. In the non-fiction arena, she writes school planners for Catholic schools, saint stories for Saint Connection, and reviews of business products for Top Ten Reviews. She helped found the Catholic Writers Guild and coordinates the online conference. She and her husband, Rob, have collaborated on four wonderful children, currently ages 15-22.

Learn more about Karina and her books at http://fabianspace.com.

Published by Full Quiver Publishing
PO Box 244
Pakenham, ON K0A 2X0
Canada
www.fullquiverpublishing.com

CPSIA information can be obtained
at www.ICGtesting.com
Printed in the USA
BVOW04s1845281116
469110BV00001B/37/P